THE HAUNTED TREE

Book One of The Magus Family Chronicles

by Scott Robert Scheller

"Few men are a threat to a fully trained wizard."
Oren the Wise

PsiScribe

ISBN: 151224709X
ISBN-13: 978-1512247091

Acknowledgements

As this is my first full-length novel to be published, there are a ton of people for me to thank. Over the years, many have helped guide my path and even, on rare occasion, given me a swift kick in the pants when needed. With so many to give credit to, I cannot begin to list them all here, but they are remembered.

My deeply grateful and heartfelt thanks to the Tuesday night writing group, led by our mentor, Elnora King. If any one person may be credited with teaching me the craft of writing, it's her. Many budding writers became published authors under her wise and patient tutelage. Including me. Thanks, Elnora, and God bless you.

With an equal measure of gratitude and love, I want to thank my parents, Bob and Becky Scheller, for all their incredible support and encouragement. When the company I co-owned closed down, I wanted more than anything to write the "great American novel". At the time I was barely making ends meet and couldn't afford a computer. My parents, even though they were retired and really couldn't spare the expense, bought me one. Wow. What can I say? It made a difference, so much that this story may not have come about without their loving help.

I also need to express my profound thanks and love to my wife, Susan. She has been more than tolerant of being a "writing widow", having to constantly share herself, my first love, with writing, my second. Many a day I would come home from work and disappear into my office to write, giving her far less attention than she deserved. In her way, she invested her time in this story as well, making it as much hers as mine.

Every writer needs outside help at one time or another. For me, it was translating English into Latin. My sincere appreciation goes out to Dr. Marshall Johnston of Fresno Pacific University for putting me in touch with Anthony J. Fredette, Latinist extraordinaire. Mr. Fredette not only superbly translated my English words and phrases into Latin, he went the extra mile and researched the most applicable forms of Latin used during my story's time setting. Amazing. Thanks, Anthony. Any error seen in how I applied his expert advice is mine, not his.

The captivating cover image, *Fog Tree*, is Copyright 2008 by Gary Philbin, and is used with his generous permission.

Of all the individuals that in some way helped me on this journey, I wish to mention two of them by name as they both participated in the genesis of Haunted Tree, and are no longer with us to see my work come to fruition.

Benjamin Gordon Brown, a good friend since college, was a font of Anglican historical facts. He encouraged my early efforts with Haunted Tree and helped me better understand the lives of the people in my story. He became so drawn in by my wanting to write, he caught the bug, too, and began a promising series featuring a blind detective. Sadly, cancer took him far too soon. I still miss ya, buddy.

Another of my post-college friends was Mariel Long. Fairly reserved, she loved F&SF stories, and seemed to really like hearing all my strange ideas for books I wanted to write. Suffering from chronic diabetes, her health continued to decline to the point she lost her kidneys. Near the end, I did what little I could to ease her spirits, often entertaining her with fanciful tales about a family of wizards who lived next to a mysterious Haunted Tree. It took a long time, but this book's for you, Mariel.

Ψ   Ψ   Ψ

If you like my work, please tell others about it. Independent authors have few avenues of promotion better than word-of-mouth. Fans are our best asset. So, please, chat me up to your friends, family, co-workers, neighbors—heck, even the clerk at your local grocery store. Maybe leave a nice review on Amazon, too. Thanks!

I appreciate feedback, both positive and negative. All I ask is that it's civil.

Ψ   Ψ   Ψ

For more information, please visit: www.scottrobertscheller.com

Chapter 1

Marc was hungry. He was cold, tired, but more than anything else, hungry. For the last two of his sixteen years, he knew nothing but desperate hardship. What had been a reasonably comfortable life changed overnight when the darkness descended upon his world. A great cold came upon the land, a winter without end. The trees produced neither leaves, flowers nor fruit. No grain grew in the fields. With each passing day, the once plentiful deer, rabbits and other game animals became ever more scarce. He feared that soon no one in Britannia would remain.

Before him loomed the fog-shrouded bluffs of Red Cliffs. There he might find food, meager though it may be. But getting to it would not be easy. The half-melted ice covering the rocks made climbing difficult. Every few steps Marc would lose his footing and slip downhill a bit, knocking loose snow which the frigid wind whisked away. As he struggled, a pair of calloused hands gave him a rude shove up the slope.

"Move!" Donald said, his displeasure naked and unrestrained. "You hold us back."

Just minutes before, Marc stood at the base of the cliffs and, following some inner urging, selected the area where they should search this day. He reluctantly faced his tormentor, knowing it would do little to change things. "If you wish to lead, do so. I told you where I thought more birds were."

Donald responded with a bitter scowl Marc knew well, one often accompanied with a less than polite reminder that he was both a year older *and* the son of the village leader. Once they had been the best of friends, but over the past year the young man behind him grew ever more arrogant and disdainful, much of it directed toward him. Marc could not remember doing anything to anger Donald during that time. The loss of their friendship was one of many hard changes brought about after the sun left them.

And Marc hated it.

"Out of my way." Donald scrabbled impatiently past him. "We have little time to waste."

Tired of this nonsense, Marc almost responded with something rude when the next boy, Sean, shook his head, indicating Marc should not irritate Donald further. Glancing behind, Marc witnessed the embarrassed looks of the younger boys; they did not care for Donald's attitude either. Following Sean, Marc considered telling Donald what he thought of him and his attitude despite Sean's peacekeeping efforts. While it would feel good to vent his frustrations, doing so would probably spark another confrontation. For now, that needed to be avoided. The good of their village mattered more.

Once they reached the bottom of the cliff face, he untied his pack and pulled out two long, braided leather ropes, handing one each to Donald and Sean. Even though Donald began to direct the group's actions, there was little need; they had done this for months now all along Red Cliffs and had it down to a routine.

Being the largest and strongest of the young men, Donald and Sean would find a secure place higher up, wedging themselves into clefts in the ruddy stone. Firmly holding their ropes, each suspended one of the smaller boys as they searched in the dim light for birds frozen within the various pockets and niches covering the face of the cliff. Often their prizes were entombed with a covering of snow and ice. After a bit of work chiseling away with a knife, the remains could be freed and tossed to the others below. It was hard, slow work, usually yielding two to three dozen birds for a day's effort. Sometimes they were lucky and found larger, meatier birds such as gulls, doves or swallows. Otherwise, the much smaller sparrows or wrens would have to do.

It had been a scant five hours of constant labor when Donald eyed the sunless sky. "We are finished. Pack up."

Marc looked upward as well. The ever-present grayish-brown haze, thicker than any thunder cloud he had seen, grew darker by the minute, leaving just enough light for them to return to their village of Oak Creek. Seeing the misery heaped upon his friends and neighbors, he deeply wished he could do something to improve their lot. Sometimes he felt as if he *should* be able to do so, but the how of it escaped him.

While lowering his charge to the ground, Donald shouted at the younger boys below. "Willie, what is the count?"

"Fifty-one," the lad said with delight, hoisting the bulging sack of birds over his head. "And many are doves."

A cheer erupted from the others.

"Fine work, all," Donald said, coiling his rope. He and Sean descended together until they stood upon a large, flat rock ten feet above Marc. Clearly in discomfort, Sean rubbed his arms and shoulders. Pink stripes marked his hands and wrists where the leather had bit into his flesh. Donald poked Sean's shoulder with a finger. "Sore, are we?"

Sean smiled. "As sore as you." He tossed his bound rope down to Marc.

Doing the same, Donald chuckled, "What we need is a good rubdown by a couple of pretty ladies."

Sean's smile drooped, his uncomfortable gaze momentarily glancing Marc's way. "If you say so."

Donald's bravado disgusted Marc. For a while now he repeatedly made advances toward many of the girls, none more so than Valeria. The thought of them pairing turned Marc's stomach. Climbing down to where the others waited, he packed away the ropes then scratched some letters on a large, reddish-brown boulder with the tip of his knife.

Sean leaned over his shoulder. "What does that say?"

Marc looked up and saw with relief Donald was elsewhere. Sean remained a good friend, treating him with respect. "Fifty-one, followed by the date. Today was good."

"Thank God. Fortune smiled upon us today. Not as many empty holes." Sean's storm-grey eyes surveyed the cliffs, then met Marc's gaze. "Every time *you* choose where to look, we seem to find more and better birds." Leaning closer, he dropped his voice and added, with amusement, "And I think Don is jealous of that special skill of yours."

Marc's stomach quailed in discomfort at his friend's compliment. He shook his head. "It's just luck, that's all." Assuming Sean would let the subject drop, he rechecked his pack, stood and hefted it onto his shoulder. "The day seemed longer. Have you noticed that of late?"

"Yes. I could almost see the sun for a while. Maybe that means things will be better soon." Hearing the tenuous, almost desperate, hope in his friend's voice renewed Marc's frustration at being powerless to improve things. Sean headed toward the path and Marc followed.

"Maybe. By the calendar it should be early spring now, but we still—" A crunch of gravel to Marc's right indicated they were no longer alone.

"No," Donald said, louder than necessary. "No spring this year, either, but me and my father will see us all through. You can rely on that." Casting him a reproachful look, Donald moved off and began gathering the boys for the trip home.

Marc ached to counter Donald's self-serving prophecy but decided it would do little to change his once-friend's negative outlook. Marc had never stopped hoping for a better future, one where life was no longer a daily struggle to merely survive the darkness. Tightening his cloak about himself, he remained silent for the rest of the journey.

By the time they neared home, the fullness of night had fallen and seeing the guiding fire far ahead gladdened him. Built some hundred feet above the surrounding terrain on the southernmost point of Rocky Hill, the fire helped them find their way in the dark. While not very large, its light shone for several miles out, visible in an arc from the east to the northwest. More than once it proved its worth, leading a lost hunter safely back.

Following the well-worn path, he and the boys passed beneath the guiding fire and entered the southern end of the village. Laid out in a long, north-south oval just east of the base of Rocky Hill, Oak Creek had a central communal area surrounded by two rings of huts spaced at intervals of twenty to thirty paces. Dominating that area was the common house—a long, low, rectangular structure large enough to hold everyone in the village with room to spare. Used for everything from meals to meetings, it was in many ways the heart of Oak Creek. Set in the middle of its floor was the knee-high stone ring that held the great fire. Nearby, the talking stone protruded four feet out of the earth. North of the common house were two smaller structures, one for storage and one for cooking. East of the cookhouse stood the Sabbath altar with a dozen log benches arranged before it. The family huts, forty-two in number, were mostly four to five paces square, with thick stone walls and steeply-pitched thatched roofs. Marc's home was the northernmost one. In all, one hundred and thirteen souls called his village home.

To the southeast of the village lay the cemetery. Marc usually avoided moving through that area for it awakened unpleasant memories. Further to the east and southeast, the rich soil of the grain fields stretched out well beyond a thousand paces. From the southeast to the southwest stood the northern edge of the great forest, thick with many leafless trees. To the west, past Rocky Hill, the trees were less numerous, mostly appearing in spotty clumps as the land gradually descended until it reached a wide, flat valley that was once lush with wild grasses and grains. Near the southern end of that valley was a landmark known as Broken Rock. Marc liked that place because it seemed mysterious. Further south, the land rose in a series of steps until reaching Red Cliffs.

Most of his neighbors had once tended the fields while others hunted or plied trades such as carpentry, metal working, woodcutting, weaving and such. Marc's family trade used to be tanning and leatherwork. But none of that mattered anymore. Now all the men were hunters and woodcutters while the women saw to the fires, cooked and cared for the other needs of the village.

Luckily, Oak Creek had stored up a surplus of wheat, oats and barley before the darkness came—but only enough to keep them from starving. That's why the men and boys hunted for game. The meat they brought back was a much needed supplement to the daily ration of grain and dried vegetables. They were too poor a village to afford any other sources of food, such as the very expensive dried fish transported from the coast by several traveling merchants.

While Donald carried the bag of birds to the women at the cookhouse as he always did, Marc and the rest of the boys joined the men in the common house and found they had a good day, too, catching a goose and two squirrels. Everyone would eat better tonight. Waiting for the meal, they rested and warmed themselves around the great fire.

"—and you should have seen it," one man said with a toothy grin. "That goose tried to fly away with the snare about its leg. The string caught on a branch, pulled tight, and that bird went all the way around the tree and bam," he said, smacking his fist on his palm, "hit the trunk, knocking itself out."

Once the laughter died out, another added, "We were lucky. Had it not got caught in that tree, it would have likely flown into the Forbidden Vale." The man's demeanor sobered. "Hungry or not, I would have let it go."

Many of the men voiced their agreement.

"Why?" Marc asked suddenly. He wasn't sure why; it just popped out. "Do we really know if that place is truly evil, or just a legend? Have any of us actually *known* someone who has gone in there and had terrible things happen to him?"

One of the older men, Domas the metalworker, gave Marc a serious look. "My grandfather knew a man who foolishly strayed into the Vale. The next day they found him wandering about, blinded, but not just blind, mind you. Skin covered over where his eyes should have been. He said he saw many frightening things, like skeletons and rotting bodies hanging from pikes with strange serpent creatures eating their putrid flesh. A few hours later he died in terrible pain."

Another nodded solemnly. "My father also told me such stories. Some date back to before the Romans left. Only the wizard Oren may pass safely through that place, for foul magic lives there. It will leave us alone if we leave it alone."

"It is haunted indeed!" a third said with a tightlipped grimace.

"But how do we *know*?" Marc's father never warned *him* of the Vale.

"We cannot," Garrett said, his voice calm and even. As the village leader, Marc respected his opinion. "Grandfathers tell fathers who tell sons. Each generation warns the next. We honor their wisdom and take it on faith they know best."

Marc felt the tap of a stick on his shin and saw it was wielded by Donald who flashed him a sly grin. "If you are curious, why not see for yourself?"

6

"That is not amusing!" Garrett said, sharply.

The boy's grin melted into a frown. "I only jested, Father."

"Well, I will go if he goes with me." Marc fought off a smile.

"That is not amusing either, Marcus," Garrett said with less fervor. The leader studied his face for a moment. "You are not planning on going in there, are you?"

All humor left Marc. "*Me*? No! I have no desire to find out if the stories are true."

The men laughed good-naturedly after which things settled down to a good round of hunting stories until dinner.

And what a grand dinner it was! The birds and squirrels went into a rich soup flavored with dried vegetables and herbs. The women took the evening ration of grain and added it to the soup instead of making the same porridge they had all tired of long ago. Topping it off, each person received a small slice of roast goose—a treat that they had not seen in a long time.

As the women cleaned up after the meal, Marc watched one of the girls in particular. By far the prettiest in the village, she was blessed with a generous bosom and sturdy hips. Her long, light brown hair was so fine the slightest breeze would fan it out in waves that reminded him of ripe stalks of grain yielding to the press of the wind. When she smiled, the sparkle in her hazel eyes caused him to go all soft inside. He cared deeply for Valeria but knew while they were lifelong friends, she did not hold the same desires for him.

Seeing Marc look her way, she came over to where he sat. "How was the meal?" Giving him a friendly smile, she reached for his empty bowl.

He fought down his want for her and smiled back. "The soup was very good and the goose—heaven itself."

Willie, seated at Marc's right, popped up and handed over his bowl with a small bow. "My thanks to the ladies for a most delicious supper."

"You are ever the gentleman, William." She moved down the line until she stood before Donald.

"Hello, Valeria." He put his hand on hers as she tried to take his bowl. "Shall we go for a walk after you are finished?" He smiled sweetly but Marc knew the sentiment to be false. More than once Donald had boasted Valeria would be his one day.

She returned the smile, retrieving both her hand and the bowl. "No, thank you."

"Well, how about sitting by the fire, then? I have many exciting stories to tell." The young man raked his fingers through his wavy, shoulder-length black hair in an attempt to draw her attention to it—many of the girls found that part of him appealing, but Marc doubted it would influence Valeria's mind in the least.

Rolling her eyes in irritation, she started to turn away. "No, Donald."

He lightly grabbed her wrist. "You will enjoy yourself, I promise. I like you," he added after a slight hesitation.

Anger flared to life within Marc, a sudden, crackling heat flowing over him; he had enough of Donald's poor manners. Rising, fists balled at his side, he started toward him but Sean earnestly gestured for him to sit.

"Let *her* deal with him," Sean whispered, a knowing look in his eyes.

Sean was right. Strong-willed and self-assured, Valeria would prefer to handle this matter herself. Reluctantly yielding to his friend's wisdom, Marc retook his seat, letting the heat encompassing him ebb away to be replaced with concern. She glanced appreciatively his way.

Valeria shook off Donald's hand, her gaze taking on a sudden hardness that caused a shiver of cold to ripple down Marc's spine. "No, I would *not* enjoy myself. You desire me for my body, not my mind or heart. You want me, but you will never have me."

Silence filled the common house as Donald's expression sagged. "Do you not like me?"

She shrugged, her glare softening. "I like you as much as any of the other men, but *not* in the lustful manner you feel for me. I like *no one* in that way."

Donald stiffened. "Why not? I lead the bo—the young men on hunts for our food. Have *I* not brought us regular amounts of birds to eat?" he boasted, pointing his thumb at his chest.

Valeria frowned, brows pinched, her impatience clearly showing. "*All* the boys work together to gather those birds and we appreciate it." Pausing, she slowly shook her head. "Why can you not admit it was Marc who remembered that thousands of birds used to nest in the cliffs? *His* wisdom has helped feed us these past months, not yours." Valeria hefted her stack of bowls to underscore the point.

Letting out a near silent chortle, Sean looked sideways at Marc, trying hard not to smile.

Standing, Donald pushed past her in a huff. "Your loss." Before leaving through the north doorway, he glared daggers at Marc, his black eyes fairly burning beneath heavy brows. Besides the obvious anger on his face, Marc thought he could feel other emotions come from him—hate, jealousy, and oddly enough, fear. Glancing at Garrett, Marc saw deep regret play across his features. He, too, disliked Donald's behavior.

With an audible sigh, Valeria looked downward. Moving to her, Marc gently touched her shoulder.

"I'm sorry Donald treats you this way."

She raised her gaze to meet his, her sad expression changing to one of thankfulness. "Do not be. It is *his* doing."

Sean came alongside of him. "Val speaks the truth. Don is foolish to treat both of you so poorly. He acts like a child."

Marc nodded, wishing the situation were different. "I pray for the day he grows up and can be our friend once more."

Giving them both a sad smile, Valeria viewed the exit Donald had left through. "As do I."

Ψ   Ψ   Ψ

Later on, while taking wood off his pile for that night's fire, a familiar voice caught Marc's attention.

"Let's do it now, before it becomes any colder." The voice belonged to his neighbor, Ethan, talking to Valeria as they started down the long northern path leading to where their animals were kept.

"May I give you a hand?" Marc called out, turning toward the path.

Ethan stopped and looked back at him, his iron brazier swinging slightly on its chain. "It would be appreciated."

Dropping the wood by the entrance to his hut, Marc grabbed his staff and caught up to them. Valeria smiled, the wavering orange glow of the coals in the brazier accentuating her soft curves. He tried not to notice. "I see it is time to open another pot."

9

She gave him an odd smile. "Yes. How did you know?"

He wondered the same thing. "I guessed. It *has* been a while since the last time."

Her expression warmed. "It has."

The two of them followed Ethan up the path, trying to avoid the trickle of snowmelt flowing along its muddy center. While the brazier's embers did little to offset the almost total black of night, illuminating a tiny circle at best, Marc knew his way from memory. The land rose gently upward for a time then leveled off at a wide glade densely covered with mature oak trees and scattered patches of melting snow. These trees belonged to Marc's family, their leaves and acorns essential for tanning hides. Continuing north, they emerged from the grove and crossed over the small creek for which their village was named. Ahead stood the shelter that housed Ethan's three pigs and four sheep.

As always, Marc approached the structure with caution, wary of predators drawn to the animals within. Built against the base of Rocky Hill, the shelter had shoulder-high stone walls with rough-hewn wood beams fastened atop. It spanned two shallow, adjoining caves that penetrated no more than ten paces into the stone of the hill, yet were deep enough to protect the animals from the elements.

Loosening the chain, Marc helped Ethan open the heavy wooden door deeply scarred by the fangs and claws of hungry wolves and bears. Valeria checked on the animals while the men headed for the southeastern corner of the shelter where dozens of large, long, cylindrical clay pots lay stacked on their sides like cordwood, over half of them open and empty. Hanging the brazier from a central beam, Ethan dropped a handful of small sticks onto the coals, causing them to quickly catch fire, thereby providing more light. He pointed at the next full pot.

"We will open this one." He looked over his shoulder and called to his daughter. "Valeria?"

From a peg on a nearby post, she removed an armful of crudely made cloth bags. "Ready, Father."

While Marc held fast the lid to the pot, Ethan used his knife to cut away the beeswax seal. Valeria handed her father a bag which he held under the opening. Easing the pressure on the lid, Marc allowed a stream of acorns to flow out. Once full, Ethan tied the bag off and started on the next one. By the time the pot was empty, they had filled twenty-one bags. Taking a quarter portion of acorns from the last bag, Valeria fed them to the animals who voraciously consumed them.

"Thank you for your help, Marc," Ethan said, hanging a bulging sack on an overhead peg and patting its side. "And thank God for your great-grandfather. If not for all those oaks he planted, my animals would have died that first winter."

Valeria struggled to lift another sack. "Do not forget Oren, Father."

Ethan deftly took it from her and placed it on the next peg. "Yes, God indeed blessed us through his wisdom. Now let us finish and return home."

On the way back, Marc followed the other two, keenly aware of Valeria's beauty. He earnestly tried to put his desire for her from his mind but could not. He had known her all his life and they had been the best of friends for as long as he could remember. But over the last few years they both changed so much; she into an attractive woman and he into a man. And with those changes, his feelings toward her grew more complex, more awkward. He often found himself unsure how to act around her.

Valeria smiled back at him, causing him to stumble into a bush, tearing the sleeve of his tunic. Paying it no mind, he returned home and collected the firewood once more. As he went to enter his house, he found her blocking his path.

"Let me mend that for you." She held up a needle and thread.

A lump grew large in his throat. "Do not worry about it." Moving around her, he parted the leathers of the door and went inside, dropping the wood beside the stone-rimmed fire pit in the center of the hut. He heard her follow, but kept his back to her. His mother paused in putting his two younger sisters to bed and looked past him, her face brightening.

"Hello, Valeria."

"Evening, Judith."

Gwen, the eldest, sat up and cheerily waved. "Hi, Val." Peeking out from beneath the blanket, Stella just smiled.

Valeria returned the gesture. "Hello, girls."

Turning, he found her standing by his bed. Before he could retreat, she grabbed the torn fabric of his sleeve. "Hold still. This will not take long."

"But this is little more than a dirty rag. It is not worthy of your skill."

"That does not matter. You helped us and now I can help you."

As her needle swiftly mended the damage, he relished the warmth of her hand against his arm, his desire for her almost painful in its intensity. Sadly, she did not feel the same toward him, or anyone else. She made that clear an hour ago in the common house. All he could ever be is her friend, nothing more. Her closeness brought to the surface fragments of dreams he recently had about her. In one of them she ran toward him, smiling. In another, she offered him a big slab of meat on a plate. But the last one was from a dream he had repeatedly experienced—her swimming naked in a small pond. *That* thought unsettled him.

She snapped off the remainder of the thread. "All finished."

Marc looked at the repair instead of her eyes. Anything but her eyes. "Perfect. Thanks, Val."

"My pleasure."

For a moment she stood there, obviously waiting for him to say something, but it was as if the power of speech had left him. Feeling self-conscious, he fidgeted and looked around until she broke the silence.

"What are you doing tomorrow? Looking for more birds?"

He shook his head a bit more firmly than necessary. "Uh, no. Garrett wants us to hunt with the men. They saw some deer tracks today." With nothing more to say, he fell silent.

"A deer? Oh, I haven't tasted venison in a long time." Her gaze flitted several times between him and his mother. "Well, I should go. Good luck tomorrow." He detected a subtle sadness to her voice.

"Thanks," he said as she left. With a sigh, he slumped down on his bed, causing the straw within the hides to crunch loudly.

"Are you all right?" his mother asked, concern deepening the creases around her eyes.

He looked at her, hoping his face would not reveal his thoughts. "Yes."

"You seem otherwise. And you were a little rude to Val."

"I did not know what to say." Marc chewed on his fingernail.

She smiled warmly. "You have known her all your life. If anything, you used to talk *too* much." Gwen and Stella giggled mischievously. His mother cast them a cautioning glance. "Shush. Go to sleep."

Marc remained silent, not wanting to further discuss Valeria. Kneeling by the stone ring, he stoked up the fire for the long, cold night. He watched the smoke twist and turn as it exited through the hole in the center of the roof. "The meal was good today," he said quietly as his mother joined him.

She nodded, holding her trembling hands nearer to the flames. "When is this darkness going to end? This is the third spring that has not warmed. It is as if the sun has gone mad."

"I think it will be warmer this year, for the snow is mostly gone in the open places. The moss on the rocks is greening up, and today Walter saw wheat shoots poking up through the ash."

Her mouth crooked into a shallow smile. "Good. Maybe this year the grain will grow, for we need it. We have only nine or ten more months' worth of stores remaining. When that is gone...." She released a shuddering sigh. "God help us." After a moment, she continued. "Still, we are very fortunate to have had Oren's help."

"Yes, we are," he murmured.

Marc recalled when the old wizard appeared in the village the month before, telling them to gather the ashes from their fires and spread them upon the snow that covered the grain fields. Everyone thought it an odd request but followed his advice. Oren later stood before the people, raised his staff high and made a series of incantations. Taking a handful of grain, he cast it out over the nearest field, making more incantations. After instructing everyone to keep out of the fields, he departed, telling them he would return soon to witness the change. And change it did. Everywhere they had spread the ashes, the snow quickly melted away.

"That wizard sure knows his magic," Marc said. "Things *are* getting better."

"I suppose, but it seems so.... Since your father died that first, hard winter, I have worried so. Even though times are terrible, you always try to find some good in it." She sighed gently, her green eyes softening. "You are much like him in that way. I wish Davi could be here to see the fine man you are becoming."

A pang of loss clenched at his insides. He, too, missed his father. While his absence affected them both, his mother shouldered the brunt of it, having changed much since the darkness came. Her once full, rosy-cheeked face was now gaunt and hollow, with dark circles under her eyes. Her pale lips and pallid skin reminded Marc of how his grandmother looked shortly before death. Still, no matter how much the hardships had ravaged her appearance, the fire in his mother's eyes had not diminished.

"You and Donald are still not getting along," she said, breaking the silence.

Staring deep into the coals, he hesitated to confess his thoughts. "He finds fault with everything I do, then points out how much better he is, yet I do not remember doing or saying anything to insult him." Whatever his former friend's reasons were for tormenting him, Marc determined not to let his own pain or anger show, or allow himself to appear weak in Donald's eyes. Or anyone else's. Somehow he would find his own way to be special, to be the best at something and make a difference.

"These are difficult times, Marcus, and that can bring out the worst in people. And young men often get a bit cocky, trying to show how big and strong they are. Donald has it by the barrow full." She patted his hand tenderly. "Patience. Someday things will be better between you. Good night." Kissing his forehead, she retired to her bed.

Long after the others had fallen asleep, Marc lay awake, watching the patterns made by the fire on the roof and walls while many thoughts occupied his mind. Yes, life was difficult, but deep down he *knew* the situation would improve and his family would come through it. The certainty of that belief puzzled him. Why did he feel that way? Was it just hopeful thinking, or could there be something more to it?

As he drifted closer to sleep, he contemplated better days with his father, learning the family craft of tanning and leatherwork at his side. He remembered sitting by the fire at night, learning to read and write. Of those who lived in the surrounding villages, few could do so. In Oak Creek, his father taught all who wished to learn. A good man and father, he encouraged Marc and his sisters to learn everything they could. Pride and love for him swelled within Marc's heart as a comforting warmth washed over him.

In his mind he heard his father's voice telling him he would one day become someone who would help many people. Where had that memory come from? He never got an answer for he finally succumbed to the gentle bonds of slumber.

Chapter 2

Up before the rest of his family, Marc stepped outside and found the dark sky held a heavy dampness, making him wonder if it might rain soon. If so, it would be a welcome change from all the snow they had seen. Going back in, he packed his things, adding an oilskin for good measure, grabbed his staff and joined the other men at the common house.

"Good morning to you all," Garrett said when everyone had gathered. "As we discussed last night, we know there are several deer somewhere in the valley north of Red Cliffs. Since that area is so large, we will need to spread out to find them. The men will travel alone through the thickest part of the forest, from the eastern side of the valley to the center. The boys will take the meadows on the west side, but they should go in twos, one elder with a younger, and no one is to cross the creek. If any of you boys spot a deer or fresh tracks, run back to Broken Rock and blow your whistle. That will be our meeting place. Don't try to be a hero." The leader's gaze paused momentarily upon Donald. "Let the men catch the deer. Remember, if we hunt well, we eat well. Good luck."

As they walked out of the village, Donald paired up the boys. "Because we are not an even number, one of the elder boys will have to go alone." Donald nodded toward Sean. "How about you? Take the westernmost position and keep others away from the creek."

Sean seemed ready to accept the task when his little brother, Scipio, tugged on his sleeve. "I want to hunt with you," the boy said quietly. Looking to Donald, he added, "Can't I go with him?"

"No, Scipi," Donald answered with a firm shake of his head. "The ground around Wiccan Creek is dangerous for someone as young as you. I would go myself, but as leader I must stay close to the middle to oversee the search."

Scipio gave him a pitiful look. "Please?"

"*No.*" Donald's tone let it be known the matter was settled. "You can hunt with me and Willie if you wish." Donald hesitantly nodded toward Marc. "Or with him."

The eldest boy's reluctance to acknowledge Marc by name was obvious to all.

Scipio's stubborn frown stated that neither offer was acceptable.

Marc agreed with the decision to keep Scipio away from the creek, for the youngster was intensely inquisitive and hard to manage. Donald proved to be a good leader in situations when anyone named Marc or Valeria were not involved. On a sudden impulse, Marc provided a solution. "I'll go in Sean's stead."

Sean looked grateful. "I appreciate it."

The seven-year-old flashed Marc a wide, toothy grin. "Thanks."

Tousling the lad's hair, Marc watched irritation grow dark on Donald's face. He did not like having his authority questioned by anyone, especially Marc. Then, Donald's expression changed into one of suppressed pleasure.

"Many perils exist there. If you should lose your footing on a slippery rock, or have an embankment crumble beneath you—" His smile deepened as he stood straighter, shoulders back. "Yes, you go," he said quickly.

Too quickly. Besides the potential hazards, Donald probably liked having him as far away as possible. The fact that the creek also bordered the Forbidden Vale was not lost on him, either. But Marc wanted to get a closer look at that area and why it was so feared. In the past, none of the boys were permitted near there lest they be tempted in a moment of foolish recklessness to satisfy their curiosity. Picking up his pace, he pulled ahead of the others.

Marc knew little of the Vale. Roughly triangular in shape, it started at the intersection of Wiccan Creek and Black Rock Hill, expanding to the north and west until it hit another row of hills, the names of which he did not know. He remembered stories of strange sounds and smells emanating from there. If true, he would soon find out.

Ahead he saw the faintest outline of Red Cliffs above to his left. Without them as a landmark, he could lose his way for the dim light and misty air made everything appear dreamlike. Distant trees looked more like disfigured faces, watching him. Ribbons of rock along the sides and peaks of hillocks became squinting eyes, stalking him. The very ground itself seemed to melt away into the gray emptiness.

Marc crossed half a dozen gentle knolls before he heard the rush of water from Wiccan Creek. Following the sound, he soon came upon it, finding it to be much more than a creek; the melting snow had filled it to nearly overflowing. He headed north, intently searching for any sign of deer.

After a half hour of finding nothing, he glanced across the creek and saw a very large bush quivering in a jerky fashion as if something fed upon it. Could it be the deer they sought? Excited at the prospect, he looked for a way to cross over and, as luck would have it, a recently felled tree provided a natural bridge a short distance upstream.

Making use of that tree, Marc crept closer to the bush, keeping his muscles taut, footsteps silent. Though the bush had no leaves, he could not see through it due to its dense tangle of branches and twigs. Arcing around, he hoped to see a deer at any moment, but saw nothing. The bush stopped moving as well. Overcome with curiosity, he approached with his staff held at the ready. Puzzled, he poked at the bush, jumping back in surprise as two hares scurried off, zig-zagging across the ground until the fog swallowed them up. Laughing at his reaction, he marveled at seeing not one but *two* of them. He had not seen any for quite some time.

"Go, my friends," he called out after them, waving goodbye. "Have many babies, for our cook pot is in need of something to fill it."

Marc looked around. He and his father had never hunted here. This must be a good place for game. How far did it extend? Even though the mist had thinned out some since leaving home, he still could not see far. A higher vantage point was needed. Moving away from the creek, he followed the natural slope of the land which became ever steeper. A hill. Perfect. If high enough, he would be able to see quite far.

After several minutes of climbing, the mist dropped away giving him an unobstructed view for miles to the east and south, all the way to Red Cliffs, the tops of which jutted from the fog like a ruddy island in a cloud sea. Even so, the shallow angle of his gaze obscured the details of the nearby region almost as much as before. He needed to go much higher, high enough to look *down* through the ground-hugging mist. Further uphill he saw a clear spot high on the right, possibly a ledge of some kind. In the center of it stood a huge tree. That would do nicely.

As he climbed, Marc began to feel odd, something akin to a mixture of dizziness and a headache. He did not seem sick or winded, yet the feeling continued to intensify. Dismissing it as hunger, he pressed on. Soon he drew close enough to see the tree was even larger than he first thought—it stood at least a hundred feet tall—and it seemed familiar in some way. Very familiar. Had he seen it before? Maybe. His father and him had hunted many times in the meadows and woods east of the creek. He had probably noticed it then but forgot about it until now.

Reaching the clearing, he looked about and found himself on a wide, level area cut into the slope of the hill, barren except for the tree. A layer of small, round stones, none larger than the end of his thumb, covered the ground. The up-slope side of the hill had been hewn away leaving the exposed rock smoothed like an enormous wall. Strange symbols were carved into it at regular intervals. Clearly this was all manmade. The north end of the ledge tapered into a path that led down into a valley with a small lake and dense forest.

Trying to shake off the strange feelings, he turned his gaze skyward. The giant tree towered majestically above him, its thicket of bare limbs stretched out in all directions. Many of its secondary branches were larger around than his waist. Marc gazed in awe at its sheer size. Never had he seen a tree this large—or fertile. Thousands of nuts—brown, wrinkled and the size of a baby's closed fist—hung from its branches. Food, and lots of it! He looked for a way up but found none; the lowest branch was ten feet away, and the massive trunk could not be climbed for there were neither footholds nor could he even begin to put his arms around it.

Turning his attention to the reason that brought him up here, Marc looked upon the valley below, the landscape dappled with varying amounts of mist. To his right, the creek flowed by the foot of this hill then headed toward the western edge of Red Cliffs. Further right lay the wooded area where he saw the hares; hundreds of acres heavily populated with trees would support much game when and if the sun returned.

Regarding the tree once more, he thought about how he might manage to harvest the nuts when another, more powerful, wave of that odd feeling rolled over him. The hairs on his neck stiffened as ice water flowed through his veins—someone, or something, watched him. Rapidly turning in place, he looked around, eyes searching for the threat but saw nothing. What about above him? Walking over to the trunk of the tree, he looked upward, bracing himself against the smooth bark.

Immediately, his head reeled as if he were falling down. A ripple of nauseous dread slithered through his core while dozens of voices mumbled incoherently. Panic replaced the odd feeling as he suddenly realized where he stood—the Forbidden Vale! In his pursuit of a higher vantage point, he unknowingly passed over the ridge line of this hill—Black Rock hill—and into the Vale.

Jaw clenched tight, he whipped out his knife and spun about in a defensive crouch, expecting to see some sort of evil denizen coming for him, but he remained alone. Sprinting to the south end of the ledge, his feet scattering handfuls of the small stones about him, Marc scampered down the slope, his heart beating so fast he feared it would burst forth from his chest. He ignored the pain of cuts and scrapes and continued his flight downhill until a drop-off blocked his path. Now well on the south side of the hill, he saw nothing followed.

Marc dropped to his knees and offered an earnest prayer of thanksgiving for having been spared a horrible death from whatever lived in the Vale. Resting to catch his breath, he thought about what just happened. When he touched the tree he heard a jumble of voices, but not with his ears. He heard them in a different way, almost as if they were *inside* him. The idea frightened him. He desperately wanted to drive the memory from his mind, to pretend it never happened. Denying it would do him no good, but answers might.

Where did these voices come from?

As he continued downhill and toward the creek, he pondered that question. Did magical or evil spirits live in the tree? Or ghosts perhaps? He shuddered, realizing they might be the specters of hunters less fortunate than himself. Maybe the tree killed them, capturing their souls for whatever reason. Another twinge of fear hit him—could the tree be responsible for some of the terrible things that had taken place in the Forbidden Vale? If so, then the tales he heard last night and countless nights before were true. Many claimed the dead haunted the Vale. Possibly, but of one thing he had no doubt— if anything could be haunted, it was that tree.

While still several hundred feet from the water, Marc paused to survey the best route down. In his haste to escape, he lost the path he took up the hill and now needed to find the fallen tree in order to cross back over. Scanning the course of the creek, he found the bridge he sought to the south. North of it were two small pools that would be good for fishing. Closer on his left lay a waterfall with a large pool behind it. Yes, that would make for even better fishing and—

His heart leapt when he saw it move. Freezing in his tracks, Marc watched carefully and it moved again. Unsure if his eyes played tricks on him, he cautiously crept closer, careful to remain hidden in the scant cover, hoping the thunder of the falls would cover any sound he might make. There it stood, right by the top of the falls—a handsome buck thrashed about in the water.

Marc could not believe his good fortune. First he ventured into the Vale and lived to tell about it, and now this. He advanced further, positioning himself behind a large tree for a better view, cheek pressed against the rough bark. The animal appeared to be stuck between two rocks that jutted up out of the torrent about four paces upstream of the falls. By the way it held itself, he knew its left-front leg was injured. Since it could not escape, he abandoned his stalking and scooted the rest of the way down.

Seeing him, the buck made a valiant effort to free itself but remained trapped by the fast moving water. All he had to do was pull it to shore and the animal was his. As Marc removed a leather rope from his pack, he once again felt the odd sensation he now knew came from the giant tree—the haunted tree. He turned to where he knew it would be and saw it perched high upon its strange ledge. Did it call to him, warning him to stay away? Or did it want him to return so it could add to its collection of souls? In either case, he would most definitely never go back there.

Putting aside those thoughts, he studied the hill and saw the waterfall sat more or less along the continuation of its ridgeline, putting both him and the deer just inside the Vale. His heart sank. Not again. He looked over at the buck he so desperately wanted and then back at the tree. Was it worth the risk to remain here?

On an impulse, he shouted up the hill. "I mean no disrespect and intend no trespass. I do not know if I am on your land or not, but there is a dying animal here that I wish to feed my people with. If I do not take it, its death will be a waste. I beg of you your patience, that you allow me to capture it and then I will be gone. If you wish me gone now, give me a sign and I shall leave."

He waited for a time, taking tense, shallow breaths, but nothing moved above him on the hill. No sound came to him other than the rush of the water and panting breaths of the buck. Even the feeling he got from the tree remained unchanged. With a mixture of apprehension and relief, he bowed his head and spoke once more. "My most humble thanks."

By now the frigid water had taken a toll on the buck for it moved less. Marc made a noose in the end of his rope then, carefully stepping on several rocks that sat just below the water's surface, eased out into the turbulent current. With a wide swing he threw the rope and missed, coming up short. He tried again. This time he caught most of the nearest antler, but before he could pull the noose tight, the animal shook it off.

After several more tries he realized he had but no choice to get closer. Another, deeper, rock lay between him and the buck. Taking a chance, he planted his left foot on it. Painfully cold, the knee-deep water tugged at his leg, but he did his best to ignore the discomfort and concentrate on snaring his next meal. The noose fell across the animal's face causing it to violently rear up in alarm. Instinctively recoiling, Marc lost his balance and fell into the churning flood.

The icy water instantly seized him in its agonizing grip, his mind suddenly screaming in panic. As he desperately tried to grab hold of something, anything, the swift current propelled him headfirst over the precipice, directly toward a nasty looking rock. Half way down, Marc felt himself abruptly move to the side and fall unharmed into the water beside it.

Gasping for air, he immediately tried to swim ashore, but the flow proved too strong, slamming him painfully against the slick boulders by the water's edge. Since that effort proved fruitless, he tried to avoid further collisions while his frantic mind raced, trying to figure out what to do. He remembered several pools lay ahead, places where the current usually slowed down. Yes! If he could ever make it to shore, those would be the best chances to try.

As the first pool approached, Marc swam as hard as he could to the west side of the creek, hoping to end up out of the faster flowing center. No sooner had he neared the edge, an eddy current pushed him back into the middle, unable to reach any handhold. With this first opportunity lost, he knew he *had* to get out at the next pool. Numbness crept over him, a feeling much like being stabbed with thousands of tiny, razor sharp knives. Soon, he knew, he would be unable to move.

Redoubling his efforts, he again swam to the side of the creek as the second pool came near only to find a large rock blocked his way, the flow parting around it like the bow of a ship. Unable to go past it, he faced it squarely, impacting the rock with bone-jarring force. Dazed and panting to regain the breath knocked from him, he held fast to its slimy surface. Struggling against the current, he slowly climbed half-way onto the rock then stopped, unable to go any further. Something had hold of his right leg.

The rope! It must have stayed with him as he went over the falls and gotten tangled around his thigh. Encouraged by this good turn, he worked it loose from his leg, gathered in what he could, then climbed the rest of the way onto the rock. Shivering, he pulled the rope taut. The other end seemed to be snagged beneath the water somewhere upstream. Not wanting to abandon what could very well be his lifeline, he tugged on it in various ways. The harder he pulled, the more he felt it start to give.

Careful to not lose his balance, he gripped the leather as tight as his cold-numbed fingers would allow, and pulled again with more force. On the third try it broke free. Quickly reeling it in, he found a bit of bark lodged in the braid. Only too late did he realize his efforts dislodged a submerged tree branch that, now freed, surfaced and rushed toward him. The branch hit his rock and slid over the top, knocking him off his feet and back into the water.

Coughing, he righted himself and got his bearings. Immediately downstream he saw the fallen tree. On instinct, he wadded the rope into a ball, held one end fast, then mustered all his fading strength and tossed the rest high into the air and toward the tree. As he raced beneath it, the loose end of the rope fell into the water next to him. Seizing it, Marc quickly tied the ends together and let out a whoop of joy. All he had to do now was climb.

That would not be easy for the frigid water had sapped much of his strength. Hand over hand, he strained against the relentless current that clawed at him. By the time he was half out of the water, his progress slowed. Each inch gained demanded more than he could give, but he found the strength somehow and advanced. Once his knees cleared the surface, he could go no further, the cramping muscles of his arms too fatigued to obey his will.

Marc's resolve crumbled. He slid back into the water, his left elbow hooked on the rope. As he prepared to accept his fate, he felt the haunted tree touch him once more. What did it want? To mock him? To tell him he may have escaped the Vale but would die anyway?

That made him mad. As his anger rose, the fear and resignation evaporated, replaced with a determination and knowledge that he *would* survive this. From deep within came a reserve he did not know he possessed, a warm ocean of power flooding his very being. Rise! he commanded his arms, and he rose. Hand over hand, briskly, tirelessly, he moved. In seconds he found himself atop the fallen tree, astounded at what happened.

Although intense shivers convulsed every muscle, Marc untied the rope and carefully moved to the western side of the creek. Thanks be to God, solid ground! Stripping off his wet clothes, he danced around for several minutes to warm up. When he felt stronger, he gathered his clothes and headed upstream, collecting dry branches and twigs along the way.

Once at the falls, he took the oilskin from his pack and donned it, tying it about his middle. He looked at the buck. From the way it barely kept its head above the water, he knew it was close to death. A pang of empathy coursed through him for he had almost shared its fate. Now that his shivering had eased, he decided to try once more to bring the deer to shore. This time he would take better precautions.

Removing another rope from his pack, Marc tied one end to the trunk of a stout sapling, the other around his waist. Well secured, he once again braved the icy water and tried to snare the animal. After several attempts he met with success and jerked the noose tight. Studying how the current had the deer trapped between the two rocks, he reasoned it could only be freed by putting himself directly upstream of it.

He moved out into the water as far as his tether would allow and pulled hard on the line affixed to the animal. At first the buck remained solidly jammed into the narrow space, but soon it became aware of his actions and put up a little fight. As it squirmed in its trap, some of the water slipped around it, allowing Marc's efforts to pay off. In less than a minute he hauled it ashore.

The unfortunate animal lay shivering at his feet, its breathing labored, its left-front leg badly broken. The buck's ribs were clearly visible under its ragged, matted fur. Marc thought about the hardships of the last two years, unconsciously touching his own all too prominent ribs.

The deer unsuccessfully tried to stand, then crumpled to the ground once more. Letting out a resigned sigh, its big, brown eyes met his gaze, pleading for him to end its suffering. Gently patting its cheek, he took out his knife and, with hands still shaking from the cold, cut deeply into the artery on the buck's neck. If the animal was half as numb as he was earlier, he doubted it even felt the blade. As its blood poured out, it went limp, relinquishing its claim on life.

With the wood he collected earlier, he started a fire between two medium-sized bushes. Next, he took two long branches that had snapped off the bridge tree when it fell and made a framework spanning the tops of the bushes, directly over the flames. After wringing out his clothes, he spread them upon the branches to dry and rested by the fire.

How would he get the deer home? It was too heavy to carry very far. If he left it here and went for help, the predators would probably find it before he returned. Blowing his whistle would do little good, either, not from this far away. The buck had to go with him somehow. A memory surfaced—his father once dragged a deer home lashed to a litter made from two poles. That would work nicely.

A half hour later his clothes had dried. Marc dressed, put out the fire, packed his things and, with a great grunt of effort, slung the deer over his shoulders. Barely able to carry the load, he carefully made his way to the bridge. Not wanting to fall into the water again, he inched his way across. Lowering his load to the ground on the far side, he hurried back for the two long branches, his pack and staff. After securing the buck to one end of the branches, he picked up the other ends and headed east.

The journey to Broken Rock drained what little strength remained in him. During that time, the presence of the haunted tree slowly faded in power as the distance grew between them. Now safely beyond its reach, Marc wondered *why* he continued to sense it. Was it, in effect, shaking an angry fist at him in frustration? Or did it inform him it would not be so lax the next time he came near? And would there be repercussions later for his trespass? He wished he knew.

Barely able to put one foot before the other, he rejoiced when the two peaks of Broken Rock came into view. Rising alone out of an otherwise flat and rock-less meadow, it stood three times the height of a man, cleaved in two as straight and clean as if a giant had struck it with an enormous ax. The mystery of its origin sparked many tall tales. Somehow, Marc knew none of them were true. For him it was a welcome place, one of pleasant memories of hunting with his father.

Reaching the rock, he dropped the litter and leaned against the face of the stone, panting for breath. After a minute's rest, he dug in his pack for his favorite possession—a wooden whistle his father had carved for him. Deeply fatigued, he climbed to the top of the rock and, cupping his hands around the whistle to better direct its sound, blew long and hard. After repeating the blast several times he heard answering whistles come from the northeast. Relieved, he slumped into a seated position and waited for the others to arrive, grateful to have survived the day.

Twice he cheated death, grand bragging rights around the fire on any day. What would he tell the others about how he discovered the buck? That he crossed into the Vale and found the haunted tree? Or would doing so make them fear he had cursed the whole village by escaping the Vale's wrath? God bless them all, he hoped not. He decided for now to keep those details to himself. His story about falling in the water and escaping would have to do.

Laying back, he gazed up at the iron sky, watching the dark mist drift slowly by. In all, he considered today to be a good day.

Chapter 3

Having finished her work, Valeria laid down on her bed to rest while waiting for the men to return. Soon fast asleep, she dreamt, finding herself walking down a path in the woods. It was a warm summer afternoon, the plants and trees lush and green. Bright patches of sunlight fell here and there, texturing the foliage and earth with contrasting highlights. The heady fragrance of wildflowers and their brilliant colors permeated the area around them. Cheerful twitters and chirps from hundreds of birds filled the air. The simple peace of it all pleased her.

Suddenly, there came an anguished wailing in the distance. Turning about, she saw a wall of seething blackness surge rapidly toward her. The churning clouds at its forefront bore a striking resemblance to tumbling skulls. Her skin prickled with fear as she sensed its menace. As the towering mass neared, the icy wind that moved before it engulfed her, the smell of it making her gag; like carrion and burnt hair, the stench of death itself. When this evil breath touched the flowers, they instantly paled and shriveled away. The leaves on the bushes and trees withered, crumbling into drifting ash. A bird tried to escape the threat but its feathers and flesh dissolved away in a puff of red gore, leaving a bleached skeleton that tumbled to the ground.

Seized with terror, Valeria tried to flee as the frigid darkness engulfed her. Nothing could be seen beyond the reach of her arm, not even the sun. Winds howled around her, mocking her feeble attempt to escape its power. She desperately tried to call out but found she had no voice. Blindly flailing about for shelter, she ran into a man. With strong hands he put her behind him. He wore a heavy, dark blue, hooded robe covered with embroidered letters and symbols of unknown meaning. Drawing out a sword of golden fire, he held it up high, brandishing it before the tempest.

With a shriek of agony, the winds ceased and the blackness fell in upon itself.

Peering around him, she saw a gigantic beast with dozens of arms and legs that sprouted from a squat and headless body; it possessed neither eyes nor ears nor mouth. Each arm gripped a fierce-looking weapon, each foot a rotting corpse. With a hideous, bone-shaking bellow, the beast began its attack, swinging wildly at the man who neatly parried each blow. The ground shook violently as it lurched about. Every so often, the man hacked off one of the attacker's hands which fell to the ground, disappearing in a cloud of putrid smoke. The injured arm would then pull back into the beast as if it had never existed. With the loss of each appendage, the others became larger and stronger.

When the man had cut off all but three of the beast's arms, it circled one of its legs around to the side, making a grab for her. Squealing, she jumped in front of the man as the scimitar-like talons of its foot snapped closed on empty air. In one fluid move, the man spun about, severed the foot and returned to deflect blows from two of the arms. As the beast reared up preparing to strike, his sword rapidly lengthened, piercing its foul heart. With an incredible rush of air, the monster collapsed and disappeared.

Rejoicing, Valeria moved to look upon the face of her savior, only to find the cloak empty. What became of the man? How did the garment remain suspended in the air while retaining the shape of being worn by someone? Reaching out, she gingerly touched the edge of the hood, pleased at how the thick, velvety fabric felt to her fingers. With a sudden movement, the cloak flew open, spun about her, then closed up tight, once again putting her in darkness, now one of warmth and protection. Turning in place, she saw a distant light approach. No longer afraid, she waited as it came near. A pure, brilliant blue—not unlike the sun in its intensity—the light flowed over her, through her, caressing her spirit. Silhouetted before it, she saw a figure of a man carrying something large over his shoulders. Her heart fluttered with gladness.

"Val," a voice said.

Strange, it did not sound like a man.

"Val," it repeated, seemingly coming from everywhere at once.

Who spoke to her? It wasn't the man in the light. Turning left and right she saw no one else. She looked at the man, able to see only the lower half of his face even though he stood almost within reach. Leaning closer, he smiled and whispered, "It's time," then vanished.

Valeria awoke with a start, confused.

"Val," her mother, Aula, said softly.

"Uh, what?"

"Wake up, dear." Aula helped her to sit up. "You were having quite a dream."

Valeria looked around, blinking, giving her mind time to adjust. She was in her home. "Oh... yes. A strange one. At the end I...." Brief snippets of her dream cascaded in her thoughts until, in a flash, she understood the man's name and what he carried. Smiling, she hugged her mother. "Praise God. The men are returning and Marc has caught a *deer*."

Aula's eyes widened in surprise. "Was it one of *those* dreams?" Val nodded. Her mother's smile held more than a little pride. "Well, we better get ready for that, now shouldn't we? Go. Greet them while I tell the others."

Jumping out of bed, Valeria hurried toward the southern entrance of the village. This was not the first time she had dreamt of things before they happened. Often these dreams—or visions, as her mother called them—were filled with vivid, yet puzzling, imagery she could only sometimes understand. When she did glean some meaning from them, they often proved to be about inconsequential happenings. Today's vision—if it came true—would be the most significant to date.

She scanned the path leading to the southwest toward Broken Rock but saw no one. Sitting on a rock she waited, contemplating the dream. While the last part of it seemed clear, the rest mystified her. What did it mean? Who was the warrior and what manner of beast did he defeat? Valeria knew of no such creature and doubted it could even exist. It must symbolize something else. And what of the cloak? What did its illustrations represent? The detail of the memory surprised her. She saw every stitch, every seam, knowing its construction intimately, as if she had sewn it herself.

30

The jubilant singing of the men and boys in the distance jolted her from her thoughts. About a minute later they exited the woods with Marc taking the lead. Behind him a large buck hung by its feet from a pole borne by two hunters. When the group got closer to the village, they draped the deer over Marc's shoulders so he could proudly bring his kill home for all to witness. Her head spun at the sight of Marc—so eerie, *exactly* as she had foreseen. A warmth flooded out of her mind and through her body as it always did when one of her visions came true.

She faced the village and cheerily shouted, "They're back. Come see. The men are back."

Laughing, Valeria ran toward Marc. His unsteady gait showed he was near exhaustion. The animal's blood darkened most of his left side; a true badge of honor for any hunter. Numerous cuts and bruises covered his exposed skin, but they must not be very painful for he gave her an ear-to-ear grin.

"You caught it," Valeria said, her voice pitched higher than normal due to her excitement. Seeing that he caught a deer—that *anyone* had caught a deer—seemed almost too good to be true.

"He sure did," Garrett bellowed from beside Marc.

Marc's gaze briefly met hers before turning downward. "Well, I didn't exactly *catch* it."

"That doesn't matter," their leader insisted with obvious pride. "You hunted well and now we'll eat well."

The men let out a long cheer, fervently shaking their fists and weapons above their heads. Seeing an embarrassed smile return to Marc's face, Valeria gave him a quick kiss on the cheek. "I'm very proud of you."

As his face reddened, she wanted to kiss him again, only this time on the lips. Intending to do just that, she leaned toward him once more, but then stopped, feeling a sensation of unease to her right. Looking that way, she saw Donald scowl, his jealousy exposed. He envied the attention she paid to Marc, attention she would never give to him. Now she understood why he treated Marc so poorly.

What made Donald so unable to face the truth? Every time he tried to win her over, she made her lack of interest quite clear. Some of the other girls thought her foolish for turning him down, citing his handsome features and that he would be a good provider and protector. As true as those points might be, she did not love him and he did not love her. Without love, nothing else mattered.

A throng of women and children poured out of the village, engulfing the hunting party. They marveled at Marc's prize, pelting him with questions. When he reached the common house, two of the men relieved Marc of his load.

Garrett put his hands upon Marc's shoulders. "Go, rest yourself. You have done quite enough for today." He turned to her and winked. "Someone should see to his wounds."

Valeria took Marc's hand, leading him toward her home. "Come, let me clean those cuts."

"I can care for myself," he protested weakly.

"I'm sure you could, but you heard Garrett. You need to rest."

"Very well." His tired smile warmed her all over.

It pleased her he was more agreeable than when she sewed up his tunic last night. Then he acted as if he did not care for her, yet she knew he did, and more. She enjoyed this chance to be alone with him. After getting a bowl of hot water along the way from the cookhouse, she took him to her family's hut and sat him on her bed. From a bag of fabric scraps, she selected a handful of blue cloth strips to use as bandages. Yes, those would look good on him.

While tending to his wounds, she savored the lean hardness of his muscles. Letting her gaze drift off task, she looked upon him. He was shorter than most of the other men, but every bit as strong. His curly red, shoulder-length hair remained much the same, but the rest of his face had changed over the last few years. His jaw now squarer, firmer, his piercing blue-gray eyes more commanding, sitting deeper beneath a pronounced brow ridge. Marc's lower, richer voice had a quality to it that made her want to listen to his words. There was something else about him, something *different*, but she could not put a word to it. Whatever it might be, it drew her to him.

She gently finished tying a strip over a one-inch gash on his left elbow, then let her fingers trail lightly, almost surreptitiously, down his forearm before reaching for another bandage. "Tell me about catching the buck."

He casually shook his head, his hair rippling as it brushed against his broad shoulders. "I didn't catch it."

"Well, I assume it didn't jump into your arms."

He laughed, his fatigue lowering his guard enough to allow his gaze to disclose how much he cared for her. That simple revelation thrilled her, but she tried not to let it show. For whatever reason, Marc was not ready to admit how he truly felt. Until then, she would have to be patient.

"No, nothing that simple," he said.

Marc told how he took the westernmost part of the search for the deer, saw the bush and rabbits, then climbed the hill to look around. He hesitated a moment before describing how he found the buck in the water, fell in, roped the fallen tree, returned to pull out the deer, then made it back home.

"You left out a part of the story," she said, tying another strip into a neat bow.

Marc tensed slightly. "Uh, no."

She instantly knew he lied. "Marc, what are you keeping from me?"

He looked away. "Nothing."

With a finger alongside of his jaw, she turned his face to meet hers. "You left out part of the story after you climbed the hill. What was it?"

He squirmed a bit, averting her gaze. "Nothing."

She felt from him a sense of—what? Discomfort? Embarrassment? Valeria touched his shoulder to reassure him, but as she did so, she knew the answer. "You're afraid of something you did. Tell me. Please. I promise to keep it secret."

He remained silent for a moment, then looked at her, trust in his gaze. "You swear?"

"Yes."

He chewed on his lip for a dozen heartbeats then said quietly, "I accidentally entered the Forbidden Vale."

His eyes told her he spoke the truth. Her heart skipped a beat as she sharply inhaled. "*What?*"

"You heard me. I trespassed into the Forbidden Vale and lived to tell about it."

Her thoughts raced madly. That was impossible, wasn't it? Why did not the evil of the place immediately strike him down?

Would it come for him any minute? Tonight, maybe? After all, evil came out after dark. She studied his face and saw he did not seem very upset at the moment. Realizing her escalating emotions were getting the better part of her, she took in a deep breath and tried to calm herself. "How?"

Marc told her the complete story. "And all the way home I kept... *feeling* that tree. I can still feel it now if I think about it. It's—" Marc suddenly looked past her, his face worried. "How long have you been standing there?"

She turned and saw their friend, Sean, in the doorway. His expression revealed he had heard more than enough. Standing, she approached him and drew him inside. "Swear to keep this secret."

His mouth agape, Sean remained silent, too stunned to say anything.

Marc joined her. "Sean, you're not going to tell what I did, are you?"

He slowly shook his head. "No. Who would believe me? *I* wouldn't believe me," he said with a weak grin. "We've always heard that no one makes it out alive, or at least unharmed. So how *did* you escape?"

"I ran like my life depended on it." The nervous smile on Marc's face melted away. "To be honest, I don't know. Good fortune, I guess. Maybe the demons, or whatever lives in there, were elsewhere."

"Swear it, Sean," Valeria insisted.

Sean grasped Marc by both forearms. "I swear. God looked after you today, my friend."

Marc nodded. "Indeed."

Sean glanced outside the hut to see if they were still alone. "So, you said there were *thousands* of nuts in that tree?"

"Forget it. I'm not going back there, ever."

"Just jesting. Still, this *would* make a great story to tell around the fire for years to come—"

"—but it's too bad that it never happened," Valeria said firmly.

Sean chuckled and met her gaze. "Don't worry. I'll take the secret to my grave."

A sudden, chilly lightheadedness overcame her as Sean's features darkened. She staggered back a step before Marc caught her.

Sean looked concerned. "You all right?"

The sensation quickly passed. "Yes. Hungry, I guess." What *had* she just experienced? It certainly was not hunger, but something deep inside her mind made her use that excuse. The sensation reminded her somewhat of how she felt when she saw a vision come true, but those felt good. This did not. Whatever it might be, the feeling was new to her.

Sean backed toward the door. As his gaze momentarily fell upon Marc's supporting arms about her waist, he flushed and looked elsewhere, trying to hide a smile. "Well, I better let you finish tending to Marc. See you at dinner."

"Bye," she said.

Letting go of her, Marc waved lazily after his friend and yawned. How she enjoyed the brief comfort of his closeness. If only he would hold her that way more often. She had him sit. "You need some sleep."

"I'll be all right. I don't want to miss dinner." He yawned again.

None of his remaining injuries were in need of further attention so she gently pushed him over, covering him with a skin. "I'll wake you when it's ready. Now, sleep."

"Very well." He closed his eyes then put his hand on her arm. "Thanks for caring for me."

She placed her hand atop his. "Anytime."

As he drifted off, she wondered what it was like to feel this tree he spoke of. That he trusted her enough to share his terrible secret meant a lot to her. How might he react if she told him about her own secret—her dreams, her visions? Would he even believe her?

Valeria decided to worry about that another day. For now, all she wanted to do was watch him sleep.

Chapter 4

"Are you certain?" Sean stared upward at the giant tree in the distance, his eyes wide in fascination. "It *looks* powerful enough, but I don't feel a thing."

"Well, *I* do." Not wanting to talk about it further, Marc approached the creek and led the way over the fallen tree.

Unease filled him at being so near the haunted tree and Forbidden Vale. He hoped he would not regret letting Sean talk him into coming all this way to hunt rabbits. Yes, the village badly needed fresh meat, and if any place could give them the chance to find some, this one would. Only his duty as a hunter brought him back this way so soon. It had been six days since he found that buck. Six days since his life changed in many ways, leaving him feeling somehow different.

Back on solid ground, Sean once again gazed at the tree, this time with a thoughtful expression. "I think I've seen this before, years ago with my father when I was little. If I remember correctly, you and your father were with us."

The memory jumped to the forefront of Marc's mind, as clear as if it had been yesterday. "We were." Tapping his friend on the shoulder, he pointed south. "The hares, if we can find any, are that way." He nodded to his right. "And that's the bush where I found them."

With a pleased grin, Sean handed him his staff, strode over to the bush, and dropped to all fours to peer underneath it. "There are rabbit tracks here, good-sized ones, too. I can see where they ate at the bark." Standing, he studied some of the limbs. "They didn't kill it, though. Plenty of leaves are budding out."

Marc looked around at the other bushes and trees, noting with relief that they, too, appeared to be waking from their long slumbers. "Everything is. I hope spring will come this time."

"Amen, my friend." Sean took back his staff and gestured forward with a wry grin. "Now, let's see if you can repeat your luck from last week."

"I'm afraid there's little chance of me coming across another injured deer," Marc said dryly, starting to walk. "I'd be happy to find a hare."

"A nice plump one, perhaps?" Sean asked teasingly.

Marc chuckled. "I'd settle for a tough, scrawny one."

"As would I. No matter what we may or may not catch, we are better off than digging birds out of the cliffs with the others. So, where should we start?"

Marc looked ahead at the ever-widening wood, then pointed at an area heavy with brush. "How about in there? Bound to be some rabbit trails that could use a well-made snare or two."

"Spoken like a true hunter," Sean said with conviction. After several steps he spoke again, his tone subdued, "I don't know why Don thinks otherwise."

Marc frowned, his mood souring. "Why did you have to mention *him*?"

"Don't let Don bother you when he's not even here. Besides, I know a few things about him that will cheer you up."

Marc pushed aside a low hanging branch with his staff. "Like what?"

"Yesterday Don spoke ill of you to some of the others, saying you just got lucky and found a deer that died from the cold. He claimed you made up the story about falling in the water."

"This is supposed to cheer me up?" Marc cast him a half-hearted glare.

Sean's face lit up with a mischievous glee. "Garrett caught him telling those lies and scolded him."

"In front of *everybody*?" Surprised and pleased, Marc did not try to hide his grin.

"Everybody. *Then* he reminded Don how *you* fed us for several days and—"

Suddenly, feeling an odd sensation not unlike the one he knew from the haunted tree, Marc reached out with lightning speed and clasped a hand over Sean's mouth. "Shh," he whispered into his friend's ear, "something's ahead of us."

Peeling off Marc's hand, Sean looked about apprehensively. "What is it?" he asked, his voice barely audible.

"I don't know."

Marc did not doubt something was there, and that puzzled him. He scrutinized the heavy shadows ahead and detected the dim image of a man who spun in place, then struck at something with a staff. Marc quickly pointed at him.

"There."

Sean scanned the spot Marc indicated. "Where?"

"There's a man, eighty paces away, just left of the tall tree."

"I see the tree, but no man."

"He's—" The figure suddenly vanished leaving Marc feeling lightheaded. "He's gone now."

"What was he doing?"

"Fighting something, I think, but I didn't see what. It's too dark over there."

Sean trotted in that direction. "Let's see if he needs help."

Together they searched for the man but found no indication that anyone had been there.

Marc shook his head. "That's strange. I clearly saw him. I *felt* something, too." He let out a ragged breath. "I felt it to my bones."

Sean's eyes widened. "Like how you feel the tree?"

Marc nodded.

"That might explain why I didn't see anything and we didn't find anything. Maybe the tree is fooling you somehow."

"No. It's not the tree's doing. I'm sure of that."

Sean looked at him a moment, eyebrows arched, then gazed around warily. "Maybe we're too close to the Forbidden Vale."

Marc shook his head. "The Vale, the tree—both feel... strange. This seemed more... friendly."

"Maybe you saw a fairy. They're supposed to be friendly."

"Fairy? They're not real."

"Says the man who just one week ago doubted the stories told about the Vale." Sean leaned on his staff, an amused glint in his eyes. "Who told you that?"

"My father. The summer before the darkness came, he told me there were no fairies, elves, things like that."

The humor in Sean's eyes advanced to his lips. "What would he have said about haunted trees?"

Marc frowned, no longer in the mood for Sean's teasing. "I saw a *man*—tall, wearing a brown robe, holding a long staff—*not* a fairy. Maybe I mistook where he stood and we've been searching in the wrong spot." Sighing, he unslung his pack and opened the flap. "Let's forget all this and set our traps."

"Agreed."

While they worked, Marc pondered what he just experienced. For the last six days, he could not keep the awareness of that cursèd tree from his mind for long. It crept into his thoughts during the day, his dreams at night—a constant reminder his life had changed in some way. He felt unsettled, as if he did not fit into his own skin.

Sean stood and admired his handiwork. "That makes seven snares. I think we can place another two before we need to return." He started toward a large group of bushes. "Let's try over here next."

Marc hurried to catch up, only to collide with him. "Why are you backing up?" As soon as the words left his lips, he understood the reason: two wolves advanced on them, growling, with teeth bared.

"God help us!" Sean said in near panic, holding out his staff in a shielding stance.

Marc's heart leapt into his throat as every muscle in his body clenched in fear. His breath came fast and shallow. These wolves were not defending their territory, they were *hunting*. "They want to eat us!" He and Sean slowly backed away, the beasts keeping about ten paces distant.

"Go hunt something else," Sean said shakily to the wolves. "You don't want us. We're tough and scrawny."

"*Sean*. This is no time to jest. We have to think of what to do."

Sean circled the bottom of his staff before him. "There's only two of them. Why don't you take the left one; I'll get the right."

"Good enough." Marc desperately wished he had a spear for it would be a far more effective defense than his staff alone. He never was that proficient in using a staff as a weapon, even though his father and Ethan had worked with him many hours to improve his skill. Too bad Ethan was not here. He could dispatch both wolves in mere seconds. Valeria, too, would be at little risk for her skill with weapons equaled her father's.

The wolves crept another pace closer.

"Why aren't they charging?" Sean asked, then quickly added, "Not that I want them to."

"They're herding us, trying to make us run." Feeling a prickly warmth on the back of his neck, Marc glanced behind and his fear surged, making him let out a cry of alarm. A dark gray female with a torn right ear slunk toward them, savage violence and hunger evident in her amber gaze. "There's another one behind us!" Marc turned to protect their rear.

Sean cursed. "We could possibly fight two, but three—"

"HELP," Marc shouted. "HEEELLLLP."

"What good will that do?" Sean asked, his voice tight with fear. "There's no one—oh, the man you saw. HELP."

Marc's mind raced wildly. He had seen the damage wolves could inflict on an animal. How could they escape? Climb a tree? No, bad idea. Maybe they could fend them off long enough to make it back to the creek. He would rather take his chances with the frigid water again than be ripped open by those snapping jaws.

While he attempted to figure out a way to escape, a thought desperately tried to surface. Something his father once told him about wolves and how they hunt. How they used diversions and ambush. Then, a sudden sense of alarm shot through Marc's body and everything went strange, moving too slow to be normal. He whirled around to see a fourth wolf, a male, larger than the rest, drifting through the air in mid leap, at the halfway point between the ground and Sean's throat. Without need of thought, Marc swung his staff hard, easily hitting the wolf's head at the back of the skull. With a crunch of bone and a momentary yelp, the creature fell hard against Sean and dropped to the ground, lifeless. The world around Marc returned to normal leaving him a bit dazed.

Sean glanced down and gasped. "Oh, God bless me. Thanks, Marc."

"It tried to ambush us from the side," Marc said, unsure of what just happened. Even so, his gaze remained on the female behind them. She looked from the body of her pack mate to him, her eyes filled with loss and hate. The dead wolf mattered to her. So clear were her emotions to him that Marc felt as if she had spoken aloud.

"You see any more?" Sean asked, bringing Marc out of his thoughts.

He quickly checked around for others. "No. One down, three left."

Now that first blood had been spilled, the remaining wolves became even more vicious, their hackles raised and muscles tensing, primed for attack. Jaws open they advanced, sharp fangs exposed, ready to tear flesh from bone. As Marc's fear reached a height he had never known, a warmth flooded over him with a calm power, the same sensation he felt when he climbed out of the icy waters of the creek.

The female began to charge.

"STOP!" he commanded, holding out his staff. Obviously startled, the animal slid to a halt, casting out a shallow wake of rotted leaves. The other two animals were equally surprised. Marc stared in disbelief.

"How did you do that?" Sean whispered in surprise.

"I—I don't know." He watched the female skitter around to join the others. The wolves looked at each other for several moments, then turned as one, sat on their haunches and regarded Marc while clearly ignoring Sean.

Seeing that, Sean grunted. "Well, that was—keep telling them what to do. Maybe they used to be tame once and learned to obey people."

"I'll try." Marc addressed the wolves in his most authoritative voice. "Do not hunt us for we do not hunt you. If you hunt us, we will kill you." He emphasized the point by kicking the body at his feet. "Now, GO, and hunt people no more!" To Marc's utter bewilderment, the wolves stood, turned and vanished into the woods.

Slack-jawed, Sean stared at Marc, equally mystified. "What the... How... ?"

Marc tried to speak but no words would form, so he shook his head and shrugged.

Gripping his shoulders, Sean looked at him with concern. "Are you all right?"

Marc nodded. He felt disconnected, as if abruptly roused from a deep sleep. Concentrating on clearing his mind, he said, "The wolves—"

"Are they coming back?" Suddenly alert, Sean carefully inspected the nearby woods, tightly gripping his staff.

"No." Marc pointed in the distance. "There."

Sean looked that way. "I see nothing."

Marc saw nothing, either, but knew the wolves would be visible at any second.

"Keep watching." As he spoke, the wolves crossed their line of sight several hundred paces away.

"Thank Heaven. They are gone," Sean said, releasing a heavy sigh of relief. After a moment, he looked down at the carcass of the dead wolf, then up at Marc. "Thanks for saving my life." Grasping his forearm firmly, Sean shook it while meeting his gaze. "I owe you a debt I cannot repay."

Marc saw a fleeting image of his friend laying down, pale and sickly. Shaking his head, the illusion disappeared along with the strange feeling. "Don't worry over it. Maybe you can return the favor one day."

"Glad to." Sean slung the dead wolf onto his shoulder. "We came for food and here it is."

Marc grimaced. "Not my idea of a tasty meal."

"No, but food is food. Maybe we should head back now before our luck changes."

"Agreed." Taking in a deep, cleansing breath, Marc let it out along with all the tension he could release. "Twice I've come to this area and twice death has drawn near. Too near."

"But you made it out safely each time," Sean said with a grin, "and with a good amount to eat."

He sighed. "There must be a safer way of finding food."

Sean laughed. "If I think of it, my friend, I'll let you know."

Ψ   Ψ   Ψ

As he and Sean neared their village, Marc heard a number of agitated voices carrying to them through the woods. Something about the nature of the sound made him cautious. Picking up the pace, they soon neared the edge of the forest and, while remaining hidden, saw the cause—three men on horseback occupied the area south of the common house. Unsure of the strangers' intentions, he motioned for Sean to follow him further back into the trees. This wouldn't be the first time others came by wanting some of their food—most would ask, but some tried to take.

Upon reaching a safe distance, Marc uncoiled a rope. "Who do you think they are?"

Sean shrugged. "Thieves?"

Marc echoed the gesture. "Could be. Whoever they are, they're not getting this." He threw one end of the rope over a moderately high limb, tied the other around the wolf's rear legs and hoisted it into the air, tying the free end off on a broken snag.

Returning, they approached the men from behind. The leader, clearly of Roman blood, stood out; the manner of his dress and posture indicated he was in charge. Dark brown hair flowed well past his shoulders and over his burnished leather armor. Worn strips of blue and white cloth tied near the end of his spear let it be known he represented the king. Of the two other men, one was Marc's size with black hair and deep brown skin, the other tall and thin, with pale skin, long hair and a close-cropped beard, both fiery red. All three were well armed and none seemed to have suffered much from the famine. Before the leader's horse stood Marc's mother and, flanking her on either side, his two sisters, their hands tightly gripping the folds of her dress. Crowded around them were the other women and children of the village. All looked upon the men with fear. Marc's gut tightened.

"Something is very wrong," he whispered to Sean.

"Yes." Sean glanced uneasily around. "None of the men have returned."

"Let's hope they do so and soon. We cannot protect the women by ourselves." The staffs he and Sean carried were no match for the unwelcome guests' spears and bows.

Marc's mother's gaze flicked his way momentarily, eyes widening in warning. Seeing her reaction, the leader looked Marc's way, his lips curling slightly in the corners, the expression remarkably similar to those worn earlier by the wolves.

"And whom might these two young men be?"

The man's authoritative tone revealed an underlying smugness. He wanted something and expected to get it judging by the fact two soldiers accompanied him. That, and his mother's worried expression, told Marc to be very careful.

"I am Marc and this is Sean," he said, stopping next to his mother. The man's narrow, angular face and large, slightly hooked nose reminded Marc a little of his grandmother, though she did not have his heavy brows or larger ears. While he looked to be about thirty years of age, something in his charcoal gray eyes made him seem much older. When Marc met the man's gaze, an uncomfortable chill tingled through him, not unlike the sensation of when an arm or leg fell asleep. "Why has the king's envoy honored us with a visit this day?"

The leader shifted on his mount and studied him for a time. "Marc. Hmmm. You are Marcus, son of the tanner, Davidus?"

"Yes, sir, but my father died not quite two years ago."

"So I have been told. As his son, you inherit your father's trade and obligations."

The way he said *obligations* sent a shiver up Marc's back. "What are you saying?"

"Your family owes a debt to the king."

The red-haired soldier shared a callous, sly smile with his shorter companion, causing Marc to feel even more concerned. Things here were not as they seemed. Hiding his reaction, he shook his head. "I know of no such debt."

"Your father had the privilege of being one of the king's favored craftsmen. For that he was to pay a yearly honorarium."

"But he's dead and can no longer sell any leather—to the king, or anyone else. That privilege is now lost."

"Possibly," the man said airily, almost as if the point were trivial. After several seconds he leaned closer, his features and voice hardening. "Even so, the debt remains."

A wash of emotions swelled within Marc—irritation that this person had the nerve to enter his village under such questionable pretenses, disgust that one such as him held the king's trust, and anger at assuming he could take advantage of Marc's father's death.

"That's foolish," Marc said heatedly. "Even if I could pay this... this *thievery*, I wouldn't." Marc stiffened as the man's face darkened and the tip of his spear dropped to hover just inches from Marc's chest.

"You have two choices," the man growled. "Pay or *die*."

"*NO!*" Marc's mother cried, lunging toward him only to be struck in the head with the butt of the black-haired soldier's spear. Staggering several steps back, she crumpled to the ground.

Gwen rushed toward her prone form. "Mother!" Gasps of alarm rose from the women and children gathered behind them.

Unable to move for fear of being impaled, Marc tightly balled his fists and watched with seething frustration as his sister helped her stand. Blood coursed down the side of his mother's head. At that moment, he would have given *anything* to be holding a spear of his own in order to plunge it into the black-haired man's heart, knowing full well the other two men would have killed him an instant later.

The leader regarded her with naked scorn. "One more word from you, woman, and I will burn your home."

"With you in it," the same soldier added with a sinister chuckle.

Marc took a step back, greatly fearing for his life and that of his family; he could do little against these bullies. Sean's grip tightened on his staff, but Marc warned him with his eyes not to act. "I cannot pay," Marc said, sounding more frightened than he wanted to. "I have nothing of value."

Cold and empty of humanity, the black ice of the man's gaze pierced him through as the muscles of his arms tensed in preparation to use his spear. "Then die," he said flatly.

Heart thrumming madly in his chest, Marc backed further away preparing to dodge the thrust when an authoritative voice cried out loudly from behind. "Hold there."

The cacophony of the villagers' upset voices stilled as everyone turned to see who spoke. A tall, lean man of advanced years strode confidently forward. He wore a long, brown, hooded robe, the hem of which barely cleared the ground. Great quantities of iron gray hair trailed down his back, his beard half the length of an arm. No one had need to ask his name for all knew of the great wizard, Oren the Wise.

"What reason do you have to do violence against this young man?" the elder demanded of the man threatening Marc.

Scowling, the leader waved a hand contemptuously at him. "This is none of your concern, old man. Be off with you for we are on the king's business."

The wizard brightened. "Ah. I know the king well. What might his business be with Marcus here?"

The man bristled defensively. "His family has neglected to pay their honorarium for over two years."

Oren's dark brown eyes narrowed, focusing more intently on the intruder who in turn stared back. Marc wondered if the old man's gaze involved magic—the same magic that made Oren all-powerful. Never had the wizard been bested in a fight, or so he had heard. Knowing he was safe, Marc relaxed a little and stood his ground.

Oren's hand settled lightly upon Marc's shoulder. "How do you expect Marcus to pay that debt when he has no money to give, *Thaddeus*?"

The man poorly hid his surprise that the wizard knew his name. "His father used to pay in leather goods, but I will accept silver—or food."

Oren snorted in disgust. "That is the true reason you are here. To rob these people of their food under the guise of collecting an honorarium. You threaten Marcus' life, counting on the good people of Oak Creek to come to his aid by giving you what you desire." He looked about, then regarded Thaddeus once more. "And when the men of the village are conveniently absent, too. Have you no shame?"

The man's shoulders tightened at that. "A debt is owed and a debt will be collected." Thaddeus redirected his spear toward Oren. "One way or another."

"*Discinde!*" the wizard barked, rapidly stepping to the side, then forward, to seize the shaft of the spear at its midpoint, his motions a blur almost too quick to follow. Snapping it in two as if it were a twig, the elder dropped the halves on the ground and retook his place beside Marc, who looked at him with awe and more than a bit of fear. "There will be no violence done here today. What is his debt?"

Visibly shaken, Thaddeus glanced in confusion at his now empty hands. "Uh, five silver coins."

Oren frowned. "I see. Tell me, whom is your master?"

"The king, of course."

"Do you serve him well?"

"Yes. What is the meaning of these questions?"

"I say that you do *not* serve him well. You serve *yourself* and your greed for the debt is only three silvers. Does not the king provide a warm place for you and your family? Does he not provide a fair wage and food?"

Thaddeus nodded, his expression empty of emotion. For some reason, that caused Marc considerable worry.

Oren subtly shook his head. "Why then must you risk losing all that for some coins? You do not honor your liege by lying to him and stealing from his subjects. I ask you again, what is their debt?"

Thaddeus lowered his gaze, the muscles of his jaw tightening. "Three," he grated through his clenched teeth. Rage practically boiled off of him.

Marc started. How did Oren know what the true debt was?

From inside his robe, the wizard produced three pieces of silver and handed them to Thaddeus. "The debt is paid. See to it that it is properly recorded. You would not like me to inform your master as to your disservice. Now, go and steal no more. If I hear it told that you are cheating any others, you will not live long enough to regret it."

Thaddeus' gaze hardened. "Do not make threats you cannot carry out. You are old and feeble; I am in my prime. Break all the spears you want. You cannot protect yourself forever, no matter how potent your magic. One day an arrow or lance will silence your mouth."

Extending his right arm, Oren said, "*Volitā!*" Marc watched in wonder as the front half of the broken spear rose up to float before Thaddeus, the blade a thumb's width from his throat. "The only one who should be silenced is you. I could kill you with nothing more than a whisper, but now is not your time. I know the day of your death and how it will come. If you knew that, you would beg to die now."

Thaddeus tried to remain stone-faced, but Marc saw the traces of defeat in his eyes. For all the man's outward bravado, he knew he could not best Oren.

The wizard leaned closer and whispered, "*Ārdē.*" Marc flinched and the villagers gasped in awe as the piece of spear burst into blue fire. "If you still wish to kill me, be my guest. Take the weapon before you. Do not fear the flames for you will have an eternity to get used to them in hell." Thaddeus warily eyed the weapon before him, his cheek twitching in terror as sweat beaded on his brow. "No? Well, you had your chance. Off with you." Oren pointed southward.

Thaddeus snarled a curse and batted the spearhead away with the back of his hand. It tumbled through the air coming to rest beneath the tall soldier's horse. With a snort of alarm, the stallion fearfully scuttled to the side, almost dislodging his rider.

"We will meet again." Pivoting his own mount, Thaddeus began to leave.

"Yes, we shall," the wizard said with certainty.

Marc studied Oren's face as he reproached Thaddeus. A faint fire blazed within the wizard's eyes—undoubtedly his magic power. That power called to Marc, touching his mind much like how the haunted tree came to him. A wisp of vertigo skittered continuously through his innards, almost as frightening as Thaddeus' attempt to kill him. He wanted nothing to do with magic, fearing both it and those who wielded its might. Even so, he was deeply grateful for Oren's protection.

The short, black-haired man was last to turn his horse about. Oren glanced at Marc, his mother, then back at the man. "Atellus," Oren said sharply.

The soldier stopped his mount and looked back at the wizard, a foul expression on his face.

"*Scinde!*" Oren commanded while snapping his fingers. With a sudden shout of pain, Atellus clamped his hand to the side of his head. Moments later, blood dribbled down his arm. "*That* is for attacking an unarmed woman. Be gone, coward."

Many of the women cheered as the man kicked his horse into a trot and caught up with his companions. Marc's savior stood still, watching the intruders ride away. Once they were out of sight, the sensation Marc felt abated and Oren turned to him.

"I doubt they will return anytime soon." The elder sounded pleased, even amused.

"I hope so, Great One." Overcome with relief and gratitude, Marc fell to his knees, bowing low. "A thousand thanks for my life and that of my family. Tell me how I may repay you."

"For your life, or the three coins?" the master of all asked, his voice gentle.

"Both."

"Stand."

Fearing him, Marc obeyed, keeping his view averted.

"There is no need to repay me. Your village has always been kind to me and thus is under the protection of the magic I command. When you saved Sean's life today, did you expect repayment?"

A chill came over Marc and his knees suddenly weakened, threatening to drop him to the ground. How could Oren possibly know about that? "Uh, no, I... I did not. But the three silver—"

The wizard waved his hand dismissively. "Not important. They are merely coins and I have more than I need. Let us discuss this later. For now, retrieve the animal that you and Sean have brought back."

Marc glanced at Sean and found him equally surprised. "Master, how did you know that?"

The old man gave him a faint, almost playful, smile. "The magic around us knows all things. I am most fortunate to have its favor. Now, go, for the sooner you bring it back, the sooner it may be prepared."

Marc hesitated, looking toward his mother; she held a bloody cloth to her temple. "But—"

"Do not worry," Oren said reassuringly. "I will see to your mother's injury. Off with you."

Marc and Sean ran to where they left their catch and found the wolf had some company—tied next to it was a fine hare, its neck still ringed with one of the snares they had set earlier.

Stunned, Sean cautiously touched it. "How did this happen?"

Marc had little doubt. "Oren."

"You think so? How would he know one of our snares had caught a hare?"

"And how would he bring it here? Magic, of course." Marc gingerly touched the rabbit's fur, half expecting to feel something out of the ordinary upon it, but it felt normal.

Sean touched it as well. "Such magic is frightening."

Marc nodded, a shiver coursing through him as he again felt the distant tree's presence. Closing his eyes, he tried to will it away. "I want nothing to do with it."

Ψ   Ψ   Ψ

Sean brought the animals back for the women to prepare while Marc hurried to his mother's side. He found her sitting upon a bench outside the cookhouse, the left side of her dress stained with blood. Oren, Valeria and his sisters stood beside her.

He dropped to one knee and carefully reached out to cup her cheek in his hand. "Mother. How are you?"

He tried to inspect her injury, but she smiled and pulled him into a one-armed hug on the clean side of her body. "Well. Oren kindly healed my wound." She touched her head just above the left ear. The wound was gone save for a faint pink line.

Grateful beyond words, Marc bowed to the wizard. "Again, my thanks."

"None is needed for I am here to serve."

Marc found the wizard's statement confusing. Something must have shown in his face for Oren cocked his head and let out a little grunt of doubt.

"You seem unwilling to believe me."

Scrambling to collect his thoughts, Marc said, "I do not understand why you say you are here to serve for you possess great power. We should be the ones serving you."

The wizard smiled, lightly stroking his beard. "I see your point. Yes, I do have much power at my command. But that does not mean I am supposed to rule the lives of others. Our Creator tells us *from those who have been given much, much is expected.*" Oren placed his large hand on Marc's shoulder and gently squeezed. "Let's pretend *you* had some of the magic power I possess, power enough to protect the innocent from those who serve evil, or—" He nodded at Marc's mother. "The power to heal. Would you demand fealty or payment for using that power to help others, or would you share it freely?"

While Marc would never desire such abilities, he understood the master's point. "Freely, most certainly."

Letting out a warm chuckle, Oren nodded. "Indeed." He turned to Marc's mother. "How are you feeling now, Judith?"

Her broad smile gladdened Marc's heart. "Much better. The headache is all but gone. God bless you." Leaning forward, she gave the wizard a hug, then kissed his cheek.

Looking a bit embarrassed, Oren winked at him. "Now *that* is a payment I am happy to accept." Several of the nearby women laughed.

Valeria eagerly touched Marc's arm, her eyes gleaming with excitement. "You should have seen how his magic healed her. The wound closed up before my eyes. Wouldn't you love to have such magic? I would."

Marc gave her what he hoped looked like an agreeable, yet noncommittal, smile. The notion of having magic further invade his life unnerved him but he wisely did not voice those thoughts for she would invariably try to convince him otherwise. Instead, he hugged his mother again. "I'm pleased you are better." As her arms embraced him, he heard excited voices to the south—the men had returned. Helping her stand, he turned to see Garrett approach their visitor and greet him with a warm handshake.

"Oren the Wise. Welcome. What good fortune brings you to our village?"

"I came to see how the crops are growing."

"Well. Very well, in fact. The rye and wheat are longer than my fingers already. If the weather does not turn against us, we should have a bountiful harvest."

Oren nodded slightly. "All signs are you will."

"Wonderful. Please, share our meal. It's not much but what we have is yours."

"You will have a good meal this day thanks to Marc and Sean." Oren nodded at Marc. "Tell him of your day's adventure."

Marc did, leaving out the parts about the mysterious man, his odd feelings and being near the Vale. "—and when we went to get the wolf out of the tree, we found a hare had been added to it."

Sean nodded in the wizard's direction. "One we didn't bring with us."

Garrett's eyebrows rose as he looked at Oren. "Your handiwork, my friend?"

Oren gave him a thin smile. "I am also here for another reason. I need help around my home. Some chores, repairs—things I am getting too old to do."

"Whatever you need, just ask, my friend."

"I will bring it up after the meal." Oren stood silent for a moment, idly playing with the cuffs of his sleeves. "Tell me, Garrett, have you ever met Thaddeus?"

"One of the king's men?" At the wizard's nod, Garrett's expression soured. "Yes, several times. A most unpleasant fellow. I don't know what the king sees in him."

"He paid the village a visit today." Oren told what took place. "There is much hatred and evil within him. He would have enjoyed killing Marc. Wanted to, in fact."

Garrett's gaze centered on Marc. Many thoughts churned within the leader's eyes, the last of which seemed to be a guarded relief. Marc had seen that same look the year before when a group of men tried to steal their food in the middle of the night. The thieves ran from home to home, hastily searching everywhere, but were driven off before finding any of the caches secreted away.

"That would have been tragic," Garrett said, his expression suddenly hardening before turning back to the wizard. "Why did you not kill him?"

Marc felt a stab of vertigo as his breath caught in his throat. That look on Garrett's face clearly revealed the man *knew* something, something secret and dangerous.

Oren returned the look. "It was not Thaddeus' time." He nodded toward Marc. "Nor Marc's."

Garrett relaxed some, giving the elder a slight bow of respect. "Thank you for protecting him and the village in our absence."

Oren waved off the compliment. "You should thank the magic. Now, if you will excuse me, I would like to walk around and visit with everyone."

As Oren departed, Garrett turned to Marc with a warm smile. "Your father would have been proud of you for defending Sean like that. I know I am."

"Me, too," Sean said. "I'm amazed how well he handled his staff. He killed that wolf with one blow. Marc has become a good hunter."

Marc felt his face redden. "I didn't do anything special. I saw the wolf and swung. Just good luck, that's all."

Garrett shook his head. "No, there's more to it than luck. You *have* improved. Tonight I intend to declare you as one of the men."

Marc staggered back a step in disbelief; this was the honor all of the boys wanted. "Sir, I—"

"You deserve it. The same goes for you, Sean. The men and I feel the time is right."

"What about Donald, sir?" Sean asked with a careful neutrality.

With a little quirk of a frown, Garrett said, "Not today." Giving Marc a pat on the back, Garrett walked away leaving them in a daze. Suddenly smiling, Sean punched him in the shoulder. "Congratulations, *Sir*."

Laughing, Marc tried to return the favor only to have Sean duck at the last moment. "That's not fair."

"Hardly the behavior of two *men*," Valeria said sternly from behind them. They stopped their horseplay and pretended to act more mature. "You're not fooling me." Suddenly grinning, she ran up to Sean and gave him a quick peck on the cheek. "Congratulations." Turning to Marc, she gave him the same followed by a hug. "I'm so proud of you."

Still locked in her embrace, he gazed deep into her hazel eyes and went all weak inside. Why did she affect him that way? It was not simply lust, for while he experienced that at times for her, this felt different. Her eyes called to him, seemingly drawing him into her soul. And more than anything, he wished he could go there.

His thoughts abruptly changed to the images of her swimming naked in that pond, but this time he watched from a more distant, ground-level viewpoint, hidden behind some bushes, knowing full well his actions were wrong. As his dream-self became embarrassed, she rose halfway out of the water, revealing the beauty of her nakedness, then looked directly at where he hid and smiled. "Marc?"

Blinking his eyes, Marc said, "Uh, yes?"

"What happened?" She wore an expression of concern.

He couldn't tell her. He just couldn't. "Happened? Uh, nothing."

Cocking her head, she gave him a cautious frown, the same frown she used the week before when he tried to avoid telling her of his trespass into the Forbidden Vale. "It wasn't nothing, You stood as still as stone."

"I did?" It must have happened during his daydream.

"And your face is red. What happened?"

Marc prayed she could not guess the nature of his thoughts. The shame would too much to bear. "Just... thinking."

Sean glanced around furtively, then quietly asked, "*Feel something again?*"

Valeria leaned toward Sean. "What do you mean, *again*?"

Sean rolled his eyes apologetically, giving Marc a sorrowful look, but that did little to undo the damage. Still, Marc was grateful for Sean's slip as it let Valeria think his daydream was about something else. With a sigh, he led them to a more private spot and told her the full story of their day.

Valeria held his hands the whole time. "Incredible. Those wolves seemed to actually obey you." Her expression turned more serious. "I thought you weren't ever going near the Vale again? The first time there *you* almost died. This time it was Sean who barely escaped. What's going to happen the next time?"

"Don't be upset at Marc," Sean said, his tone heavy with regret. "It was my fault. I talked him into it. I thought we could catch a rabbit or two there."

"And we did, so it would seem." Marc nodded toward the wizard across the way.

"I suppose Oren knows we were close to the Vale." Sean looked worried.

Marc shrugged. "I just hope he doesn't know about last week."

The returning boys caught their attention. Donald soon passed by them with the bag of birds, but he looked only at Sean, deliberately ignoring Marc and Valeria.

"Thirty eight," he boasted.

Sighing, Marc smiled at his two friends. "Let's go pick a nice place to sit for dinner while there's time."

"Somewhere close to Garrett," Sean said with a wink.

"And far from Oren," Valeria added.

"But in view of Donald so he can see us *men* after the ceremony is complete," Marc said with more than a bit of spite.

Valeria took his and Sean's arms as they walked. "It serves him right."

Sean laughed. "That it does."

Ψ   Ψ   Ψ

The three of them remained near the common house central fire until it was time to eat. While Sean busied himself entertaining his younger brother, Valeria and Marc quietly watched as the old wizard went from person to person, talking with the adults and performing some feat of magic for the children. Seeing how his face lit up when the little ones giggled and laughed made Marc realize that despite Oren's great power and serious manner, inside him lived a gentle man.

The meal turned out better than Marc expected. Even so, wolf-rabbit-bird stew would never be a favorite of his. Afterward, Garrett asked that he and Sean recount their hunt, as was the custom. Rising in place at the table, they took turns telling a simpler version of their day, one wisely omitting their nearness to the Vale and how it affected Marc. When Sean acted out with great enthusiasm how Marc's skill with the staff had killed the wolf, Marc did his best not to blush. As they started to retake their seats, Garrett motioned for them to wait. Ascending the talking stone, Garrett spoke to all.

"Marc and Sean, come forward."

With his heart in his throat, Marc turned and followed his equally nervous friend toward their leader. Glancing back, he saw Valeria now sat next to his family. The four women watched with unabashed pride as he took his place before the village. He needed every bit of his willpower to keep a silly grin off his face. After all, this was a serious moment.

Garrett gazed at both of them, his countenance as stoic as granite, and yet Marc spied the smile that could not be hidden within the man's eyes. Looking out over the people, Oak Creek's leader waited until the room was silent and every eye had turned

55

his way, then spoke with conviction and purpose. "Marcus. Sean. All here have witnessed your deeds. You have worked hard to feed us, to protect us, to keep us strong. You have proved yourselves able-bodied and brave, as men, not boys. Do each of you swear, on your honor, to always put the good of the village before that of your own, to share what you have with all, to keep us in your hearts and minds as brothers and sisters?"

"I do," Marc and Sean said together.

Garrett smiled. "Turn and face your village."

It was done. He was a man now. With new eyes Marc looked upon the people he knew so well. All were happy except Donald, whose displeasure seemed to press against him like a foul wind, his eyes blazing with anger and resentment. Though younger than Donald, Marc was now in a position of authority over him. For a moment that pleased Marc, but then he realized it was wrong to think that way for it made him no better than his former friend. Marc let the childish thought go.

Garrett stretched his arms out wide, palms facing inward as if embracing the crowd before him. "Citizens of Oak Creek, it is our great honor to welcome these two men into our village."

A great cheer arose from the crowd, filling Marc with a humble sense of pride. Grinning ear-to-ear, Garrett shook hands with him and Sean in the manner used by the men of the village—a warrior's grip, hand to forearm. Engulfed by the throng, Marc gladly received the many hugs and handshakes from his newly extended family. Once things quieted back down, he and Sean returned to their seats as Garrett stood before the village once more.

"Tonight we are privileged to have Oren the Wise among us. Without his wisdom and magic, many of us would not have lived this long." Garrett gave the wizard standing to his left a respectful nod. "Even today he protected us from three of the King's men. Let us all welcome his words."

Marc felt a sense of foreboding come over him as Oren took his place upon the stone, the nearby fire illuminating him in a most unusual way. His gray hair had an eerie glow about it and the contrasting shadows of his features made him appear all the more imposing. The crowd stared expectantly.

"Thank you for those kind words, Garrett, and thanks to all of you for sharing your meal with me. Today I came by for more than just a visit. I am in need of someone to help me at my home for a year's time. Of course, I will pay for these services."

Marc wondered what kind of help a powerful wizard might need when Sean suddenly stood. "I will help, Master. You need not pay me. Your aid to our village has been payment enough."

Oren acknowledged him with a gracious nod and indicated he should sit. "Most kind of you, however I need someone who can read and write."

Seeing his friend's face fall, Marc gave him a supportive look. Donald then rose.

"I can read some, wise one, and I'm a hard worker."

Marc could easily guess Donald's intentions. By working for Oren he would gain higher status within the village as well as earn the favor of the wizard. Marc suspected he also wanted to learn the old man's magic. Fine. Donald could do that for all he cared.

"Thank you, Donald, but I need someone who can read well. Besides, you are needed most here." Oren scanned the crowd. "Anyone else?"

Marc wondered who he would pick. There were several in the village who could read fairly well. Then, he felt a warm jolt as Oren's gaze stopped upon him.

"How about you? I know you can read and write."

"Me?" What did Oren see in him? There had to be somebody better.

"Yes. You have skills I could use."

"Like leather work?" Marc wondered what good that would be given the current shortage of animals.

"That, and others." Oren regarded him for a moment, then frowned. "If you would rather not—"

Marc felt a sudden twinge of regret over his thoughtless, almost rude, response. Only a fool would deliberately insult a wizard. "Oh, no, Master Oren. I'd be happy to serve you. That way I could repay some of my debt. I only worry about who will look after my family."

Garrett raised his hand. "I will assume that responsibility in his absence."

Ethan stood. "As will I."

Soon all the men pledged their support.

Oren nodded gently. "Now are you willing?"

"Yes," Marc answered, momentarily bowing his head. His mother seemed both sad and pleased while his sisters had yet to understand what his departure meant. The disappointment in Valeria's eyes gave him the only real reason to stay.

"Good. I need one other, an artist preferably." Several people volunteered and Oren thanked them but indicated that there was someone better suited for the position. "Valeria. How about you?"

Marc's heart leapt within him. As to why, he was not certain.

With a little squeal of delight, Valeria turned to her parents who encouraged her to accept. "Yes, wise one. I would be honored to serve."

"You are still skilled with the needle, are you not?"

"I am," she said proudly.

"And how is your hand with the quill?"

Her enthusiasm ebbed some. "Fair to good. I read better than I am able to write."

"Well, you will have ample time to improve." The villagers responded with gentle laughter as she reddened. "Many thanks to the rest of you for offering your help. May you all sleep well tonight." Stepping down from the stone, Oren approached Marc and motioned for Valeria to join him. "Gather your belongings tonight. We leave at first light."

Chapter 5

Despite the morning chill, Oren moved surprisingly fast for a man of his years. Marc initially assumed it would take at least half a day to walk to the wizard's house, but at their current pace he figured the entire journey would take about three hours. Although he had never been there, he knew its general location. Many in the village did as well, but few found reasons compelling enough to disturb the mighty Oren the Wise.

Ever since last night, many thoughts ran through Marc's mind. Like what the wizard wanted with him and Valeria. Chores were mentioned—probably chopping firewood, fetching water, hauling ashes and such—but why was he so interested in their ability to read and write? Maybe the old man's eyes were getting too weak. That made sense. Marc also worried about all he had left behind—his mother, sisters, Sean and other friends. Subtle pangs of homesickness told him he would even miss the village itself. Now that he was finally a man, it seemed unfair he would be unable to serve as one. For the next year, anyway.

But, more than anything else, Marc thought about magic. Now that he would constantly be near a powerful wizard, it made him very uneasy to think there was some all-powerful force surrounding him, watching him. Would it interfere in his life, or that of the people he knew and cared for? That unknown bothered him a great deal. He wished he could avoid magic altogether, but for some reason it relentlessly shadowed him since he encountered the haunted tree.

As they climbed a small hill, Marc noticed a faint warmth lightly caress his right cheek and neck. Looking that way, he saw a dim, circular outline part way up the eastern sky. Stunned, he stopped dead in his tracks and stared at it. Was it real? Did his eyes play tricks on him? Yesterday he thought he saw someone in the shadows before the wolves attacked, and yet no evidence of the man could be found. No, this seemed real. Quite real.

"Master. Val," he said, uncertainty making his voice waver. "The sun. I can see the sun."

Halting, Valeria followed his gaze and gasped. "Praise God. It's been so long." She glanced at the wizard. "Is this a good omen, Master?"

Oren calmly faced them without looking upward. "It is not an omen, only a sign things will continue to improve."

Marc did not understand why his master seemed so unaffected by this miracle. "Why are you not excited about it?"

"I foresaw the sun's return."

"You *knew* this would happen?" Valeria asked while still marveling at the hazy orange disc.

"Yes." Planting his staff, the wizard turned and continued down the path. "Come. There is much to do."

Puzzled over Oren's indifference at the good news, Marc fell in behind and glanced repeatedly at the sun, remembering how different his life was the last time he saw it. Then he was warm and well fed. His father and grandmother still lived. He, Valeria, Sean and Donald were the best of friends. And no one named Thaddeus had ever tried to kill him.

Turning his thoughts from the past to the present, he inwardly rejoiced that his prayers had been answered. Seemingly overnight the evidence of their deliverance sprang up everywhere. As Marc made his way up the slope, the tips of young grasses tickled the sides of his feet. This wondrous carpet of green covered nearly every inch of soil within view. Tiny specks of pink, white and yellow peppered the trees and bushes, blossoms just beginning to awaken from their long sleep. Soon the air would be filled with their heavy perfume. He could hardly wait.

Cresting the hill, he glanced left and saw the haunted tree in the distance, exactly where he knew it would be. Although he did his best to ignore it, the disquieting presence of his invisible and silent companion had grown stronger all morning. Tapping Valeria on the arm, he held a finger to his lips and pointed toward it.

Her eyes widened with surprise. Leaning close, she whispered into his ear, "Do you feel it?"

He nodded.

"You may talk openly about the Great Tree," Oren said without breaking stride. "I know you have been there, Marc. Such things cannot be kept secret from the magic." Marc and Valeria shot each other a worried glance. "There is no need for concern. You are not in any trouble over entering the Forbidden Vale."

His spine stiff, Marc stared at the back of his master, wondering how much he really knew. Without him intending to, the thoughts in his mind found a voice. "How do you know all this?" Realizing he may have spoken too boldly, he respectfully added, "If I may ask?"

"Of course you may. How else are you to learn? Both of you may ask me anything, but you may not always receive an answer you like. Now, as for your question, what do *you* think the answer is?"

"I know it has something to do with the forces of magic, Wise One. What I meant was by what *means* do you know this?"

"Ah, let this be your first lesson: when chosen correctly, words possess great power."

Marc wondered what he meant by *first lesson*. "Yes, sir. I will try to speak more clearly."

"Good. The answer to your question is not an easy one if you do not understand how magic works." Oren stopped and faced him. "Stand still. Close your eyes." Marc did so. "Tell me about the world around you."

He hesitated. "Uh, I'm not sure—"

"What do you smell?"

Marc took several sniffs of the air. "Well, I smell the growing plants... the damp earth... water." He didn't add that he also scented the dried lilac blossoms Valeria had rubbed into her hair that morning.

"What else can you sense?"

"There's a cool, light wind coming from the direction we are headed, uh, northwest, I believe. I can also feel where the sun is." He shifted his concentration to his ears. "I hear water faintly in the distance, probably Wiccan creek. Your staff just touched the ground and Val shifted the weight of her pack."

"Now, open your eyes and tell me what you see."

Marc looked about and was flooded with details he ordinarily took for granted. "Much more. While my ears and nose gave me some information, my eyes yielded a thousand fold more."

The wizard acknowledged him with a single approving nod. "Magic is much like having another pair of eyes. It allows me to sense many more things."

Marc wondered what those things might be. All he or anyone else could know came from their God-given senses. "I think I understand, Master. It must be interesting to feel this magic only wizards can know."

Oren gave him a thin smile. "That it is."

Valeria lightly touched his arm. "But you've already felt magic, Marc."

He gave her an uncomfortable look, hoping she would take the hint to let the subject drop.

Her gaze let him know she was not about to. "You've *felt* the Tree's magic. You feel it now."

With a sigh, he realized it served no purpose to pretend otherwise. Marc looked at the old man expectantly. "Is that magic?"

"Not exactly. What you feel is due to magic, though. Good observation, Valeria."

She grinned modestly for a moment, then asked, "Does that make Marc a wizard?"

Her hopeful look caused Marc to cringe. "Val!"

Oren gently laughed. "You act as if being a wizard is a bad thing. I assure you it is not. Feeling the Tree does not necessarily mean one is a wizard. There are times in many people's lives where they will occasionally encounter magic as Marc did."

Marc recalled the fear of that moment. "It was when I touched it."

"There you go. Having felt it that closely, you are still able to sense it because you know it is there." Giving him an odd look, Oren pointed a finger at Marc. "And, in a way, it knows where you are, too."

Marc squirmed at the thought. "Is there any way to make it forget about me?"

Blinking, the wizard paused for a long moment. "Why do you ask that?"

"It wants me dead. It tried to kill me once already."

Oren studied him a moment. "Explain."

While Marc told all that happened that day, Oren idly stroked his beard, nodding from time to time. Feeling a bit embarrassed, Marc avoided his master's gaze. "I was lucky to escape with my life."

"Do you know why you were not harmed in the Vale?" The wizard's expression made Marc think he should already know the answer.

"No, Master. Why?"

"The magic knew you would come serve me one day. You, and Valeria, are safe from any magic in there."

"Then we can walk into the Vale at any time?" Valeria asked, intrigued.

"Yes, but I would prefer to guide you through it first. It holds dangers that have nothing to do with magic."

"I want to see the haunted tree." Her eagerness made Marc uneasy.

A flicker of a smile played upon Oren's lips. "If you wish, but understand the Great Tree is not as it appears." The master said the words *Great Tree* with an inflection bordering on reverence. "It is also not haunted."

Marc thought otherwise but held his tongue, not wanting to discuss magic any more. "How much further to your home, Master?"

"One half hour."

As they walked on in silence, Marc thought about his good fortune at having been chosen to serve Oren. Without that protection, he would have surely perished in the Vale. Even though the wizard said he would be safe, Marc decided to keep far from the Tree. The power of its magic frightened him. Even now, if he listened to its call, he could hear the whispers of the souls trapped within.

Trying to push those thoughts from his mind, Marc studied the landscape. This area had more rocks showing than he was used to. They looked different, too, being darker than most. Some were even made of a curious, glossy black stone. Soon they encountered a tiny stream that gave off wispy clouds of steam. Amazed, he touched the water and found it fairly warm.

"Master, what kind of magic is this?"

"None. There is a hot spring nearby. Its waters are warmed by great fires within the earth."

Valeria squatted by the stream. "That sounds like magic to me." Wetting her fingers, she brought them to her nose. "It smells a little like rotten eggs."

Glancing first at Marc, Oren smiled at her. "Would you like to see the spring?"

She quickly stood. "Please."

Marc just nodded, still impressed by the ribbon of vapor rising along the water's length. Oren continued down the path until he came to a narrow rut heading to the left. Following it, they soon came upon the stream again where several large, flat stones were arranged in a crude bridge. Crossing over, they climbed a short but moderately steep slope. For some reason Marc found the area quite familiar. Reaching the top he looked down at a pond no larger than ten paces across. It steamed like a giant cook pot.

Standing at the water's edge, he *knew* he had seen this before. Valeria glanced around as if it were familiar to her, too. When their gaze met he instantly saw flashes of her swimming naked. Valeria quickly looked away, leaving him feeling very strange; this was the place in his dream. A very real place. How could this be possible? He had never been here before, yet he knew the placement of every stone, every plant as if he visited it daily. A warm buzz of dread prickled over his skin as he realized the dreams were magic's doing and it had invaded his life long before his journey to the Tree. Forcing the tightness in his chest to subside, he calmed his thoughts and looked toward the wizard.

Using his staff, Oren played at the water's surface, sending out a series of ripples that caused the reflected image of the trees beyond to shimmer. "This is a good place to soak. It takes some of the cold out of these old bones." The master regarded him for a long moment, his face unreadable, then turned away. "It is close, too. My home is over the next rise. Come." He led them back to the path and on to their destination.

When he first saw Oren's property from the top of the hill, Marc was impressed. The path led up to a wide iron gate set in a heavy stone arch towering well over twice his height. Upon the apex of the arch perched a carved likeness of a raven, apparently crafted from that smooth, black stone he saw earlier. To either side of the gate, high stone walls ran for hundreds of paces to the west and north before intersecting the hill behind, creating a great triangle of land within. In the center of the gate hung an iron bell the size of his head.

"Welcome to Raven's Gate," Oren said with a sweep of his arm, indicating that Marc should enter first.

Putting his hands upon the rough, cold bars, he pushed but it did not open. Pulling, it remained equally fast. He searched for a latch of some kind but found none. The right side of the gate had three hinges and the left had two thick rods that disappeared within slots cut deep into the stone of the column. Peering closer, Marc figured something inside must be holding onto the rods.

"It is locked, Master."

Oren waved his hand with a practiced ease and commanded, "*Aperīte!*"

Marc heard a sharp clunk of metal sliding upon metal come from within the pillar and the gate now yielded to his hands, slowly swinging wide. Hastily releasing it, he inspected his palms, worried that he had once more touched something enchanted, but he sensed nothing unusual. It felt normal. He looked to Oren to find the man watching him closely. "It was locked by magic?"

"You could say that." The master gestured them forward. "Enter, and welcome to your new home."

"Amazing." Valeria took a few hesitant steps while watching the gate come to a rest.

Marc followed her and Oren through the arch and looked about in fascination at the quantity of land before him. To the left were many trees, mostly fruit and nut varieties from what he could see. On his right sprawled an striking patchwork of rectangular garden plots, most of which lay barren. In the center of the area, a wide, stone-ringed well rose waist-high. At the very back of the enclosure, centered up against the hill, sat the largest house he had ever seen. Between the gate, well and house ran a broad path. A foot higher than the surrounding ground, it was covered with what seemed to be the same small, rounded stones he found littered beneath the haunted tree.

Unsure what to make of the similarity, Marc gestured around. "Is all of this for growing food?"

"No. I also grow plants for medicines, potions and other needs."

Valeria smiled. "It's beautiful. Did you build all this yourself?"

The wizard shook his head. "I inherited it from the wizard before me, and he from the one before him and so on. Each of us have made improvements, though. I added the plum trees, for example."

"And the walls surrounding all this? Who added those?" Marc asked as they passed the well. "They are most impressive."

Oren grunted in agreement. "A grateful Roman official, almost two hundred years ago. One of my predecessors did him a favor."

Marc chuckled. "It must have been quite a favor." Noticing the gray soil around the trees, he veered off the path, stooped to gather a handful, and examined it while returning to his place behind the master. "I see you spread ashes upon your land, too. That magic melted the snow fast."

"I must confess it is due to nature's laws, not magic."

Casting the dirt to the side, Marc dusted off his hands. "How so?"

After a long moment, the wizard asked, "What happens if something is left out in the summer sun?"

Not sure what his master wanted, Marc said the first thing that came into his head. "It becomes warm?"

Oren glanced back over his shoulder at him, a pleased glint in his eyes. "Exactly. And dark things get much warmer than lighter things, correct?" Marc nodded remembering how hot iron could get—sometimes painfully so. "Spreading the ash on the snow made it darker. Even with our weak sun, it melted faster than it would have otherwise."

Marc found the simplicity of it intriguing.

"That's clever, Master," Valeria said, equally impressed. "Did your magic teach you that?"

"No. I have studied the collective knowledge of the great societies: the Romans, Greeks, Egyptians and Sumerians, to name a few. Their wisdom is mine and will be yours, too."

She shot Marc a look. "Ours?"

"In return for your services, I intend to teach both of you all that I know. How is your Greek?"

Marc met Valeria's gaze and she shook her head. "Neither of us know any," he said.

"Not to worry. You will be adept by this time next year. Well, we are finally here," Oren said, stepping to the side.

Welcoming the opportunity to learn new things, Marc turned his view toward the house when a sudden pain in his arm jerked his attention to Valeria; her fingers gripped him so tightly that her nails had pierced his skin, drawing blood. "Val! What's wrong?"

Her eyes wide with fear, she nodded toward the house. "B-bones!"

Marc followed her gaze and saw with alarm what shocked her. On either side of the door inclined an iron pike, and upon the end of each perched a human skull.

Chapter 6

With a sharp intake of air, Marc's focus locked upon the dry, bleached bones of what used to be two living souls. The dark hollows of the skulls' eye sockets sought Marc out, drawing him into their empty gaze, tracking his every move. A cold knot of dread tightened in his stomach as Valeria, quaking in fear, clung even tighter to him. With such symbols of death on display, he suddenly worried if Oren might be a practitioner of dark magic. Who better to have command over the evil in the Forbidden Vale? Taking a step back, he pointed at the nearest skull, his voice tight, "Master! What evil is this?"

"None. They are my guards," the wizard said, his voice calm and unconcerned. "Effective, are they not?"

Whipping his head about, he stared at the old man as if he had lost his mind. "*What?*"

"They are my guards—well, they used to be. They keep some of the less determined from disturbing me." Oren's eyes met his and Marc felt a slight pulse of heat come out of them—clearly the master's power. While not coming across as threatening—and Marc was unsure *why* he understood that fact—it did convey he needed to comply. "Calm yourselves. There is no reason to fear them."

Swallowing hard, Marc nodded and faced the doorway, this time noticing that several feet below each skull stood a flat-topped, square stone pillar bearing a mound of precisely stacked bones. Were they pillars, or sacrificial altars? No, his imagination was getting the best of him. Oren said not to be afraid. Closing his eyes, he took in a deep breath and let it out slowly along with as much of his tension as he could manage. Valeria, too, had quieted. Releasing his arm, she looked away, embarrassed. Marc viewed the unsettling scene once more, then asked, "How did they... come to be here?"

Oren moved to stand between the pillars. "My predecessor, Arturius, saved the lives of several children belonging to two brothers. In gratitude the brothers insisted upon taking turns guarding Raven's Gate. They proved useful in sorting out those who had no real need of Arturius' power. After my master's passing, I told them to return to their families as I had no need of guards. They refused, saying that since I had inherited Arturius' responsibilities, I also inherited them."

"So why are their remains displayed this way?" Marc asked, curiosity outweighing concern.

"They wished to continue serving their wizard—even after death." A look of sadness passed through Oren's eyes as he touched the nearest pillar, his voice softening. "And so I honored their request. I do not see two sets of bones here but reminders of old friends—Crotious on the left, Gastus on the right."

Now that he knew why the bones were there, Marc's trepidation all but vanished. Feeling the warmth of Valeria's hand upon his skin, he found her swabbing away the blood trickling down his arm with the hem of her tunic. As if sensing his gaze, she turned her face toward his, regret evident in her expression.

Turning her attention back to his wounds, she quietly said, "Forgive me, Master Oren, for assuming the worst when I saw your guards."

Visibly pleased, the wizard momentarily closed his eyes and gave her a respectful nod. "The second lesson of the day: False assumptions often arise out of ignorance. In the future, seek more information before making decisions. Things are often different than they initially appear."

While Oren undid the chain on the door, Marc said, "Since you no longer keep any more guards—uh, living ones, to dissuade unwelcome visitors, I take it times have improved since then."

"I would not say that."

That surprised Marc. "But father told me the king had brought peace to the land."

Pursing his lips, Oren nodded slightly. "For a time. If I read the signs correctly, that will soon change. Then we will see many more visitors like Thaddeus." Leaning forward, he grasped Marc's injured arm and pulled it closer, inspecting the wounds. "Hold still."

Marc did as he was told. With eyes closed, the old man hovered his free hand a finger's width above the injuries while making a slow, circular motion. "*Coalescere... coalescere... coalescere.*" At once the area felt warm and tingly. When the wizard withdrew his hand, Marc gasped aloud, amazed to see the wounds had completely closed. He stared in near disbelief at the arc of thin, pale lines, half expecting them to burst open an any moment and bleed anew.

Valeria gingerly touched his arm and, regarding the wizard with much respect, managed a weak smile. "That's what he did for your mother." Oren opened the door and motioned her forward. Entering, she said, "You *could* thank him, Marc."

Realizing his inexcusable rudeness, Marc immediately gave the wizard a short bow. "Oh, yes, I beg your pardon, Master Oren. Thank you very much."

"You are welcome. Now, go inside."

Putting his hand upon the door, Marc felt its considerable mass. Made from heavy wood beams thicker than the width of his palm, it hung in a dense wall of mortared stone, a smaller version of the great walls surrounding the property. Above it sloped a roof covered with flat slabs of slate rock. The wizard's house was nearly a fortress.

Marc stepped through the opening into a dark place. A musty dampness tinged with herbs and smoke hung in the air. From what he could tell it was a narrow room, more deep than wide. As his eyes adjusted to the dim light, he began to see more detail. More of that slate covered the floor, the stones knit tightly together to form a near perfect whole. Along the wall to his left hung iron sconces made to hold candles or oil lamps. Several narrow benches sat against the wall to his right. Ahead, a large square table made from stout oak planks bound with wide iron straps dominated the space. Beyond that, dark brown curtains of heavy wool stretched across the room.

Sandals scuffing softly on the floor, Oren passed him and pointed at the table. "Put your bundles there." While Marc helped Valeria take off her pack, the wizard gestured about himself. "This is the receiving room. When people come to call, I meet with them here. No visitor is allowed in the remainder of the house. Come."

Parting the curtain, Oren moved past it. Marc followed and found himself in almost total darkness. Valeria took his hand and sidled up close while the wizard did something ahead. Suddenly, light streamed into the room from an opening in the wall.

"I am so used to my house that I can find my way in the dark," Oren said, tying up a leather flap. "Normally I keep this covered."

Square and about the length of his forearm on each side, it was not a simple hole in the wall as Marc first assumed. Something filled up its space, something clear, like the ice that forms on top of puddles in winter. It even had fine bubbles in it like ice. Intrigued, he walked over and touched it, finding it smooth and as hard as stone. Through it he saw the distorted images of trees.

"Is this your magic, Master?"

"No. It is called glass. The Romans make it. It lets the light in and keeps the wind and rain out. I have more of it throughout my home."

For some reason Marc felt a little disappointed it wasn't magical. "Even so, it is a wonder."

"Ah, yes. You will learn of many more wonders during your stay here."

Moving around a clay urn, Oren started for the far end of the space. "This is my storeroom. Past here is the fire room where I spend a good part of my day."

Marc looked about. Numerous sacks and bundles of all kinds and sizes were piled upon the floor or hanging from pegs on the wall. One corner held a number of small kegs that had a stack of folded skins heaped upon them. Suspended above were a dozen or so coils of rope.

Separating the storeroom from the next room hung a tall curtain made of hides from sheep with black hair. He knew such coloration to be rare and wondered if it had any magical significance. Following the wizard, he entered a rectangular room twice as wide as deep. Two of the walls each held two pieces of that intriguing glass, and opposite him a chest-high square recess sank deeply into the stone of the wall.

That puzzled him. Clearly it was made for some purpose, but what? A thick layer of ash covered the bottom and soot darkened the stones of the wall near the top of the opening. "Master, what is this?"

"It is where I light my fire."

Marc studied the large niche again then looked up at the ceiling and saw no hole for the smoke to leave through. Odd. "Where does the smoke go?"

"Ah, look inside the fireplace. At the top you will find a chimney—a hollow column of stones that carry the smoke away."

Peering within, he saw just what Oren described. "But why go through all this trouble?"

"With a hole in the roof, too much rain and wind get in while the heat easily leaves. The fireplace solves those problems. I stay quite warm in here and use much less wood. Why not light a fire to see how it works?"

Although dubious how well it might function, Marc was eager to give it a try. "Yes, Master." From the nearby wood stack he selected a small, dry stick, peeling thin strips from it with his knife. After cutting some larger pieces, he cleared away the ash in the center of the fireplace and built a kindling pile. He glanced about. "Where is your flint rock?"

"No need for that in this house." Oren slowly waved a hand over the pile and said, "*Ārdē!*" A tiny flame appeared at the bottom of the kindling and quickly spread upward. Amazed, Marc watched the first curls of smoke rise and vanish into the chimney.

Valeria cried out in delight. "Master, you must teach us that magic!"

"It *can* be most useful, especially in this weather. But—" He paused, his tone becoming more understanding, more apologetic. "I cannot teach magic to just anyone. Only those destined to command the great power may learn it."

Valeria's smile fell along with the cast of her shoulders. "Oh. Then I suppose the same is true for how you healed Marc's arm."

"I am afraid so, my child."

A heavy blanket of regret descended upon Marc. Something about it made him associate it with Valeria, almost as if he could feel her disappointment. Hoping to distract her thoughts, he offered her a smile and a slender stick. "Help me with the fire?" Her soft gaze met his wherein he saw her emotion shift toward gratitude. With a nod she knelt beside him, took the stick and snapped it into several pieces, feeding them to the growing flames. Looking up at their master, Marc saw him watch her with a warm, almost parental smile. Oren's gaze swung to him and he nodded approvingly. Embarrassed, Marc turned back to the fire.

After adding three larger pieces of wood to the blaze, Valeria stood and dusted off her hands. "That should burn for a while."

The wizard guided them to the south side of the room. "Over here is the kitchen."

They entered into a wedge-shaped space. Marc was surprised to see the arched top of a clay bread oven in the far corner of the room; never had he seen one built *inside* a home. To the right, a hip-high, slate covered work surface ran half the length of the glass studded outside wall. Opposite it, against the wall by the oven, stood an oblong wooden table. Atop it sat a large stone mortar and pestle for grinding grain. On the wall by the table ran four shallow shelves populated with many small containers. Much of the remainder of the room was crowded with kegs and barrels of all sizes, sacks, clay pots, and other stores. A glance at Valeria let him see that she, too, looked about the room trying to take it all in.

Oren gestured toward a narrow doorway near the table. "That is a small sleeping chamber. It will be yours, Marc."

Marc stuck his head in there and saw it was indeed small, little more than a bed and a shallow ledge upon which to place a few belongings.

Retracing their path, the wizard led them to a third doorway on the northern side of the fire room. Stepping through a hide curtain smaller than the one to the storeroom, they entered into a short alcove having three more openings to other rooms, two on the right covered with floor-to-ceiling heavy wool curtains, one on the left holding a wide wooden door.

Oren pointed at the curtain nearest the fire room. "This is my chamber." He then indicated the second curtain. "And this will be yours, Valeria. It is larger than the rest. Sufficient, I hope, for you to prepare garments in."

Knifing her extended fingers into the gap between the fabric and the wall, she moved the curtain aside and looked within.

"Yes, Master. It is more than enough for my needs. Why is a sleeping chamber this large?"

"Some of the past wizards had many children." Turning about, Oren lifted the latch on the wooden door and ushered them into the third room. "This is my workshop."

The room was quite spacious—easily larger than any of the others. Along the right wall four pieces of glass let in a fair amount of light. Under them sat a long, deep and sturdy workbench littered with tools, pieces of wood and metal, bits of leather and cloth. In the center of the room stood an elevated fire pit with an anvil to one side and a large copper hood suspended over it. Beyond that was a large table similar to the one in the receiving area. At the far end of the space, another heavy wooden door led somewhere, but this one was strange, its featureless surface having no handle or latch with which to open it. Left of the door, hundreds of scrolls were stacked neatly in an array of bins stretching the full height of the wall.

Marc pointed at the scrolls. "What are those, Master?"

"Knowledge. Remember, I said you would learn the wisdom of the great societies."

Impressed, Marc attempted to estimate their number when Valeria's gasp broke his concentration.

"Half of the room is made from solid stone," she said in wonder.

He studied the workshop. Just past the fire pit the wall changed from mortared rocks to unbroken stone. Tracing the dividing line with his gaze, Marc followed it over the ceiling and down the other wall at the point where it encompassed the far half of the workbench. The wall holding the strange door was also a sheet of smooth rock. With a start, Marc realized what it meant. "This workshop extends into the hill behind the house."

"It does." Oren touched the rock overhead. "Hewn from the living stone with magic."

Awestruck, Marc said nothing for a time, trying to understand the amount of magical power it took to cut away the hill so precisely. "And what lies behind that door?"

"A special room filled with secrets."

Intrigued, Marc approached the door and studied it closely, seeking any hole or slot that might conceal a hidden latch. The even face of the wood revealed no such opening. "And protected by a door no one can open."

"No one except wizards," Valeria said, touching its surface with respect. "Will we be allowed in there?"

"Not today. Both of you, sit at the table." While Oren rummaged among the scrolls, Marc and Valeria each perched upon a stool. "Ah, some Greek history. This will do nicely." He plucked one from an upper bin and returned to the table.

Marc listened as their master told of a great leader named Alexander, followed by story of an epic war between the Greeks and Trojans. Marc found the tales so fascinating that the hours quickly passed.

Oren stood and stretched. "Enough. It is too dark to read any more. Time for our evening meal."

Marc suddenly realized he forgot all about finding tonight's dinner. Glancing at the glass in the wall he saw it was nearly dark outside. "Forgive me, Master. I did not go hunting."

Oren gently shook his head and motioned for him to be calm. "There is nothing to forgive. During your time here there will be no need to hunt. I have more than sufficient stores to last the three of us for the next year. Later on, you may hunt from time to time to provide us a little fresh meat, but for now I want you to concentrate your efforts on your work." He started toward the door. "I will see to our meal. Put those scrolls away then join me in the kitchen."

Valeria reached for a parchment, her eyes bright. "That was interesting. Especially the story about the soldiers hiding in that horse. Very clever."

"I bet they were surprised." Marc rolled and tied his scroll. When Valeria had finished with hers, he picked it up. "I'll put it away for you."

She gently held his arm, keeping him from moving. "I'm sorry I injured you."

"Injured me?"

"When I saw the skulls—" Her embarrassed gaze darted to his arm.

"Oh. Oren healed me so don't worry about it."

"Do they hurt?" she asked, running her fingertips lightly over the faint wounds, the sensation making his breath catch.

He tried to ignore the pleasure of her touch. Part of him wanted to believe the caress went beyond her regret over hurting him, but such thoughts were foolish. "No, just itches now and then." Depositing the scrolls in the proper bins, he gestured toward the exit. "Let's go eat." With a demure smile, Valeria nodded and followed him to the kitchen.

During their meal, Oren spoke to them in Latin, testing the extent of their vocabulary. Marc thought he knew it reasonably well, but soon discovered he and Valeria had much to learn. That night, seated before the fire, Oren began their lessons in that language.

After being dismissed, Marc took care of his private needs and headed for bed. Just as he was getting comfortable, a presence loomed over him in the darkness.

"Sleep well, Marc," Oren said softly, "for tomorrow you will begin to learn the ways of magic."

Chapter 7

Marc slept poorly that night, greatly worried about what Oren had said. The shock of that revelation had yet to fully set in. Just being *around* magic put him ill at ease. The very thought of having to *learn* and then *use* it scared him. If only he could refuse his master's wishes, but that was not an option. Resigned to his fate, he decided to learn what he must and, once his year of service had ended, forget it as soon as possible.

Stiff, sore and far from rested, he dressed and wandered back through the house and found Valeria sitting before the fire on a large, thick cushion. He yawned. "Morning."

She gave him a bright, eager smile. "Morning. Ready to start your day?"

He knelt beside her and automatically held his palms toward the warming flames. "Not really. I didn't sleep very well." He looked about the room. "Where's Oren?"

"He left for the hot springs a while ago." She poked at the embers with a stick. "I'm excited for you."

He studied her face for a several heartbeats, wondering if she were serious or making light of him. "Excited? About what?"

She playfully jabbed him in the side with a finger. "*Marc.* Learning magic, of course."

His stomach fluttered. So, the master had shared that with her as well. With a single shake of his head, he looked away. "I'd rather not."

"You are jesting, yes?"

"No. Why does he want *me* to learn it? You should ask him to teach you instead."

"I will. I'd love to learn magic."

"You wouldn't think so if you had touched that haunted Tree."

She leaned closer and gave him that sly grin he knew so well. "I will today."

"Huh?"

Valeria stood and smoothed the fabric of her dress. "Oren wants us to meet him at the waterfall. He said you'd know where."

His stomach tightened further, somehow knowing he would not like the reason for going there. "I do, but why—"

"He's going to show us through the Forbidden Vale."

Marc's heart skipped a beat. This had to happen sometime, but why now? Regaining his feet, he let out a labored sigh. "When?"

"As soon as we get there." She patted a small leather sack tied to her waist. "I'm bringing some nuts and dried fruit along for breakfast. Shall we go?" Without waiting for an answer, she headed toward the front.

Following, he collected his staff along the way. Outside, the chill in the air nipped at him. The ghostly image of the sun's ruddy disk hung just above the eastern hills. Halfway to the gate, he saw the master had not left it open. "How are we to leave? The gate is locked."

"Oren said it will open for us."

He glanced at her, head cocked in doubt. "Just like that? Yesterday he needed a spell. Are we supposed to do anything?"

"He didn't say."

They walked on in silence, the crunch of the stone underfoot marking their progress. When they were ten paces from the gate, he heard the clunk within the pillar. Fascinated, he watched the gate slowly open on its own. Unsure how long it would remain so, he took Valeria's hand and hurried under the arch. They turned about in time to see it close and lock.

"Marvelous," she said with a grin.

Marc suddenly felt a subtle tingling wash over the surface of his skin. The sensation reminded him of being near the Tree or, even better, his encounter with the wolves, yet it did not seem threatening in any way. With a start, he wondered if it was magic's presence. If so, it would be rude not to acknowledge its help. "Thank you," he said to the air above him.

Patting the back of his hand, Valeria looked away from the gate. "Which way?"

Three paths converged at the arch. One ran northeast into a thickly wooded area. Marc knew only that it led to the village of Bitter Well and other regions north. The middle path led to the hot springs, Broken Rock, then on to their village. The other path briefly headed west alongside the wall then veered southwest into the forest, following the gentle slope down to Wiccan Creek, down to the Forbidden Vale.

"This way." He headed west.

"Here." She handed him a dried plum.

"Thanks."

Taking a small bite of it, he barely appreciated the luxury of a morning meal, his thoughts too occupied with what lay ahead. He was to *learn the ways of magic*. What did that mean? And how quickly would the master expect him to learn it? Marc hoped he could suppress his fear of magic well enough to succeed. He did not want to displease Oren for he was indeed powerful, and that demanded both respect and obedience.

Soon they came upon a narrower path branching to the left.

"Where does that go?" Valeria asked casually.

"The hot springs," he answered without even thinking about it.

She gave him a questioning glance. "It does? How do you know?"

Yes, how *did* he know? Had the Tree put that knowledge in his head? He hoped not. Perhaps he erred in thinking he had never been on this trail before. Maybe when he was very young he traveled it with his father and had forgotten it until now. As much as he wished that to be true, deep down he knew otherwise. The magic, he feared, was having its way with him. But he did not want to tell her that.

"Well, it seems obvious. That's the direction the springs should be in, and it's important to Master Oren, so there'd be a path to it."

Valeria accepted his reasoning and proceeded to ask many questions about what they would see in and around the Forbidden Vale. He shared all he could recall, much of it already told to her the week before. Still, he welcomed it for doing so eased his growing apprehension.

"I wonder how close we are," she said. "I hear the creek quite well."

Marc stepped over a small birch tree that had recently fallen across the path. "Very close. We'll be out of the woods in another minute." He helped her over the obstacle.

She gave him another questioning look, this one more intense than the last. "How do you know that? You've never been on this path, have you?"

"I believe not. Yet I know where to go." It disturbed him how well he knew this trail. Damned magic.

"Is it the Tree?" She took his hand, concern in her voice. "I know it... bothers you."

"It does. Even now it is with me, growing stronger with every step, but I cannot say if it is telling me how to walk this path." Marc said no more, not wanting to further explain how the macabre beacon guided him.

Exiting the woods upstream of the large pool, they entered a wide, treeless area that bordered the eastern side of the creek for some distance. In several month's time the green stubble would grow into a lush meadow rich with game.

Valeria gazed expectantly at the Tree across the way. "It's huge!"

He reluctantly glanced at it. "It has grown fat on the souls of those unlucky enough to come under its spell."

"It doesn't seem so dangerous," she said with a quick shake of her head.

"Why do you doubt me?" he snapped. Her confused and injured expression dissolved his burst of anger. Embarrassed, he hung his head. "Forgive me. I... I didn't mean that." He looked to the Tree once more, acutely aware of its power, its *being,* flooding into him. "If you had touched it before, you'd understand." Without further comment, she took his right hand and laced her fingers into his, indicating all was well between them.

They walked south along the creek until reaching the falls. There he indicated the route he took over the water, up the hill to the haunted tree, and down to where he found the buck. He then pointed at the violent churning beneath the falls. "That's where I went over."

Viewing that place, her face darkened with concern. "It's a wonder you didn't drown."

The sight brought back many uneasy feelings, ones he did not care to relive. "Yes. It's strange how—" Something caught his attention and made him look behind. Oren approached. "The Master is here."

Valeria cheerfully waved at the old man. When she looked back at Marc, her smile dimmed. "Why do you frown? We'll be safe with Master Oren."

He tried to give her a reassuring smile but doubted it looked genuine. "It's not that. I remember the fear I felt that day. It—it changed me." She said nothing, but her gaze held warmth and support.

Still twenty paces from them, Oren gestured toward the creek. "Shall we cross over and begin our journey?"

"Certainly, Master." Valeria took Marc's hand and pulled him toward the fallen tree. After several steps she let go and giggled in surprise. She no longer moved forward, but upward, her feet already well above the ground.

Marc stared after her, transfixed, all worries of the Tree gone from his mind. "Such powerful magic," he gasped.

Oren came up beside him. "It is, and safer than crossing over on that log."

Valeria drifted over the creek like a dandelion seed floating on a gentle breeze, laughing and flapping her arms as if she were a bird. After coming to rest on the other side, she let out a wordless cry of joy and danced about. "*Thank you*, Master Oren."

Acknowledging her with a nod, the wizard faced him, an amused gleam in his eyes. "Now your turn. Keep still and pay close attention." Nervous, Marc watched as Oren extended both hands before him, waist high, palms up. "*Volitā!*" he commanded, slowly raising his hands.

Marc instantly felt a warm, tingling sensation envelope him. His head spun, his stomach lurched and everything became bathed in a faint blue fog as the ground dropped away. After a moment of fear he accepted it as something to be marveled. Below him raced deadly waters and yet he hung effortlessly over it all, lighter than a feather, safe in Oren's magic. His arms and legs moved effortlessly for the earth no longer pulled at them. By the time he reached the far side he found himself laughing out loud.

Valeria wrapped her arms around him, giggling loudly. "Isn't that fantastic? I'd love to learn to do that. Wouldn't you?"

Returning her embrace, he laughed again. "Absolutely!" He savored the moment, thrilled at the experience magic just afforded him and, more importantly, holding her close to his heart.

Valeria turned to Oren as he landed beside them. "Master, since you intend to teach Marc magic, why not start by teaching him *that*."

Raising an eyebrow, the wizard regarded Marc for a moment, then looked back at Valeria. "Floating requires advanced magic. I will start by teaching him much simpler things." Oren met his gaze. "If he proves himself worthy, magic may then choose to bestow power such as that upon him."

Marc found the prospect of learning to Float anything but frightening, more like useful. Maybe he was rash in thinking everything about magic was bad.

The master began to ascend the hill. "Let us first visit the Great Tree."

And maybe not. Reluctantly following, Marc looked up at their destination, deeply worried what might happen there. Would he have to touch it? Its many voices already whispered in his mind—there was no need to make them louder. And how would it affect Valeria? If only he could shield her from its menace.

She turned to him, placing a hand on his forearm. "You seem troubled."

He shrugged off her comment and hand together.

Her concerned face drew closer and she spoke in a near-whisper. "Marc, what is it?"

He knew that look. If he did not tell her now, she would pester him until he did. "I don't want you to feel the Tree's evil."

"And why do you think it is evil?" Oren's tone made it more command than question.

Marc averted the elder's gaze hoping he had not offended him. "Because it feels that way. The voices, they... come after me, chase me. They try to draw me in, to take something from me, but I can't say what, or why."

The master gave out an affirming breath, a hint of a smile on his lips. "Trust me when I tell you it is *not* evil. Very strong magic exists there and your mind cannot yet understand it. That will change in time. Come, and learn."

Marc wanted to believe Oren—the Master seemed so certain—but part of him refused to let go of his fear. Caution outweighed trust. The Tree's presence continued to intensify, reinforcing how powerless he felt against it.

Once they reached the ledge, Valeria eagerly studied the Great Tree. "Master, this is *truly* the largest tree I have ever seen."

Marc wished he could share in her innocent wonder. Not only did the Tree's power pull at him, so did the earth surrounding it. It felt *warm*, making his feet tingle. Why did Oren want him to learn more about this place? While willing to try, he doubted he could ever think of it as anything but evil.

Valeria looked straight up, her face alight with amazement. "The nearest branch is so far away. If I were twice my height, I still could not touch it." She walked around slowly, scrutinizing the ground. "There is—this place is very special." She closed her eyes for a moment, then looked at Marc oddly, strode forward and grabbed the trunk, then jumped back in surprise. "OH!"

He hurried to her side. "Val?"

Her eyes held a far-off look. "I felt it—felt *them*. I see what you mean. It's so strange. But I don't feel anything evil." She glanced at the surrounding ledge once more, then took his hands, gazing deeply into his eyes. "We are *supposed* to be here," she said, her voice serious, even respectful. "Somehow I know that. Come." She led him up to the Tree.

He pulled away at first, but something in her face quieted much of his apprehension. Touching the bark, he braced himself for its attack. None came. Instead, the voices intensified, as he had expected, plus something else slowly came upon him. Something new. Pain. His lungs hurt. So did his stomach. Then, from the center of his chest, a great discomfort radiated outwards and into his left arm. Stumbling back, he dropped to his knees, fiercely clutching his aching arm while gasping for breath.

"What's wrong?" Valeria squatted before him and touched his cheek gently, her gaze filled with worry.

"Pain!" he grunted through clenched teeth. "I feel—" Whatever had beset him vanished. "No, it's gone now. But I felt pain, felt death, I think." A icy prickle dashed over the skin of his arms causing the hairs to bristle. He looked to Oren. "Is that true?"

The wizard nodded, clearly pleased. "Yes. Excellent."

Taken aback, Marc stood. "How is that excellent? Its attack was very unpleasant."

"The Tree did not attack you. You experienced the Magic trying to tell you something."

Letting out a huff of frustration, Marc wished it could find a less objectionable way to communicate.

Oren turned to Valeria. "Did you find it disagreeable?"

"No. I felt some alarm at first, but only because it was so unusual." She touched it once more. "It's not unpleasant at all."

"Indeed. Valeria, leave your right hand upon the trunk. Marc, take her right."

Cautiously, he did so, expecting more of the pain. Instead, a jumble of things that made no sense flowed through him. The voices remained, but his overall impression changed considerably, becoming almost peaceful. That surprised him.

"Both of you may let go. Now, what did you feel this time, Marc?"

"Well, no pain—that's good—but I don't know how to describe the rest. A hundred strange thoughts went into me, and—" He shrugged. How could he explain it? It felt like a dream or long lost memory, yet composed of much more than thought. It included sensations, sounds, smells, even tastes, but none of them distinct enough to describe.

"What made it different when I stood between him and the Tree?" Valeria asked while trailing her fingertips along the bark.

Again Oren looked pleased. "The magic of this place is filled with many things. Its power talks to you, in a manner of speaking. If you touch the Great Tree while thinking dark thoughts, then you will only hear that in its voice. Your mind, Valeria, was open, unclouded. When he held your hand, he shared *your* perceptions, heard it as you do. I know neither of you understand that now, but in time you will."

Feeling a bit foolish for his earlier misgivings, Marc regarded the Tree with a fresh, even curious, outlook. Hearing a low chuckle, he turned toward the master.

"I am pleased you both gained wisdom here this day." Oren moved northward. "We have more to see. I encourage you to visit here often." No sooner had Marc wondered what purpose that would serve, the master added, "Especially you, Marc. Every time you do, you will learn something new."

"Yes, Master." Apparently these journeys would be part of his schooling in magic. So what did he learn today? That the Tree held no evil? Maybe, but spirits most definitely resided there, so it remained haunted, just in a different way.

The wizard led them downward along a narrow, winding path through the trees into the wide valley that made up most of the Forbidden Vale. Its serene beauty gave Marc no indication of the dangers within. Except for scattered outcroppings of that shiny, black stone, he saw little difference between the Vale and the surrounding land. Across the valley, a diagonal row of hills marked the northern boundary. Intersecting Black Rock Hill several miles to the west, the hills ran northeast past Oren's home. Because of his elevation, Marc could clearly see the south wall of Raven's Gate even though it was well over a mile away.

As the trail flattened out, they came upon a low cairn of rounded, head-sized stones stained with a variety of pale oranges, yellows and browns. Surrounding the mound at a distance of ten paces were a ring of six, shoulder-high vertical iron bars. Atop each, an animal's skull sat facing outward. Marc considered whether the similarity of that tableau to Crotious' and Gastus' remains flanking the Master's door was more than chance. Probably. It, too, likely served to discourage the unwanted. Right before they reached the nearest bar, Oren abruptly raised his hand.

"Stop here."

They did, and Marc looked upon the mound with interest and more than a little trepidation.

Oren regarded them with a most serious expression. "Deadly vapors sometimes erupt from beneath these stones. They kill quickly and horribly." Oren turned his gaze upon Marc. "Even wizards can die from them. Today it sleeps."

Valeria gingerly sniffed the air, frowning in disgust. "It smells like the hot springs, only much stronger."

"Yes, but when the vapors come forth, the smell is terrible, even from afar. Your eyes will weep and your throat will burn as if on fire. You would be wise to avoid this place."

"Or at least stay upwind of it," Marc said. "Does it have a name?"

"My predecessors called it *Devil's Breath*."

Valeria warily eyed the rocks. "*Is* it from the Devil?"

The wizard chuckled. "No. It is a natural part of the earth."

Moving several steps closer, she inspected it for a long moment, then retreated, ending up next to Marc. "Our world is a curious place."

And dangerous, thought Marc.

Oren led them past other features of the Vale, including a small lake to the west and a mysterious rock that seized Marc's knife to itself as surely as if it had invisible hands. They ended up at the northeastern corner of the Vale, next to a series of small waterfalls. Studying the water's course, Marc found it to be the upper portion of Wiccan creek. Immediately to the east, tucked against the base of the hill, perched a small, isolated ledge on the far side of the creek.

The Master pointed toward it. "There is one more thing to see. A cave."

Marc liked caves. Eagerly searching the ledge, he quickly spotted the cave's dark maw mostly hidden by a dense clump of trees. Repeating his earlier magic, the wizard Floated them across the water to the ledge. The cavern's hole looked to be two paces high by four wide, expanding into a larger sized pocket within the hill. The overall shape reminded Marc of a half-open mouth. He looked toward his master.

"I take it this cave is special in some way?"

The old man nodded. "It is indeed. This is how we shall return home."

Marc wondered by what magic a cave could bring them to Oren's home.

Valeria looked equally confused. "I don't understand."

The wizard strode purposefully inside, his cloak flaring out behind him. "You will shortly." They followed him until it was too dark to continue.

"Uh, *Master*?" Valeria called out, her voice echoing back from the cave's depths. "We cannot see."

Marc heard the master's footsteps halt, then move close to the wall on their left. "*Ārdē!*" Seconds later a torch caught flame. Taking it from its holder, Oren held it high. "Is this better?"

"Much," she said.

Oren gave them an odd look coupled with the slightest trace of a smile. "You are unable to see in the dark?"

"And you *can*?" Marc blurted in disbelief.

"Yes. Here." Handing him the torch, Oren proceeded further into the cave. "Magic tells me where things are, letting me move through the dark with ease." After a moment the elder added, "Would you care to learn how, young Marcus?"

Valeria flashed him a delighted smile, reflecting his own excitement. "Indeed, Master. Such a skill would be valuable on long, dark nights." If he knew how to see in the dark, unseen threats lurking outside of the fire's light would no longer remain hidden. Bears, wolves and even the occasional thief could be found and dealt with. Shaking his head, he suppressed a chuckle at having found another positive aspect of magic.

Soon the cave narrowed to a tall crevice just wide enough to walk through. At that point a light wooden door blocked further travel. Oren swung it open. "This keeps the bats out of the deeper recesses."

Once past the door, they threaded their way through seemingly endless twisting passages, the floor of which was filled in and leveled with a fine gravel. Heavy with moisture, the air smelled a bit of wet earth and mold. Marc found the journey both thrilling and mystifying; he had no idea one could go this far into the ground. The rock around them felt warm to the touch, and every so often he spied bands of different color stone meandering up the wall. After several minutes, the crevice before them abruptly closed up to little more than a crack; they had reached a dead end.

"Where to now, Master?" Marc asked.

Pointing upward, Oren commanded, "*Volitā!*"

Again the magic enveloped Marc. Still holding the torch, he rose through the blackness until coming to rest in a continuance of the fissure higher up. Peering over the edge, he looked down at Valeria who looked back with a wide grin. The distance between them seemed to be about thirty feet.

"Val, there's more cave up here."

In short order, Oren's magic deposited her beside him. They found themselves in an oblong chamber, three paces wide by seven deep, filled with an ample quantity of stores similar to those kept in the house.

Valeria patted a nearby keg as Oren joined them. "Master, why do you have so many supplies this deep in a cave? Are they not difficult to get to?"

"No." When she gave him a puzzled look, he calmly added, "You will see."

The wizard moved past them into another passage and, after a few steps, took a sharp right turn into a corridor that was clearly man-made. It immediately widened into a medium, rectangular room, also man-made, with multiple niches hewn into the rock walls on either side. The space reminded Marc of the part of the workshop cut into the hill. At the far end, Oren stopped before a wide wooden door and faced them.

"This room contains my most important possessions. I show you this because we will soon be working with them. I know I can trust you both to keep this room, and the caves beyond, secret."

Honored, Marc bowed his head.

Oren took the torch from him and placed it in a sconce on the wall. From a small shelf above the door he took an oil lamp and, raising it to the torch, lit it, then handed it to Marc. Moving to the center of the room, the wizard reached deep into the shadow of a larger niche and brought out a very thick object wrapped in a light brown suede. Tucking it beneath his arm, he returned to the door.

"As you can see, this door has no visible latch. Within the heart of the door is an iron bolt that slides into a hole in the stone. To pass, magic must be used to move the bolt out of the stone and further into the door. Marc, do you remember the spell I used to open my gate yesterday?"

"Yes."

The Master gazed intently at him. "Say it."

Marc's stomach lurched with fear. "Do I have to?"

"Yes."

His master's tone was sufficient to convey he could not avoid this task. Passing Valeria the lamp, he took a deep breath, braced himself—against what threat he did not know—and quickly spat out a half-hearted, "*Aperīte.*" Nothing happened. The remaining air escaped his lungs in a sigh of relief.

"What was *that*?" Oren was not pleased.

"I said it correctly, did I not?"

"You used the right word, but the importance lies in *how* you say it. It is not a request or a statement, it is a *command*. It must come from the very core of your being. The magic will not work its wonders for you if you merely ask. Try it again. This time take charge."

Marc repeated the command several times, fearing what would happen. Who was *he* to utter a mere word and command the great power of magic? But Oren persisted, and soon, with authority, Marc commanded the door to open.

"Better. Now concentrate your thoughts upon what you want to happen. As you speak the command, you must also will the magic to slide the bolt over."

Will the magic? What did that mean? "How do I do that?"

"See the bolt in your mind. Imagine your hand upon it. Then, as you speak the spell, think *move* to the bolt."

Again Marc repeated the task, this time gesturing like he had seen Oren do. He imagined seeing in his mind what the bolt might look like, but had difficulty maintaining that likeness while doing everything else. Taking Marc's hand, the wizard held it near the door. Immediately, the same sensation he felt when Oren Floated him over the water enveloped his arm—magic's power!

"Again," Oren said, helping him through the motion.

With great surprise, Marc suddenly sensed the bolt. He did not see it as with his eyes, nor did he feel it as he would with his fingers, yet somehow he perceived it as if both of those senses were at work. Seizing the moment, he imagined seeing the bolt slide as he commanded, "*Aperīte!*"

The iron shaft sprang to life within the door, making a loud clunk as it slid. Jumping back, Marc yelped in pleased astonishment. Oren nodded approvingly.

Val hugged him with glee. "Fabulous! You learned your first magic spell."

Oren separated them. "Try it again, but this time lock it."

"I don't know the command."

Arching an eyebrow, the master tilted his head. "Tell it to lock."

Suppressing an embarrassed chuckle, Marc said, "Yes, of course." He tried to concentrate on the bolt but could not sense it as before. Maybe it would work anyway. "*Claudite!*" he firmly commanded while trying to will the bolt to move. Nothing happened. The elation of unlocking the door evaporated. "I'm sorry, Master. I—"

"Do not worry. You have learned all the parts of spell casting except how to talk to the magic. When you unlocked the door, I helped you connect with the magic, but you did the rest. Now, hold your hand out to the door. Take the memory of how it felt to sense the bolt and move it down your arm and into your fingers. Will it to happen."

"I'll try."

Wondering how he would accomplish that, Marc fixed his thoughts upon how it felt when Oren assisted him. With much effort he finally managed to find, then extend, that sensation down to his hand. The power bathed his mind and body, feeling both odd yet familiar. He thought about the door and gasped when the bolt's image jumped into his mind, clear and precise. Quickly, he uttered the command once more while willing the bolt to move. A satisfying thud echoed in the cave.

"Excellent." Oren patted him on the back while Valeria clapped. "Now unlock it again."

Marc easily did so. "Amazing!" His heart beat wildly within him as the magic tingled on his skin.

"Absolutely." Valeria grabbed his hand, then abruptly dropped it, backing up. "Oh. Your hand is... hot." She examined her fingers as if something coated them. "Well, not really *hot*, but—Master, did I just feel magic?"

"Yes."

When she touched him, Marc felt a surge of familiarity toward her. Curious to learn more about it, he reached toward her.

"I would not advise that," Oren said gently, blocking his arm before he made contact. "Release the magic."

Marc did so, withdrawing his hand. "My apologies."

"Do not move the magic from you into another person until you are trained. Use it only on objects." Oren pushed the door open and stepped through to the next room. "Come."

Marc didn't intend to do anything wrong, but he apparently had. Another reason to not like magic. Chagrined, he reached to usher Valeria through the doorway, but with a worried look, she stepped back.

"Sorry, Val. The magic is gone now."

She relaxed. "Oh, good. I'm sorry, too. I touched you first, and—"

"Are you coming?" Oren called from the next room.

"I'll tell you later," she whispered. Firmly taking his hand, she led him after the wizard.

Passing through the doorway, Marc found himself in a well lit place—the workshop. So now he knew what lay behind that strange door. With a grin, he pushed the door closed and cast the spell to lock it and the thrill of the act returned. Oren sat at the large table, indicated they were to sit opposite him, then began unwrapping the suede covered bundle with great care. Intrigued, Marc sat without taking his eyes off the object and soon saw it was a large and very old book.

"This is the great book of magic. For hundreds of years it has been passed down from wizard to wizard. Within it is the knowledge a wizard needs to know." Taking the lamp from Valeria, Oren held it over the cover as he opened it. "As you can see, it is far past its prime."

Marc saw that more than a few pages had pulled free of the lacing that once bound them. Many others had frayed and torn edges from long years of handling. He reached for the book, then paused. "May I?" Oren nodded his permission. Gingerly pulling on the suede beneath it, Marc slid it closer and examined its contents. Although it had aged considerably, he could tell the vellum used for the pages had once been of the highest quality. The grain of the leather—tight and smooth, without blemish. The edges—straight and even. Skilled hands had carefully crafted each page.

The same held true for the lettering and artwork. The first few pages recorded who the book belonged to at various points in history. The last entry chronicled where Arturius passed it on to Oren. Further in were incantations, most penned in Latin, but some had letters he did not know. Could this be the Greek Oren mentioned? Many of the spells had explanations about when and how to use them. Illustrations accompanied others. Every so often he found strange symbols drawn in the margins.

Valeria bent closer. "It's beautiful."

"Yes, it is." Marc ran his hand lightly over the surface of a page and detected a faint, though familiar, tingling—magic. That was to be expected. "I take it you want me to craft another to replace it. That's why you wanted my leather working skills." He continued thumbing through the pages.

The Master gave a single nod. "That is one reason you are here."

Marc felt a humble sense of pride at being asked to perform such an important duty. "I am greatly honored, Master Oren. I will do my best work; however, I cannot draw illustrations such as this." He indicated a dragon snaking its way up the right margin of a page.

"That's my task," Valeria said. Her bright gaze swung up to meet the master's. "Am I right?"

Oren smiled slightly. "You are. Between the two of you the book will be restored. In addition, there are newer spells to be added."

"How soon am I to complete it?" Marc asked. "I have no leather to work with."

"There will be plenty of time and I already have the needed supplies. But before we do that, Marc—" Oren waved meaningfully at the tome. "I want you to learn all of these spells."

Stunned, Marc gauged the book's considerable thickness. "Master, I-I can't learn all of these. There must be hundreds, maybe even thousands."

"You can and will learn them. After mastering the more basic skills, the others will become easier."

Marc had a nagging hunch Oren hid something from him, but what? For some reason he knew it had to do with magic. "So you selected me for more than my leather skills and chopping wood. You want me to learn all this magic, too. Why?"

As soon as the words left his mouth the answer began to form in his mind, but not in time to soften the blow of his master's response.

"You are to be my replacement."

Chapter 8

Oren's words chilled Marc to his core. His *replacement*? The very thought scared him. "I- I don't want to be a wizard. I didn't ask to be one, and I'm not suited to be one. Respectfully, sir, choose someone else."

Oren looked him square in the eye. "The magic chose you, not I. From the moment of your birth you were destined to walk the path of service and magic."

Marc barely heard Valeria's gasp of surprise, his thoughts too occupied with Oren's revelation. *Destined*? It couldn't be—for him, anyway. He was meant to tan hides, craft leather goods. How could he become Oren's replacement when he did not even *like* magic? His mouth suddenly dry, he struggled to speak. "Master, *please*, I do not want this. Having magic is wrong. Why should a few have magic's favor when the many do not?" Marc expected Oren to be displeased, angry even. Instead, the elder nodded in understanding.

"Tell me, Marc. If a man is a skilled hunter, does he not use that skill to feed his family and neighbors?"

"If he is honorable, yes."

"And what of a builder? Should he not build bridges to cross over rivers, roads to travel on and walls to keep out the enemy?"

"Yes."

Oren gestured toward Valeria. "Consider Valeria here. She is a gifted seamstress, is she not?"

Marc smiled at her. "She and Aula are known far and wide for the beautiful garments they craft." Valeria gave him a humble smile, then looked bashfully away.

"Do you know any others with their skill?"

Marc shook his head.

"Many have been blessed with skills others do not possess. Our lives are enriched when they use these talents—these *gifts*—to help others. The same is true for wizards. *Magic* is their gift."

"Those people were given their skills by God, but I'm not so sure about wizards. Magic comes from somewhere else." Marc did not want to go so far as to claim magic was evil.

Oren took in and released a deep breath, clearly trying to remain patient. "*All* things come from God, good and evil. It is up to each of us to choose between the two." Leaning past the edge of the table, the master pointed to his side. "That knife at your waist, is it good or evil?"

Marc glanced at the weapon tucked into its leather scabbard. "Neither."

"What is it, then?"

He thought about it for a moment. "It is a tool. I cut things with it, dig with it." The image of his blade piercing the buck's neck flashed through his mind. "And kill things with it if necessary."

The master leaned closer, his brows narrowing. "And if you used it to kill an innocent man? Good... or evil?"

"That would be evil, but the evil would be upon me, not the knife."

Straightening, Oren slowly nodded. "You show wisdom, Marc. Open your mind and realize that magic, too, is only a tool. Have you ever heard that I used magic in a wrongful way?"

"Never."

"So, what am I? Good or evil?"

The master had well made his point. Marc could no longer assume magic was something it was not. "Well, good, of course."

"I try to be. I use my knowledge and magic to help others. When I foresaw the darkness we are now emerging from, I could have remained safely here while the world starved around me. Instead, I warned everyone I could. Your village listened and survived."

Marc squirmed uncomfortably on his stool. "I don't want to be responsible for people's lives like that. I'm not a leader, that much I know."

Oren studied him for a moment, his eyes afire with magic. "In time you will become many things you are now not." While Marc wondered what that meant, the master rose. "Look through the book. Pick out a few simple spells and learn them. Also practice more with the door. Meanwhile, Valeria and I will make bread for supper." He motioned for her to follow.

She stood and humbly dipped her head. "Master, might I stay a short while? I would like to learn these, too."

Marc looked to the wizard, hopeful for any sign of agreement—he very much wanted Valeria's support—but the man only repeated the gesture. "He alone must study the book."

As they left, a trickle of panic seeped into Marc's mind. How would he learn all this? And what if he should fail? He turned several pages, examining the spells on them. It looked overwhelming. Surely Oren erred in thinking he could become a wizard. Marc owed him his life, so he would do his best to memorize the spells. But learning magic and practicing it as a profession were two different things. And as for being Oren's replacement? Marc could not see himself confronting a man like Thaddeus, someone who could end his life with one swift arrow. No, he could not be the wizard Oren hoped for.

Standing, he cleared his thoughts and regarded the cave door. On a whim, he cast the spell from the far side of the room, easily unlocking the bolt. A cautious grin spread across his face, all fears of wizardry suppressed for the moment. A half hour ago he would not have believed he could do what was now a simple task. Maybe it *would* be easier than he thought to learn all this magic. Returning his attention to the book, he began to study.

Ψ   Ψ   Ψ

Valeria followed Oren into the kitchen, her mind not on the bread to be made but what she had just witnessed. What a marvelous gift Marc had been given. She always knew he was special in some way. While glad for him and, if she were honest with herself, maybe a bit jealous, it frustrated her to be so close to the magic she yearned for and yet so removed from it.

Oren started a small fire in the oven, warming the stones enough for the bread to rise. Taking a large measure each of wheat and barley, Valeria ground them into flour, mixed up the dough, and put it into the oven to rise. All this time Oren had patiently observed her.

He frowned slightly. "You are unhappy about being excluded from learning magic. Do not worry so."

"I don't mean to be rude, Master, but why can't I learn it along with Marc?"

"Today you touched the Great Tree and felt its power. Do you feel it now?"

"No. Should I?"

"If you were meant to command the magic that Marc must learn, you would."

Her heart sank. Ever since yesterday morning she believed she might learn *some* of the master's spells. Even after being told she could not light a fire or heal a wound, she still figured the simpler aspects of magic were attainable. "So that means I will never learn to use magic?"

He gave her a sympathetic shrug. "What must be, will be. If in the future the magic decides you are to learn the spells, that will be made known to you." Oren settled on a stool. "Speaking of the *future*, why do you assume there is no magic in your life?"

Valeria thought about it. Of course she had magic in her life; Oren, and now Marc, used it. But why had he mentioned the word future in that way? Did the look in his eyes mean—

"My dreams? Magic causes my dreams?"

The corner of his mouth twitched upward. "In a way."

She found herself suddenly bewildered. "How do you know about them? I've told no one but my mother, not even Marc." Keeping silent, the wizard stared expectantly at her, one brow raised. It took her more than a moment to understand why. "Oh, how foolish of me. The magic told you, like it tells you everything else."

"Yes. It would be difficult for me *not* to know about someone so strongly blessed with the gift of prophesy." His intent gaze met hers. "Something rare among those favored by magic."

Valeria doubted her own ears. Did she hear him correctly, or only what she wanted to hear? "So, I *was* right to think I have a connection with magic?" Oren's nod seemed to convey more than agreement. Seizing her first thought, she blurted it out. "You chose Marc and I for our magic, not our other skills. You *knew* you would choose us long before coming to our village."

The wizard's lips curled ever so slightly upward. "There is some truth in that, but both of you really do have skills I need. Now, tell me of your visions."

Elated, Valeria detailed every dream, ending with the one where Marc returned carrying the deer. "Most of my dreams are very strange, making little sense. Why is that so, Master?"

"Magic talks to us in its own language. At first it appears to speak in riddles, but after you learn *how* to listen, the meaning will become clearer. It will take time for you to hear its true voice."

"Do you understand my dreams?"

"Portions, but it is not for me to say what they mean. Your visions are just that: yours."

Her visions. The concept finally sunk in. Joy overflowed within her. She wanted to hug Oren, but something in his expression told her not to. He was the master, she the servant. Words would have to do. "Thank you for choosing me. I want to learn how to listen better to the magic."

"You shall." Oren's gaze shifted to the oven. "We have talked long enough for the bread to rise. Light the oven. I will see how Marc is doing." He stood and left.

Valeria tried to awaken the fire by blowing on the ashes, but the embers had died out. She built a new kindling pile, then headed for the fireplace to fetch a burning stick. Midway there, she paused. Why not try using magic to light it?

Recalling Oren's instructions to Marc, she imagined how the magic felt, concentrated on the kindling and evoked the spell. "*Ārdē!*" Nothing happened. Focusing more intently and putting all the authority she could into her voice, she tried again. Still nothing. With a sigh of frustration, she decided to light the fire the normal way. After the oven reached the proper temperature, she put the loaf in to bake.

With nothing more to do, she headed outside. Looking about, she viewed the world anew. The vibrant green of life suffused everything. A gentle breeze danced about her, bringing with it the delightful fragrances of newly opened blossoms. And the fruit and nut trees were adorned in the deepest of pinks, the brightest purples and whites so pure that snow seemed dim in comparison. Bees sang to her as they lazily drifted from flower to flower. Hearing the quiet rush of air slipping past wings, she looked up to see a flock of geese pass by. She counted fifteen. What a welcome sight!

Laughing, Valeria ran to the gate. Grasping the bars, she surveyed the land beyond. The mist that usually shrouded everything had lifted, allowing her to see for miles. She gazed along the southern path which led toward home. Just over the rise, occasional wisps of steam rose from the hot springs. A warm bath sounded most inviting, but it would have to wait.

For a time she wandered about the compound, thinking on what it meant to have the gift of prophecy. Why did *she* have it as opposed to someone else? How should she use it? Oren could perform magic at will, but her visions came upon her sporadically and only during sleep. If there came a need for seeing into the future, would she have to wait days, or even weeks, for a dream to come upon her? She let out a gentle sigh. It was too soon to worry about such things.

Returning to the kitchen, she found the bread only half baked, so she headed to her room. She reached for the curtain covering her doorway, then hesitated, glancing at the workshop door. What were the master and Marc doing in there? As if to answer her, the door swung open. Both men sat at the table. Knowing one of them used their magic on the door gave her a bit of a thrill.

When she moved to look into the workshop, Oren gestured her way. "Come in. See what else Marc has learned."

She quickly entered and took a seat. "Show me."

Marc placed a wooden bowl before him and cast a spell. Amazed, she watched it rise until it hung a foot above the table, bobbling slightly. How did the magic hold it up? She waved her hand under and over it, feeling nothing except a slight warmth. As the vessel settled back on the table, she clapped enthusiastically. "That's wonderful. Can you make anything else fly?"

"If it's not too heavy. Master Oren wants me to move the anvil over there, but I can't do it."

"Yet," Oren said pointedly. "Your will must be stronger. The magic can only work as hard as you do. Practice it every chance you get." He stood with a groan. "These old bones are getting stiff. A good walk will loosen them up. Valeria, help him find different things to levitate, but remember the bread."

"Yes, Master." Glancing around, she pointed at the lamp. "Move that." She watched Marc with great interest. His eyes sparkled with the excitement of performing the spell. If only he would look at her like that. And the way his lips were pursed in concentration—perfect for kissing her.

"How's this?" he asked as the lamp floated several inches above the table while slowly rotating.

"Very good. I'm proud of you."

Keeping his gaze fixed upon the object, he grinned. "Thanks.

"Our master seems pleased, too."

Marc lowered the lamp to the table's surface then looked at her, his face serious. "I hope so. I'd rather not have him angry at me."

"You're afraid of him?"

"No, but mindful. I've displeased him twice today." Marc leaned closer and lowered his voice. "He tells me if I do well in my studies, I may one day learn the Great Secret of magic."

A tingle crept over her. "Great Secret? Magic *itself* is secret. Whatever it is, it must be very important." She held his hands. "I also have something important to share." How to tell him? Certainly he would be glad for her, but he might also be hurt that she kept it to herself until now. "I just found out I can do a little magic, too."

His eyes lit up in surprise. "That's wonderful! What is it?"

"I sometimes see things *before* they happen. I see them in my dreams." She told him about some of them. "That's why I knew to greet you when you brought back the deer."

"Fascinating. Will you be learning the spells, too, then?" He nodded toward the book.

She shook her head, all too aware the sum of magic's knowledge was within her reach. "Master Oren says I don't have the same connection to magic you do."

"Maybe not, but you do have your *own* special kind, and that pleases me." He gave her a hearty but all-too-brief hug. "Tell me when you have any more visions."

"I shall." She wished the hug lasted longer. Why did he not act on the way she knew he felt toward her? "Are your feelings hurt that I never told you about my dreams until now?"

"No. Why would you think so?"

"You told me your secrets, going into the Vale and everything. You trusted me enough to tell me."

Marc laughed, mischief flashing in his eyes. "Only *after* you forced me."

"But still, I could have told you—"

"No. You had no reason to. Your dreams are private. I'm glad I told you and Sean about going into the Vale. I could have brought ruin upon our village. Sharing it eased that burden." He leaned forward and tenderly kissed her forehead. "Thanks for being so curious."

The room spun about her and her skin flushed with sudden warmth. "Glad to," she mumbled. With his touch a cacophony of images flooded her mind. Images of him. Some from past occurrences, but most of times unknown. The experience made her recall what took place earlier by the cave door.

"One more thing, Marc. Before, when I said your hand was hot—" How could she explain something so abstract? "I saw images of you like I do in my dreams, but none of them made any sense."

"Some day they will. Tell me then."

"I promise." She tried not to blush.

He smiled, warm and genuine, awakening the memory of his kiss. She let it linger until he reminded her to check the bread.

The remainder of the day passed and Valeria retired to her chamber to sleep, her mind filled with the remarkable events she experienced. Memories of the Great Tree and the Forbidden Vale flitted through her head before being replaced with seeing Marc perform his first spell. He seemed as thrilled as her when he learned that bit of magic.

Soon memories drifted into dreams as she imagined him standing before the people of their village, performing great feats of magic. The crowd cheered and applauded his every move. But something felt wrong. She knew someone was missing. Donald? He would not want to witness Marc being praised. Searching through the thin blue haze, she saw him next to his father, clapping along with the rest.

That troubled her. Things were not right. Aside from Donald's behavior, something else seemed terribly wrong. But what? Why did everything look so strange? And that smell?

Smoke! Thick, billowing clouds of it blew through the crowd who ignored it while continuing to celebrate Marc's prowess. She desperately tried to warn them the village burned, but they did not hear her. Maybe Marc would.

Looking back to where he once stood she found no one. Whirling about, she now found herself standing in the graveyard, alone. The trees were gone, replaced with giant spears thrust blade-first into the ground. Impaled into their shafts were hundreds of arrows arranged in ghastly caricatures of branches and boughs. Above them rivers of blood flowed through the near-black sky.

Frightened, she cried out Marc's name. The only answer— the icy wind. Once again she tried, shouting. With a great clap of thunder, the heavens burst open and a magnificent sword of golden fire tumbled to earth, landing in a hole before her. She leaned over the edge and saw what she feared most: Marc lay in an open grave, covered with blood. Her tears fell upon him and his eyes snapped open. A terrible scream of pain and rage tore from his lips and split the world in two, leaving her in silent blackness.

Heart pounding, Valeria gasped for air. She felt about herself—blankets and skins surrounded her. She was in bed. Dread overcame her. "Oh, God, no." While she desperately tried to convince herself it was just a dream, she knew better. It was a vision. A very bad vision.

About Marc.

"Oh, God, *please*, no," she quietly cried into her pillow. "Don't let it be so."

Chapter 9

Whistling a tune, Marc strode briskly through the woods, enjoying the early morning air. He was in a good mood. No lessons today. No chores. After a quick visit to the Great Tree, he would be free to leave and spend the day with his mother and sisters. To top it all off, the weather looked to be perfect.

For six weeks straight he and Valeria had served Oren well and today was to be their first day of rest. In that time, he learned much about the cultivation and application of the many herbs the master used for healing and potions. His continuing lessons on Latin, Greek, history, medicine and the writings of great minds, gave him a deeper understanding of the world. But his progression in the ways of magic surprised Marc the most—he had learned nearly one-quarter of the spells in the book. Throughout it all, the master's expert guidance and encouragement made his tasks easier. The knowledge and wisdom Oren had gained over the years amazed Marc. He hungered to learn it all.

Exiting the trees into the meadow east of the creek, he waded through a knee-deep sea of wild flowers. Insects darted everywhere while mice and other small creatures scurried underfoot. When he came to the large pool behind the waterfall, he saw dozens of fingerlings swimming about; Wiccan creek had calmed now that the last snows had melted. The return of these long-absent things comforted him.

Marc climbed the hill, letting the magic of the Great Tree flow into his mind. With each previous journey his discomfort toward it diminished, transforming as of late into curiosity. Its intense magic had a purpose, but what? Oren would not say. Once at the ledge, he put his hands upon the massive trunk expecting a rush of emotion or a sensation of some sort, but other than feeling its raw power, the Tree remained quiet.

Waiting to see if that would change, his thoughts turned to the village. It would be good to see everyone again, but he worried about what questions they might ask and which answers to give. Sean would surely pounce upon him and Val, demanding to be filled in to the last detail. How much should he be told? Val wanted to tell her mother the reason for her visions. Marc wondered if it would be wise to tell *anyone* about the magic, for doing so might very well change how the others treated him.

With a sigh, he let go of the bark and sat facing the valley, his back against the trunk. Scanning the land below, he found his gaze kept halting upon one particular spot on the hillside across the way. Why did it catch his interest so? There was little to see but trees and rocks. After some thought, he realized the hot spring lay on the far side of that place. Why would that be important right now?

Shrugging it off, he decided the Tree had determined to remain mute, and headed back to Oren's house. As he walked, his thoughts returned to Val, recalling little snippets of her handing him bread, stretching to get something off a high shelf, kneeling in the master's garden and running after a goose. Then, suddenly, a surge of vertigo welled up, causing him to stagger to a nearby tree for support. The daydream of her swimming naked at the hot springs returned with a vivid intensity he had not previously experienced. Not only could he see everything more clearly, he also heard her splashing about and singing. The crisp scent of the water and the plants living around it came strongly to his nose. The absolute *realness* of the mental picture both fascinated and worried him. Pushing it aside, he continued on.

Ahead he saw the branch in the path. To the left, Oren's home. To the right, the springs. Determined to prove to himself these thoughts were only fantasies of his lustful mind, Marc veered right and quickened his pace. All the way there he continued to see her swim about as if he floated bird-like, high in the air over the spring. The strength of his thoughts distressed him—they seemed so genuine, but, of course, that could not be.

With deliberate care, he slowly climbed the rocky path to the spring. Keeping low and to the left, he hugged the hillside and silently pushed his way into the vegetation at the water's edge, trusting the gurgle of the spring would mask any noises he might make. Slightly parting the last layer of bushes, he cautiously peered out over the water. His heart leapt. Not fifteen feet away swam Val! Although her back was to him, he could tell she was indeed naked, just as he had seen. Marc swallowed hard, trying to control the fear and excitement surging through him. *Could* this be real? Or just a figment of the Tree's magic?

No, it *had* to be real. He *felt* the bushes against his skin, the grit of the rocky soil pressing sharply into his knees, the heat radiating off the water. Valeria looked real enough, too. And yet he hid from her like a frightened animal. His fear melted away to be replaced with shame—he should not be doing this. As he started to back away, she quickly looked with alarm in his direction.

"Hello?" Sinking up to her chin, she carefully scanned the area around his hiding place. "Is anyone there?"

He froze, desperately hoping to remain undiscovered. She looked around several more times before moving to the far side of the spring. When she turned away, Marc retreated down the rocks and back to the path. Crossing over the tiny stream, he stopped and looked behind him in dismay. What just happened? Surely the Tree had a hand in this—what he saw on the way here *was* real—but there was more to it. Did magic itself want to tell him something?

Concern for Val pushed those worries aside. As he thought about how frightened she must be, his mind snapped back to the bird's-eye view of the spring. She now stood next to the water, dressing. Forcing the image from his mind, he ran toward Oren's house, afraid of what he had done and filled with questions he could not answer. Should he ask the master about what happened? Would he be punished?

Blurting out the spell, he opened the gate and hurried down the path toward the house. He had not gone far before spotting his master off to the left, far back in the trees, next to the wall. The old man knelt upon the ground, eyes downcast. Marc found that odd. Oren never kneeled, not even to pray. He said doing so caused him too much pain. Moments later, the wizard stood and inspected the branches above him. By the time Marc caught up with him, Oren had moved several trees closer to the house. He glanced at Marc before returning his attention to the immature fruit.

"Ah. How was the visit to the Tree?"

In his brief look at Oren's face, he saw the man's eyes were moist. While momentarily curious about the master's doings, his visions of Valeria concerned him more. Marc tried to keep the panic from voice. "Nothing happened there, but on the way back I started having visions—powerful ones—and then I saw they were real."

"Visions?" Oren asked calmly. "Of what?"

Marc took in a ragged breath. "I saw—now please don't be angry. I didn't ask for them." He paused, fought back his jittery nerves, and took another breath. "I had visions of—"

"Valeria!" Oren looked past him, his face lined in concern. "What is the matter?"

Marc swiveled to see her running up the path.

"Master. Marc. Someone spied on me while I bathed at the spring." She darted up to Oren and grabbed his hand. When her agitated gaze met his own, Marc felt a pang of guilt.

Oren placed his other hand atop hers. "Be calm, for you are in no danger. Who was it?"

Biting her lower lip, she shook her head. "I don't know. I didn't see them."

"Then how do you know you were being watched?"

"I- I can't say why I know, I just do. I *felt* it."

Oren nodded and lightly pulled at his beard. "Ah. There may have been someone, or it may have been the magic. It sometimes feels that way when it comes to you."

"Can you tell if anyone is still there?"

The wizard nodded. Closing his eyes he faced skyward, spreading his arms out from his sides. Marc wondered what kind of magic he used. His own experience of seeing Valeria swimming must be insignificant to the powers the master could summon. After a moment, Oren returned his gaze to her. "I Envisioned the area around the spring and found no one."

Valeria visibly relaxed. "So it was magic I felt?"

"I believe magic was involved." Oren gave Marc a subtle, knowing glance before adding, "To some degree."

She turned to Marc. "Did *you* see anyone this morning?"

Marc desperately tried to swallow the hard lump in his throat. Should he tell her the truth? Doing so was sure to upset her, but he did not want to lie to her, either. "The only people I've seen this morning were you and Master Oren." Even though he spoke the literal truth, it felt like a lie. A terrible lie. *Again* the magic he never wanted brought trouble into his life. Only this time it spilled over into Valeria's life as well. Filled with frustration and shame, he averted her gaze.

Valeria drew closer, the fingers of her right hand coming to rest on his forearm. "What's wrong?"

When Marc glanced at the master, the wizard gestured encouragingly toward Valeria with his eyes. What was he trying to say? That she suspected something? If so, she would not rest until she rooted out the truth. It would be better to confess now than later. Putting his hand on hers, he faced her. "It... was me," he said, quietly.

"What?"

"It was me you sensed." He looked into her eyes expecting to see anger, shock, or, at the very least, disapproval. Instead he found concern.

"Explain."

He told her everything he experienced after leaving the Tree. "I honestly did not intend to spy upon you. I just—I had to know if what I saw was real."

Her face brightened. "Don't worry yourself for what happened was magic's will." She faced Oren. "Yes?" The wizard nodded. "I am thrilled about the gift my best friend has received." Giving him a quick hug, she turned toward the house. "I'm going to gather my things for the journey. Are you coming?"

Caught off guard by her rapid change in attitude, it took him a moment to answer. "Uh, soon." After she was out of earshot, Marc addressed Oren with a subtle bow. "I trust you knew what happened even before I confessed."

"Yes."

"So what *did* happen? How was I able to see visions of Val from so far away?"

"Visions are images of what will *be*. This morning you *Envisioned*—seeing what is happening now. To a wizard, this is a most valuable aspect of magic."

"So the magic *talked* to me?" Marc asked slowly, unsure of his thoughts.

"In a way."

A jolt of excitement rippled through him. To hear magic's voice meant he had its favor—well, some favor, anyway. "I am honored." He remembered how Oren Envisioned the spring a minute ago. "Will I be able to Envision at will someday?"

"You already did, seeing Valeria at the springs, and can do so now. Center a thought in your mind about someone or some place. Then concentrate on *wanting* to view them or it. It is easier to Envision people or places you know well, and much more difficult to see things unknown." The master smiled at him. "Tell me what your mother is doing at this moment."

Marc eagerly focused on knowing his mother's whereabouts and first thought she might be at the family hut. Nothing came to him. He tried harder, wishing to see his mother inside the hut. No change. "I see nothing, Master." He explained how he tried.

"That is because you wanted to see both her *and* the hut. Magic cannot show you what is not there. I assure you she is not in the hut. Try Envisioning just the hut alone."

Marc did, and after a dozen or so heartbeats, the image of his home popped into his mind just like the springs did earlier. "Yes! I see it. No one is home."

"Very good. Now try thinking only of your mother."

He did and quickly found her, Gwen and Stella gathering reeds from the marsh east of the oak grove. As before, he saw the scene from high above. Wondering if he could get a closer look, he tried redirecting his viewpoint and was thrilled to find it instantly responded to his will. He watched his mother cut the base of the reeds with her knife, pass them to Stella, who then stacked them horizontally in Gwen's arms. The scene was as true and clear as if he stood beside them.

Releasing the magic with a chuckle, he looked to his master. "This is incredible."

"It is, but use it responsibly." Oren regarded him closely, his expression most serious. "Wizards must *always* respect people's privacy."

Oren's caution sobered his excitement, reminding him of how he frightened Valeria and then, like a coward, tried to lie to her. Marc nodded his understanding. "It seems magic gave me a perfect example of what not to do."

Releasing a gentle sigh, the master patted him on the shoulder. "I admit, the timing could have been better. Now, off with you. You have an adventure awaiting you."

Relieved, Marc headed to the house and set to loading his pack. For some reason he felt the need to take a blanket *and* a skin, plus extra rations of nuts and dried fruit. After Valeria was ready, they said goodbye to Oren and headed down the path to Oak Creek.

At first they did not talk, only sharing a small loaf of bread she brought along. Seeing a blackbird eyeing them, he tossed a large crumb to the side of the path and watched it swoop down from its perch to snatch up the morsel. He thought it only fair since enough of the bird's cousins had fed him in the past. When they neared the small path that led to the spring, Valeria took his hand. Her touch roused the memories of her bathing, making him feel embarrassed.

She gave him a warm, reassuring smile, almost as if in answer to his unspoken apology. "I'm glad it was you that saw me, not some stranger. Looking back on it, I realize I never actually felt threatened. I also sensed a faint kind of magic coming from where you hid. At the time I was too distracted to realize it strongly reminded me of yours."

He avoided her gaze. "How so?"

"Like I've told you before, your magic feels, well, *hot* to me. Oren and the Tree only feel warm. What I felt earlier was just like yours. What do you think?"

Calming himself, he gave it some thought. "I believe you are right. I sometimes feel the presence of you or Oren. Maybe this means the magic is starting to talk to you."

Her grip tightened. "Oh, I'd love that." She let out a joyous little giggle.

Sweeter than any music, her laughter eased his desires. Even so, it could not return things to how they once were. For some time her beauty called strongly to him, but he had always managed to push those thoughts aside. Today changed all that. He wanted her yet knew he could never have her. Even someone as important as Donald was not worthy in her eyes. For as long as he and Valeria served in their master's house, Marc vowed to remain a gentleman.

Ψ   Ψ   Ψ

Lost in thought, Oren lingered at the gate long after his two wards disappeared from sight. Would they notice how much they had changed, especially Marc? It surprised him how quickly the young man learned to use his gifts despite the conflicts warring within him. Oren wished he could tell Marc why part of him feared magic, but doing so would change what would be. What had to be.

Leaving the gate, he slowly walked up the path, contemplating his future. With each passing month, the aches in his legs and back continued to worsen as his energy, eyesight and hearing also declined. He felt fortunate to have his magic to fall back on, but even that had its limits. Would he remain strong enough to face the coming tribulations? And after over eight decades on this earth, would he live long enough to teach Marc everything he needed to know in order to survive those tests? He hoped so, trusting all would progress according to the Lord's plan.

Oren approached a favorite plum tree, one of three he and his wife had planted on their wedding day. It remained barren; no flowers or leaves had come forth. He gently bent a twig. Its brittle snap told him that the darkness had claimed yet another life. Sadly, he knew it had to be removed to make way for a new sapling, one full of life and vigor. A wry smile crossed his face. He, too, would soon be replaced in kind.

Continuing deeper into the orchard, he came to the place he was at when Marc returned earlier. He knelt. The pain that shot through his knees paled against the ache and emptiness in his heart. Reaching down, he delicately caressed two flat, featureless stones set flush in the ground, opening his mind to the feelings his magic enabled him to receive.

"I miss you, my darlings," he said gently. "I still feel you strongly even though you have been absent for so long. I wish you could meet my apprentices. You would love them both. They are so innocent, yet soon will learn the harsh truths of the world. Pain will find them, especially Marc. But they will be strong. Our Creator has seen to that. I am honored to be His instrument to guide them."

He visited a while longer before struggling to his feet—he avoided using magic out of respect for his wife and daughter. Wiping the tears from his eyes, he made his way to the house. From within the caves he retrieved medicinal herbs, extra blankets and other supplies. Returning to the house, he carried them into the fireplace room. It was time to ready things for tonight.

Chapter 10

"Hurry, Marc." Valeria tugged eagerly on his arm. "We're almost there."

Above them a thin curl of smoke drifted skyward from the remnants of the previous night's guiding fire.

Laughing, he broke into a jog. She had not changed since childhood. "You just can't wait to tell your mother."

Her eyes flashed playfully. "And what's wrong with that?"

He laughed again. "Nothing, as long as it's only—"

"Marc! Valeria! What a pleasure this is." Garrett hurried toward them through the underbrush.

Marc extended a hand. "Greetings." The village leader firmly shook it in the manner used between the men. Valeria gave him a quick hug.

Garret beamed. "What brings the two of you here? Some task for Oren?"

"No, just a free day to visit. How is the hunt lately?"

"Very good indeed. We—"

Valeria started to slip away. "I don't mean to be rude, but I'll go see my mother while you two talk."

Garrett laughed as she hurried off. "Good-bye, then." He looked back at Marc, a gleam in his eye. "The hunt? Much improved. Sean has brought in dozens of hares since you left. Seems he has a secret hunting place and won't tell where. We're starting to see some deer, even does with fawns. Lord knows where they've been hiding, but I'm glad they haven't died off. There are many geese as well."

"It's good to see everything is changing for the better."

"Your life is changing, too." Garrett glanced about as if to ensure they were not observed, then spoke quietly. "How are your studies in the ways of magic coming along?"

Startled, Marc met his gaze. "How do you know that?"

"Oren told me the night he selected you to help him, but I've been expecting it. Since you were a little boy he knew you would be favored with magic. Your father had some in him, too, right?"

Gasping in a choked breath, Marc managed a stunned, "*What?*"

Furrowing his brows, Garrett regarded him for a long moment. "He never told you?"

Giving his head a slow shake, Marc searched his memories. "He talked *about* magic a few times, but nothing concerning him— uh, us having any. I do remember him asking if I had any interest in it. But—" Marc looked away, not wanting Garrett to see the hurt in his eyes. "Not long after that he died."

Recalling his father's memory awakened some of the pain he felt at losing him. While knowing they shared a connection to magic gladdened his heart, he wondered what other secrets may have died with him. Images and emotions of that terrible night tried to surface, but Marc firmly repressed them. Even so, something about it nagged at him, something important but very unpleasant. Best to change the subject.

"This morning I saw Oren kneeling in the trees by the south wall. When I came up to him, he looked sorrowful. Do you have any idea why that might be so?"

Garrett nodded sadly. "His wife and child are buried there."

That fact surprised Marc. "Oh. I never knew he had married."

"They died many years ago, well before my time. He never remarried, either. He must have loved her very much." Putting an arm around Marc's shoulder, Garrett directed him toward the village. "Enough of that," he said with forced cheer. "Let's get you home so you can greet everybody."

Thinking of those whom he would soon see, he suddenly became worried. "Who else knows about my studies?"

"No one."

"Not even Don?" Marc worried about Donald's reaction should he find out.

Garrett scoffed loudly. "Especially him. He still thinks as a boy and until his attitude changes, he will be treated as such."

It startled Marc to hear Garrett speak so frankly about his son. "He'll come around."

Garrett gave him a nod of appreciation. "I pray for that every day. Come."

It did not take long for the villagers to notice his return. Within a minute, a small crowd surrounded Marc, eager to hear of his time with the wizard. He patiently explained what he could, carefully avoiding anything that even hinted of learning magic. The nagging sensations associated with his father's death continued to escalate to the point that, once free of the crowd, he could no longer repress the unwanted memories. Stumbling toward a nearby bench, he collapsed onto it as the nightmare he often suffered surged into the forefront of his mind.

Marc found himself in the woods at night, clutching a sword in one hand and an antler in the other. His head spun as his heart pounded madly in fear. A figure cloaked in black snuck about the darkness, sliding from shadow to shadow, stalking him. An overwhelming sense of evil hung about this presence—evil directed at him. And the terrible smell of the place, singed hair and charred meat, burned his nose and throat. The dream always ended the same way—the figure rose into the air, burst into flames and vanished.

"What is the matter?" a man's voice asked. "Are you ill?"

Realizing he was slumped forward, head in hands, Marc sat up and opened his eyes to see Domas, the metal worker, looking concerned. "No. Just tired." He put on what he hoped appeared to be a natural smile and stood. "Had to rest my eyes a bit."

Relieved, Domas said, "Good health to you, then," and headed off.

Marc trembled a little. Was it from fear? Being assaulted by the unwanted nightmare had definitely unsettled him. But there was more to his unease than just the dream. What that might be, he didn't know. Looking around, he determined no one else had seen him lose control of himself. Grateful for that, he took in a deep breath, calmed himself and resumed his walk.

Passing by Sean's home, he heard his friend's voice inside. Turning up the short, stone-lined path, he stopped in the doorway and saw him talking with Valeria.

"Marc!" Sean bounded over and nearly squeezed the life from him. "It's good to see you."

Marc squeezed harder. "And you, my friend."

"Valeria has spoken much about your time at Oren's. She also told me why you were not harmed when you entered the Vale. Amazing, isn't it? And you said you'd never go back there. Ha!"

Marc shot Valeria a quick glance, worried she let slip the secret they agreed to keep. Her clever smile eased his concern. "Yes, the Great Tree is not so frightening now. What else has she talked about?"

"She started to tell me about Oren's many scrolls."

"You'd love them. Grand tales of adventure and exploration."

"And poetry," Valeria said.

"Yes. Val's taken quite a liking to poetry. She'll tell you about it while I go see my mother. Let's talk more later." He shook Sean's hand and retreated outside, walking the short distance home. Entering, he found his mother and sisters weaving reed baskets, giving him a momentary thrill when he recalled Envisioning them at the marsh just hours before. They quickly set their work aside and greeted him.

"We've missed you so much," Judith said, clutching him firmly to her.

He hugged her back. "I have as well."

"Are you here to stay?" Gwen asked, somehow managing to worm between them. "I won't mind letting you take over chopping all the wood."

Stella lifted her older sister's arm, squeezing the biceps. "Look how strong she's getting."

Marc chuckled as Gwen yanked her arm back with a frown. "No, I'm only here for the day. Why don't the two of you get back to your weaving. I need to speak with mother." After hugging his sisters, he motioned for his mother to follow him outside.

"What is it, Son?"

"We need to talk in private. Away from here." He gestured up the northern path.

She studied his face for a moment, then nodded. "Very well."

While leading her to Ethan's shed, he repeated what he told the villagers about his time at Oren's. After ensuring they were alone, he unfastened the door and bade her enter.

Tightening the shawl about her shoulders, she gazed at him uneasily. "Why are we here?"

"I want no one to hear us speak."

A flicker of concern crossed her face. "Are you in some kind of trouble?"

"No. I—" How would he tell her? Just blurt it out or ease into it? Oren told him that when making important decisions, he should think first with this mind, but then let his heart make the final choice. "Did father ever talk about having a connection to magic?"

She cocked her head in puzzlement. "Magic?"

"Did he know things about it? Did he ever mention it?"

"No. Why do you ask this?"

"Because I found out he not only knew about magic, but had some in him as well."

Her eyebrows narrowed. "That's nonsense. Where did you get such a silly idea?"

He took her hands in his and faced her. "I, too, have magic."

Initially shocked, her expression changed into one of confusion. "Marc? Why—why would you say something like that?"

"Because it's true. Oren is teaching me to use magic. He wants me to become a wizard." Marc saw a thick clump of flowers growing near the sheep pen. "I'll prove it to you. See those flowers over there?" He pointed them out. "I will bring them to you using magic. Don't be frightened." Lowering his voice, he gently said, *"Flōrēs, ad mātrem meam īte."*

She gasped seeing a handful of blossoms break free and float toward her. The color drained from her face as she backed away, bumping into a hanging sack of acorns. "How—?" His mother glanced nervously between him and the flowers hanging in space before her.

"They won't hurt you," he said reassuringly.

Hesitantly, she reached out and accepted them. "Thank you."

"I'm sorry to shock you this way, but I didn't know how else to make you believe me."

She smiled weakly. "I see. How long have you been using magic?"

"Since my second day with Oren." Marc briefly described his studies, during which the apprehension in her gaze faded.

"Does Valeria know about this?" she asked.

"Yes. She's helping me improve my skills."

Judith squeezed his hand affectionately. "Then study hard and learn well. Oren is giving you a wonderful gift."

"He is, but it's not always wonderful. Sometimes I fear magic. It reminds me of the terrible dreams I had after father died." That nagging feeling returned, unsettling his stomach. "Somehow I know they are related."

His mother hugged him. "Those were only dreams. They couldn't hurt you, Son. If you hadn't been the one to find him—"

The memories of that terrible night surfaced full force. It was late evening and his father had not returned from hunting, so the men and older boys went in search of him. Donald and Sean helped Marc look in an area his father favored. At one point, Marc thought he heard his father's voice calling to him from the other side of a thicket. Pushing through the brush, he found him sprawled backward over a log, lifeless eyes staring vacantly into the black sky, his hands gripping an antler protruding from his chest.

Marc instantly knew he was dead. Releasing a gut-wrenching cry of loss, he dropped to his knees in the snow and touched his father's face. It was cold, nearly frozen. While Donald ran to alert the men, Marc moved to pull out the antler. Upon touching it, a hot, tingling sensation rushed into him.

Jumping back, he fearfully regarded his father's ashen form in the flickering torch light. Cautiously, he tried once more. The heat and energy again assailed him, this time with greater intensity. Seeing he could not remove it, Sean did it for him. Later, the men searched in vain for a one-antlered buck. How the animal managed to gore his father remained a mystery.

Two years ago, Marc knew nothing of magic or how it felt, but now he understood the antler had a strong connection to it. A cold, chill sweat trickled down his back as the truth became evident. He embraced his mother.

"Oh, God! I know why I fear magic as I do." He told her of straying into the Forbidden Vale, feeling the Tree, and how its magic related to that of the antler's. "Why was the antler so strongly charged with magic? Did the magic kill him?" That last thought greatly worried Marc.

"I wouldn't know, Son." She reached out to caress his cheek.

When her hand touched him, he again saw quick flashes of the nightmare, only this time with new images. The dark figure skulked about as before, but now he saw it watch as his father knelt before a fallen buck, knife in hand, preparing to clean it. Stepping from the shadows, the figure approached his father, who stood and looked upon the man with familiarity. The figure suddenly drew a sword and plunged it into his father's heart. Next, Marc saw the antler being thrust into the wound and his father's lifeless hands positioned around it.

"Marc?"

Shaking his head, Marc fought off the effects of the dream—no, not dream. *Vision.*

"Marc? What is happening?" she asked, distressed.

Taking her hands in his, he met her gaze. "I just had a vision."

Some of her earlier apprehension returned to her eyes. "You get visions?"

"Not often, but this one revealed something terrible." Anger welled up within him as he understood what the vision meant. "Father was not gored by a buck. He was *murdered.*" Gritting his teeth, he gripped her upper arms. "Murdered with a sword wielded by someone he *knew.*"

Pain filled her eyes. "Who?"

Who indeed, Marc wondered. While the magic revealed some much needed information, it also withheld the most important part. Seeing he was hurting her, Marc relaxed his grip and reined in his temper.

"I don't know, Mother. But I'll find out and avenge father."

"How? It's been over two years."

"Magic, that's how." Holding her to him, he released what anger he could and calmly said, "I swear on father's honor, and my own, that I will find a way to use magic to expose the killer."

Patting his back, she said, "Ask Oren for guidance."

Ask Oren. The man who knew everything, to whom everyone turned when they needed direction. "He says I am to become a wizard like he is, that I am to replace him one day. While I am fairly good at magic, I don't want to be a wizard for they are also leaders. We all expect Oren to solve our problems. I can't be responsible for other people's lives." He met her gaze. "I can't do that."

A loving, knowing smile blossomed on her face. "You can, and I'll tell you why. You don't see yourself as others do. Many of your father's strengths are within you. You put the needs of others ahead of your own. You listen before speaking. You never think of yourself as better or more important. You *care*. And you are very smart." She tenderly placed the palm of her right hand on his chest. "The leader you claim not to be is already inside. All you have to do is let him out. I know that. And so does Oren."

Marc saw pride and love in his mother's eyes, plus one other thing—certainty. She truly believed it. A sense of peace came over him. Embracing her once more, he felt a warm, familiar sensation come from his left.

"I know that, too." Valeria walked into the shed. Her expression matched his mother's.

"Val!" He ached to hold her tight.

She smiled at him, then looked at his mother. "I see he told you."

"Yes. Quite a surprise. I'm not sure how to adjust to this. How did you do it?"

Valeria gave her a crooked little smile. "I'm still adjusting. Sometimes it's a little strange, but Marc is learning it well." They exchanged a knowing nod. He had seen women do this before, but never understood its meaning. This time proved no different.

His mother kissed his cheek. "I'm proud of you." She moved toward the door. "I need to help with dinner. Let's talk after." She glanced at the bouquet, then smiled. "Thank you for the flowers."

Valeria followed. "I'll help, Judith."

She held out her hand. "No. Stay. He has something to tell you." Ducking through the doorway, she left.

Valeria flashed him a curious grin. "I thought you weren't going to tell her?"

"I wasn't." He told her what Garrett said about his father's magic. "I had to ask her. She thought it was all nonsense. I showed her it wasn't."

"So this is what you're supposed to tell me?"

Marc shook his head. "I know why I once feared magic."

Her brows rose slightly. "Why you *once* feared magic? What changed your mind?"

He explained about the antler. "I didn't put the pieces together before because I hated to remember that night." He paused, unsure how to share the terrible news. "And then a few minutes ago I learned something more." He told how a vision uncovered his father's murder.

Stepping closer, she affectionately looked into his eyes. "I'm sorry those memories hurt you. We'll solve this together." Her soft embrace comforted him.

Chapter 11

After several hours of constant talking with friends and neighbors, Marc felt in need of some quieter time, so he talked Valeria into visiting the grain fields. "I'm eager to see how high the oats are," he said, leading her past the stone altar used for the Sabbath worship. Behind it stood a simple wooden cross fashioned from braided saplings. "Sean says Garrett expects—" Seeing that Valeria no longer walked beside him, he glanced back and found her standing motionless before the altar, staring blankly at the cross.

"Val? Are you all right?"

When he touched her arm she blinked, gasped and took a few uncertain steps back. "Oh!"

Grasping her elbow, he steadied her until she found her balance. "What happened?"

She gave him a curious smile. "A vision, I think. When I looked upon the cross, I suddenly saw a man lying on the ground."

A rush of delight leapt within him. "A vision? *While awake?* Wonderful. What does it mean?"

"I'm not sure, but—" Her forehead crinkled in concern. "Somehow I know he's in need of help."

"Can you tell where he is?"

She looked at him, uncertain. "No, I didn't see enough to recognize the place."

Thinking about his own experience that morning, he guided her to a bench, then settled next to her. "I believe I can help. Close your eyes. Remember how you saw him."

Closing them, she nodded. "All right. Now what?"

"Remember how it *felt*."

After half a minute, she frowned and gently shook her head. "I keep losing the memory."

"Try again. You must *want* to know the area around him. Make it important to you."

While she struggled with the task, he noticed a faint blue light surrounded her, clinging like a second skin. As he began to wonder what it might be, the light momentarily intensified and she bolted to her feet. "OH!"

He stood as well. "Well?"

A wide smile burst upon her face and her eyes blazed in elation. "Oh, yes! It's a wonder. It truly is. I saw him, Marc. I saw him try to sit up as clearly as if I were standing there before him. He's just off the path to Broken Rock, near the big patch of roses. If we don't help him, he'll die." Valeria took his hands, her touch warm with the power he knew well. Several tears rolled from the corners of her eyes as joy radiated from her. "The magic came, Marc. It showed me everything I needed to know. Thank you." She threw her arms around him in a brief, but intense, hug, then turned and hurried toward the southern path.

"Val, wait," he called out, moving after her.

Stopping, she waited for him to catch up. "What?"

"Shouldn't we take our packs? Also, we need to tell someone we are leaving, otherwise they'll wonder why we disappeared and come looking for us."

She pursed her lips in a thoughtful frown. "You're right, but what do we tell them? That I had a vision?"

"Tell your mother the truth and I'll tell mine the magic has revealed something we need to take care of."

After hastily informing his mother, Marc collected his pack, met up with Valeria and rushed down the path leading to Broken Rock. He thought about why the man needed help. Had he injured himself? Been attacked by some beast, or worse, set upon by thieves? Whatever it might be, the three remaining hours of light should be enough to find him and help him back to Oak Creek.

Eager to reach the man, Valeria stayed ahead of Marc. Several hundred paces before the woods gave way to the wide meadow, she veered left into the trees and brush. "We're close, Marc."

The magic must have given her as vivid a picture of the man as he had of her that morning. If so, she would know the place as surely as if she had already been there. In less than a minute they came into a small clearing fifteen paces across. Curled up in a ball, the man lay shivering against a fallen tree.

Panting for breath, Valeria knelt and touched his forehead. "Sir, do not be alarmed. We are here to help you."

He was a small man, somewhere in his early forties, clothed in a filthy, brown robe that covered him save for his bald head, hands and sandaled feet. White with fever, his gaunt face clearly showed he had not eaten for some time. The stench that arose from him made it apparent he was quite ill. Marc's heart went out to him.

The man peered out through slightly opened eyes. "Oh, thank God," he wheezed, breaking into a wet cough.

Slipping the strap of his water skin off his shoulder, Marc crouched and offered it to him. "Who are you?"

"Gildas." The man feebly took the skin and swallowed four mouthfuls before resting. "Bless you. I have not drank for two days, too sick to move from this spot."

Valeria softly patted his shoulder. "Rest easy, for we will care for you, Brother Gildas." A look of surprise crossed her face. "You *are* a monk, yes?" Gildas nodded weakly. "Well, Gildas, I'm Valeria, and this is Marc." She touched his forehead once more. "You have quite a fever. How long has it been since you have eaten?"

The monk coughed before answering. "Six days."

Marc removed a small cloth bag from his pack and opened it. "I have dried fruit, nuts and a little bread. You are welcome to it all."

Valeria took the bread. "Drink more water, then eat this."

Gildas' eyes opened wide; the fist-sized bit of bread must have been more food than he had seen in a long time. He put a shivering hand on Valeria's. "Our Lord has richly blessed me by bringing both of you here, but," he pushed her hand away, "I cannot take your food from you."

"Please do," Marc said. "We have enough to eat."

Again Valeria offered it. "You need it to get well."

Gently accepting it, Gildas said a quick prayer of thanks and devoured the morsel.

Valeria pointed at a bundle lying nearby. "Do you have any other clothing in there?"

"No."

"Well, we need to get you out of that robe. It's wet and quite soiled."

Again Marc dug inside his pack. "He can use this blanket and hide." Setting both on the ground, he stood. "I'll get wood for a fire to warm him."

While scavenging about for fuel, he thought of Valeria's vision. How fortunate for Gildas—and her—that the magic chose *this* day to speak to her. Smiling, he recalled the heat of her magic flooding into him. It pleased him that he helped her just as the Great Tree had helped him. Even now he sensed its raw power, knew its direction and distance.

A feeling of awe overcame him as he realized the true importance of this day. The Tree had not kept silent this morning—the entire *day* was his lesson! A taste of Envisioning earlier let him know how to help Val later on. Marc discovered much about his father, and through that, even more about himself. But of all the things that took place today, the most important was losing his fear of magic.

Then there was Gildas. Was he part of that lesson as well? Were they destined to find him? Is that why, earlier that morning, he felt the deep-seated need to bring a blanket, skin and extra food? Or was it just chance they were nearby and the magic used that opportunity to teach Val more about her visions? Oren would know.

Bending to get one last stick, he headed back, eyeing the sky through the treetops. The deepening mass of clouds concerned him. For the monk's sake, he hoped it would not rain tonight. Returning to the clearing, he found Gildas bundled within the blanket and hide, with only the man's black hair showing. Downwind of them sat the robe.

Valeria put a finger to her lips and spoke quietly. "He's sleeping. He ate three pieces of fruit and drank the rest of the water." She raised the empty water skin by its strap. "I need to get some more."

Marc nodded. "You should wash his robe as well. It'll dry by the fire."

"I'll do that." She glanced back at Gildas with a pitiful expression. "That poor man's so wasted away, little more than a skeleton. He's been starving for some time."

"He'll recover," he said confidently.

She cast him a questioning glance. "You sound so certain."

"The magic guided you here for a reason. I believe to rescue him. Therefore, he'll recover."

She appeared thoughtful for a long moment, then gave him a look of admiration, or possibly respect. "I think so, too."

He quietly set the wood down. "We'll stay the night. By morning he might regain enough strength to walk."

Glancing back at the prostrate form, she shrugged. "Maybe. I'll get the water."

While she headed off, Marc started on the fire. Gildas was weary indeed, for he slept through the noise of snapping wood and the knife against the flint. While the fire steadily grew, he pieced together a framework upon which to dry the robe. With a quiet chuckle to himself, he recalled doing much the same the day he went over the falls. Valeria returned just as he finished.

"All clean." She handed him the damp ball of cloth, set the water skin aside, and sat cross-legged next to the fire. Draping the robe over the frame, he settled beside her and poked silently at the embers.

Her gaze searched questioningly over his face. "What are you thinking about?"

"What to do with Gildas tomorrow. He still needs much care. It would be better to take him to Oren's—it's closer than the village—but I'm not sure if our master will welcome him."

"The magic led us to Gildas. How could Oren refuse?"

Nodding his acceptance of her logic, he again inspected the sky. The darkening clouds looked even thicker and the breeze had strengthened, bringing with it a chill dampness. "I'm worried it might rain this evening. Even if it doesn't, it will be cold. Gildas will need both my blanket and hide. All we have left is your blanket to keep warm." He glanced over and saw her gaze was fixed upon the flames.

"We can share it like when we were younger."

"But we were much smaller then."

She faced him, a trace of a smile on her lips. "Then we'll snuggle up close. That will keep us warmer."

Yes, *too* warm. Nothing short of torture. "And if it rains? A short, light rain should not be a problem, but this looks like a downpour to me."

She gestured at the monk, then shrugged. "There's little we can do about it now."

Sighing in agreement, he stood. "We'll need more wood, then, to last the night."

Grabbing a rope from his pack, he headed back into the trees. His task did not take long for many trees had dead limbs that snapped off easily. He also came across two long, stout branches as thick as his forearm—ideal for making a tent should the need arise. Tying the firewood into a bundle, Marc lugged it back.

He found Valeria, still by the fire, braiding wildflowers into a necklace. As he sat beside her, she draped what she had completed below her neck. "Doesn't this make me look beautiful?"

"You don't need those flowers to be beautiful."

"You think I'm beautiful?" She gazed at him expectantly, her eyes soft and dreamy.

Marc silently chastised himself for revealing too much of his feelings for her. Quickly staring at the ground, he pulled up a few blades of grass. "Absolutely." His confession shocked him. Why did the words escape his lips as if under their own power? He certainly didn't want to tell her that. Or did he?

She took his hand. "Marc—"

An urgent rush of warmth shot through his insides. She was about to speak further, but Gildas awoke in a sudden fit of coughing. The mood broken, Valeria moved to the man's side. When the spell subsided, she felt his face.

"Your fever has eased some, Brother. How do you feel?"

His smile appeared stronger than before but his voice remained shaky. "Better. The food and water helped me greatly. Again, my thanks to you and your husband for coming to my aid."

She grinned briefly. "Oh, we're not married. We're from Oak Creek, a nearby village. We were—" Her uncertain gaze flicked Marc's way for a moment, her thoughts very likely close to his.

How *would* they explain finding him?

"We were returning to the home of our master when we came upon you," Marc said. "When you are well enough to travel, we will take you there to further recuperate."

"That is most kind. Please, tell me of your master."

Marc knew he had to choose his words carefully. "Oren is very wise and has been teaching us many things, including Latin and Greek."

The monk gave him a look of approval. "An educated man."

"That he is. From his many scrolls we have learned—" A faint noise in the distance caught his ear. "Do you hear that, Val?" He pointed in the direction of the stream.

Pulling her hair back, she cocked her head. "A goose. It sounds pretty excited about something. Let's take a look."

Together they moved toward the ruckus which rapidly grew louder. All of a sudden, a gander popped out of the brush and half flew, half ran to the center of the clearing. Right on its tail was a fox, which upon spotting them, abandoned its prey and made a hasty retreat. Marc laughed and watched as Valeria chased after the injured bird. Its bloody left wing hung limply at its side. As it tried to fly with its good wing, it rotated around and ended up landing on its back. Valeria made several grabs for it, but each time it managed to elude her. Gildas started to laugh as well but ended up coughing violently.

Marc chuckled. "Let me do it *my* way!" Saying a retrieval spell, he brought the panic stricken gander to his waiting hands. "See. No running needed."

The monk gasped in terror. "What evil magic is this?" Fear filled his eyes as he fished out a wooden cross from beneath the blanket and held it in a tightly clenched fist.

Marc put his arm around the bird to quiet its flapping wing. "It's not evil, Brother Gildas. I learned it from our master, the great wizard, Oren the Wise. He's a good man."

"Impossible!" Gildas pointed an accusatory finger Marc's way. "Practitioners of magic serve the evil one, not our Heavenly Father."

Sitting next to Gildas, Valeria took that hand between hers. "Oren *is* a good and God fearing man. He gives a blessing to God at each meal and prays daily. Our master helps and heals many people. He foresaw the great darkness and warned our village two years before it came. We were able to store up enough food in that time to survive. Is that something an evil man would do?"

"Evil often disguises itself in the clothing of good. Because of his warning your village now owes him a great debt."

Marc moved closer to him. "One he has never tried to collect on. A while ago he saved me from death at the hands of one of the king's men. Why would an evil man do that?"

"You are his servant."

"I wasn't at that time. In gratitude I offered him anything he wanted, but he forgave my debt."

"That proves nothing for here you are in bondage to him."

Valeria caught Gildas' gaze. "We serve him *voluntarily*. He asked for our help and both of us gladly agreed. We didn't know then, but the real reason he wanted our help was because we were blessed with the magic."

Gildas looked warily at Valeria. "You, too?"

"Yes. I sometimes see powerful visions. They used to frighten me until Oren explained they were a gift from God." She reached out and gently touched the monk's cross, then gestured around them. "This afternoon, while standing before the holy altar in our village, I saw a vision of you laying here and knew you needed help. That's how we found you."

Gasping, Gildas crossed himself.

Marc nodded. "Oren commands us to only use magic for good. How is that evil?"

The monk's thoughtful gaze shifted between him and Valeria several times. With a sigh that ended in a cough, Gildas smiled weakly. "It is tempting to trust the two of you for you have shown me nothing but kindness. I also trust that my Lord will not deliver me into the hands of evil. While I am not ready to believe that magic can be good, I will go with you to your master's home."

Marc grinned. "Well enough. Now, are you hungry for some roast goose?"

Gildas' eyes lit up. "Indeed."

The bird made a fine meal. By the time they had eaten their fill, the chill dark of night had arrived. Gildas tried to refuse the use of Marc's blanket, insisting his now dry robe and the hide would suffice to keep him warm. Valeria convinced him that because of his fever he needed the warmth of the extra blanket.

After Gildas fell asleep, Marc stoked up the fire so it would last the night. Valeria crawled under the blanket with him and soon fell asleep holding his back.

Keenly feeling her warmth against him, her sweet breath upon his neck, he could not help but think about how close her beautiful body was to his, only a few thin layers of cloth away. Preparing to fight off his rising lust, he found it never fully manifested, for other feelings, more powerful and important feelings, tempered his carnality. Feelings of a shared friendship so deep, so complete, that he could never remember a time it did not exist. Feelings of comfort—just being in her presence put him at ease. And he truly *cared* for her, more than any other of his friends, almost as if—

He gasped aloud, unable to contain his surprise. Did he *love* her? Not just the best friend kind of love, but the man and woman get married, have kids, die of old age together kind? Maybe so. But did she love him back? It was obvious she liked him, even cared for him as well, but at what point did *like* become *love*? A hundred memories of the feelings he'd had toward her tumbled about his mind, all clamoring for attention. He'd never been in love before. What was it supposed to be like? He thought of his parents, how they used to relate to each other, the little looks and touches, the way they talked. He and Valeria acted like that sometimes. Wishing he had answers to those questions, he resolved to think about it awhile.

Marc made an earnest prayer for understanding and strength, asking that he take no action that might damage their relationship. Turning his thoughts elsewhere, he reflected on the events of the day and how their lives had forever changed. Magic itself had changed for him, too. Not just that he no longer feared it, but today was the first time he had participated in magic that did something good—a life had been saved. While he contemplated these things, sleep finally came.

Ψ   Ψ   Ψ

"Wake up, Marc," a voice said, urgently.

Confused, he felt someone shake his shoulder. His cheek was wet. Why? Suddenly his mind focused and he realized the rain he feared had arrived. Opening his eyes, he saw Valeria's face hovering over his. Seeing he was awake, she gave him a hint of a smile, then moved away. With a resigned sigh, he cast off the sodden blanket and rolled to his feet. While icy cold, the rain fell fairly lightly. No downpour—so far. From the position of the quarter-crescent moon just visible through a gray veil of clouds, he knew four or five hours remained until dawn. The fire had died back, but its low flames and glowing embers provided enough light to see in the immediate vicinity.

Valeria seemed mildly upset. "You were right, it rained. Let's make a tent out of the blankets."

"No, Gildas will become too chilled if we wait out the storm here. This rain is bound to last for hours." He glanced over at the monk. "We have no choice but to get him to Oren's."

She knelt, placing her palm on the man's forehead. "How? He's still too weak to walk."

Marc wished he knew more magic. The Floating spell would have made it much easier to move Gildas to safety. Marc hit upon an idea. "We'll carry him."

"Carry him? How?"

"Lay him on the hide, then attach a rope to each corner." He pointed at the pile of firewood. "We'll run the ropes over those two long branches and put them on our shoulders like poles, slinging him between us. It should take about an hour and a half to get home. We'll be wet and cold, but the house is warm and dry."

She looked doubtfully at the branches, then Gildas.

"You'll be able to carry him, Val. He doesn't weigh very much."

After a moment of consideration, she nodded in agreement.

While she woke the monk and told him of the plan, Marc rigged up the sling. Once Gildas was loaded onto the hide, they covered him with one of the blankets, and draped the other over the branches as a makeshift tent. Taking the lead position, Marc headed for the path north. The wind picked up as the fullness of the storm swelled, pelting them with a frigid barrage of stinging raindrops that sucked the heat out of their flesh. The partial moon provided adequate light when it shone freely, but the fast-moving clouds often hid it from view, diffusing its illumination to the point where he could barely distinguish between tree and open space.

Despite that, and the continuous trickle of water in his eyes, he somehow kept to the path.

After over an hour of travel it seemed as if the branches had burrowed deep into the flesh of his throbbing shoulders. His feet were two blocks of unfeeling ice, and his calves ached with the added effort of carrying the monk. Completely soaked through, his clothing clung coldly to him, weighing him down, fighting his every move. By the way Valeria staggered about, Marc knew she would soon buckle under the load. They both needed to rest. Ahead lay the hill south of the springs. To the east, he remembered seeing a small outcropping of rock that would provide some protection from the elements.

"This way." He moved off the path and toward the outcropping, trying to keep his footing in the deepening mud.

"Where are we going?" she asked, her voice weak and breathy.

"To rest."

Hearing her grunt of agreement, Marc led the way around several piles of rocks until they were under the meager overhang. Fortunately, it was almost dry and fairly protected from the wind. Upon setting Gildas down, Valeria sank to her knees with a quiet whimper. Knowing where his own muscles smarted from the task, he began massaging those same areas on her. In time, he felt her tension subside.

She squeezed his hand. "Thanks. I'm much better. Let's get going again. I'm cold. Walking will warm me up."

Reluctantly shouldering their burden once more, they returned to the path. As they climbed the hill, he realized that while rubbing her, not once did his thoughts drift toward the carnal. That pleased him. Cresting the hill, Valeria gave out a tired sigh.

"Do you need to rest again, Val?"

"No," she moaned. "Keep... going."

Soon they were before the large iron gate. Relieved, Marc cast the spell and entered the compound.

Hearing the groan of the hinges, Gildas stirred. "Where are we?"

Marc realized the man had slept the entire time. "We've reached Raven's Gate—Oren's home."

"Oh, God bless both of you! I will keep you in my prayers, always."

The monk's praise made Marc feel somewhat embarrassed. Unsure how to respond, he simply said, "You are welcome."

Valeria's labored breathing and unsteady gait told him she was too exhausted to go much further. His own fatigue gnawed heavily at his resolve.

"You can do it, Val," he said, encouraging himself as much as her. "We're almost there."

"Yes," she panted.

Eyeing the path ahead, he put one foot before the other, maintaining the rhythm until they reached the stone of the entry steps. Marc prepared to cast the spell upon the door when it creaked open. Oren stepped out into the rain and smiled down at the monk.

"Gildas the Wise, Abbot and servant of our Lord. Welcome to my home."

Chapter 12

"*Volitā*," Oren quietly said, waving his arms upward.

The branches gently rose from Marc's shoulders—how he wished he could do that. Stepping aside, he watched as the entire sling floated through the door with the master trailing behind it. Following, he stopped short as Oren waved him off.

"See to Valeria."

Marc turned and saw that she stood very unsteadily in place. Lifting her into his arms, he carried her inside. "You look exhausted." He felt more than heard a little chuckle come from her.

"I do? I can't understand why." Putting her arms around his neck, she smiled, closed her eyes and snuggled into his chest.

Resisting the temptation to kiss the top of her head, Marc responded with a chuckle of his own. "Let's go find a nice, warm fire." Casting the spell, he closed the door behind them. When they entered the fireplace room, he saw with surprise that Oren already had Gildas situated on a bed placed close to the fire. "Master, there's so much to tell you about what happened today. We—"

The wizard stopped him with a curt gesture. "In the morning. Go to the workshop. There you will find warm broth, dry clothes and a place made ready for sleep. I will tend to our guest. Go."

By Oren's subtle smile, Marc knew the master was pleased even though his terse dismissal might be interpreted differently. "Yes, Master. Good night. And a good night to you, Gildas."

The monk began to speak but Oren urged him to save his strength. Marc carried Valeria into the workshop, finding it warm from a fire that had burned for hours. He deposited her on a stool and found two piles of clothing on the table. Sitting upon the stone fire ring were two large mugs of lightly steaming broth. Taking both, he put one into Valeria's hands.

"Drink, Val. This will warm you up."

With grateful eyes, she lifted it to her lips and tasted it. "Mmmm, delicious." Then, in one motion, she proceeded to swallow all of it.

Laughing, Marc did the same, noticing Oren had steeped medicinal herbs in it as well, most notably rose hips. Collecting his clothing from off the table, he headed for the cave door. "I'll change in here. Let me know when you're finished."

She looked at her pile and slowly nodded.

Saying the spell, he entered the cave and saw the oil lamp burning brightly upon its shelf. That was unexpected. He peeled off his wet garments and stood to dry in the warmth of the space. Glancing again at the lamp, he realized Oren must have known well ahead of time they would return with a guest in need of care. Why else did he meet them at the door and welcome the monk by name, never mind all the other preparations? The master's magic was indeed powerful.

Donning the dry clothes, he listened at the door to see if Valeria had finished changing. Hearing nothing, he lightly knocked.

"Val? Are you finished?"

Still nothing. Did she leave the room? Cautiously Envisioning the workshop, he found her half-undressed and slumped against the table, asleep. He called out louder this time. "Val?"

"Whaaa?" she said, groggily.

"Are you dressed yet?"

She stirred. "No. Wait." After a long moment, he heard the sound of wet cloth slapping the stone floor. A minute later she sighed heavily. "Finished."

Leaving the cave, he saw her slowly kneeling on the pallet of blankets and skins spread upon the floor. With a low groan, she half-rolled, half-fell onto her side. He took another blanket and covered her. She was already asleep. Giving in to his own weariness, he laid down as well, closed his eyes and joined her.

Ψ   Ψ   Ψ

The remainder of the night passed quickly for Oren. The gentle patter of rain on the slate roof was broken only by the occasional cough of his guest. He knew this man was special in some way—important enough to awaken Valeria's visions—but his magic could disclose nothing further about him. Any answers would have to wait, for magic would reveal the truth according to its schedule, not his.

Several hours after dawn, he looked in on Marc and Valeria and found them sleeping soundly; she laying against Marc, her head and arm resting on his chest, his arm curved protectively about her back. The power surrounding them had grown since the day before, especially hers. That surprised Oren, for he expected her development to be more gradual. It mattered not, for the day proved them worthy of their destiny. Now the next phase of their training could begin.

Shortly before noon, Gildas awoke and struggled up into a stooped posture.

"How do you feel?" Oren asked.

No longer displaying the ashen pall of the night before, the monk turned to face him, his gaze hesitant. "Still weak, but better, thank you. I believe the fever has left me." He looked around the room, taking it in for the first time. "Where might I see to my... private needs?"

Oren stood and approached him. "Outside and to the right. Let me help you."

Holding up an unsteady hand, Gildas shook his head. "No magic, please."

"I intended to help you the normal way." Extending his hand, the monk took it and allowed himself to be assisted to and from the privy. Once Gildas returned to his bed, Oren gave him a bowl of oat porridge. Accepting it with a murmur of thanks, Gildas said a quick prayer then silently ate it, occasionally looking at him.

Oren acutely felt the apprehension and uncertainty of his guest. "There is no need to fear me."

Pausing in his meal, the monk studied him for a long moment. "That is what your servants said, but I have my doubts. Last night you summoned unnatural forces to make me fly. And—" Fear rose within the man and he looked away, his voice shaky. "You knew my name without being told."

"My knowing your name gives me no power over you. We all wear our names and other information about ourselves like a cloak. The magic sees it and tells me what it thinks I need to know."

"Which gives you an advantage over me."

Giving it some thought, Oren nodded. "I suppose you could say that." He gestured to the nearby blaze. "That fire is very much like magic. Both are mysteries of nature that possess great power. Do you understand how fire works?"

"No."

"Neither do I, but like you, I have learned to use it for my needs. It will warm my home, cook my food and chase the darkness away, but only if I respect its power and use it wisely. If I am careless, it can cause great injury and damage. Now, pretend you had never seen fire before. What would you think if you saw someone using it? Me, for example."

Gildas paused, then flicked him an understanding glance. "I would fear it... and you as well."

"And once you learned to use it for yourself?"

The monk nodded. "I would no longer fear it. But I cannot learn to use magic, can I?"

"No. True magic chooses those who may learn its mysteries."

"*True* magic? Is there any other kind?"

"Sadly, many are those who claim to command the great power, but are only tricksters who fool people into parting with their money. These thieves often call upon pagan gods, or worse, the forces of wickedness and evil, trying to make themselves appear great and powerful. They accomplish naught but to soil the reputations of real wizards. That is why you think of magic as you do."

While Gildas pondered his words, Marc and Valeria shuffled into the room. Gesturing between them and himself, Oren continued. "Watch us during your stay, *then* judge whether magic is evil. Like you, Marc also feared magic when he arrived here. Only yesterday did he come to understand the full measure of his error."

A spark flashed through Marc's half-closed eyes, one more of amusement than surprise. "My master speaks the truth, Gildas," Marc said, covering up a yawn. He began to stretch, but stopped, wincing. "Ow!"

Both of his students remained partially hunched over. "I see the two of you are still experiencing the consequences of last night."

Marc's eyes rolled upward. "Unfortunately."

"Other than that, how are you feeling?"

"Hungry, and still a little tired." Marc turned toward Valeria. "You?"

"The same."

Oren pointed at two stools near the fire. "Rest there."

As they took their seats, Gildas spoke up. "I regret that you suffer on my account. I wish I could do something to help." The monk's gaze shifted to Valeria. "Thank you so much for finding me."

An embarrassed smile grew on her face. "There's no need to thank me, Brother. It is *I* who should thank *you* instead."

Gildas blinked in surprise. "Why?"

"Because you were in need, the magic came and opened my mind to its power. I've had visions before, but always during sleep and they were difficult to understand. But I saw your plight while still awake, and, with Marc's help, I learned to strengthen the vision enough to find you. Yesterday was a very special day for me." She looked toward Marc, her gaze softening. "For both of us."

Pride for her blossomed within Oren; she understood her relationship with magic while remaining humble about it. He started for the kitchen. "I have several loaves in the oven that should be ready. Be gentle with our guest for he needs his rest."

Reaching into the oven, he lightly tapped each loaf; both yielded a satisfying hollow thump. Removing them to cool on the table, he took down a small crock of honey from a high shelf. What better way to celebrate than with a luxury of that kind? From another shelf he fetched a wide, shallow basket and four bowls. When the breads had sufficiently cooled, he placed them in the basket, collected the bowls and honey and returned to the other room.

"Come, let us feast. Hot barley and rye breads topped off with honey." He passes Gildas the basket. "Would you kindly give the blessing, Brother?"

It took a moment for the monk to recover from the sight of so much bread, but after a quick prayer, they indeed feasted. Soon nothing remained but the warm fragrance of the meal.

Ψ   Ψ   Ψ

Afterward, Marc followed Oren and Valeria to the workshop to give Gildas some more time to sleep. Once seated about the large table, the master had them recount their adventures of the day before. Once they were through, Oren asked if they had any questions. Marc went first.

"When we first came upon Gildas, Val called him *Brother*. How did she know that? He wore only a simple travelling cloak. Nothing pointed to him being a monk."

"Being a novice with her visions, she could understand only the simplest part of what magic tried to reveal to her—that he was ill and where he was. By touching him, she understood a bit more, that he was a monk. If she understood how to *Read* the magic better, she would have known his name and other things."

Valeria eagerly leaned forward on her elbows. "It was amazing, Master. Please teach me how to do this better."

With a pleased nod, Oren patted her hand. "In time *both* of you will master this magic. Next question." He looked pointedly at Marc, as if already knowing what was on his mind.

Taking in a nervous breath, Marc broached the subject that had lingered on his mind since the talk with his mother. "Did you already know about how my father died? About the magic in the antler?"

Oren met and kept his gaze. "Yes."

"And that he was actually murdered by someone he knew?" Marc did nothing to conceal the pain the memory evoked.

"Yes."

He stared at the table, balling his fists in frustration to keep the anger from his voice. "Why didn't you tell me that when I first came here? That way I wouldn't have feared magic as I did. Why keep it secret?"

The master's shoulders sagged with regret. "Since you discovered the Great Tree before you began your studies here, your perception of magic became falsely directed. You saw it as evil because it reconnected you with the terror of finding your father's body. If I *had* told you about that night right away, you would not have completely accepted my explanation. By discovering the facts on your own, and at a time when you better understood magic, you truly came to understand why you feared magic, and why you reacted to the Tree the way you did."

A rapid flux of emotions ran through Marc as he tried sorting his fractured thoughts into a whole he could comprehend. "I think I understand, but—." He met Oren's gaze again. "There's more to it, isn't there?" The master's silence proved answer enough. Then, between one heartbeat and the next, his confusion vanished leaving him suddenly *aware*. Marc jumped to his feet and pointed excitedly at his master. "You know everything about what happened. Somehow, I *know* you do." Marc felt both alarmed and pleased with his outburst.

Oren gave him that satisfied little smile he used whenever he or Valeria did something exceptionally well. "Yes, I do. Your magic serves you well. Now, sit."

Releasing an anxious breath, Marc retook his stool as Valeria curiously eyed him. "So you know who killed my father."

Nodding, Oren held up his hand to ward off Marc's next question. "But, as before, I cannot tell you. The answer must come to you when the time is right."

"Is it something I've forgotten? Like the antler?"

"No."

His frustration began to rise once more. "Why *can't* you tell me? Shouldn't the killer be brought to justice?"

The wizard gestured for Marc to calm himself. "In time you will discover the truth, but only when your magic is strong enough to confront the guilty party. To learn it before then would alter your destiny."

Accepting his master's words, Marc let go of the tension in his muscles, causing him to slump toward the table. "I pray that day comes soon."

A distant look came over Oren's eyes and his voice grew quieter, more guarded. "If you knew the events of that day, you would not pray for its hastening."

Again Marc felt *aware*. His teacher desperately *wanted* to tell him, to warn him. "Are you able to tell me when this will happen?"

"No."

"What awaits him? Valeria asked, a touch of panic in her voice. "Some kind of danger?"

Seeing her worry, Oren momentarily closed his eyes, his features tense. "One could say it is a test. A test of Marc's skill with magic." The master's gaze shifted to Marc. "And of his character."

"And if I should fail this test?"

The elder quickly straightened and emphatically shook his head. "You *must not* fail. Everything you learn between now and then will be critical to your success."

Feeling the burden of an unknown responsibility settle upon him, Marc stared at the table in silence, idly tracing the edge of the iron band with his thumbnail. Moving to stand beside him, Valeria put her hand on his shoulder and gently squeezed . Marc smiled at her show of support, then looked Oren in the eye with determination. "Then I won't fail. Teach me what I need to know."

Oren warmly placed a hand on Marc's other shoulder. "I shall, and more."

Ψ   Ψ   Ψ

A sea of mottled, light gray clouds hung low, dense enough to block the warming rays of the sun, but holding too little moisture to further threaten rain. The winds were all but gone, and the air still had a slight nip to it, pleasant enough weather for a trip to the Great Tree. Marc had just visited it yesterday—the day his whole world changed. This afternoon's experience would be new and unique, maybe even pleasant. While he no longer feared magic, the apprehension of facing some unknown future test weighed heavily on his thoughts.

He looked at Valeria as she walked next to him, the tall grass swishing quietly against her dress. "Do you feel it yet?"

"Nothing." Traces of disappointment showed on her face.

"We're so close. I thought you would by now."

"How does it feel to you?"

"Strong. As if I were already next to it." Lifting his gaze from the path, he studied the still-distant Great Tree. It felt different this time—warmer, open, and even welcoming. The master was correct. Its magic had not changed at all, only his perception of it.

A huff of amusement came from her. "What are you smiling about?"

"The Tree." He explained his thoughts.

"I'm glad to hear that." She looked up at the Tree, unsure.

He knew her so well he could almost hear her thoughts. "If Oren says you'll feel the Tree as he and I do, then you will." Marc did his best to sound reassuring.

Valeria gave him an impatient frown. "But will I *today*?"

Taking her hand, he gently squeezed it. "If not today, then soon. Try to be patient."

She smiled. "I'll do my best." Letting go, she sprinted toward the log that spanned the creek. "I'm first."

While she scampered across, Marc directed his thoughts fully upon the Tree. Why did it ignore her? She already heard magic's call; her visions were proof of that. If only he could talk to the Tree, reason with it. If she was destined to connect with it someday, why not now? Then her lessons could begin that much sooner.

"Marc," she called from across the water, her voice sounding distracted.

"Coming." He hopped up on the log and started over.

She let out a quiet sigh. "I... I feel it." Her face glowed in wonder. "I feel it!" Not waiting, she started up the hill with a purpose.

Quickening his pace, he caught up to her. "Are you certain?"

"What else could it be?"

He touched her arm and felt magic's warmth upon her—clearly from the Tree. Marc let out a whoop of joy. As they scrambled up the slope, he wondered if he somehow influenced the Tree's actions. Upon reaching the ledge, he gestured for her to approach the Tree.

Valeria shook her head. "I'm not ready yet. You first."

"Nervous?" he asked with a chuckle. "All right." Stepping forward, he placed both hands upon the Tree and invited its power to enter him. "Let me learn my magic well. Help me pass this test I must face." The Tree's magic surged, sending tingling waves of energy flowing through him. A gasp from Valeria made him look her way. "What is it?"

She stared at him strangely. "You're *blue*."

"Blue?" He immediately inspected his arms and lower body. "No I'm not."

"I mean there's a blue light all around you. Like how coals in a fire glow." She arced around him, her gaze traveling down his body and up again. "It's very clear to me."

Letting go, Marc again examined himself. "I see nothing."

"Oh," she said, cocking her head in surprise. "It's gone now. It began when you spoke to the Tree. What did you feel right then?"

"Its magic became stronger." He backed away and gestured her forward. "Your turn."

She hesitantly moved closer to the massive trunk, hands held close to her chest, palms out. "I feel the might of its power even from here." Reaching out, she touched the bark with the tip of a finger. "Oh, my!" She yanked back her hand and, wiggling her digit, inspected it. "Marc, that's—" She gave him an odd smile. "It's nothing like the last time I touched it."

He chuckled once more; she was so eager a minute ago. "Feel all of it. Grab it."

She planted both hands on the Tree and giggled. "Oh! This is quite strange. I'm Envisioning us from high above." She gave him a teasing grin. "Much like how you saw me at the spring yesterday."

Ignoring her attempt to embarrass him, he grinned back. "What else?"

"I hear sounds, like a bunch of people mumbling nearby. It makes no sense."

"I hear that, too."

As she leaned closer, a bluish light grew about her as it did during her vision of Gildas the day before, only more intense. This must be what she had seen around him.

"You're blue as well."

Remaining silent, she stared blankly at the Tree, much like when she first Envisioned Gildas at the village altar.

"What is it? What do you see?"

Still unresponsive, her arms began to tremble. Now concerned, Marc moved next to her. "*Val?*" The trembling intensified, spreading to her entire body. Tears streamed down her face. Dread clutched his insides. Was the Tree harming her, or magic itself? "Val! Let go!"

Her eyes rolled up as she violently arched backward. Jerking her away from the trunk, he carefully lowered her to the rocky ground. Patting her face, he tried to snap her out of the trance, or whatever had hold of her.

"*Please*. Wake up."

Her face turned toward him, glazed eyes focused on some distant point. "Beware the Magus of Power," she blurted before passing out.

All efforts to rouse her failed. Panic overcame him. For a moment he thought her dead, but she still breathed, deep and regular. After a slight hesitation, he put an ear to her chest and found her heartbeat strong. Why had the magic done this? He just came to accept it and now had another reason to fear it.

Gathering her into his arms, he hurried for home. "I'll get you to Oren. He'll know what to do." Marc prayed for that to be true.

Chapter 13

"Valeria," soothed a deep, gentle voice in the darkness.

It sounded familiar, but when she tried to connect it with a face or name, the knowledge seemed to recede from her, keeping just out of reach. Why did she feel so peculiar, so disconnected? And where was she? She started to open her eyes but quickly snapped them shut—the candle's light too painful to bear. Then she noticed the searing headache accompanied by dizziness and nausea. Something bad had happened to her.

"Where... ?" she rasped.

"You're back home, Val," another, more familiar, voice whispered. It held power, moving over her spirit in a way most welcome. "I brought you here after you passed out."

Home? Whose home? And... passing out? Someone took her hand causing a pleasant warmth to flood through her—this person cared for her.

"Marc?"

"Yes, Val. You had me quite worried for a time."

Holding his hand tighter, she eagerly drew in more of his warmth, more of his... *magic!* She began to remember. Marc had carried her here, just like the night before. But why did he have need to? Had she become injured? Maybe the terrible headache meant she fell and hit her head. She reached to feel her face but another hand intercepted hers. It, too, had magic, but different.

"Master Oren?"

"I am here."

Yes, the first voice she heard. "I remember being... somewhere, then Marc brought me here."

"Correct."

"What happened?"

Marc cradled her hand against his chest. "Don't you remember going to the Great Tree?"

144

As he spoke the final two words, a fiery wind of magical power blew through her being, making her instantly aware of the Tree, why she went there and what took place.

"Master, I felt the Tree. I—." She swallowed. "I feel it now. It gave me a great vision I can't quite explain." The memory of it began reform in her mind, frightening her.

Oren patted her hand. "Do not try right now. When you have recovered, then we will discuss it."

She carefully nodded, each movement sending icy spikes of pain through her head. "Why did I pass out? And why does my head hurt so bad?"

"At the Tree you became fully aware of the magic that Marc and I know. That would be enough of a strain on you, but at the same time your ability to see visions was also greatly strengthened. Your head hurts because the vision took control of you, overwhelming your mind. I will teach you to control it. Now rest. Marc will stay with you while I see to Gildas." With a gentle squeeze of her hand, Oren rose and left.

She pulled Marc's hand to her cheek, resisting the urge to kiss it. "Thanks for rescuing me."

His magic warmed further. "Any time."

"Where am I?"

"On your bed."

Still with eyes closed, she felt around and found he knelt on the floor. "Those stones can't be comfortable." She carefully shifted to the far side of the bed and patted a spot next to her. "Sit here." After a moment, he perched on the edge. "Closer. Your magic comforts me." Reaching around his waist, she guided him toward her until his back rested against her hip. More of his magic flowed into her, easing the throbbing agony that began at the back of her eyes, tore through her head and burned down her spine.

"Better," she sighed. "Tell me what you saw happen to me."

As he detailed what took place, she pictured in her mind's eye what he must have seen. "I was blue, too?"

"Yes."

"We've got to ask Oren what that means."

"I already did, hours ago."

"*Hours* ago?"

"You've been asleep for five or six hours. I worried at first, but Oren assured me you were in no danger."

"Oh. That's good. And the blue?"

"Magic. Well, not exactly. The Master says it's a way of seeing the magic that is, uh, attached to things. I don't understand all of what he told me, but he did say we would soon be able to see this light at will."

When Marc said *we*, he gently firmed his grip on her hand. The message was understood. "Am I to start learning the spells, then?"

"I asked Oren that question and saw him trying not to smile."

A rush of delight filled her. "Teach me."

"Gladly—if he permits it. But otherwise—"

"I know." Ignoring the pain, she sat up, put her arms around him and whispered in his ear. "Thanks." Kissing his cheek, she eased herself back to the comfort of her pillow.

He turned toward her more. "What did you see in your vision?"

Valeria deeply wished he had not asked that. The vision was most unpleasant, and she feared it had something to do with the test he must face. What could she possibly tell him that would not make him dread his future further? I saw you all bloody? In a grave? Or that someone shoots an arrow at you? No, it would be better to keep it to herself for now.

"I'm not certain of its meaning. I should talk with Master Oren about it first."

"Very well. But tell me, what did you mean when you said, 'Beware the Magus of Power'?"

A cold sensation suddenly radiated outward from her core, its cause unknown to her. "I don't know. I have no memory of saying those words."

Patting her hand, he gently placed it on her stomach and stood. "You better get some more sleep. I'll spend the rest of the night in the workshop. If you need anything, call me." She heard his sandals scuff across the floor.

"Marc?"

"Yes?"

"With all the things we've experienced the past two days...."

"It's been quite an adventure, hasn't it?"

"Thanks for being such a good friend."

"You, too. I wouldn't want to share it with anyone else. Good night."

Chapter 14

Valeria awoke to the chirping of birds outside. What little light managed to leak in around the leather flap covering the window told her the sun had yet to rise. The events of yesterday seemed more remote than they should, as if but a dream. Someone else's dream. *That* person journeyed to the Great Tree, became overwhelmed by magic and woke in the middle of the night, confused and in pain. But she knew that someone was her.

Two things remained from the night before: her headache—now greatly lessened—and a keen awareness of the Great Tree. It remained a constant presence in her mind, not unlike the sound of a nearby waterfall. Now she understood why Marc considered it haunted and had such difficulty finding words to illustrate the experience.

Tossing the blanket aside, she rose and stepped into the tiny alcove where the doorways to the nearby rooms converged. Peeking past the hide curtain to the fireplace room, she saw that both Gildas and her master still slept. Next, she quietly lifted the latch on the workshop door and inched it open until she could slip inside. Marc also slept, curled up on a blanket spread upon the stone floor, his chest rising in slow, even breaths. She watched him for a minute, wanting to sit by him, or better, lay by him, for his presence comforted her. But at the moment there was something she desired more.

Leaving him be, she tip-toed over to the cave door. Placing her hands upon its heavy planks, she recalled every detail of Oren's instructions when Marc learned his earliest spell. She knew she needed to remember how the magic felt and to make that feeling move down into her hand. But how *did* it feel? The magic of her visions, or how Marc or Oren felt when she touched them, were different from being Floated over the stream. Concentrating, she tried to recreate the latter.

"That will not work," a voice whispered into her ear.

Valeria's heart leapt into her throat as she spun about and saw—"Master! Forgive me, I—"

Putting a finger to his lips, he pointed at the still sleeping Marc, then motioned for her to follow. She was devastated. The master *had* to be displeased. Why couldn't she have waited? Oren would have taught her in time. But now her impatience may have cost her dearly. Humbled, she trailed behind as he led her outside and over toward the well. He sat on the bench facing the trees and nodded at the space next to him. Sitting, she kept her eyes focused on the ground, not wanting to see his anger.

"Eager, are we not?" His voice betrayed no emotion.

"I'm so sorry, Master," she said meekly, unable to keep the tremor out of her words. "I don't know what came over me."

"Be calm, Valeria. I am not angry." His hand briefly settled upon hers.

She looked up and saw warmth in his gaze. "But I tried to use magic without your permission."

A grin sprang to life on his face. "Without *my* permission? What did I tell you about learning magic?"

"That *it* would choose if I were worthy." She paused, realizing the source of Oren's amusement. "And since I can feel the Tree from afar, I am now permitted to start learning the spells."

"Later today," he said with a wink.

A rush of excitement ran through her.

Oren held up a finger. "But first, tell me of your vision at the Tree."

Her thrill quickly tempered into unease. "I don't remember it as well as my other dreams."

"Do your best."

She nodded. "It began with Marc walking through a great fire of some kind which parted around him as he moved. I saw anger on his face, but—" She sighed. "Somehow I knew he had been deceived. I *felt* it."

The corner of his mouth quirked up. "Go on."

"Next, I saw a hand draw back a bowstring. I'm certain it was somebody I knew, but the vision would not reveal who. That person felt cold, felt... evil. Then I saw Marc covered in blood, crying." She clutched at her quivering stomach, trying to will away her rising panic. "After that, the cold man sneered, but I saw only his mouth. The rest of his face remained hidden in shadow. Next, Marc knelt upon the ground, looking up at someone; the cold man, I think. An arrow flew through the air, but strangely, for it moved slowly, like a feather floating by." She clutched the master's hand so tightly he flinched in pain. Taking an unsteady breath, she forced out the words she feared to speak. "Then Marc lay in an open grave, screaming."

That memory sent a shudder down her spine. Should she tell Oren she'd dreamt it before? Something in his gaze made her think it would be best kept to herself for now.

"And how did that vision make you feel?" he asked gently.

"Frightened. I worry it means he will die."

The master looked momentarily troubled. "Have you ever *seen* him as being dead?"

"No, but I know death is involved. Should I go on?" He nodded. "The last image is the strangest. The cold man possessed a sword and a quiver of arrows, both of which flew off to the side as he rose up into the air, moving away from me. A great wall of flame erupted between us and the vision ended." Releasing a silent sigh, she relaxed a little, grateful to have shared her burden.

The master idly toyed with the cuffs of his sleeves for a half-minute before speaking. "Interesting. The most difficult part of interpreting visions is to remove the influence your emotions have upon them." He looked at her in a way she had never seen before. Tenderly. "Your feelings for him may cloud the truth."

Suddenly unsettled, she searched his face for clues. Did the master know how deeply she cared for Marc, or was he only referring to the fact that they had been good friends all their lives? "I think I understand what you mean. There's one other thing. Marc told me I said something before passing out, but I don't remember saying it."

Oren nodded. "'Beware the Magus of Power'. As for what it means?" He shrugged. "It might be a portent of something yet to come. Visions need not have any images. They can be only a smell, a taste, how something feels, or even sounds. In your case, words that are spoken."

"Then what purpose did that part of the vision serve if I'm unable to remember it?"

"It is difficult to say. I trust in time we will discover why. Do remember, though, visions often contain many messages mixed together. If something is important, you will usually see it more than once."

Valeria tensed, now even more concerned about seeing Marc lying in a grave for that signified death. Or did it? True, she never saw anything indicating he was *actually* dead, but what if it meant he would be seriously wounded?

"These images of Marc worry me, Master. Shouldn't I tell him about them?"

Oren sternly shook his head. "No, not until you are certain of their meaning. Giving false information is worse than giving none." He stood. "Do not fear your visions for they serve a higher purpose. Come." She followed him toward the house. "From now on, you and Marc will spend most of your day learning the spells. He will teach you what he has mastered so far, which is considerable. I expect you to learn quickly and learn well."

"I shall!" Oh, how she wanted Marc to instruct her in the ways of magic.

The old wizard chuckled. "Of that I have no doubt." He opened the door and bade her enter first. "I have a special task for you. My wizard's robe is far past its prime. I want you to craft me a new one."

"Gladly."

Together they returned to the workshop, entering as Marc stretched and yawned loudly. "Morning, Master, Val." He looked at her with a caring eye. "How are you feeling?"

His concern gladdened her heart. "Much better. Just a small headache." She glanced over to see Oren entering the cave door, then flashed Marc a big grin. "I have some good news for you."

His eyebrows rose. "What?"

For a moment she thought about teasing him, making him try and guess the answer, but her impatience won out. "Master Oren has decided to take on a second apprentice. Me."

Marc hugged her with enthusiasm. The sudden contact with his body and magic made her mind reel with delight. "That's wonderful! When do *we* start your lessons?" His playful smile caught her off guard.

"You already knew?" His smile broadened, causing an understanding to form in her mind. Planting both hands on her hips, she gave him the most irritated glare she could muster. "Last night, when I asked you to teach me magic, you *already* knew you'd be doing so, didn't you?"

"Yes. Oren and I discussed it before you woke. I didn't tell you because I knew that, despite having a terrible headache, you'd want to start learning then and there."

"You're right," she said with a laugh. "I would have."

Ψ   Ψ   Ψ

The first part of her morning crept by. Oren detailed at length how he wanted his new robe constructed, with all kinds of inside pockets and secret places not visible from the outside. She did not understand why he needed those additions but knew better than to ask. After taking his measurements, they ate the morning meal during which she fidgeted nervously, barely able to stand the wait. Marc took great pleasure in tormenting her by eating slowly, pretending he had nothing important to do. When he finally finished, she took his hand and eagerly led him to the cave door.

Marc laughed. "Shall we begin?"

"Of course."

"Since you already know how to properly utter the command, let's move on to feeling the magic."

"Yes, let's." Hearing the scrape of the workshop door upon the floor, she turned to see Oren had escorted Gildas into the room.

"Never mind us," Oren said, gesturing for her to look away.

So she would have an audience. Not a problem. Holding her right hand out toward the door, she looked at Marc. She had dreamt of this moment for weeks. "Ready."

When he took her hand in both of his, she immediately felt magic's power flowing through him. Its heat made her skin tingle all the way up to her elbow.

"Do you feel that?" he asked.

"Very much."

"Good. Now, make it move up your arm and into your head."

Without the slightest idea how to do that, she nodded in agreement. What would make it move? She wiggled her arm but the magic stayed put. Flexing her muscles did no good, either.

"Talk to it," Marc said gently.

Talk to it? How? She thought about finding Gildas the other day and how she made the vision stronger. What worked then might work now. Concentrating her thoughts on finding the magic, she stared intently at their hands. A gasp erupted from her as she saw—no, it couldn't be. Blue! Why didn't she see it before? Opening her mind much as one would step out of another's way, she gazed deeply into the glow and cleared a path that the power immediately took.

Instantly, the tingle washed over her entire body. For a moment her head spun as if she were about to faint, but the sensation passed, leaving her acutely aware of the door before her.

"I— I see the door," she said, almost reverently.

"Wonderful. Now find the bolt."

"With ease."

"You know what to do."

"*Aperīte!*" The bolt hastily moved within the planks. "I did it!" She jumped up on Marc who caught her, laughing.

"Yes, you did."

Sliding off him, she danced around like a young child. She felt suddenly free, as if something trapped deep within her had managed to escape its bonds. The sound of clapping drew her attention to the far side of the workshop. Gildas applauded her. Oren, too, nodded in appreciation.

"Thank you," she said with a bow. Whirling about, she ran up to Marc and hugged him once more. "And thank you, too."

"You're welcome." His arms encircled her in a heavenly embrace. If possible, she would have clung to him forever, but soon his grip relaxed and he stepped away. "Now do it on your own."

Reaching out, she tried to see the door once more. Nothing. While weak, the magic had not completely left her. Focusing all her willpower on that small remainder, she tried to make it grow. At first, her efforts were ineffective. Success came when she found out how to control her thoughts and thereby the magic. As soon as she located the bolt she wasted no time in acting upon it.

"*Claudite!*" The thud echoed within the room.

"Marvelous." Gildas clapped louder than before.

Pleased with herself, she released the magic. Without warning, light-headedness swept through her, making her knees buckle.

Marc's strong hands steadied her. "Easy."

The discomfort passed. "Does this always happen?"

"No. You'll adjust to it soon. That was an acceptable performance—for a beginner." Admiration filled his gaze.

"Acceptable? Ha! It was perfection."

"It must be because you have such a skilled teacher."

She gave him a stern look, then broke into laughter. "Yes. It must be that."

Ψ   Ψ   Ψ

Marc worked with Valeria until mid-afternoon; in all she learned over a dozen spells. He was proud of her and wished he could have had her enthusiasm when he began the lessons. No telling where he would be today. Leaving her to start work on their master's new robe, Marc joined Oren on a walk. After discussing Valeria's progress, the wizard's demeanor became more serious.

"You and Valeria have experienced many changes these past few days, changes that will continue as I teach you ever more powerful forms of magic, such as starting a fire, floating in the air, healing wounds, knowing things about others—" Oren winked at him. "Something Valeria has already done a measure of."

Marc tried not to smile. "I look forward to learning new things, Master."

Oren continued. "You will also learn about mankind. Since you will often deal with people in stressful situations, the more knowledge you have about how and why they behave, the better off you will be."

"Would the way you handled Thaddeus be an example?"

"Yes. Although I used magic at one point, I mostly put him in his place by understanding what he wanted."

"And what was that?"

"Power and wealth. Too often people become seduced by those. They achieve a measure of control over others and find they like it, believing themselves better than everyone else. Eventually they no longer follow the rule of law and custom, and others suffer

154

because of it. Such a man is Thaddeus. His heart holds no love or compassion, only a greed for what he can take and control. A hunger which can never be sated."

"Cannot the power magic provides corrupt us as well?"

Oren smiled. "Indeed. We are expected to use this great gift with humility and kindness, to share it freely with others."

"I understand." Marc was about to ask another question when his stomach growled loudly.

Oren chuckled. "Hungry?"

"I am."

"We are near enough to the creek. How does fish sound?"

"Delicious."

"Gather up some firewood, then."

As they made their way, Marc gleaned dry twigs and sticks from the litter on the forest floor. "Master, why go through all the trouble of catching, cleaning and cooking the fish when you could just cast a spell and make food appear?"

"Magic does not allow it, for to do so is wasteful and lazy. Neither could I have produced food enough for all during the darkness, because that would have altered destiny. However, magic *did* enable me to give everyone two years notice of the coming hardships, allowing them time to lay up sufficient stores."

Marc well remembered that particular meeting. Oren not only spoke with Garrett and the men of Oak Creek, but also the leaders of the surrounding villages, including those of their two nearest neighbors, Leahenfehr of Bitter Well to the north, and Patrick of Fox Glen to the south. That very day Garrett directed every able-bodied villager, women and children included, to begin clearing many new acres of land, nearly tripling the size of the grain and vegetable fields. Later, they increased their hunting efforts and amassed a large cache of dried meat.

"So magic gives us just as much guidance as direct help."

The master chortled. "Excellent, Marc."

"May we aid others in any way as long as magic permits it?"

"Absolutely."

Marc thought much on that. He had always helped his neighbors. Having had the idea to search Red Cliffs for birds frozen in their nests gave him a fulfilling sense of purpose. So did saving Gildas. The master did say he was meant to *walk the path of service and magic.* If being a wizard meant he could help others all the time, then he looked forward to becoming the best wizard possible.

Once at the creek, Marc dropped the wood on a sandy patch of ground. Oren walked to the edge of the water and winked at him. "Being a wizard does have its advantages." Extending his arm, he said a quick retrieval spell and a fat brown trout leapt from the water into his hand. "Now, you try."

Marc moved to the bank and watched the fish dart about the stones on the bottom. Spying a nice one, he said the spell but only got a handful of water.

"What?" He stared at his dripping fingers. "How did that happen."

"See the fish with your magic, not your eyes. The surface of the water plays tricks on you."

Doing as he was told, Marc soon had a fish in hand. "I see what you mean."

Oren handed over his fish. "Prepare both while I make the fire."

Squatting by the stream, Marc cleaned, then skewered each on a long stick for roasting. By this time the fire was ready. He held out the stick containing his master's fish, but the wizard waved him back.

"You cook for I am about to begin a lesson."

The elder's tone revealed a certain tension. Had something upset him? Marc saw nothing in Oren's face to indicate that. Kneeling, he suspended both fish over the flames. "What will the lesson be about?"

"You will see shortly. For now, remain silent."

Again, Marc sensed that tension. And why was he to keep silent? Perhaps the lesson used a difficult spell and the master needed to concentrate. No matter, he would do as he was told and returned his full attention to the meal.

Then, in one sickening instant, Marc understood the reason for the edge in Oren's voice. The sound of a sword being drawn from its scabbard was unmistakable.

"I will take those fish," commanded a deep voice behind them.

Panicked, Marc froze momentarily but Oren smoothly faced the intruder. "They are not yours."

"Now they are." The man sounded quite confident of that.

Turning, Marc saw the man and fear filled him. Heavily muscled and tall—at least a full head higher than himself—he held the broad point of a gladius inches from his master's chest. The man's eyes narrowed to dark slits, his malevolent smile showing many missing teeth. With an icy stab of terror, Marc suddenly recalled the night of his father's death. Why had that memory come to mind just now?

Oren calmly crossed his arms. "What kind of man would attack another who is unarmed?"

"A hungry one."

Looking the man over, Oren frowned in disgust. "You appear to be a soldier, not a common robber. Have you no honor? Permit me to arm myself and I will do battle with you."

A hearty, rolling guffaw burst out of the man. "What will you fight me with, old man? Your gray hair? You have no weapons."

Oren selected a feeble stick from the woodpile, one no bigger around than his little finger. "I have this."

The man laughed again, his heavily-scarred hand wielding his weapon with a practiced flourish. "My sword against your stick? Ha! I'll fight you, but I'll give you one more chance. Yield the fish and live, fight me and die."

Marc almost handed over their meal, but Oren's hard glance instructed him otherwise. "So you say, but we are keeping them. I must warn you there is more to me than meets the eye."

For the first time the robber looked at Marc. "Is he mad?"

Somehow, Marc found the courage to respond. "No, but *you* are if you fight him."

"You're *both* mad," he snorted, holding his sword at the ready. "Very well. Defend yourself, ancient one."

Oren whispered a spell, ceremoniously tapped the stick with two fingers and held it before him in a defensive posture. The man lunged with a stabbing thrust but the wizard deftly stepped aside, swatting the attacker on the thigh with the stick. A howl of pain erupted from the brute as a six-inch gash appeared on the spot. All humor left the man who swung again with a vengeance, making a wide, horizontal sweep directed at the master's midsection. Once more, Oren avoided the blade, this time tapping his opponent on the arm. Another wound appeared. Purple-faced with rage, the soldier raised his sword high and, with gritted teeth, slashed downward at Oren's head. Spinning to the side, Oren struck the gladius near the hilt. With a loud ring, the blade broke off and fell clattering to the ground.

The assailant halted his attack and stared in bewilderment at the remainder of his weapon. "What... ?" Glancing at his wounds, anger flared anew in his eyes and he started toward Oren.

"Hold, there," the wizard ordered, brandishing the stick before him. "The next stroke will remove your arm, *Portaeus*."

The light of reason awoke within the man, who stopped and took a step back, looking once more at the stub of his broken sword. "Who *are* you? How did you do this and... how do you know my name?"

Marc came along side his master. "He is the powerful wizard, Oren. You should be more careful whom you choose to rob." Hearing the conviction in his own voice surprised Marc, for it held none of the anxiety he felt.

The man drew in a sharp breath as his eyes widened. "Forgive me. I did not know." Dropping to one knee, he hung his head.

Oren gazed sternly upon him. "Why should I forgive you? Had I not been a wizard, you would have done as you said. You are able to hunt and fish for your own needs, but you choose instead to take from others. Tell me why I should not kill you now?"

"I will never steal again, I promise." Portaeus quaked with fear.

The master's voice took on a cold hardness Marc had never heard him use before. "Know this: I am the protector of all who live within a five-days walk. If I hear that you have been so much as *impolite* to one of my people, I will send my demons after you. Behold!" Oren pointed up the slope behind Marc.

Looking in that direction, the robber unleashed an agonizing shriek and cowered at Oren's feet. "Spare me, mighty wizard!"

Marc turned and, with a start, saw two man-like creatures with blood-red skin and black, leathery wings. Within seconds they vanished. Filled with more astonishment than fear, Marc faced Oren and gasped, "*Master?*"

Holding up a silencing hand, Oren ignored him and addressed Portaeus with authority. "Always remember that I spared your life so you may warn others to leave my people be. Go, and depart from my land."

Without a word, their former attacker jumped to his feet and fled south.

"Why didn't you kill him?" Marc asked, glancing nervously at the spot where the demons had stood.

"He will serve our needs at a future time." Casually breaking the stick in two, Oren dropped the pieces in the fire. "How are the fish?"

After all that had taken place, Marc was amazed how his master remained so composed. "Uh, not quite ready." He put the fish back over the flames, eating the last thing on his mind. "How did you make the stick so powerful? It cut through leather and flesh like a finely honed blade. And breaking his sword. And the—" His voice softened to express a quiet sense of wonder. "—the *demons*. Incredible."

The wizard chuckled. "So you found the lesson interesting. Good. I did not fear him because I Envisioned him stalking us. Remember, young Marcus, few men are a threat to a fully trained wizard. However, the most important part of the lesson had little to do with magic. It had to do with guile."

Marc looked up at his master, head cocked in interest. "Guile?"

"Yes. A bit of deception can greatly enhance our abilities. The stick had no power of its own for I could have inflicted the same damage to him without it. When you learn the more advanced skills, I will explain this further. The stick acted as a distraction, something for that wretch to pay attention to. In his world there was no way a mere twig could do that. The impossible became possible, confusing and frightening him. *That* changed his offensive attitude to a defensive one, giving me influence over his will."

"And the demons?"

Oren perched on a nearby rock. "The illusions you both saw did not actually exist. I do not have the power to command demons."

"*Illusions?* But I *saw*—"

"I know. It involves more advanced magic. Some day you will be able to do that, too."

Marc did not understand all his master had told him, but looked forward to learning those mysteries. Soon, he hoped.

Chapter 15

Marc awoke to the sound of someone moving about nearby, whispering. Opening his eyes, he found the only light entering his sleeping chamber came from a flickering candle in the kitchen. Obviously, the sun had not risen, yet he heard grain being ground for bread. He rose and exited his alcove. Standing at the large table, Gildas energetically wielded a pestle while reciting scripture to himself. Even though the man was still quite thin, he had gained much in both weight and strength over the past month. As of late, he insisted on earning his keep by tending the gardens and preparing meals so Marc and Valeria could concentrate on their studies.

"Good morning, Brother Gildas," Marc said, breaking into a yawn.

The monk turned toward him and smiled, the rhythm of his work unchanging. "A good morning to you, also, Marcus. I trust you slept well?"

Marc nodded. "You're up early."

"This is a special day."

"How so?"

"Today I will resume my journey."

The man's statement caught Marc unawares for until now there had been no mention of Gildas' departure. He realized with disappointment that the person he had come to think of as a friend would soon be gone.

"You are leaving? Why?"

"I am in good health and do not desire to be a further burden on your master. He—" Gildas paused, then gave him a grateful smile. "*All* of you have been most generous to share your home and food with me."

Oren entered the kitchen and nodded a greeting toward Marc. "You are not a burden, Brother. You chose a life of service to others as have I. Therefore, it is an honor for me to serve you."

"And I thank you, but I must be moving on."

"You came to us very near death. In the time since you have recovered enough to feel better, but not enough to endure the elements. Stay. Let your recovery be complete."

Gildas halted in his task and studied the old wizard. "It seems there is another reason you wish me to remain."

A twinkle flashed in Oren's eyes. "Correct. It is not time for you to go. The magic is quite clear on that."

"The magic, you say? Explain."

"If you left now your life would be at risk. I cannot say more than that."

"Cannot, or *will not*?" The monk raised a questioning eyebrow.

Quelling a laugh, Marc found it refreshing to see someone other than himself frustrated by Oren's incomplete explanations.

Oren smiled. "Both. Will you stay, then?"

"Yes." Gildas returned to grinding. "I trust you will tell me when it *is* time to leave."

"Without fail."

"Very well. Go teach Marc something and leave me to my work and verses."

With a chuckle, Oren left, motioning for Marc to follow him to the workshop. Once there, Marc started to ask him what the magic had revealed about Gildas, but Oren sidestepped the issue and engaged him in some cleaning up. As they worked, his master glanced at him several times and smiled, but said nothing. Marc suspected he had something to tell him, but knew it was best to remain patient.

After breakfast, Oren had Valeria escort Gildas to the hot springs so he could bathe and enjoy the heat. Marc wondered why his teacher did that, for the monk could easily journey there and back and already knew the location of the springs. Clearly the master wanted them out of the way.

Once they were alone, Oren took Marc into the workshop and closed the door. He pointed to a stool by the large table. "Be seated." His master stood before him, nervously pulling at the cuffs of the robe Valeria had recently completed. "I have something to tell you. It is important that you listen carefully for I will now reveal the great truth of magic."

Gasping aloud, Marc quickly clamped a hand over his mouth.

With a slight smile, Oren pulled up a stool and sat opposite him. "I dare say you will most likely be shocked. I was when my master told me."

Marc's heart raced as a hundred thoughts reeled within him. The Great Secret. What could it be? The spell of all spells? The power to call down lightning bolts or make the earth quake? It had to be something fantastic. Why else would it be so carefully kept? Fighting to keep his composure, he bowed his head reverently. "I'm honored, Master Oren."

"You have surprised me, Marc, for although I knew your powers were strong, I did not expect you to develop so quickly and so well. Normally, you would serve several years as an apprentice before—" Oren sighed, clearly concerned about something. "I think it is better you learn this truth before we encounter... certain future events."

A sense of dread overcame Marc. What could be serious enough to bother his teacher this much? Unless— "Are you saying you might die soon?"

Oren grinned briefly. "Heavens. I hope not."

"Then what worries you so?" The master avoided his gaze, causing Marc to wonder if he should be worried as well. "Does it concern my test?"

The wizard released a silent sigh. "I have foreseen things that indicate your training needs to be hastened." Picking up the book of spells, Oren gave it to him. "Have you learned everything within this?"

"No, Master."

"True. Now, tell me, have I ever lied to you?"

"No."

Oren's steeled gaze locked with his. "I have."

Again Marc gasped, this time too astounded to cover it up. Oren's admission must be a prank or a test of some kind. He had no reason to lie because a powerful wizard feared nothing. Or did he? What were these future events he just mentioned? "Master—"

Oren silenced him with a gentle wave of a hand. "Concealing the great truth necessitated I misdirect you. For all time wizards initially had to withhold the full truth from their apprentices. But what I tell you now is no lie. This secret of secrets must never be told to anyone except those so chosen by the magic. Do you promise to keep this secret to your grave?"

Seeing the resolute edge in Oren's eyes, Marc swallowed hard, fearing himself unworthy of such terrible knowledge. Taking care to keep his voice firm and clear, he spoke the three words that would forever change his life. "I so promise."

"Good. I will first ask you a question. Think very carefully before answering it." Oren watched him closely. "When you do magic, where do you feel the power come from? Outside you... or from within?"

For Marc, the answer was obvious. "From within."

A wide, satisfied smile broke upon the man's face. "Excellent! When Arturius asked me that question so very long ago, I answered incorrectly at first."

Marc's stomach dropped to somewhere around his ankles. "*That's* the secret? How is that so shocking?"

Oren leaned close and quietly said, "Because there is no such thing as magic."

Stunned, Marc rocked back so far he nearly fell off his stool. Scrabbling for balance, he righted himself, then stared blankly at his teacher. What Oren said made no sense. Of course there was magic. Just what had he been learning, and *doing,* if not magic? "*What?*"

"You heard me. There is no such thing as magic—at least as you know it."

"But—" Marc's pulse hammered in his ears. Had the old wizard gone insane?

"I know you feel otherwise, but believe me, every spell you have learned is a lie."

Deeply confused, Marc looked upon the book in his hands. For months it had been the center of his world, and now to be told it was false seemed almost too much to comprehend. "How... how can that be so? I do magic every day."

"You said it yourself, Marc. The power comes from *inside* you." His elder nodded meaningfully toward the book. "The spells you cast, the incantations you speak—they are but shadows. Those words do nothing, for if they did, then any man or woman could do magic. You and I were born different than most other people." Oren pointed at the workbench. "Bring that ball of string to me without speaking or thinking a spell."

Certain it could not be done, Marc visualized the string with his magic and willed it to move. The object immediately sailed across the room to Oren's waiting hand. Marc jumped to his feet in astonishment. He immediately remembered how he learned his first spell—unlocking the cave door. Even though he spoke the command correctly, it did nothing until he pictured the bolt moving within his mind. His master spoke the truth! Suddenly annoyed, Marc roughly thrust the book into Oren's hands. "Then why did you make me learn these spells?"

Carefully placing the book upon the table, Oren opened the cover and idly leafed through the pages. "They are for show. To impress the people you perform magic for."

Marc took and released a deep breath, suppressing a seed of rising anger. "Why would I want to do that?"

Closing the book, Oren thoughtfully stroked his beard, eyes closed momentarily in thought. "That requires a fair bit of explaining, so please bear with me."

Trusting his feelings toward his teacher, as well as becoming more curious by the second, Marc nodded his assent.

"People with our abilities are quite rare, yet we have always been part of mankind. Unfortunately, humans often fear things they do not understand. Long ago our kind were either banished or killed, our powers considered evil." The wizard winked at him. "At one time *you* also thought that way."

Marc felt shame over his past prejudice. "Until you showed me otherwise. I can see how people would fear—should we still call it magic?"

"We might as well since we do not truly understand how our abilities manifest themselves."

"If everyone fears it so, then why call attention to ourselves?" He tapped the book to reinforce his point.

"Many years past some very clever wizards invented the concept of magic. They told everyone it was a powerful, living force that existed everywhere, and that no one could harm it or escape its power. They said if someone hurt or killed one of its servants—" Oren gave him a sly wink. "That's us—the magic would take a terrible revenge on them. Since this perception by others protects us so well, we have had little reason to change things. It allows us to use our gifts to help others while making a living at it.

"This false magic also allows us to hide our limitations. We cannot conjure up a pile of gold, raise the dead, change the weather, or make a person fall in love." A wry smile flickered across the old man's face. "Many have asked me to do such things. All we can do is influence items around us and learn things from people and objects. If we are asked to do what we know we cannot, or *should not* do, we simply say the magic will not allow it. Magic sets the rules, and we, as its servants, cannot change them."

A sense of relief washed over Marc. "That's clever. And—" He paused, shrugged, then humbly gestured toward the spell book. "It's good we don't have too much power."

From the kindling pile, the master selected a slender twig. Twirling it in his fingers, Oren looked him in the eye. "But what we *do* have can be very powerful when used in the right manner. Remember how I dealt with Portaeus?"

Oren handed him the stick. Marc regarded it while recalling the ease with which his master defeated the thief. "The stick, and the spell you pretended to put on it, were meant to fool him and—his wounds! How did you do that?"

"It is called the Magic Blade. You will learn it soon."

Marc eagerly clapped his hands together. "Yes, please."

Oren chuckled. "I thought you would like that. Now the reason I made you learn the spells first was to ensure that *you* believed in them and, as a result, be convincing to others. Always use the same phrase for the same task, otherwise people might become suspicious. If there is some difficult task to achieve, be sure to have the spell fail the first time or two. Use a larger, more fanciful spell the second or third time. Make it rhyme. Get some of the witnesses to hold hands, or kneel, or do something else special. Remember, the bigger the show you put on, the more powerful your magic appears to be."

Marc imagined himself casting spells before a crowd, waving his arms in grand gestures while hoping no one would realize his deception. Unsettled at the thought, he shook his head. "I would feel like a liar doing that."

"Do not. If you are to be a wizard, that is the part you must play. It is expected of us. Think back on my past visits to Oak Creek."

Memories of Marc's youth flooded through him, of the many times Oren came to his village and how he and the other children eagerly ran to greet him. One day in particular came to mind. Marc was ten and playing with Valeria, Sean and Donald, when the wizard approached them.

"Good day, young Marcus. I see you and your friends are enjoying yourselves."

Self-conscious at being singled out, Marc just nodded.

"How would you like to help me do some magic?"

Valeria gasped and looked at Marc with an infectious grin. "Say yes, say yes."

Catching her excitement, he smiled at Oren and asked, "What do I have to do?"

The wizard gestured at a leather pouch sitting on the ground before Marc's crossed legs. "Just empty out your acorn bag."

Donald's eyes widened and he drew back slightly, his voice nervous. "How do you know he has acorns in there?" Marc wondered the same thing.

Valeria let out a titter of amusement. "Because he's a *wizard*, Donnie."

"There's that," Oren said, giving her a nod, then tapping a finger beside his right eye, "plus I've been paying attention."

Undoing the drawstrings, Marc upended the bag and dumped several dozen acorns upon the ground. "Now what?"

"Hold it open to the sky because I'm going to catch some of the heavens and put them inside." Marc and his friends watched in fascination as Oren slowly lifted his arms above his head and majestically opened them as if in supplication, all while casting his spell with a sure and steady tone. After a minute of this, the wizard placed both hands, one atop the other, above Marc's head and said, "Hold your right hand palm down over your bag." Marc did so. "Now say 'let the sky come to me'."

As soon as Marc spoke the words, the bag gave a little hop, brushing against his hand.

"Look inside," Oren instructed, watching him closely.

Tugging the edges of the opening wide, Marc gazed within and saw a flash of reflected light. Tipping the bag up onto his left hand, he gasped as a nearly perfect sphere rolled to a stop against his thumb. Almost as clear as water, it had a light blue tint that spoke to him of cold, cloudless winter skies.

Valeria leaned over his hand, inspecting it close. "It *is* a piece of the sky," she whispered reverently.

Oren chuckled. "You could say that."

Marc rolled it around his palm with the tip of a finger. The stone, or whatever it was, had a curious warmth to it. "My thanks, wise one. I will treasure it always."

Returning his thoughts to the now, Marc Envisioned his sleeping chamber and the shallow ledge above his bed. Seizing the object he wanted with his thoughts—his *magic*—it drifted through the house, four feet above the floor, and to the table's surface before him. Tiny reflections of the fire on his left shone on its glossy exterior. Marc met the master's gaze.

"You knew even then, didn't you? Knew I'd have the... the power we share. That I'd be your replacement."

A smile lurked within the elder's eyes. "I did."

Picking it up, Marc held it between his thumb and forefinger, inspecting it with a casual ease. "I've always treasured this. For a time after my father passed, I would hold this piece of the sky and find some comfort in it." He gave Oren a knowing look. "The way you presented it to me made it special, gave it meaning. If you had just handed it to me without such ceremony, or *show*, as you call it, it would not have mattered nearly as much."

With a gentle flick of his wrist, he tossed the stone into the air and, with his thoughts, caused it to slow, then hover a couple of feet above the table, slowly spinning in place. Giving his teacher a respectful nod, he gestured at the stone with a dramatic wave of his hand. "I understand the need for wizards to use show."

Marc felt the trickle of magic that stretched between him and the blue orb. His will alone kept it aloft, and that act seemed...

Normal? Natural? It required almost no effort to maintain, yet what was easy for him was impossible for anyone else. Why?

"Master, if our power comes from within us, where do we get it from? Why are we different from others?"

"No wizard can answer that for certain, but I believe the Creator gives it to us. There is no need of spells, potions, amulets and such. We just will it and it happens. I see our gifts as having the tiniest little sliver of God's power inside us." Oren gently placed a hand on Marc's shoulder, his voice taking on a humble tone. "What else could that be besides *true* magic?"

God's power? The very idea filled Marc with awe and humility. What made *him* so special as to receive such a wondrous gift? Distracted by that thought, he lost control of the stone and it dropped to the table with a sharp crack.

As if reading his mind, Oren shrugged. "None of us know why we have these gifts, we just do."

Letting out an amused snort, Marc turned his attention to the book sitting between them. "I suppose I should continue to learn the remainder of the spells?"

"Yes, along with other important things I will teach you." The wizard watched him a moment before saying, —*This is your first lesson in the new magic.*—

"What lesson—" Marc froze. Something seemed very odd. He understood his master's words, yet Oren's lips neither moved, nor did Marc hear anything with his ears. Gasping, he took a hasty step back from the table. "What!? How... how did you do that?"

Oren regarded him calmly. —*Do what?*—

The master's words passed through him like a hot wind. "I... I can hear you even though you are not speaking. It's as if you are invading my thoughts." A surge of discomfort welled up inside Marc. "Please don't do that."

—*Do not be concerned. This is normal for wizards. You can do this , too.*—

Marc's anxiety subsided to a general unease. "That may be, but I still don't like you in my mind."

—*I am not inside your mind. I am talking with my thoughts and your mind hears it as your ears would hear my voice.*—

Sitting, Marc tried to clear away the confusion churning within him. Magic wasn't really magic, yet it was. And this power he possessed—how far would it progress? What other mysteries would be revealed? He felt strangely dizzy. "So many changes. I feel quite odd."

—That is because your magic is trying to talk like this. Do not resist it. Let it happen.—

Part of Marc wanted very much to learn this magic. Another part feared giving in to it. The room spun sickeningly. "Master, I—" He tried to stand, but the vertigo swelled and he crumpled toward the floor. Weakly putting out an arm, he attempted to break his fall, but the impact never came. It took him a moment to realize Oren's magic had caught him and returned him to the stool. The woozy feeling lessened. Taking a deep breath, he wiped the sweat from his forehead with the back of his hand.

—Thanks, Master. I— Marc's eyes opened wide and, unsure of what just happened, he hesitantly pointed at his head, then Oren's.

—Yes, I heard you. We wizards call this Linking.—

All reservation left Marc. *—This is remarkable! How far away can we talk—Link—like this?—*

—It depends on the strength of each persons' magic. I could easily communicate with Arturius when he was at a distance of several days journey.—

"Incredible." *—Sorry. This is still new to me.—*

—You are doing fine.— The master gave him a pleased smile.

Ψ   Ψ   Ψ

Marc practiced more Linking, but soon the strain of it gave him quite a headache. Even so, he was glad to have learned it; the excitement he felt equaled that of unlocking the workshop door for the first time. Receiving Oren's permission to take a break, Marc left the house and walked down the stone-covered path, looking about. Everything seemed slightly different. Could it be his imagination, or did learning the Great Secret change him somehow? The surroundings appeared the same physically, yet he sensed there were other aspects he could not quite identify.

As he approached the large iron gate, Marc caught himself about to wave his hand and utter the spell like so many times before. Smiling, he did neither. Seeing the locking bar with his mind, he moved it, letting the gate swing free. With a satisfied laugh, he stepped through the arch, closed the gate behind him and idly strolled down the southern path.

Elated, he felt freed of a burden that until now he did not know he bore. An intense hunger grew within him, a hunger to learn all he could about the new magic—the true magic. He felt so foolish for fearing it in the beginning. If only his first encounter with the Great Tree could have been on different terms. Suddenly, he realized the Tree presented an even greater mystery than before. How did his awareness of magic awake under its influence? Was it due to *his* magic, or did it have some of its own? Oren probably knew. Marc considered whether it was worth further aggravating his headache to Link to his master for an immediate answer. No, it could wait until he returned. For now, he wanted to rest and enjoy the fine day.

Chapter 16

Marc knocked at the workshop door. "Master?"

"Come," came the muffled reply. Marc half expected his master to Link his answer instead.

He entered, finding Oren seated at the large table, the book of spells before him. The old man gestured at the stool opposite him.

"Feeling better?"

"Much," Marc said, sitting.

Oren regarded him for a moment. "You have questions."

Marc smiled. "Yes, many. The Great Tree. How do I sense it? *Why* do I sense it? And why does it affect me so? Does it have magic within it like we do?"

The elder nodded in a pleased manner which implied he expected those questions. "The spot upon which it stands is unique. A power flows out of the earth much like water does at the hot spring. It is something we can feel and even draw into ourselves. But the Tree cannot use or guide that power as we do." Oren gave a half shrug. "I do not know why this is so, it just is."

"If I had not gone to the Tree, would I have ever discovered the magic within me?

"Possibly not to the degree you understand it now, but since I knew you were destined to become a wizard, I would have sought you out regardless." Oren eyed him for a long moment, a faint smile upon his lips. "You should know you had already used some of your gifts before coming here."

A flutter of surprise danced in Marc's belly. "I did?"

"For one, you had many little visions." The master's smile broadened. "Mostly of Valeria."

Feeling his face heat, Marc looked away in embarrassment. "But those were not as life changing as touching the Tree."

"True. After that experience you became open to other things. When you and Sean encountered the wolves, the magic in your mind sensed when the attack would come. It also commanded the wolves to stop attacking and leave."

Marc blinked in disbelief. "You must be jesting. I didn't actually *talk* to them, did I?" Closing his eyes, he recalled seeing the female wolf's startled reaction to his command. "Maybe so. But how?"

"In a way you did a simple version of Linking. Wolves are intelligent creatures. They understood you to say *stop* and *go away*."

Amazed, Marc took in a deep breath and let it out slow. "But I hadn't learned to Link yet."

"Sometimes, a severe stress such as having your life threatened will make your powers awaken, if only momentarily." Oren leaned closer, his eyebrows raised. "Like when you escaped from the creek on the day you found the buck."

Marc remembered the icy grip of the water and how he almost gave up. Only after becoming angry did he find the strength needed to climb the rope. "What did I do?"

The wizard raised his hand with a flourish. "You learned to fly."

Instead of being shocked, Marc immediately realized Oren was right. He recalled how the warmth spread throughout his body, his magic coming alive. "Like how you floated me over the water?"

"Exactly like that."

By the tightness in his cheeks Marc knew he wore a silly grin, but he did not care. "Master, I must learn this right away."

Oren laughed. "You shall."

The workshop door swung open and Valeria bustled inside, causing Marc's fantasy of soaring with the hawks to come crashing back to reality. In one hand she gripped her sewing bag, and in the other she held up a thick bundle of a coarse, tan fabric bound crosswise with twine.

"Master, I found that cloth you want—" Halting, she looked self-consciously between him and Oren, then started to back out. "Pardon me. I didn't mean to disturb the lesson."

"Nonsense," Oren said reassuringly, waving her over. "We need your help."

"We?" Marc blurted out. The wizard ignored him.

Valeria's face brightened. "Yes, Master?"

"Take that cloth and make monk's robes for both Marc and myself, only do a poorer job of sewing them."

After a brief pause, she nodded in understanding. "You want them to look like monks made them, not a seamstress."

Oren graciously dipped his head toward her. "Correct. Give them deep hoods to better hide our faces and large sleeves as well. And include some hidden pockets, much like you did for this fine robe you made me."

Marc watched as the master paused and appreciatively inspected his own garment. The rich, dark green fabric matched the color of pine needles in the deepest shadows of the forest. Marc especially liked the ornate borders of yellow and white that Valeria embroidered on the cuffs, hem and hood—truly a work of art. Wondering what purpose the monk's robes would serve, he only half-listened as his master stood and moved slowly around the table.

"We will discuss their construction further after supper. However, before you begin those, I have a more important task for you to complete." Oren stopped behind him. "I need you to make another wizard's robe for Marcus here. As of today he is no longer an apprentice, but a junior wizard."

All other thoughts vanished as he stood and faced his teacher. "*I am?*"

Valeria jumped at Marc, flinging her arms around him as the bundle of fabric tumbled to the floor. "I'm so proud of you!"

The soft warmth of her embrace smelled of flowers and freshly baked bread. Returning the hug, he was surprised to feel her mould her body to his. Marc liked that feeling. He liked it very much.

Oren moved toward the door. "Measure him for both robes. I have a chore to attend to. In the meantime, keep studying, *wizard.*"

Marc quelled a laugh. "I will."

As Oren left the room, Marc felt his master's mind once more. *—Remember, tell her nothing of the secret.—*

—Yes, Master.— Marc realized something else had come through the Link. An emotion. Oren was proud of him.

Valeria brought her hands together in a gleeful clap. "A wizard. That's wonderful. Everyone back home will be so excited when they find out." She eagerly hugged him once more.

Again her body conformed to his, the warmth of her ample bosom painfully apparent even through two layers of cloth. Fighting his surfacing lust, he gently separated himself from her embrace. "Let's not tell them yet. I need to learn more first."

"Oh." She sagged, disappointment replacing her grin. "As you wish, Marc." Her gaze flicked downward, voice taking on a remote edge. "Or should I call you Master now?"

Placing a hand on hers he gently squeezed. "Don't call me that. I'm no master. I'm still a student like you."

Her smile returned along with a quiet sigh of relief. "Good. Now, let me get your measurements, oh wise junior wizard." Retrieving a measuring string from her bag, she gestured at him. "Off with your tunic." Marc peeled off the garment and she eyed his chest and arms with delight. "My, you've got more muscles than I remember."

Her gaze ignited a fluttering tingle low in his belly. "It's from chopping all that wood for our master's many fires."

"Hold out your arms, like a bird with outstretched wings."

As he complied, she placed one end of the string between his shoulder blades, holding it fast with her left hand. With her right, she pressed it lightly against his skin and slowly slid her hand across his back, drawing the cord over his shoulder and down his arm to his wrist. His breathing quickened at the intimate warmth of the caress. Next, she reached around his chest with the string, again moving with a sensuous grace. When her hands met at the front, she nestled herself against his bare back.

"Do you like me, Marc?" she asked, softly.

"Uh, yes." Why did she act so strangely? She almost seemed—

"I mean as *a woman.*"

His heart raced at the heat in her voice. Could she possibly have *those* feelings for him? The same ones he felt for her over the last several years?

Her lips drifted next to his ear, brushing ever so lightly against his flesh. "And by that I mean—"

She did! "I know what you mean, Val," he said, his voice barely more than a whisper. Excited and confused, his head spun. What should he to do? He placed his hands over hers. "I do like you... very much... and have feelings for you I don't know how to describe." *Like*? Why was *love* so difficult to say? The urge to speak that word—no, to shout it—raged inside of him, yet it would not come. "I've never felt this way before."

She moved around to face him. "I can't help but feel we are supposed to be together." She gazed deeply into his eyes.

A lightning bolt blazed through his mind, a flash of pure magical force more powerful than he had ever felt. Cut off from his senses, he floated in a void, empty save for a magnificent radiance before him. Valeria. Their minds existed together in a place separate from their bodies. They knew what the other thought, felt what the other felt. No secrets could be concealed here, no hiding behind false modesty, no resisting the truth for fear of another discovering one's weaknesses. They were truly one, and he knew with absolute certainty they would remain so for the rest of their days. Then, just as suddenly, his awareness returned to his body.

"I love you," they said simultaneously. Laughing, they shared a long, deep kiss, one more of love and familiarity than raw passion.

Enraptured by the experience, neither of them said a word for a time, happy only to cling to one another. Wiping a tear from her cheek, Valeria spoke first. "You are a great wizard, Marc. What kind of magic was that?"

"I do not know."

Valeria touched the side of his face with great tenderness. "I know things about you that I shouldn't be able to. Like what you felt the first time you touched the Great Tree, how cruel Donald has been to you, and—" She giggled. "Your many visions of me swimming naked at the springs." Leaning forward, she whispered in his ear. "You *liked* seeing me that way."

Those images returned stronger than ever and, for the first time, he felt no guilt over them. "You've loved me always and I was a fool to not see it before" He chuckled. "I also know you tried using magic without the master's permission."

"True, but I like *this* magic much better. It still tingles all over me. I can feel you, too." Sliding out of his embrace, she plucked his tunic off the table and held before her, gently kneading the fabric in her fingers. "Like on this. I *feel* you on it. I *know* this is yours." Wonder filled her gaze. "How can that be?"

Marc stood tall and did his best to imitate Oren's *you should know that answer* stare. Valeria backed away several steps, a mischievous smile on her lips. By the way she held the garment, he knew she was about to throw it at him. Laughing, she swung her arm. He quickly blurted out the spell "*Cōnsiste!*" and the would-be weapon froze in mid-air.

She snatched it back. "That's cheating." While he laughed, she showed him the sleeve. "Remember this?"

"You sewed it up the night before I found the deer at the falls."

"Yes. Now I know why you acted so strange. You desired me but were embarrassed about it."

Why deny it? "Yes. And you wanted me as well."

Nodding, her moist eyes closed, freeing several tears to roll down her cheeks. "I followed you inside, hoping your mother and sisters were elsewhere." She held him close, planting little kisses on his neck. "I still feel that way. I love you so much."

He caressed her back, his fingertips gliding down either side of her spine before coming to rest at the top of her hips. Again, he felt her surrender and knew he could have his way with her. But deep down he also knew that now was not the time. A strange, yet somehow familiar, power entered him, quenching his passions, calming his thoughts. Tenderly, he pushed her away.

"It's too soon," he whispered, placing his forehead against hers. "We're not married, Val. We're not even betrothed."

An almost silent laugh bubbled out of her as she lazily trailed a hand over his chest. "I think we are now." She met his gaze. "I have always felt your love for me even though you've never openly expressed it, and I have always wanted to be your wife."

Brushing a lock of hair from her face, he softly kissed her. "And I your husband."

"Then let us be wed as soon as Gildas returns."

Once more that strange power let its presence be felt. He shook his head. "No."

She looked at him, puzzled and a bit wounded. "Why not?"

"I want to, but somehow I know, I just *know*, it's not the right time. Maybe the magic is telling me that." Closing his eyes, he took several deep, cleansing breaths. "Let's try to put this aside for now."

"All right." She stepped back and collected herself in much the same way. "Where were we?"

He gave her a taunting grin . "You were seducing me while pretending to take my measurements."

Heat flashed in her eyes. "*Marc!* I take offense to that." The indignation in her voice was belied by the sly smile on her lips. "I really *did* get your measurements."

Chapter 17

Valeria placed the bolt of cloth on the workshop table and rolled out a length. Letting the tips of her fingers skate across its velvety surface, she marveled at the most luxurious fabric she had ever beheld, its beautiful deep-blue color fit for a king. Her king.

Over an hour had passed since her magical encounter with Marc, and yet the sensation of being one with him had not abated. An unbreakable bond had been forged between them; knowing they would remain together for life thrilled and contented her. She wondered if the magic ordained their pairing early on. It must have, for she had always loved him, but until today did not understand its depth and completeness. On top of that, the incredible force of his mind amazed her. Having recently learned to command the magic herself allowed her to truly understand his power, tendrils of which even now flowed warmly in and around her. Would her own also grow as strong? She hoped so.

With string and chalk, she quickly laid out the various parts of Marc's robe, already knowing how to craft it, having seen it in her vision of him returning with the deer. That vivid memory filled her mind, rich in every detail, as if she had already sewn it. It fascinated her how the magic could reveal such things long before they happened. It could tell her other things, too. Closing her eyes, she let the magic rise and concentrated on knowing Marc's location. An image of him and Oren sitting on rocks came to her. The area looked familiar, somewhere on the western path to the Forbidden Vale. As she focused more closely upon Marc, he looked up in her direction and smiled, a ripple of his comforting presence brushing over her.

Her heart leapt with joy. He *felt* her.

Ψ　　　Ψ　　　Ψ

"Marc?"

Refocusing his thoughts, Marc returned his gaze to Oren. "Excuse me, Master. I felt Val watching us."

The wizard nodded slightly, the corner of his mouth twitching upward. " I must show both of you how to Envision in a less obvious manner. Shall I continue?"

His teacher had just begun to tell of things that lay in Marc's future before Valeria intruded. Nervously wiping the dampness from his palms on his pants, he said, eagerly, "Please."

"In time you will be the master to many wizards for your gifts are quite strong." Oren paused a dramatic moment before adding, "So, too, in the woman you will take as your wife."

Marc straightened in surprise. "You've had a vision about her?".

"Several. Together you will bring forth a magical family line that will continue for many centuries. I have been greatly blessed to foresee it."

Excited, Marc wished to know everything the master had seen. How many generations would there be? Where would they live? And would his heirs all be wizards? Before he could voice these thoughts, he caught himself. It would not do for him to chatter on like an inexperienced apprentice. He was more than that now. Wizards, even junior ones, were to carry themselves with a greater decorum. The answers would come in time. Relaxing, Marc gave his master a respectful nod.

"Val will be pleased to hear that."

A large smile spread across Oren's wrinkled face. "I thought you would know by now. Have you shared each other yet?"

Fearing his master assumed the worst, Marc's cheeks burned. "Oh, no, Sir! We have behaved most properly. I—"

Oren laughed. "I did not mean in the carnal sense. No, have your minds joined, become one?"

"Oh... uh, yes." Greatly relieved, Marc explained what took place, leaving out the more embarrassing parts. "I'm glad her power is as strong as ours."

"Why do you think that?" Oren's questioning gaze pierced him through.

"I don't think it. Somehow I *know* it," Marc said, mystified as to how he could perceive such a thing.

The old wizard gave him a satisfied smile. "Very good. Soon you will begin to see future events, not like the partial visions you had before, but true visions. When that happens, you will be my equal."

Marc's heart nearly stopped. "*Never*, Master."

The elder's brows rose. "You think I am mistaken?"

"No, Sir, but—" At a loss for words, Marc communicated his confusion with a slow shrug.

Oren gently laughed, putting a hand upon Marc's shoulder. "It will happen, my young mage. Before the end of my days on this earth, *you* will be the master, and *I* the student."

Part of him believed Oren, knowing the statement to be true, but another part of him remained doubtful, for accepting the master's words would mean he would be greater than the man before him. "How can that be? You have lived many years as a master wizard. I am still a novice and have much to learn. Surely you have learned all there is."

"One never stops learning, Marc. Even this morning I had a vision and discovered something I did not know before." Oren's expression held something Marc could not quite discern. Was it awe? Incredulity? "Many generations from now a great conflict will rise up between the forces of good and evil. Champions of good, your descendants will be in the thick of it."

Gladness swelled within Marc. "What about your descendants? Will they also not—" As soon as he spoke he deeply regretted it. "Forgive me, Master. I did not mean to—"

Oren cut him off with a wave of his hand. "You did nothing wrong in asking that." Composing himself, the wizard took and released a deep breath. "I have no descendants. My wife was unable—" An ancient pain furrowed the master's brow as he looked away, focused on nothing. "Four times she became with child but lost it before it could be born. The fifth child lived, but she and my wife died of a sickness the following year. I still miss them after all these years."

Waves of sorrow washed over Marc, almost as if he could feel his Master's emotions. But that could not be. He must be imagining it. "I'm sorry I brought it up."

Oren shook his head. "In truth, it is good to share it with someone." He gave Marc a sad, gentle smile. "Had she lived, my daughter would have been older than your grandmother Etta."

The woman's face came to life in Marc's mind. He had loved her so much, but those feelings could not have stopped the fever that took her only months after his father— her son—died. She lived to be fifty nine, the oldest person he ever knew. Until now. He looked his master over. While his hair was completely gray, he seemed pretty fit and healthy for an elderly man.

"Master, may I ask how old you are?"

"Of course, but rather than me telling you, why not find out for yourself. Examine the area around me with your magic and pull the information you want out of it."

"I can *do* that?" Oren nodded. With a shrug, Marc extended his senses much like he did when Envisioning, exploring the area directly around the master. At first he perceived nothing more than Oren's clothing, but then tried touching upon the magic surrounding him. Suddenly, many bits of knowledge entered his mind as if they had always been there. Marc thought about wanting to know Oren's age and a number immediately came to mind. He frowned. "I must be wrong. You can't be eighty seven."

"I sometimes think so as well."

How could it be? That meant Oren was born about the same time as his great, great grandfather. "But anyone that old is weak and sick, laying on their deathbed."

The wizard laughed. "As you can see, I am doing much better than that."

"Have you lived this long because of the magic inside you?"

"Not that I know of. I have always been healthy. Maybe I was destined to live this long in order to train you and Valeria."

Marc now saw his master in a new way. "When is Val to be told the truth about magic?"

"Very soon. She already suspects it, but so far only in the back of her mind." Leaning toward him, Oren met his gaze. "Both of you posses a strength of magic far greater than my own."

That disclosure astonished Marc. Oren's magic seemed to come so easily, while his own efforts took much work and often resulted in less than perfect execution. "How do you know that?"

"By the strength of your auras—that blue light you have seen about Valeria. Yours are the brightest I have ever seen."

Marc looked Oren up and down, both with his eyes and magic, then studied his own hands. "I see nothing."

"That is because our magic is at rest, making our auras faint." The wizard stood. "You cannot smell the fragrance of a single flower held at arm's length. You must bring it to your nose. So, too, with the faint magic about people and things." Oren moved to another cluster of rocks that jutted into the path and gestured at them. "Find the magic that is here and pull it back into your mind."

Joining his teacher, Marc deeply probed the weak magic of the rocks and brought it back into himself. Suddenly, he felt a multitude of sensations, emotions and memories. "There are many things mixed together in the magic on these rocks."

"Choose one and follow it."

The jumble reminded him of a writhing mass of earthworms. Studying it, one stood out above the others, familiar in some way. He trailed after it until it was before him, large and accessible. With his mind he touched it. "Ow!" His toe suddenly hurt. Lifting his foot, he felt it with his hand but found no injury; the pain was in someone else's toe. They had just stubbed it and hopped over to these rocks to sit down. Amazed at how real it felt, Marc understood it to be a memory of some kind.

"This is... incredible. A man hurt his toe and sat here. It's like it happened to me."

"Tell me his name," Oren said, his voice low and serious.

For a moment Marc wondered how to do that, but then it seemed obvious. He Envisioned seeing the injured toe, then moved his view up the body to the face. Nothing prepared him for what he saw. For a moment joy filled him only to be replaced with sadness. Breaking contact with the magic, he looked at the old wizard. "Davidus. My father."

"Correct. Now, tell me when and why he was here."

Marc hesitated. As much as he marveled at what his magic let him do, he also feared it might awaken other, less pleasant memories.

"Marc," Oren said reassuringly, "the Traces that remain here will not cause you pain. They are but the moment of that day, nothing more. Trust me."

"Yes, Master." Oren deserved his trust. Marc reconnected with the—what did the wizard call it?—the *Trace* of his father. For several moments, he held back, steeling himself against what may be, then pulled it into his thoughts. Something had made his father happy and he ran to tell Oren the good news. Marc strained to uncover this deeper layer, then laughed. "He came to tell you his son had been born. To tell you about me."

A smile came to his master's face. "Indeed. A most delightful day. Well done." Oren stepped away from the rocks. "Practice this skill often. Master it, for it is by far the most useful form of magic."

"I will. Thank you for bringing me here, for letting me feel a moment from my father's life."

The wizard answered him with a single nod. "Now, look at me as you did when you felt the Traces."

In seconds he sensed what he could not before; a faint blue glow surrounded his master. "I see it now."

"Very good. Practice that as well."

Briefly revisiting the Trace left upon the rocks, Marc relished how richly it filled part of the void left by his father's absence. He wondered what other objects would have similar Traces on them. Surely the whistle would, his father's tools and clothing—Clothing! "Val felt my Trace on my tunic today."

Oren's eyebrows rose. "Interesting. Both of you continue to surprise—" The distant clanging of a bell caught their attention. "Someone is at our gate. Tell me who."

Marc Envisioned the gate. "Sean. He looks worried."

"The news he has is most urgent. Come." Together they hurried for home.

"You know why Sean is here, don't you, Master."

"His thoughts are quite agitated."

"You know what's in his mind?" Marc asked with surprise.

"Only what is on the surface. I sense that much as I do when I receive a Link. Emotions are easier than actual thoughts. When we get close to him, try to feel his mind. Go past the emotions. Learn what worries him."

Marc would have been more excited about this new form of magic, but knowing Sean was troubled dampened much of the thrill. Had someone taken ill or died? If so, whom? His mother, one of his sisters, someone like Garrett? Soon they were within sight of the gate.

Sean ran to meet them. Out of breath, his face flushed, he bowed his head toward Oren. "Mighty wizard. Marc. I have terrible news."

—*Sense his thoughts,*— Oren instructed.

Marc probed his friend's mind and quickly knew the terrible burden he carried. "The king has died."

Sean looked at him, startled. "Yes. Did someone else bring you the news?"

"No. Only you."

"But I haven't said anything." Sean looked confused.

—*Very good. Now learn how he died.*—

Again, Marc let the emotions and thoughts radiating from Sean enter him while suppressing the embarrassment of invading another's mind. "He died fighting his nephew."

Clearly unsettled, Sean took a step back. "How do you know that?"

—*Tell him,*— Oren said.

—*I don't know if I'm ready to. What will he think of me? I might lose him as a friend.*—

—*If he truly is your friend, he will remain so.*—

"I'm a junior wizard, Sean. Master Oren has been teaching me magic." Marc expected him to be shocked, but instead a broad grin spread across Sean's face.

"I knew it! I knew there was a reason you survived being in the Forbidden Vale. And the wolves! Only a wizard could have acted as you did." Sean turned toward Oren. "You have chosen well in your apprentice, Great One. I know of no person better suited for that honor than Marc."

"I agree, but the magic chose him, not I. How is the village taking the news?"

Sean's smile vanished. "Not well. Everyone is worried, especially Garrett. He fears the factions that were once unified under the king will now fight for control of the throne."

Oren nodded. "That concerns me as well." —*Invite him to stay the night.*—

—*I thought outsiders were not to be allowed past the greeting room?*—

—*Sean is a trustworthy and honorable man. He has kept his pledge to not reveal your first encounter with the Great Tree.*—

Marc shook Sean's hand and pulled him into a brief embrace. "Despite the reason for your visit, I'm glad to see you. The day grows late. There is no need for you to return home in the darkness. Please, stay the night as our guest."

Sean's smile returned. "Only if you will do one thing."

"What?"

"Tell me all about how you became a wizard."

Marc chuckled. "It's going to be a long night, then."

Chapter 18

Marc, Sean and Oren approached the gate. Putting his hands upon the bars, Sean studied them and the surrounding stonework.

"I've been here before... when I was little." His gaze traced the curve of the structure above him. "This arch seemed huge to me then. It still does."

Marc nodded in the direction of the house. "After you."

Sean tried to enter. "It's holding fast. I see no way to open it."

"This gate is magical. Watch." Marc swept his arm in an impressive gesture and commanded, "*Aperīte!*"

Sean gasped, his eyes following the door as it swung along its arc. "Amazing! Such powerful magic."

"Come," Oren said, walking past them. —*Good use of show, Marc.*—

Marc fought off a smile as he ushered Sean in. "Actually, it's simple magic. It's the first spell I learned."

"Oh." Sean eyed the gate a moment before asking, "What was the second?"

Again Marc put on a show. "*Claudite!*"

As the gate closed, Sean chuckled. "Of course."

"This way," Marc said, following his master. After several steps, he felt an odd, prickly sensation on the side of his face and found Sean studying him. "What is it?"

Sean dropped his gaze, embarrassed. "Sorry. I didn't mean to stare, but finding out my best friend's a wizard is a bit of a shock. I wanted to see if there was any difference in how you looked."

"There isn't. What *has* changed is I can listen to and speak with the magic."

Sean nodded, seemingly accepting Marc's words, then looked around at the wizard's land. "You have so much inside your walls, Great One. I especially like your many trees."

"Call me by my name," Oren said.

Sean shot Marc a questioning glance. "Uh, yes... Oren."

That surprised Marc as well. *—Master?—*

—We can be less formal with him. He will be your faithful friend for the rest of his days.—

Hearing that pleased him. *—And I, his.—*

Oren veered off the path and into the trees. "I planted most of these myself, Sean."

As Oren talked with Sean about his orchard, Marc remained where he was and thought about what might happen now that the king had died. While he knew little of the power structure that once surrounded the king, he did know of one member of the inner circle who often expressed views opposite those of his monarch: Crowe. It was widely rumored he bragged he would be king one day. Maybe now he would seize his chance. That did not concern Marc much for he had no say about who would be the next king.

What did concern him were men like Thaddeus—those who thirsted for wealth and power and would do anything to achieve it. Men who showed their enemies little or no mercy. A chill slid down Marc's spine as he hoped Thaddeus would be too occupied with filling his pockets elsewhere to think about returning to Oak Creek to seek revenge upon him or Oren. Further worries fell away as a familiar sensation came from his right. He turned toward the house to see Valeria bounding toward him.

"I thought I felt you," she said as she neared..

Her arms encircled him, her lips finding his. Warm and sweet, Marc enjoyed her kiss before remembering they had an audience. "Uh, I haven't told—"

"The Master?" She gave him a playful smile and tousled his hair. "I'm sure he already knows. He seems to know everything."

"No, not Oren." Before he could explain, she looked past him and clapped with delight.

"Sean!" Hurrying over to their friend, she gave him a heartfelt hug. "It's so good to see you."

"You, too." Sporting an amused expression, he looked from her to Marc and back again. "I see you and Marc *finally* realized how much you care for each other."

Marc studied the knowing smile on his friend's face. "How could you tell?"

Sean's eyes rolled upward. "*Please.* It's obvious. The way you've looked at each other for some time now. Even Don sees it, that's why he's so jealous." His smile warmed. "I'm happy for both of you."

"Thanks." Valeria gave him another quick hug and returned to Marc's side.

As Valeria's arm slipped around his waist, he realized there was much more to his friend than he ever saw before. *—Sean is wise, Master. He should become village leader after Garrett, not Donald.—*

—While he would indeed serve well as Garrett's successor, that is not his destiny.—

Interested that the master knew something of Sean's future, he asked, eagerly, *—What is it, then?—*

—Your will learn that later,— came Oren's guarded reply.

Feeling the shift in his master's demeanor, Marc tried to read his emotions but got nothing. The wizard, as always, liked keeping his secrets.

"Why have you traveled all the way here, Sean?" Valeria asked.

Before Sean could answer, a rush of alarm spread out from her. Seeing her glow rise sharply, Marc did a quick probe of her mind and found she felt a great sense of dread towards their friend. It took but a moment to realize what that represented. Death.

Noticing the subtle change in Valeria, Sean regarded her with concern. "You don't look so good."

She flashed him an embarrassed smile. "I'm just excited to see you."

Their visitor's manner became more somber. "I came bearing bad news. The king has died."

As Sean told her the rest of the story, Marc felt Valeria's spirit quickly lighten. Somehow she must have unknowingly sensed Sean's emotions concerning the king's death. This intrigued Marc, for only this day had he learned to perceive another's thoughts, yet she did so without any training or knowledge of Linking.

Oren extended his arm toward the door of their home. "Valeria, please show our guest the house. Do not go beyond the workshop." After they were alone, Oren turned to him. "It appears your future wife's talents are surfacing more each day."

Marc chuffed out a brief laugh. "Indeed."

"How well have you observed our other guest these past weeks?"

The change in topic momentarily confused Marc. "Who, Gildas?"

"Yes. Do you know how he speaks, what he says, how he moves? At times you will have to pose as someone other than yourself to go unrecognized among the people."

"Other than as a wizard."

His master smiled. "I am pleased you see yourself that way."

Marc thought about it a moment. "I could pretend to be a monk. When are we to do this?"

"Soon."

"This is because of the king's death, isn't it?"

Oren nodded. "His loss will result in a considerable shift in power. I fear whomever replaces him will be far less of a leader."

"You don't know who it will be?"

"No. Perhaps Valeria will see something. Her gift of vision is unusually strong."

Not to mention empathy, Marc thought. "What *do* you see coming?"

Sadness emanated from his master. "Great violence. Death."

Marc shared Oren's feelings. "It's unfortunate we cannot use our magic to find the next king and put him in power. Maybe that would prevent any violence."

Oren watched him dispassionately for several breaths. "Do not underestimate your influence. Our abilities give us considerable power to affect the affairs of others if the need arises." His master's voice had a waver to it that concerned him.

He again tried reading Oren's emotions and face, but neither provided a clue. "I have seen... portions of your futures."

"*Futures?* More than one?"

"Your life can take different directions depending upon your actions from this point forward. In one, you play a part in the struggle over who will be king."

Marc blinked in surprise, unsure how to take that. "I will, er, might?"

The set of Oren's eyes hardened, his gaze distant. "In another, you do not."

In a flash, Marc knew what that meant. "It's the test I must face." Although the words flowed smoothly from his lips, a stark hollowness opened up deep within him. "The king's death might very well result in my own."

"That is not what I meant."

"But it could happen. His death is involved with my test."

His master sighed and raised a placating hand. "It is only the first step of that journey."

"And how soon will the journey end?"

"I do not know the day." Oren smiled slightly. "But by then you should have all the skills needed to face any test."

Knowing the future was partially in his own hands gave Marc some comfort. "Then teach me well, Master."

"I will teach as I always have. *You* must *learn* well."

Oren's use of humor implied he was not unduly worried, which further lightened Marc's spirits. "As *I* always have."

The sparkle returned to his master's eyes. "Good. Remember, few men are a threat—"

"—to a fully trained wizard. I'll be ready."

Ψ   Ψ   Ψ

While Gildas prepared the evening meal, Sean and Valeria sat by the fireplace as Marc demonstrated some of the magic he had learned. Until now he kept his studies secret, worried what Sean and others might think. Seeing the delight in his friend's eyes made Marc realize his concerns were for nothing. After making two pieces of firewood dance about then jump into the fire, Marc saw Gildas nod at Oren. Dinner was ready.

Sean clapped and laughed. "Marvelous. What other wonders are there?"

With a smile, Marc extended his right arm and said, "*Convīvium profer!*" One by one, he magically conveyed the food containers into the fire room and onto the table, each followed by Sean's rapt gaze. Once finished, he bowed toward Sean. "Dinner is served."

Stepping up to the table, Sean inspected everything with amazement. "There's so much. Breads, dried fruit, nuts and—" Bending, he sniffed at a large copper pot. "Venison stew?" His gaze met Marc's. "Life as a wizard is indeed privileged."

"Not so," Oren said, guiding their visitor toward a stool. "Our fare is usually quite simple. But today we have an honored guest, so a feast is in order." Looking a little self conscious, Sean sat. Oren glanced at Gildas with a smile. "Brother."

Bidding them join hands, Gildas gave a longer than normal blessing, but Marc figured this special meal deserved an equally special benediction. Once over, they began to eat.

"Tell me, Brother Gildas," Sean asked, "how did you manage to survive the last few years? Did Oren warn your people as he did ours?"

The monk's countenance sagged and he shook his head. "I heard no warning. When the darkness first came upon us, I and my brethren were filled with fear, not knowing why the sun had left us as it did. People came to us for help, begging us to pray to God to end it. We were already trying that, but nothing changed. Some of the people abandoned the Almighty and reverted to the false gods of Rome's past. Great piles of precious food were burned in unholy offerings to them." As if to underscore his point, the monk lifted a piece of bread before him.

"After that, things continued to worsen. While I did not witness it myself, I heard tales of human sacrifices and other such horrors. Some of my brethren also gave up their faith and fled. Those of us who remained managed to survive on roots we dug up. When the darkness began to leave us, I went in search of a village or town that might take pity on a humble monk. I came upon more than one settlement where no one remained. Whether they died, or moved elsewhere, I do not know. After walking for many days, I took sick. Soon, I could go no further and laid down expecting to die." He looked toward Valeria, giving her a respectful nod. "I would have, too, if not for Valeria's magic."

Cocking his head to the side, Sean looked at her in surprise. "You, too?"

A flicker of a smile danced about the corners of her mouth. "Yes, I'm learning magic, but I'm not as advanced as Marc." She briefly told of her visions and how she found Gildas.

"Amazing. My two best friends, a wizard and a witch." Dipping a crust of bread into his stew, Sean chewed it thoughtfully before asking, "Tell me, Oren, have many wizards lived in this house?"

"Yes. Wizards were among the earliest Romans to come to this land. One of my kind first settled this property over four hundred years ago. Each wizard passes it down to his replacement. I will do the same to Marc and Valeria one day."

"Are many wizards Roman, then?"

"Men and woman of magic come from every part of the world, including Rome and its territories. At one time, many Romans lived here, and a few of them served magic and the people around them. The Romans improved our lands. They built cities, roads." Oren waved his hand in a slow arc around him. "They even built the wall around my home. Sadly, they left some time ago."

Gildas gave a snort of disgust. "Rome has long since cast us off, disregarded for more pressing concerns. They do not care Britannia is being overrun by the Saxon menace." He looked down and shook his head. "Many among us have forgotten what it was like before the victory at Mount Badon—what has it been, now? Forty-two years? The invaders were soundly defeated, but since then the people have become complacent and lazy, leaving us ripe for conquest. Man's evil has caused God to set his wrath against us."

Marc felt deep conflicts over mankind and magic war within Gildas. "Wrath?"

Gildas' eyes burned with the fire of righteousness. "The great darkness we have just endured. Thanks be to God it has passed." The monk reverently crossed himself.

Oren let out a gentle sigh Marc knew well; his master often used it before correcting him on some error in judgment. "You believe the darkness was a punishment of some kind."

Gildas answered him with a curt nod. "Most surely. God snatched the sun from the world to show His anger with our sins." He studied Oren for a moment. "You believe otherwise?"

After stroking his beard a few times, the wizard shrugged. "I cannot say whether it was punishment or not, but I *do* know the sun never left us. Instead, a tremendous cloud of dust covered all the earth for that time."

"Dust?" Gildas said with a frown. "That is impossible."

"So you say, but our Creator's world is capable of many wondrous and frightful things. Far to the east, deep into the southern part of the Orient, stood an island, a great volcano. For many years fires burned at its peak, the smoke of which could be seen from a great distance. Then the island rose up out of the sea with a great violence and burst open, casting itself upon the wind and was no more. For weeks a huge column of dust rose from its grave, fouling the air even this far away."

Again the monk studied Oren, but longer this time. "If this is true, how could you know this?"

"I have... communicated with other wizards in far off lands." Oren surreptitiously winked at Marc. "One of my kind who lived in the Orient told of hearing a tremendous sound in the distance, a roar like a thousand claps of thunder, only lasting much longer. Hours later, towering waves came out of the sea, flowing far inland and wreaking unbelievable destruction, killing many thousands. Then great quantities of yellow dust fell upon his land as the darkness descended."

While Gildas absorbed that information, Marc took advantage of the pause. —*We can Link that far?*—

—*At times, but only with those whose magic is about as strong as our own.*—

Marc liked the thought of Linking with someone so distant.

Gildas shifted on his seat. "Pardon my skepticism, Oren, but are you telling me the truth?"

The elder lifted his hand as if taking an oath. "I swear on my life."

Nodding slowly, the monk leaned against the table. "These other wizards, what do they say now? Have their lands come out of the darkness as we have?"

A ripple of sorrow emanated from Oren and Marc saw his eyes mist up. "Sadly, many of them fell silent in the first year. I fear the cold or hunger took them from us."

Marc saw several flashes of violent mobs attacking persons he knew to be fellow wizards. Shocked, he wondered if this knowledge came from Oren, or that mysterious something else which seemed to place whole thoughts into his mind as if they had been there all along.

"Or the hands of murderers," Marc muttered.

"That as well," Oren said with a grimace. "But those who remain have reported the sun has returned."

"Thank God. I am sorry for your brethren."

Oren nodded his acceptance of Gildas' condolence. "Marc and Valeria are the future of those who serve magic. They will help many people overcome the hardships of life." As Oren looked at them, Marc felt Valeria's hand seek his, her thumb tenderly rubbing against his palm. Seeing that, the wizard smiled and returned his attention to Gildas. "I know you have a dim view of mankind and think that evil is everywhere. In my many years on this earth I, too, have seen all kinds of evil wrought by the hand of man. But I have also seen far more good. People are always helping one another, generously sharing what they have, willing to put themselves at risk to save their neighbor. The light of brotherly love pierces the blackness of evil."

"I pray you are right."

"I, too," Sean added.

Marc agreed as well. He glanced over at Valeria to see her reaction but found her staring blankly into space.

"Val?"

She did not respond and her hand felt cooler than it had a moment before.

"Are you having a vision?"

He probed her mind but felt nothing—no thoughts, emotions, or anything else. She glowed with strong magic, yet it seemed as if her spirit were elsewhere.

"*Val?*"

Slowly, she turned her head toward him, her eyes vacant, unfocused. He touched her cheek and her arms sprang closed around him, squeezing hard.

"No! No, Marc! Please no!" An immense wave of fear flowed from her.

"What is it, Val? What's wrong?" Her grip relaxed as she began to sob. "Tell me what frightens you so." She shook her head as other emotions spilled out—anger, frustration, loss. "Was it a vision?" After a pause, she nodded, avoiding his gaze. "Was I in it?" She nodded again. "Did I do something wrong?"

"No." Biting her lip, she said nothing more.

What could be so terrible that she would act this way? His own fear began to match hers. "Then what is it?"

She looked at him in anguish, her reddened eyes flooded with tears. "I saw you die."

Chapter 19

"*What?*" Marc heard Valeria clearly enough—what she said was just too much to accept at the moment.

Oren leaned forward, his lips pulled into two thin lines. "Tell us of your vision, Valeria."

Wiping the tears from her eyes, she glanced nervously at Marc before answering their master. "There is someone who desperately wants to kill Marc. He... he *burns* with the need to do so. At first he will fail, taking another's life instead."

"Who wants to kill me?" Marc asked quickly, desperate for the truth. "And who will die?"

Her shoulders slumping in despair, Valeria slowly shook her head. "I do not know."

The master placed a hand gently on hers. "I, also, have had this vision. Marc should survive the attack."

"The first one, yes." Trembling, she stared at the fire. "But not the second."

Oren stiffened. "A *second* attack? I have never foreseen it. Tell me more."

Sensing her rising anxiety, Marc took her hand between his and looked into her eyes, concerned more for her wellbeing than his own. "Easy, Val. Tell us what you can."

Gripping his fingers tightly, she forced out her next words in a quiet, even voice. "A great evil stalks you, my love. It hates everything you are and can be. It is filled with violence, deceit and a terrible anger." Her tearful gaze swung to his. "It waits for you to challenge it."

He swallowed hard. "*Challenge* it?"

She nodded. "Only one will survive. It is crafty, hiding its weapons away. No one knows its true strength until too late." Leaning against him, she rested her head upon his shoulder.

Marc looked toward Oren. "You said I had a future, that my heirs would fight a great battle of good and evil. How can that happen if I die?"

"Future visions can change. Valeria may also see what will happen many years from now." Marc had never seen Oren appear so worried.

"No," Valeria said, firmly. "It will be soon. Of that I am certain."

Marc's heart leapt; her visions were often true. "*Master*?" he asked, nearly pleading.

Oren nervously rubbed a hand over his mouth. "Are you *certain* he dies? In your earlier visions—"

Valeria cut him off with a harsh shake of her head, her tone even more forceful, assured. "I saw it clearly. Caught off guard, Marc is struck with a dagger thrown from behind. It... it pierces his heart and he dies." Her strength melted away and she began sobbing once more.

Cradling her in his arms, Marc found this hard to accept. While he did not fear death, he hoped to live for many years before that day came. "Master, now that we are forewarned, is there any way to change what her vision reveals?"

"Possibly. Valeria and I see conflicting futures, much like you and I discussed earlier this afternoon." Oren gently put his hand on Valeria's head. "Do not mourn him yet. While your vision is powerful and seems to be true, it may not come to pass. Other events may alter what will be."

She sniffed back her tears. "I pray that is so." Kissing her forehead, Marc silently agreed.

They all remained quiet for the better part of a minute before Sean asked, "How may I help?"

"Do as Valeria," Gildas said. "Pray hard and often. Our Lord hears those whose supplications are humble and true."

"I shall. I'll urge the entire village to do so." Sean turned to his host. "Ask anything of me, Oren. I will do whatever it takes to see that Marc is safe."

For a moment, the master regarded Sean with a look of deep respect. Bowing his head, he said, "You are indeed Marc's truest friend." Visibly calmer, Oren faced his two students. "Marc.

Valeria. Be at peace, for what will be is in the Creator's hands. Do you not agree, Brother Gildas?"

"Yes. We must trust His plan will benefit all."

With a deep sigh, Oren stood. "It is probably best we all retire for the night."

The mood now spoiled, the others took the master's advice. After they bid each other well, Valeria took to her room and Marc gave Sean his sleep chamber, returning to the workshop to bed down. Unable to let go of Valeria's vision, he found it difficult to sleep. Would he really die soon? Could it be prevented somehow? Marc began praying for guidance when he heard the hushed scrape of the door opening, followed by bare feet padding toward him across the stone floor. Valeria knelt by him in the dark and the pleasant scent of lilac met his nose.

"I see you are still awake." Her voice trembled slightly.

"Who could sleep after hearing they were going to die?" His attempt at humor had the opposite effect, eliciting a moment of pain from her. "Sorry, Val. I didn't mean to—"

"Come." Taking his hand, she led him to her chamber, climbed onto her bed and pulled him after her. "Lay next to me," she whispered.

He did, lying on his left side, with her clinging to his back. Wondering what her intentions were, he probed her mind and felt sadness mixed with guilt and regret, but more than balanced by a rich and bottomless love.

She gently kissed the back of his neck. "Forgive me." Her touch filled him with a warm sense of peace.

"For what?"

"Hurting you."

"You did nothing to hurt me."

"If I hadn't had my vision, you would not be worried now." Her arm slid beneath his tunic, tenderly holding his chest.

"And I would not know what might happen. But now I have a chance to prepare, to quite possibly *prevent* that future. Maybe that was the purpose of the vision. I cannot thank you enough."

A surge of relief came from her as she held him tighter. "I love you so much. It would be terribly cruel if you were taken from me so soon. You are the man the magic has chosen for me."

"I love you, too, Val. I want nothing more than to grow old with you."

"But what if we *can't?*" Her renewed despair edged close to panic. "Oren foresaw us having heirs. That means we have to have children—at least one." She rolled away from him and pushed his tunic up until it lay bunched around his shoulders. Rolling back, she clung to him once more. The soft heat of her bare breasts against his skin startled Marc. "Make love to me, Marc. Give me our child now before anything can happen to you."

Lightheadedness washed over him; the press of her flesh against his so wonderfully intoxicating. "Val, I—"

"I know. I'm being too forward, but what else can I do? In our hearts we know we are already married. Be my husband now. Gildas can marry us in the morn, but be my husband now."

Marc had dreamt of this moment for years, and now that it was here, he did not know what to do. Turning over, he jerked his tunic the rest of the way off and began kissing her, lightly at first. Moaning with pleasure, she eagerly returned his attentions, running her hands all over his back. As their passions rose within them, the same calming inner voice he had heard before called to him. He tried to ignore it, but it persisted, gaining further hold by the second and soon managed to push aside all other thoughts. With a sigh of frustration, he let go of her and rolled onto his back.

"We can't."

Rising to rest upon an elbow, she looked at him in the dim light. "I don't understand." He clearly heard disappointment and confusion in her voice.

"We're about to make love for the wrong reason. You love me, yes, but your heart is also filled with fear and desperation."

She gently caressed his cheek. "Your love will make them depart."

"My physical love can't, but I know what will."

Holding her close, he merged their spirits as before, letting the inner voice talk to her as well. He knew her fear and panic had opened a raw, gaping wound in her soul. Letting his love flood over her, he gradually closed up that wound and washed away her pain.

After a time her mind quieted, her breathing became slow and regular. Even though she slept, the love she felt for him permeated her being, comforting him. He vowed to do whatever it took to change the outcome of her vision, if for nothing more than to give her peace of mind.

Ψ   Ψ   Ψ

Valeria found herself walking in a dense forest. While it seemed familiar, she could not identify the place. Beneath her feet, a thick carpet of leaves and humus yielded with every step. An intense, deep-blue sky spread out above her, the hue more vibrant than she had ever seen. A warm, gentle breeze spiced with the scent of flowers and trees played lightly against her bare skin. Bare skin? A quick glance down told her she was indeed nude. While unsure of the reason for her lack of dress, her state did not bother her at the moment. Looking about, she saw no one else within view, but did notice something that caught her absolute attention. To the south, through a gap in the trees, the distant sky boiled with a mass of black storm clouds. *This* she recognized.

Alarmed and feeling quite vulnerable, she took several steps back, bumping into a tree whereupon one of its branches quickly wrapped around her waist. Grasping the limb, she found it soft and warm—very un-branch-like. Smiling to herself, she realized this was a dream or vision. Could she end this now or did it have to play out? If she *were* dreaming, then she must be asleep somewhere—her bed most likely. Concentrating, she remembered bringing Marc to her bed and how his magic calmed her. She looked down at the branch around her waist. What could it represent? Of course, Marc's arm. Placing both hands on the branch, she directed her mind to wake up. Immediately her world began to fade. The sky dimmed out, objects around her melted away, vanishing into the emptiness. When everything about her had gone, Valeria opened her eyes.

Early morning light streamed horizontally through the window glass and cast its orange fire upon the far wall. Marc lay sleeping behind her, his arm curved protectively around her middle, his breath hot upon her shoulder. Having him cuddled next to her felt incredibly right. The warm strength of his body conveyed a sense of safety. And the magic! Oh, yes, the magic coming from him was tremendous. She felt privileged to hear its call, to share it with the one she loved.

The memories of last night surfaced anew, her vision of seeing him die. The pain of it had gone somehow, cleansed because of his love for her and the thing he called his inner voice. She instinctively knew the voice did not come from inside Marc, but elsewhere. It had an immense power beyond that of magic, or at least what she knew of magic. Whatever it might be, it changed and strengthened her. For that she gave thanks.

Low, muffled voices carried through the wall; the others were awake and moving about. Turning onto her other side, she faced Marc, kissing him on the mouth. A moment passed before his eyelids fluttered briefly, then opened. His lips curled into a lazy smile.

"Good morning." His fingers gently caressed the skin of her back, sending little sparks of pleasure throughout her body. "How are you feeling?"

Valeria returned the massage. "Wonderful. Thank you for easing my pain last night." She snuggled closer. "I love you so much. I wish we could stay here all day." The light in his eyes told her he agreed. "But it's time to begin the day."

"Yes, Sean will be leaving soon." Marc's gaze drifted down her body. His appreciative smile pleased her. "I should leave so you may dress."

"If you must." She wanted to bring up marriage once more but decided the time was not right.

"I must, but before I go, I want to tell you of a special dream I had last night. A dream, or possibly a vision."

"A vision?" He had had small visions before, mostly of her. She studied his face for any clue. "Was I in it?"

"You alone. I saw our wedding day—well, part of it."

Wedding day. Those two words sent a rush of excitement through her. "Tell me!"

His eyes sparkled with mischief. "I saw you in the dress you made for our wedding."

Her heart leapt within her. "What dress?"

His smile, while warm, had a bit of smugness about it. "The pale green one with the lace and embroidered flowers on it. You've kept it secret all this time. Even your mother doesn't know you've been working on it. I saw you wearing it, standing before me, your hair in braids. I've never seen you look more beautiful, Val."

Joy overcame her as his hand caressed her cheek. "Marc—" That same hand placed a finger across her lips.

"I know that day will come. That is why we can wait." He kissed her briefly, then rose. For a moment, he towered over her, watching. Bending, he picked up his tunic, smiled in an impish manner, then yanked the blanket off of her, revealing all to his view. With an affectionate laugh, he dropped the blanket on her and left.

Rolling onto her back, she threw up her arms and kicked her legs with glee, sending the blanket flying. Marc had seen their *wedding*, and she knew his vision was true. How fitting he had learned of the dress that way; the magic knew all along he was to be hers. She did not, though. Hoped, yes, and prayed as well. Her heart had been filled with him as far back as she could remember. And the dress was a manifestation of her heart's desire. Each stitch placed with him in mind, that he would be the one for which she would wear it. A cry of happiness escaped her lips.

Waiting would be easy.

Ψ   Ψ   Ψ

The morning proved pleasant enough. While no one brought up the topic of last night's disturbing vision, Valeria sensed an undercurrent of tension, especially from Sean. The banter over breakfast dealt with light topics—when the crops would come in, what their yield might be, preparations for winter. Valeria even read some of her poetry. Sean seemed to like it.

After the meal, Sean knelt by the fireplace, gathering his things to leave. "Thank you for welcoming me into your home, Oren. I know what a rare honor it is."

The master bowed slightly. "You are always welcome here." He started for the workshop. "Do not leave yet. I have something for you."

Sean glanced questioningly at Marc, then her. They both shrugged and shook their heads.

Gildas took advantage of the silence. "May the Lord grant you a safe journey home, Sean."

"Thank you." He looked thoughtfully at the monk for a moment. "Why don't you come with me to Oak Creek? Tomorrow's the Sabbath and it would be good to have you lead our services. I know you would be most welcome."

Gildas' face perked up. "That would please me very much. However, I do not know if Oren will permit me to leave." He turned toward her and Marc and winked. "It seems I am to stay here a while longer."

The rustle of hides caused Valeria to look behind her. Oren returned with something clenched in his fist.

"Sabbath in the village? By all means, Brother. The walk is not overly far and fairly level, so you will not become weakened. Return in two days time." The master nodded at Marc and Sean. "Face each other."

They complied, standing several feet apart. Oren opened his hand and an oval stone the size of a thumb tumbled out, jerking to a stop by a lace threaded through one end of it. Nearly clear, the stone had a faint, milky-green vein meandering through its center that reminded Valeria of rising smoke on a windless afternoon. The well-polished surface reflected the flames of the nearby fire.

"Extend your right hands, palm up," he said, placing the lace in Sean's hand. "Hold this tightly." Sean's fingers closed about the leather. Oren then settled the stone into Marc's palm. "Leave your hand open. This amulet will allow Sean to contact you if an important need arises."

As Sean watched in wide-eyed fascination, the master held his hand over Marc's and began a long incantation, during which the stone hovered inches above Marc's hand. Keen to learn this new magic, Valeria drank in every word. Never before had she witnessed the master working with charms or amulets, so she knew this had to be special indeed.

"Done," Oren said, placing the amulet about Sean's neck. "Keep this with you always. Should something important happen we need to know about, take it loosely in your right hand and *think* strongly about Marc. Call to him. If the magic believes your message is worthy, the stone will move within your fingers. Release it and it will float in the air before you. When it does this, speak aloud and the magic will convey your words to him."

Awestruck, Sean gaped at the stone hanging from his neck. "I... I'm not worthy of this."

Oren smiled. "Of course you are. The magic would not have allowed it otherwise."

Gingerly touching it, Sean let out a long breath. "But this holds great power."

"As do you."

"Pardon?" Sean's doubtful gaze met the master's.

Valeria found herself equally surprised.

"Your influence, your actions—they can, and will, shape Marc's future. The power within the amulet pales before that."

"I don't understand."

Oren put his hand on Sean's shoulder. "All of us here play a part in shaping Marc's destiny, but *you* will have one opportunity in particular to do so. For now, do not concern yourself with it. When that time comes, you will know what to do. Trust me in this."

"I guess... I mean, yes, I will."

While Sean further examined his gift, Oren pulled Gildas off to the far corner of the fireplace room to talk in private. Burning with curiosity, Valeria instinctively began to Envision them. As the image formed in her mind, she suddenly heard Oren say —*NO!*— Startled, she lost the vision and found Marc pulling her toward the kitchen.

"Let's gather some food for them to take on the journey home," Marc said, glancing back at the Master.

How did Oren do that? And why did her head spin so?

"They can have the bread left over from breakfast."

She looked at him, confused. "What? Why did you drag me—"

"And some dried plums. Those will do nicely." He dropped his voice to a whisper. "You were rude to listen to the master's conversation."

"I didn't mean to." She suddenly realized something. "He *talked* to me, but I heard it *inside* my mind. Then I felt odd. I still do."

He tenderly embraced her. "You'll feel better in a minute."

"What happened just now?"

"The master put his thoughts into your mind. He's done it to me, too." Letting go, he smiled at her and picked up a small square of cloth. "Now, let's gather the food I mentioned."

By the time they placed the food on the cloth and tied it into a bundle, the strange feeling had abated and they rejoined the others. Sean and Gildas said their good-byes and left. Making no mention of her transgression, Oren indicated she was to complete the robes with all due speed. He left with Marc, saying he would return by noon to give her a special lesson. Looking forward to it, she hoped the master would be in a good mood.

Chapter 20

As they left the house, Marc felt tension pouring off his master. Something worried him, but what? This was to be a teaching walk and somehow Marc knew it concerned the lesson for the day. Opening the gate, he spoke his mind.

"I sense you are troubled, Master Oren. It's about today's lesson, is it not?"

A brief chortle erupted from the old wizard as they passed under the stone arch. "Indeed. You use your talent well. However, the lesson is not one, but three. Circumstances dictate you must learn all of them today—if you are able."

Taking the path toward the Great Tree, Marc wondered why the wizard seemed doubtful. "I have learned many kinds of magic in less than an hour. Surely in one day—"

"With more rudimentary tasks, yes. But these take much practice to learn and great skill to use. They are not mastered in a day, even by those as gifted as you."

"Then show me the most basic forms and I will work through the night to learn them well. I *will* succeed, for I know I must."

Oren smiled. "Wisely said."

"So, what are they?"

"The ability to Float, create a Spark, and the magic Blade we discussed yesterday."

Rather than being daunted by the difficulty of the three tasks, Marc found himself impatient to begin, especially since he had some experience with the first one. "Float? I already did that the day I fell in Wiccan Creek."

"Yes, but you have yet to do so at will."

"I've done it before and, with your help, I'll do it again."

"Your eagerness is commendable, but a clear mind will serve you much better. Given our limited time, I may be less patient with you today."

"Do what you must."

"Very well." Marc heard the amused lilt in Oren's voice but did not have time to think about it. With a violent lurch of his stomach, he sped skyward. In seconds he found himself hovering above the highest treetops, able to see distant things with perfect clarity. Looking down, a sudden sense of falling shot through his center. Everything spun about in his mind and he instinctively flailed his arms about for balance. Suppressing his panic, he relaxed and dropped his arms to his sides, knowing Oren would keep him safe.

—*Look about yourself with the same magic you use for reading Traces,*— Oren Linked. —*What do you see?*—

While his eyes revealed nothing, Marc slowly inched his magic away from his body. When it was nearly at arm's length, he detected a considerable change in the area surrounding him. Fascinated, he checked again in several different directions learning more about its makeup. —*There is something like a fine rain falling down around me. I'm in a hollow space shaped like a cocoon, or a bubble. It appears to keep that rain out.*—

—*Correct. Find out how to push against that rain, as you call it.*—

Marc tried interacting with the boundary but found it quite frustrating, likening it to catching smoke in his hand. After several fruitless minutes without success, he studied how his master's magic touched the bubble. That gave him the clue he needed; Marc could now push at it in places.

His master's chuckle carried over the Link. —*That is cheating.*—

—*No, Master. That is learning.*—

—*Then learn to make your own bubble.*—

The rain-free space around Marc vanished and he plummeted earthward, the sudden wind whipping his cloak about his face. Fighting the panic clawing at his mind, he frantically pushed at the rain around him, but could not make anything even close to resembling Oren's bubble. As the ground rushed up to strike him, he snapped his eyes shut. Nothing happened. Opening them, he found himself settling gently upon a log. The bubble had reappeared at the last moment.

Arms crossed, Oren stood before him, a smile upon his lips. "Do you still think you will learn it this day?"

"Yes." Marc stepped down, his heart pounding from both fear and excitement.

"You now know the basics of Floating. Improve on them. I suggest you try imagining the bubble as a whole, willing it into being. The next two lessons are, in concept, quite simple, employing the same magic you just used, and yet many wizards find them most difficult to learn." From beside the path a thin twig rose to Oren's hand.

"Say you wish to light the end of this. First surround it with the proper kind of magic, then concentrate it very quickly into a tiny spot on the tip." Oren demonstrated the concept by holding up his right hand, fingers spread wide, then rapidly closing them into a fist. "Understand?"

It sounded easy enough, but so did making a bubble at first. "Yes. May I observe you do it once?"

"Certainly."

A spherical pool of the master's blue magic swirled about the end of the twig as if it were a living thing. Then, almost too quick to sense, it disappeared into the wood which caught fire.

Oren handed him the twig. "That is how you make a Spark."

Marc stared at the inch-high flame, impressed by his master's skill. "I've never made magic move that fast before."

"You will learn. Now, the magic Blade is even more difficult because you have to hold the concentrated magic together much longer than with the Spark. And, instead of making it move to a single spot, you form it into a line that functions much like the edge of a metal blade."

That seemed logical. "Understood. What will this magic cut?"

"Anything, provided you wield it skillfully enough." Oren pointed at a nearby rock. "That stone there. Suspend it before me."

As big as his head, Marc seized the stone with his magic and positioned it in front of his master, waist high. "The magic Blade can cut this?"

"With ease. Observe." Oren's magic formed above the stone, gathering itself into a short, tight line just above the surface. Once complete, it leapt rapidly at the rock, which cleanly cracked in two with barely a sound. The edges of the cut were perfectly smooth and straight.

In his surprise, Marc let go of the pieces which dropped to the earth with a twin thud. "Master! No sword could ever cleave it that way. How does this magic work?"

Oren shrugged. "If one could answer that question, they would be wiser than Solomon." Oren suspended one of the halves before him. "Now you try."

"But this is the most difficult of the three. Should I not try the Spark first?"

"I have watched you use your magic to throw rocks. In doing that, you have already learned to partially concentrate it. You need only learn how to squeeze your magic further."

Fixing his gaze upon the stone, Marc made his magic flow toward it and gather into a small cylinder. He squeezed it ever smaller, but could not make a line anywhere near as good as the master's—thin as a thread and perfectly straight. His own was larger than boot lacing and crooked as a briar branch. Thrusting it against the rock caused a few small flakes to be shed from its surface. He frowned in disappointment.

Oren grunted, then nodded. "Not bad for a first try. Concentrate on making the line smaller, straighter and striking with more force."

Pushing all other thoughts from his mind, Marc repeated the effort. The line was tighter this time and he struck it with everything he had. He was satisfied to see a chunk the size of his thumb fly from the stone.

"Excellent, Marc. I do believe that by the end of this day you may indeed split a stone, albeit a smaller one."

Oren's praise filled him with confidence. This was the most difficult of the three skills, and yet he had quickly learned to perform it. But what of the other two? The Spark seemed within his grasp since it was so close to the Blade. Floating, however, did not look easier by any account. Concentrating magic was straightforward enough, but how was he supposed to make a bubble? The only thing that gave him hope was the fact that he had done it once before. Now if he could only remember how.

Marc shared his concerns with Oren. "What advice can you give me on making bubbles?"

"Much, my young wizard. Let us continue on our way to the Forbidden Vale while I enlighten you."

As they walked, Oren shared that his greatest difficulty in learning to Float was not pushing back the rain or making the bubble, but overcoming his fear of heights. Being more than a few feet above the ground had terrified him. Marc realized his master had never before revealed a weakness to him; a clear indication he had gained the wizard's trust.

Upon entering the Vale, Oren stopped and pointed up at the Great Tree. "What can you tell me of the magic that surrounds the tree?"

Marc paused, trying to understand just what question was being asked. Sensing his elder's mood, he assumed it was posed more philosophically than literally. "It has no reason for being there and yet it is. It is neither good nor evil. Those with magic in them can feel its magic even when their own is hidden from them. It awakens that hidden self. It reveals truths that need to be learned. It strengthens the magic of those that seek it." Marc smiled, understanding the question's purpose. "It will strengthen *my* magic this day so that I may learn the lessons more quickly."

Oren beamed. "Exactly. Destiny has chosen well in bestowing magic's gifts upon you." His master walked toward the hill. "Make haste. I have little more time to spend with you."

Once at the tree, Oren worked with him at making a proper bubble. Uneven and misshapen, his first ones worked well enough for him to Float, but in order for him to actually go anywhere, he also had to simultaneously use the magic with which he moved objects. Manipulating both at the same time proved very awkward, reminding him of the time he tried to juggle. Still, he kept at it until he met with success.

"Master, this is most exciting!" Marc marveled at the foot of space between the ground and his sandals. Gently pushing up, he rose several more feet. "This is almost effortless."

Leaning on his staff, Oren gave him a wry smile and pointed past the Great Tree. "Try moving sideways."

Marc pushed horizontally and barely moved. Using much more force, he managed a casual walking speed. "This is difficult, like wading through deep water. Why is that?"

"I do not know. However, the larger the bubble, the more effort it requires to move sideways." The master paused, then added, "Since our magic comes from within us, using it tires the body much like physical work does. The more strenuous the magic, the faster we tire. This is especially true for the three skills you will learn today. If you use too much magic, eating something sweet like fruit or honey helps you regain some strength." Oren turned and began walking toward home. "Practice, young wizard. If you have an important question, Link to me but do not disturb me unnecessarily for I have much to do."

"Yes, Master."

Continuing to Float, Marc moved northward and down the path into the valley that made up the Forbidden Vale, keeping close to the ground. Nearing the bottom of the hill, he heard a faint noise reminiscent of a gentle wind blowing through trees. As he continued forward, the sound grew louder and more breath-like— a deep, continuous exhale. A terrible stench enveloped him, causing his eyes to water and the back of his throat to sting.

Alarm shot through him—the Devil's Breath! Sure enough, it sat no more than a dozen paces before him. He tried to retreat, but in his haste lost control of the bubble and tumbled to the ground, skinning up his left hip and thigh. Scrambling back up the path, he warily viewed the source of these noxious vapors—a low cairn of stones stained with whatever leaked out from beneath them. Plucking up a handful of grass, he tossed it into the air and it drifted northeast, away from him. The wind should have blown the smell away yet some still reached him—powerful vapors indeed.

Months before, when Oren warned of the dangers of this place, he said the vapors came from deep within the ground. Marc wondered just how deep. Extending his Envisioning into the earth, he followed the path the gas took through a maze of cracks and crevices until he came upon an area of shattered rock where many wedge-shaped slabs nestled together. Playing with them, he found one loose enough to move. Sliding it to one side, he widened the crack until it spanned the width of two fingers. After about fifteen seconds, a great rush of gas shrieked loudly as it erupted from the stones of the Devil's Breath.

Even though he knew the reason for the noise, it unnerved him, awakening something primal in the dark recesses of his mind. He could understand how the uninformed would fear this and equate it with evil. Lifting his gaze above the rocks, he discovered the vapors could be seen as well. Everything viewed through them shimmered and danced as if possessed. Fascinated, he followed the distortions upward and saw their effects gradually diminish.

Not far beyond the gas column, two ravens flew his way. One veered off to the side while the other continued straight into the plume. It immediately cawed loudly and flapped about, rapidly changing direction several times. Seconds later it fell to the ground, flopped twice, then lay dead. Gasping, he feared he had just unleashed a horrible danger upon the world. Earnestly hoping it could be undone, Marc quickly shifted the slab back to where he found it, and the flow ebbed, returning to where it had started.

Relieved, he decided his time was better spent practicing the lessons. Having had some initial success with Floating and the magic Blade, it was time to try the Spark. He searched the ground for something to burn. Finding a short stick, he peeled the bark off one end exposing bare wood. Nervous, Marc focused his attention on the end and gave it his all. Nothing happened. Touching the wood, he found it quite warm, but nowhere near hot enough to ignite. Again he tried, and got the same result. Frustrated, he tried six more times, adding a bit of anger to the effort. Still no change.

Perhaps the stick was too large for the magic he could create right now; the twig Oren used earlier was a third the size. Marc needed something tiny. Looking around, he found little but the abundant grass, and it was too green to burn. Then he remembered the ring of dead grass and weeds surrounding the Devil's Breath. Tinder dry, it would require much less effort to light. Fetching a few blades with his magic, he held one before him and Sparked it. A wisp of smoke briefly curled up from the pale yellow stem. He laughed. While not a complete success, it was certainly close enough.

After two more attempts, it caught fire. Exhilarated, he selected another blade and repeated his accomplishment on the first try. Challenging himself, he moved nearer to the Devil's Breath to see if he could Spark the grass around it from a distance. Wary of the scant vapors still leaking from there, he moved fully upwind and kept five paces away. Choosing a lone blade as his target, he Sparked it.

Suddenly, an incredibly loud noise and immense flash of light assaulted him as a great force slammed into his body, flinging him backwards through the air, depositing him on his already sore left side. Rolling to his feet, he shook his head to clear his mind and the ringing in his ears, then stared at where he had stood the moment before. Whatever it was had just moved him a good ten feet! Then he saw something that surprised him even more; a four-foot-tall flame rose from the center of the rocks. Incredulous, he cautiously circled around it, not knowing what to expect. Was it caused by the burning grass? No. While all the dry grass was now afire, it burned quietly with a low, calm flame. The large flame clearly came from where the vapors exited the earth.

The Vapors burn! It seemed miraculous that something unseen burned as if a great pile of wood were in its place. How large would the flame become if he were to let more of the vapors escape? Eager to see, he ran fifty paces up the path toward the Great Tree and moved the slab once more. After the same delay as before, the flame sprang to life, rapidly growing until it towered over thirty feet high. A great roar fill his ears, mightier than the rapids of a river, and its light rivaled that of the sun. He approached it but soon stopped—thirty paces distant—for the heat became too intense to venture further. Worried that the nearby trees might catch fire, he moved the slab fully back into its crevice, even tighter than before. The flame soon dwindled to a small flicker which sputtered away to nothing.

Squatting on his heels, Marc stared at the opening in the rocks. This truly was a marvel. He remembered Oren talking about show. This was definitely the best kind of show he could imagine. It should have an equally impressive name as well, something akin to Devil's Breath that described how a massive flame might come from the earth. A terror so frightful one might think the very gates of Hell had opened, letting slip some of the fire used to torment the sinful. A wide grin expanded on his face. Yes, *Hell's Gate* sounded perfect. Chuckling, Marc realized he was becoming quite comfortable with his role as a wizard. Did any of his predecessors know that the vapors burned in this fashion? He imagined seeing Oren's master, Arturius, demonstrating to the nearby villagers why they should not enter the Forbidden Vale. A great fire from Hell's Gate would have been enough to keep even the most skeptical person away. Even him. Well, the *old* him.

Elated, Marc could not wait to share his discovery. — *Master. I've got great news—*

—*Not now,—* Oren said, then abruptly broke the Link. Instead of being irritated at being disturbed, the master seemed excited about something. While curious as to what Oren was up to, he quickly suppressed the temptation to Envision him. If it was something he needed to know, the master would tell him later. Rising, he stomped out the remnants of the burning grass and made sure no fire remained to threaten the forest.

Thrilled that he had learned the spark fairly well, Marc concentrated the rest of his time on practicing Floating and the Blade. Each time he felt his ability and understanding had improved enough, he moved further away from the Great Tree's influence. If he was to truly learn these skills, it would have to be without any outside help.

It was late in the afternoon and he was about five hundred paces from the tree when he felt Valeria's spirit touch him—she was cheerful to the point of bursting. Less than a minute later, he again he felt her joy. Was she trying to contact him? Risking Oren's displeasure, Marc allowed himself a brief peek. His magic found her in the workshop, dancing about the room while Oren looked on, smiling. The master looked in his direction, nodding in acknowledgment. Marc *knew* why she was so happy.

—*Val just learned the Great Secret, hasn't she, Master?—*

Chapter 21

Exhausted, Marc walked on. Even with the help of the Great Tree, the day's practice had drained him, both mentally and physically, and he looked forward to getting home. Cresting the last rise, his heart leapt as he caught sight of the great stone wall. Almost there. As he neared it, the structure loomed over him, nearly twice his height, its shadow trailing off some ten paces in the late afternoon sun. Turning, he walked along its length, running his hand across the surface. Even though he had done this dozens of times, he still marveled at the variety of textures and colors of the rocks used to build it. Some were rough to the touch, light gray granite, flecked with bits of black, blue and pink. Others were smoother, like quartz, with irregular ribbons of dark stone running through a translucent dirty-white. Then there was the black, shiny stone; he knew of no name for it. Its surface was nearly perfect in its smoothness, with edges formed of jagged crests that were as sharp as a well-honed knife. Framing everything was a mantle of gray-white mortar.

In a way, the wall gave him comfort. It meant something to him, but he wasn't sure what. Maybe the protection it offered, or perhaps it spoke of the reverence shown to past wizards. Marc knew that these walls, and the area inside of them, were part of him. He belonged here. This was his home now, not Oak Creek. Slipping through the gate, he hurried toward the house, eager to share the day with Val and Master Oren.

She met him at the door, her smile wide and eager, her eyes alive with excitement. As she kissed him firmly, it surprised him to hear, —*I love you, Marc.*—

Breaking the kiss, he gently held her face with both hands and looked into her eyes, Linking as gently as he could, —*And I love you.*— She winced, causing him to remember his own pain when he first learned to communicate mind to mind. "No more

Linking for now." He kissed her forehead. "I'm so happy for you. Now you will learn everything."

Valeria stepped back, looking him up and down with interest. "Your power has grown much since this morning and—" Her gaze fell upon his left side. "You're injured. What happened to your leg?"

He gave her a lopsided grin. "I had a few mishaps while practicing my lessons."

"Come in and let Valeria attend to your injuries," Oren called from the doorway. "She needs a rest from learning magic, and I from teaching it. Having two apprentices is much work for this old wizard." With a heavy sigh, the elder reentered the house.

Taking Marc's hand, Valeria led him inside. "I want to hear all about today."

After being deposited near the fireplace, Marc told of his training and practice while Valeria cleansed his wounds. When he spoke of altering the flow of the vapors, Oren took great interest.

"At one time I sought the source of the Devil's Breath, but it seemed to have no bottom. Tell me more."

"I found no bottom, either. But I did find a place where I can change how the vapors come out." As Marc shared his experience, his audience listened with rapt attention.

"Remarkable." Oren said. "If my memory is correct, no wizard has ever controlled the vapors in that way. Let us refer to the wizard's journal."

Wizard's journal? Marc had not heard of this before. The master's magic extended beyond him into the workshop. Moments later, a large, flat book glided into the room and through the air to Oren's hands.

"This is a chronicle of the major events that have taken place in the lives of the wizards who have served here. The first entry was made three hundred and ninety six years ago." Opening it, Oren searched through the aged parchment. "There was a time when the Breath flowed strongly for years."

Valeria carefully touched the binding of the book. "Why have you not shown us this until now?"

"The journal is to be seen only by those wizards who know the great truth for the entries herein are written openly. No pretense to casting spells is mentioned. Even so, we are careful to

217

avoid any mention of the secret should this somehow fall into the wrong hands." Oren's finger slid down the outside margin of the vellum and stopped near the bottom. "Yes, here it is. Elnorus reports of a time the earth shook all over the land. That day he found the Devil's Breath to be yielding a much larger quantity of vapors, so much that even from a half-mile away the air was most unpleasant. He tried everything to halt it but the flow continued." Oren scanned further ahead. "Ah. Almost six years later it ceased after the ground shook once more." Closing the book, Oren Floated it over to the table, then smiled at him. "Marc, you are the first wizard to master the Devil's Breath. Well done." A look of fatherly pride almost glowed from the master's face.

While he appreciated Oren's compliment, Marc could hardly contain himself. "But that is nothing compared to what happened next." He quickly told about making a spark near the vapors. "It was hotter than a hundred fires. Then I undid everything and the flame died away. I'm thinking of calling it Hell's Gate. What do you think?"

Oren, who until now had been bent forward, focused on Marc's every word, leaned back into the cushions behind him. "Astounding." His mouth moved silently as if searching for words. "Utterly astounding. I must see this."

Val took Marc's hand, squeezing it almost to the point of pain. "I must as well. Let's see it now."

The keen glint in her eyes told him she was ready to run there if need be, but he did not feel like making the journey. Not only was he very tired, but his left knee and hip had grown more tender as the evening progressed. "I need to rest and so does Master Oren."

"Very much so," Oren said, putting a foot upon a stool. "He will demonstrate this remarkable discovery in the morning." Valeria began to protest but Oren lifted his hand in the manner he often used while teaching. "As we discussed earlier, madam witch, someone with our powers needs to be in better control of their impulses."

She deflated like a water skin being poured out. "Yes, Master. Today was so grand, so exciting—" Her smile returned. "To have seen the great flame would have been the perfect end to the day."

"Then tomorrow it will be all the more special." The master looked at Marc. "What happened after you learned to open *Hell's Gate?*" Oren chuckled. "Good name."

Marc could not help but grin. "Thanks."

While telling about the remainder of his day, the aroma of baking bread grew ever stronger. After the meal, Oren retired for the night and Valeria shared her adventure. Halfway through it, she yawned, stretched out and rested her head in his lap. Stroking her silken tresses through his fingers, Marc heard little more of her tale for within a minute she had fallen asleep.

Ψ   Ψ   Ψ

Eager to see Hell's Gate, Valeria woke Oren and Marc up at dawn and hurried them down the path to the Forbidden Vale. Marc found it amusing that his master needed little encouragement. On the way, Oren had him teach Valeria to read Traces. She was most adept. By the time they reached Wiccan creek, her skill was equal to his. He asked the wizard why that was so.

"Men and women usually differ in their magical strengths. The gentler of the two," Oren said, gesturing toward Valeria, "are often blessed with a greater ability in some magical areas—visions, reading Traces and sensing other's thoughts and emotions. Men tend to be stronger in the physical aspects—moving things, Floating, the Spark and the Blade. The remaining abilities do not seem to favor either gender." Oren pointed his staff over the creek. "Show us how well you have mastered Floating. Carry us to the other side."

Marc's gut tightened. "I'm not ready. I can barely Float me, but to do you or Val—"

Valeria took his hand and squeezed it. "You can do it. Send me first for I am lighter than Master Oren."

Looking toward his master, Marc saw an encouraging nod. "Go easy. Concentrate."

Taking a deep breath, Marc cleared his thoughts and faced Valeria. "Hold still." He surrounded her with his magic and, with great care, slowly crafted a bubble. The quality of it surprised him. Never had he made one about himself that good. As she rose into the air, she remained calm and relaxed. Her trust bolstered his confidence. Slowly pushing her across the water, he gently lowered her to the earth and released the bubble.

"Very smooth," she said, clapping. Her smile warmed his heart. "Now the Master."

With a short bow in his direction, Oren folded his arms across his chest and stood ready. In moments Marc had him airborne and, shortly thereafter, deposited next to Valeria. For the third time he created a bubble, this time about himself. It lacked the quality of his first two but proved adequate enough. As he landed next to the others, Oren clapped.

"Well done. As you see, creating your own bubble is the most difficult."

Marc was about to discuss that oddity when Valeria took his hand and pulled him westward. "On to the flame."

Laughing, he let her lead the way. When they reached the Devil's Breath it was quiet; no vapors rose from its stones. Once they were safely positioned over fifty paces upwind, Marc first demonstrated how the unlit vapors screamed as they left the earth.

"It is very loud," Valeria shouted over the noise.

"Quite," Oren agreed.

—You may have the honor of Sparking it, Master,— Marc said.

A surge of delight came from the old man. *—Thank you.—*

Oren began an incantation, then caught himself, causing Marc and Valeria to laugh. Marc felt the pulse of magic fly from his master toward the source of the vapors. Immediately, it seemed as if the entire sky was alight in a blinding flash. At the same instant a great clap of thunder hammered painfully against his ears. All three of them ducked and put their hands to the sides of their heads, but by then the worst of it had passed. The great flame stood tall and strong, long tendrils of fire spiraling through its length.

Marc observed the others. Valeria fought her fear, but enjoyed the experience just the same. Oren, on the other hand, laughed like a boy, his face aglow from more than just the fire; wonder graced his master's countenance. Oren gave him a quick embrace.

—This is fabulous, Marc. For all my life I have seen such a fire in my dreams, but until now I did not know what it was. Thank you so much.—

As his master turned back toward the flame, Marc grasped what had just happened. His discovery of Hell's Gate had been foreseen long before his birth or even that of his grandfather. That fact overwhelmed him. He had experienced several visions of his own, but until now never truly recognized them for the awesome miracle they were—gifts from God. Only He knew the future and could pass that knowledge on in the form of visions. Marc wondered again why he was one so privileged.

After he extinguished the flame, they made their way to the tree. There Valeria quickly learned to read other's thoughts and emotions. While glad for her, he also found himself slightly envious that her abilities in these areas exceeded his own.

The remainder of the day was spent teaching Valeria to Float—or trying to. Although she continued to give it her best effort, she was unable to create the magic that made the bubble. Hours had passed when Valeria sat on the ground and hung her head in frustration.

"Oh, it cannot be done."

Marc regretted his earlier jealousy toward her. He had to help somehow. Kneeling beside her, he looked up at Oren. "Do you know how I can help her?"

"Yes. The answer can be found if you think like a wizard. Consider it a lesson."

Marc thought hard. How could he tell her in a way that he had not already tried? Words were so inadequate when it came to describing the way magic worked. He learned to make his own bubbles by copying Oren, but she already tried that and could not sense the magic. If she could only experience it like he did. He chuckled. Of course, the answer was obvious.

He rose. "Stand." When she was before him, he gazed deeply into her eyes and merged their spirits. While so joined, he demonstrated how he created the proper magic, allowing her to know it as intimately he did. Once she was able to duplicate it without his help, he separated from her. "Try it."

Slowly and unsteadily, Valeria created a crude bubble about herself and Floated up several feet. She began to clap which upset part of the bubble, toppling her onto the ground. "Ow." She inspected the skinned palms of her hands then smiled at him despite the pain he knew she felt.

He pointed at his bruised knee. "I did that a few times, too. That was good."

She held him tightly, trembling with excitement. "Thanks."

"I wish I had thought of that sooner."

Oren smiled warmly at them. "Well done, Valeria."

She let go of him and gave the wizard a little bow. "Thank you, Master."

"Practice it often. Your progress will be slower than Marc's, but you will improve. Do not worry about the spark or the Blade. Save those for another day." The master retrieved his staff and faced Marc. "Do not return until she can do so unassisted by way of the caves." Oren turned and left.

Valeria took a deep breath and let it out, squaring her shoulders. "It seems I have been challenged. Do you think I will learn it well enough to do as the master has ordered?"

He kissed her on the tip of her nose. "That depends if you clap any more."

"Ha!" A playful gleam flashed in her eyes. "I'll learn it so well that *you* will be the one clapping."

Marc put his hands on her hips and pulled her close. "Brave talk from a lowly apprentice. You should be cautious of angering the mighty wizard who teaches you."

"But I know how to calm the wizard's temper." She kissed him passionately for a moment.

"Indeed you do." He gazed into her eyes and felt his knees weaken. "You command a great and mysterious magic—" Marc quickly Floated up beyond her reach. "—but only if I am near. Cast your spell on me now, witch."

Looking up, she smiled mischievously. "I shall before this day is over."

Chapter 22

It was a warm, sunny morning and Marc tended the garden along with Valeria and Gildas. He had just finished tying up the last row of berry vines when the master led him and Valeria to the woods outside the compound.

"I am pleased with the progress you both have made. In the two weeks since learning to Float, you have come close to mastering that necessary skill. Today you will learn another, equally important, form of magic: illusion. Tell me, have either of you seen a dragon?"

Marc thrilled at the thought. "No, but I'd certainly like to."

Valeria's eyes widened. "I have heard many tales of dragons. Do they really breathe fire?"

The wizard chuckled. "They do whatever you want them to."

"Pardon?"

"They exist only in the imaginations of skilled wizards." Oren suddenly extended his staff to his right, pointing at the treetops. "Look. Over there, above that chestnut tree."

Following his master's gaze, Marc froze in place for, several hundred paces away, a great beast flew through the air. Its long, snake-like body writhed with each beat of its wide, leathery wings. Its color was that of dried blood and each massive foot hung low, heavy with wickedly curved claws. Taking a faltering step back, Valeria gasped loudly and the dragon whipped its gaze in their direction.

Oren let out a little cluck of dismay. "It appears we have been discovered."

Marc's pulse pounded in his ears. "How does one defend against a dragon?" he asked, his voice almost breaking from the tension. Also alarmed, Valeria slid behind him as the master thoughtfully pulled on his beard.

"A good question for I have never been attacked by one," Oren said as if casually discussing the weather.

The creature stretched wide its wings, wheeled sharply in the sky and sped straight for them. A chill sweat broke on Marc's brow and part of his thoughts screamed for him to flee to the safety of the trees. How could Oren remain so calm? "Master! Do something."

"Why? There is nothing to fear."

Pulling his gaze from the approaching threat, Marc reached for his weapon but found only empty space at his side; he had left the house without his knife. What about a magical weapon? The Blade? Could it be used against a moving target? Glancing about, he sought shelter.

There was none they could reach in time.

The dragon drew close enough that Marc saw its malevolent eyes; two glowing embers fixed keenly upon him. He watched in terror as its mouth snapped open, spitting out a stream of boiling fire. Whirling about, he did his best to shield Valeria as the flames engulfed them. He braced himself for the searing pain that never came.

"What?" He quickly looked about but saw no trace of the beast. "Where did it go?"

The master began to laugh and Valeria joined him. "Where did what go?" Oren laughed harder.

Marc then remembered the two demons used to scare Portaeus and began to laugh himself. "It's an illusion. You tricked us."

"No, you tricked yourselves. I clearly stated dragons do not exist, but you *wanted* to believe they did. Learn this lesson well. People will often believe what they want to, even after being told the truth."

"But it seemed so real," Valeria said, grinning. "I'm impressed."

The master dipped his head her way. "Thank you. I am proud of my little pet. It is my best illusion."

Marc wiped the perspiration off his face with his sleeve. "Your pet?"

"In a way. I spent decades perfecting that dragon. It has become a part of me."

He glanced once more at the now empty sky. "How did you make us see it?"

"I first created the image of the dragon in my mind, down to the last detail. While it may sound simple enough, it is difficult to maintain the needed concentration. If it is not vivid to me, it will not be so for those whom I wish to influence. Then I *Pushed* the illusion of the dragon into your minds. Pushing is essentially the opposite of probing another's thoughts."

"But I didn't just see it," Valeria said, "I heard it, too."

"Illusions can include any of the senses as well as emotions, but images are the most challenging. Also, the more people you wish to affect, the more difficult it becomes." Oren leaned on his staff and chuckled. "Seeing the two of you react to my illusion was most satisfying."

"Teach us this, Master," Valeria asked.

"Yes," Marc said. "Illusions would be most useful, especially if guile is needed."

Oren shared a crafty little smile with them. "Exactly. Let us begin the lesson."

Ψ   Ψ   Ψ

As with all the higher forms of magic, illusion required much effort and time to learn. Marc had meager success but Valeria took to it quickly, first learning how to Push sounds and thereafter making every nearby object talk to him. While entertaining at first, it soon became annoying, especially when it distracted him from his own efforts.

Moving away from the others, he found a quiet place to practice. He tried to create something simple, the image of an egg, but could not maintain it for more than a few seconds because a lightheaded feeling repeatedly came over him. At first he wondered if Valeria was trying something else out on him. No, her illusions—her magic—had a certain texture to them. Using the knowledge he had learned so far, Marc narrowed the sensation down to one of two things—a form of Linking or a thought probe. Again he felt it and immediately opened his magic to observe it. The source of it surprised him.

—*Master. Val. Sean is trying to contact me.*—

Excited, he quickly Envisioned Sean and found him standing in the doorway of Garrett's home, holding onto the amulet as he had been told. Reaching out over the miles between them, Marc tried to connect with the stone. Only after focusing all of his mind on the task could he make the stone quiver within Sean's hand. With a start, Sean opened his fingers and Marc suspended it before the other's face.

—*Can Marc hear me?*— Sean asked the amulet, wide-eyed in wonder. Marc made it bob once. Taking a nervous gulp of air, Sean continued. —*Thaddeus just left here. He said we have one day in which to swear allegiance to lord Crowe as the new king. He will return tomorrow for our answer. Garrett wants Oren to come right away.*—

The news so startled Marc that he lost control over the stone and it fell back to Sean's chest. Shaking off his lapse, he lifted the stone once more but did not know how to acknowledge the message. Two sets of footfalls rapidly approached, Valeria and Oren. "Master—"

"We have Envisioned it as well. Valeria, use your new magic to tell Sean we will be there by nightfall."

She quickly looked at the master, eyebrows raised. "I can Push an illusion that far?"

"I believe so. Have the stone speak to him only."

Valeria nodded her assent, closed her eyes and went still in concentration. Her glow brightened for a short time after which Sean nodded. —*Thank you, magic stone.*—

Marc released the stone and ended the Envisioning. "What did you say?"

"To make it more special I had the amulet speak in poetic verse. I said:

> *The magic has heard your words,*
> *and passed along your plight.*
> *Two wizards and a witch will help,*
> *they journey here tonight.*"

Placing a hand gently on her shoulder, Oren said, "Excellent use of show, Valeria." The elder's pleasure faded to be replaced with unease. "I feared something like this would happen. We leave for Oak Creek as soon as we are packed."

Ψ　　　Ψ　　　Ψ

Grunting, Marc struggled under the load strapped to his shoulders. His pack bulged with the many things the master wanted to take: two monks robes, a week's worth of food for the three of them, all kinds of dried herbs and medicinal powders, several blankets and skins plus other assorted supplies.

"Too tight?" Valeria tugged on his right strap.

"No, too heavy. Let me help you with yours."

Valeria faced the large table in the greeting room, picked up her pack and handed it to him. Threading one arm through a strap, she turned so he could lift the other side onto her shoulder. While not as full as his, her burden was far from light. As he adjusted her straps, Oren and Gildas entered the room.

The master briefly examined the packs. With a nod to them, Oren turned to the monk. "We will be off, Brother. Now is the time for you to go as well for this place will no longer be safe. Head north to Bitter Well, the next village. Seek out Leahenfehr. Tell him what has happened at Oak Creek and that they will not support Crowe." Oren put his hand on Gildas' shoulder and looked him in the eye. "Tell him *I* said Crowe is not to be trusted."

Marc knew that while Leahenfehr was a decent enough leader, he rarely took advice from outside of his inner circle. Oren counted on using the reputation he had developed over the years to ensure the man would do as he wished. Marc wondered if he would ever be that highly regarded.

Gildas nodded respectfully. "I will do so my friend."

"Take much food with you and whatever you may need in the way of supplies. Take this as well." From beneath his robe Oren produced a fist-sized bag of coins, so full that the stitching of the seams pulled taut, and placed it in Gildas' hand.

"I cannot." Shaking his head, Gildas tried to give it back but Oren refused.

"Many will kindly give you shelter and food on your journeys. This is for those who will not."

Gildas drew the bag to his chest and bowed slightly. "You are most generous."

"No more than our God has been to me."

"Amen. Thank you for your hospitality, friendship and wisdom." Gildas addressed Marc and Valeria. "And I again thank both of you for my life. I know now that our Heavenly Father led you to me."

Marc felt a wry smile grow on his lips. "Then you accept that magic is not evil."

Gildas smiled and nodded slightly. "I must confess, the magic the three of you command is good. I cannot speak thus for any other magic."

He chuckled warmly. "I'll take that as a yes."

With a satisfied grin, Valeria leaned toward the monk and kissed his cheek, causing him to blush.

After their final good-byes, Gildas sent them on their way with a heartfelt blessing. Barely past the gate, Marc realized how much he would miss his friend; the memory of this monk would last for the rest of his life.

"Master, you once said Gildas had an important destiny. Do you know what it is?"

"Yes, but perhaps Valeria can tell us something of his future."

"I'll try." She stopped and closed her eyes, her aura brightening. "He will be well known for many years, centuries even. His writings will be read by great scholars. I believe he will be... an historian."

"Very good. Will you ever meet him again?"

"Oh, yes. Several times."

The old wizard leaned on his staff, pride clearly showing on his face. "Even though you are both still new to the ways of magic, your gifts have borne fruit. Let us make haste for the village awaits us."

Ψ   Ψ   Ψ

When they were about an hour from Oak Creek, Oren led them eastward off the path and toward the northern end of Rocky Hill. Marc glanced at the steep and nearly impassable slope ahead.

"Why are we going this way?"

"A shortcut to save us time."

Marc knew of no shortcut in this area. The remainder of the path led south around the hill for good reason—it was far easier going that way than trying to climb over it. But that limitation did not apply to wizards.

"You intend to Float over Rocky Hill."

"Correct. While I would prefer not to reduce the strength of our magic, the need to arrive quickly prevails. The heart of the village lies directly across from this point."

That sounded fine to Marc. His feet—and back—could use the rest. Following Oren, he and Valeria rose high into the air and drifted toward Oak Creek. He knew being this far above the ground bothered her, but she did not complain and kept up with them. Marc worried about another matter; it seemed certain the test he was to face would likely take place in the next day or two.

What few things he had learned about the coming trial passed through his mind. Like Valeria's vision of the dagger piercing his heart, and the evil, black-robed man who wanted him dead. Could this be the same faceless specter who haunted his own dreams? Was he part of the test? Marc hated not knowing when the trial would come and what it would be.

"Marc," Valeria said, enthusiastically pointing downward, "look at our village. It's very different when viewed from above."

Releasing his concerns, he gazed at the approaching rooftops. Not many people were visible, but those he saw moved about with a purpose. None were aware of three wizards descending into their midst. A blue-gray column of smoke rose from the hole in the roof of the common house, a sure sign the men were discussing what to do about Thaddeus' visit. Would they choose to give in to Crowe's threat, or be making plans for war? If he knew the other men as well as he thought he did, it would be war.

Glancing to the left, he looked at his mother's house. That struck him oddly. *His mother's house.* By now he was so used to living in the home of the wizards that he no longer considered the humble structure below to be his. Had he really changed that much? Looking again he saw his two sisters next to the doorway. The eldest stopped suddenly as if hearing a noise and turned to look directly at him. As she shrieked, he felt fear, then amazement, come from her.

"Marc?" she called out, shielding her eyes with a hand.

"It's me, Gwen." He laughed as she began running around, shouting for everyone to look up. Observing her closer, he saw something that truly surprised him. "Master, my sister has *magic*. It's weak, but I see her glow."

"Both of your sisters have magic in them for they are also children of your father."

Stunned, Marc could not yet voice the next question forming in his mind, but apparently Valeria's thoughts paralleled his own. "Will you teach them to use their magic as well?"

"There will come a time to do so but their gifts are less than yours and Marc's. They may never come to know the true secret. Do not speak to them of this for now."

Gwen's actions caused quite a number of villagers to come out into the open and stare upward. Some were fearful, some fascinated, but all focused on either him or Valeria. Oren guided them toward the space north of the common house where most of the people had gathered.

—*Good show, Master.*—

—*I am pleased you noticed. This grand entrance will leave no doubt that you and Valeria are powerful in the ways of magic.*—

As Marc's feet touched the ground, Gwen and Stella rushed forward and quickly hugged him, then Valeria.

"You can fly!" Gwen said, nearly squealing in her glee.

He gave his sisters a big smile. "Yes, we can, and it's fun." That set them to giggling. The other villagers held back, seemingly unsure about the situation. Garrett exited the common house and came forward to shake their hands. "Thank you all for arriving so soon. Come in and rest as we plan how to defend our homes."

War it was.

Once everyone had crowded into the common house, Garrett summarized what had been discussed so far. Most of it had to do with different ways to lie in wait for Crowe's men and what additional weapons could be fashioned in the time remaining. Oren listened patiently to everyone, then spoke.

"Do we know their number?"

Garrett shook his head. "No. We were talking about sending out scouts when you arrived."

"That would be dangerous, both for the scouts and for the village. Crowe will be expecting that. If the scouts are detected, he will immediately move on Oak Creek."

Many of the people nodded their heads. Garrett sighed. "That was our concern as well. But we *must* know how many men he has and where they are in order to plan our attack. Who knows, he might only have a handful. This could be little more than a bluff."

Ethan stood. "I am willing to risk my life to scout for the village."

Marc felt Valeria's concern and took her hand. If any in their midst could successfully spy on Crowe, it would be Ethan. His stealth and hunting prowess were renowned. Marc remembered that many of the hides he and his father had tanned were the result of Ethan's bow.

"I, too, will scout," said another.

"I would be honored to do so." Marc knew that voice well. Donald stood with the other two.

Garret waved for his son to sit. "Only the men are permitted."

Anger flashed through Donald's eyes. "What *better* way to prove I am worthy of manhood."

Oren rose. "There is no need for any of you to put yourselves at risk. Marc and I will scout."

Marc's body tensed at hearing that. While willing to risk his life, it would have been better if Oren had asked him first. Silence filled the space as everyone gave them curious looks.

"As many of you have guessed by now, Marc and Valeria are learning magic from me. They are well on their way to becoming an accomplished wizard and witch." He paused a moment before continuing. "The magic is not pleased with Crowe or his motives for coming to your village. It is our ally against such evil and will help us in our fight. The magic will allow Marc and I to spy unseen."

As a murmur of appreciation rose up, Marc saw Donald scowling at him and Valeria. His former friend's gaze shifted downward, clearly noticing they held hands. Marc could not help but feel the raw hostility that filled Donald's mind. With one last spiteful glance, Donald moved past them and slipped outside.

Valeria squeezed his hand. —*We have to tell him about us.*—

Marc gazed at her with sadness. —*He already knows.*—

Ψ   Ψ   Ψ

After the meeting, Oren told Marc to join him south of the village, near the edge of the great forest.

"I am here, Master."

"Are we being observed?"

Stretching out his magic, Marc found no one within several hundred paces. "No."

"The sun has just set and the time is good to see what we can find out about Crowe. Float up higher than you have ever done before. From there you will be able to see a great distance. Look for movements of men on the roads and paths. For once your eyes will serve you better than your magic."

"Am I to do this alone?"

"My own eyes are too weak for the task."

"Well, if I can see them, can they not also see me?"

"You will be but a speck in the sky. Once you see anything worth investigating, return to the ground and we will Envision it to learn more."

That made sense. Floating up several feet, he crossed his legs, ankles atop opposing thighs, and gathered the bottom of his robe into his lap before rising skyward.

—*Why did you do that?*— Oren asked.

—*To look less like a man. From a distance I will appear more like a bird.*—

Oren laughed through the Link. —*Quite clever of you.*—

Marc continued to rise until he was indeed higher than he had ever been before. Looking straight down, he fought the queasy feeling trying to overcome him. He estimated his elevation at nearly a mile. —*Is this high enough?*—

—*Quite. What do you see?*—

Looking to the northwest, he saw home, the Great Tree, the hot springs and many other landmarks he knew well. Turning southward, he clearly saw the pattern the paths and roads made on the land. There was Broken Rock and the area where Gildas had lain. Scrutinizing the roads beyond, Marc saw little sign of an army.

—*I see no one on the roads.*— A brown smudge further off caught his attention. It looked to be a thin, horizontal cloud that spread out to the east for many miles. It seemed to originate just to the east of Red Cliffs and, judging from its proximity to the Roman road, it probably came from their nearest neighbor.

—I see smoke in the distance. I believe from Fox Glen.—

After a brief pause, Oren tersely Linked, *—Return to my side.—*

Marc rapidly dropped down, slowing in time to make a gentle landing. Expecting a compliment from his master, he instead found him to be upset. "What is wrong?"

"See the evil man can do," Oren said, bitterly. "Envision Fox Glen."

Marc brought the image of that village into his mind—and nearly threw up. He saw the remains of a hut, its burned-out shell still smoldering. In the center of it lay the charred corpses of two adults and a child, their bodies twisted into grim shapes. A quick check of other nearby huts found more of the same grisly visage. In all, over half the village was lost to fire. Elsewhere bodies covered the ground, most with savage wounds from swords and battle axes. Unable to take any more, Marc pushed the vision away. Fighting off nausea, he struggled to keep his voice steady.

"Dear God! They were butchered without mercy." A wave of anger washed over him as a clear thought came hard to the forefront of his mind. "Crowe did this."

A tear rolled down the old wizard's cheek. "It seems obvious he is responsible. We must journey there to be certain." Oren sighed heavily. "I am sorry you had to experience that, but this is one reason you have been given your power. You, Valeria and I are here to protect others from those like Crowe." Shaking his head, the wizard started for Oak Creek. "We will discuss this later. After it is fully dark, we will once more search for Crowe's camp. Their fires will lead us to them."

Marc made a silent vow that whomever committed these heinous acts would pay for their sins. No matter how much risk he would have to take, justice would be meted out. And then, in that moment, he realized this must be the test he would face.

Chapter 23

Marc sat on one of the benches before the village altar, away from his former neighbors, and ate his meal in silence. Images of murdered villagers haunted him, still vivid in his mind. He knew some of those people and it seemed difficult to accept they were dead. That the whole of Fox Glen was gone, no more. Maybe some of them managed to escape. He hoped so. He struggled to understand how anyone could slaughter an *entire* village. What kind of madness possessed them? The mindless carnage of it sickened his soul. Footfalls interrupted his thoughts as Oren and Valeria came to sit on either side of him. He sensed the elder's unease.

"Master?"

The old wizard regarded them a moment before speaking. "I have to tell you something important, but I have been reluctant to do so until now." Oren stared at the ground. "It is difficult." Regret and sadness emanated from his teacher

Valeria leaned past Marc and put her hand atop Oren's. "If we are to know this, then speak it without fear of how we might react. Truth is truth."

The master's face rose to meet hers. "You are a wise and gentle person. I pray you remain so." Patting her hand, Oren sat up straight. "There is no easy way to say this so I will be blunt." The wizard's gaze locked with Marc's, sending a chill through his body. "There will come a day when one or both of you will have to kill someone."

Shocked, Marc recoiled a bit, bumping against Valeria. "You want us to commit *murder*?"

"*Never*. But you will undoubtedly encounter evil men who lack goodness or mercy in their hearts, their souls filled with wickedness. The worst of these criminals are the ones you may have to act against." The wizard's voice softened. "Like the men who murdered the people of Fox Glen."

What did Oren ask of him? Criminal or not, Marc had no wish to become an executioner. "I could kill, but only in defense of myself or another. Even then I would rather use my magic to render them harmless in some way, much as you did with Portaeus."

Oren slowly nodded. "That is often the best choice. Still, there will be occasions when you *must* kill because otherwise the person will continue to do evil. You and Valeria are able to judge them wisely for you can look into their minds and know their crimes and intentions. After we encountered Portaeus, you asked me why I spared his life. Even then, without the skills you now possess, you knew he was corrupt and unworthy of the life the Creator had given him. Did he not deserve to die?"

"Yes, but you changed him, put the fear of God in him."

"No, I put the fear of *me* in him. Once away from us he reverted to his old ways." Oren stood and faced them, a sorrowful cast to his gaze. "Think much on this. I will be with Garrett if you need me."

Once the master left, Marc turned to Valeria. "I need to walk about. Join me?"

Her smile lifted his spirits. "Certainly."

Departing the village center, they headed east into the trees. The cool fragrance of the forest and the warmth of her hand in his did little to settle his thoughts. Until now he believed being a wizard only meant helping people, a role he gladly accepted. But this new responsibility promised to be most unwelcome.

Valeria pulled him closer, bringing their sides together. "Your thoughts reflect mine."

She always found a way to make him feel better. Sometimes it only took her presence. "Who am I to judge someone's fate? I'm as sinful as the next man." They walked a while in silence before he quietly asked, "Could you kill someone, Val?"

They continued for several dozen paces, then she sighed and gave a single, firm nod. "If need be. Remember the day you fought off the wolves, when Thaddeus pointed that spear at you? If I had command of my magic that day, I would have killed him and felt no guilt over it. And it's not just because I love you, but because he intended to murder another."

"But Oren didn't—" Marc froze in place, his whole being tingling.

Still holding on to him, Valeria stopped as well, dropping her voice to a whisper. "What's wrong?"

—Keep silent. I sense a threat nearby.—

She looked about. *—Where?—*

He stretched out his magic and found a man trying to approach the village unseen. *—Southeast. See him?—*

Her magic surged outward, heading in the direction he indicated. Moments later, he felt her Envision the stranger. *—Yes. He may be a spy for Crowe's camp.—*

—We better warn the village.— Marc Linked to Oren. *— Master?—*

—Yes?—

—A man is creeping toward the village, about four hundred paces off to the southeast. He carries only a short sword with no pack or torch. We think he may be a spy.—

—Return immediately. I will have everyone hide the weapons they have been making, then meet in the common house. We must make the spy believe we intend to side with Crowe.—

As he and Valeria hurried back, Marc appreciated all the practice Oren had put him through. Without it he may have never sharpened his skills enough to detect the spy so early.

Entering the village near the common house, Valeria veered to the right. "Oren hasn't finished telling everyone yet. I'll take the people to the north. You go south."

"Agreed." Quickly sweeping the arc of huts to his left, Marc quietly informed everyone of the news then headed for the common house with the rest of the villagers. The tense emotions in the room ran high, nearly overloading him. Doing his best to push the sensations aside, he turned his attention back to the intruder.

Hopping onto the talking stone, Garrett silenced the people, talking low. "The wizards tell us there is a spy drawing near, possibly a member of Crowe's forces. He must be made to think we are ready to submit to Crowe's rule, otherwise we will be attacked. Do you all understand?"

A sea of nodding faces responded as Garrett looked to Oren. "How close is he now?"

"Seventy-five paces, but he's moving faster now," Marc answered, his heartbeat quickening.

"And he is most definitely Crowe's man," Valeria added in a quick, loud whisper. That she could read the man's thoughts from this far, especially with the distractions of everyone's fear and excitement, impressed Marc.

With a nod of acknowledgement, the village leader spoke even quieter to all, "Our visitor is close. Let us begin." Speaking quite loudly, he continued. "And, as I said before, the agent for Lord Crowe assured us that we would receive the same protection from him as we did from the old king."

—*The spy heard Garrett speak just now,*— Valeria Linked to Marc and Oren. She then caught Garrett's eye, pointed to her ear, then to the southeast. The leader nodded in understanding.

While Garrett continued his ruse, Marc followed the spy as he moved directly toward the common house. Reaching the edge of the trees, the man looked about then dashed over to the building's wall, crouching between two barrels. Valeria whispered into her father's ear, who then grinned slyly and spoke up.

"What of the taxes on our crops and livestock?"

Marc and his fellow wizards pointed energetically at the wall behind them. Garrett nodded again. "Lord Crowe was a faithful servant to our former king, God rest his soul. I trust he will be as fair, carrying on the tradition of his predecessor. Well, we have discussed this for hours. It is time to decide. Do we agree to swear allegiance to Crowe?" A great noise of affirmation rose from the crowd, loud enough that Valeria covered her ears. "Good. Now return to your homes and sleep well. Tomorrow we will make preparations to welcome our new king."

Feeling the spy's surge of satisfaction as he slipped back into the woods, Marc laughed inwardly knowing those *preparations* included arrows and spears. A fine welcome indeed.

Oren headed out the doorway as he Linked with Marc. —*I will follow the spy. Stay here for a short time to be sure no others are watching. Afterward, float up high and find their campfires. See what you can learn but take great care not to be discovered.*—

—Yes, Master.—

Garrett and several others, including Sean, approached. The leader pointed at the wall, eyebrows raised.

"The spy is gone," Marc said. "Oren is following him."

"Good. My thanks to both of you for learning of his approach. Had he caught us preparing to fight—"

"There is no need to thank us for the magic wanted you to know of the danger he posed."

The ease at which those words came to him intrigued Marc. While their usual purpose was to remind others of the false premise that magic held the true power, he actually meant what he said. His abilities were not earned, but God-given. No amount of labor or study could make them come forth to those not so destined. This knowledge humbled him. Realizing Oren also understood this made Marc respect him even more.

Separating Garrett and Sean from the others, he led them to an empty corner of the room, his heart heavy with the information he needed to share. "Has Oren spoken to you of Fox Glen?"

Curious, Garrett shook his head. "Not a word."

"Nothing," Sean said.

"You should know that resisting Crowe is very dangerous." He told what happened earlier that day. Sean was shocked, but Garrett only shook his head again.

"Even more reason why he should not be king." The man's gaze hardened. "Our only choice is to fight, but we have an advantage that Fox Glen did not. Forewarning, plus two wizards and a witch."

"Then victory is ours," Sean said with confidence.

"Not necessarily," Valeria said.

Sean looked at her, puzzled. "What do you mean? I thought magic is all-powerful."

"It is, but we are not. Magic allows us some things, denies us others." She took Marc's hand. "But the power we *are* allowed makes us a formidable enemy."

Sean smiled slightly. "Then that will be enough."

Marc hoped his friend was right.

Ψ   Ψ   Ψ

After several checks of the area around Oak Creek, Marc and Valeria found no others lurking nearby. When he was about to Float up high, she insisted on going with him.

"You clothing is too light," he said. "You might be seen."

"Not a problem. Come."

Wondering what she meant, he followed her to her parent's house. They were alone. From within her pack she pulled out a dark brown wizards robe and held it against her body, smoothing out the larger wrinkles in the fabric. "I started on this after learning the Great Secret. It's not completed yet—no pockets or secret folds—but the rest of it is wearable."

Eyeing it carefully, he noticed the cut of it to be much more feminine than his own robe or that of Oren's. "It's beautiful, just like the woman who made it."

Smiling, she gave him a peck on the lips. "Guard the door." As he blocked the entrance to the hut, Valeria quickly stripped off her travel cloak and donned the robe. He tried to ignore the beauty of her form, but his thoughts must have betrayed him for she sashayed over and gave him a more languid kiss. "I like how you look, too." With a breezy laugh, she squeezed past him. Trying not to laugh himself, he moved after her.

Hurrying south into the woods, they Floated up as he had done earlier. Marc found the view astounding, even better than during the day. Far to the west, the ruddy remnants of sunset ebbed away. Below, the dim contours of the landscape could be seen, the textures softening with increasing distance. Forests, a deep blue-gray with a hint of turquoise. Open spaces, slightly lighter with a bit more green. Bare earth clearly stood out, especially roads and paths, visible as ghostly gray lines. All illumination came from the stars; the moon had yet to rise.

"It's beautiful," Valeria said with near reverence as she slowly looked around.

"Yes, it is. With everything so dark we should easily spot any fires."

"I see one already—no, make that two, close together." She pointed at them.

He saw them as well, two bright points of flickering light off to the southeast. "It must be Crowe's camp. That's the direction the spy came from." To be thorough, Marc searched further. "I see more fires. Due south but further away. I wonder who is there?"

"If you'll Envision those, I'll do the first two."

"Fair enough." Concentrating his thoughts, he guided his magic along his line of view and the image of three widely spaced fires arranged in a large triangle blossomed within his mind. Enclosed inside the triangle were several good-sized tents and many warriors. He tried to count them but found it difficult because they moved about. Some tended to their weapons, others cleared spaces to bed down. Several men prepared a boar for cooking. Widening his view, Marc found six men on patrol outside the camp.

"What did you find?" Valeria asked.

"A big camp. It's hard to tell exactly, but I would guess there are around fifty-five men. All armed fighters. I can't see much detail Envisioning from this far. I need to get closer. What of yours?"

"Only eleven men, all heavily armed, and Oren is watching them. Should I contact him?"

"Certainly." Marc lightly grasped her forearm to share in her Link.

—*Master?*—

—*Valeria. I see you are also searching for Crowe's men. What have you found?*—

—*Two camps for some reason. The one you are at and another further south with over fifty men.*—

Marc thought it strange for Crowe to have two camps. — *What of the spy?*— he asked.

—*He came directly here and reported to Crowe. Our ruse worked. Go to the far camp and learn what you can. Go with God.*—

Oren's concern carried over the Link, giving the emotion a kind of weight all its own. They knew the danger they faced and the fear they needed to contain. —*And with you, Master.*—

Returning to the ground, they headed south at a brisk walk, making better time than they could by Floating, plus saving the strength of their magic. Even so, it took over an hour to reach the camp. They halted at a distance of about fifty paces outside of the path of the patrolling guards. Valeria's skills had not advanced enough to repel arrows and spears sent her way, so Marc sought a secure place from which she could watch. Spotting a nearby tall tree, he pointed at an upper branch. —*That looks safe enough, Val.*—

Letting out a near silent huff of resignation, she Floated up into the tree and lowered herself into a sitting position on the limb. —*Be careful.*—

Because the moon had recently risen, he lifted himself to treetop level and approached the camp from the west so as not to be seen silhouetted against it. The pleasant aroma of roasting pork met his nose as he drew close to the nearest fire. Finding a sizable, mushroom-shaped tree with dense foliage, he settled into the top of the canopy, squatting on an upper branch. The leaves blocked the firelight yet allowed him to be within twenty feet of the ground. Immediately below, a patrolling guard passed by unaware of his presence. To his left, two men guarded a large tent while many others sat around the fire.

Skimming over their emotions, Marc found some of them unsettled, others wished they were elsewhere. A few gave off a sense of mild excitement, the nature of which roused his curiosity. One man in particular strongly radiated this yet unknown emotion. After pondering it for a time Marc realized its nature: the thrill of the hunt. Stalking prey. Chasing it. Killing it. Delving deeper into the man's emotions, a sudden wave of nausea swelled within Marc.

The *prey* he pursued was his own kind. People.

Steeling himself, Marc continued to read the man—Tomar—and saw brief images of women, children and unarmed men being mercilessly slaughtered, coupled with a lustful pleasure of killing. Able to tolerate no more, Marc withdrew his contact and took a ragged breath—this man overflowed with true evil. An evil which displaced all kindness, compassion and love, separating Tomar's soul from his mind and leaving behind nothing in its place but an emptiness devoid of anything human. No, the malicious corruption he sensed felt *more* than just empty. Tomar was filled with *Nothingness*.

Valeria's mind touched his. —*What's wrong?*—

With a heavy heart, he told her. —*Tomar, and others here, enjoyed murdering the people of Fox Glen. Read him and see the evil within. I call it Nothingness.*—

Moments later, the horror and sadness she felt came across their Link. —*He's barely human any more. Evil has eaten away all of the good in him. There are others like him in camp, too.*—

—*Yes. Let us inspect the remainder of the men and be gone from this wretched place.*— Rising, he began to move west but too late realized the hem of his robe had snagged on a small branch. Breaking free, the limb snapped back into place with a loud rustle.

"Who goes there?" shouted a nearby guard.

Marc instantly stopped, his pulse thumping in his ears. The guard circled around the tree looking upward, an arrow at the ready. Marc knew he could not Float up quickly enough to prevent being spotted. Or shot. Two other guards ran up.

"What is it?" one of them asked.

"Not sure. A noise came from up in that tree."

Marc's mind hazed over with panic.

—*Hold still,*— Valeria said as a gray blur whisked by him and vanished into the leaves of the tree. Immediately a frenzied owl burst out, flying rapidly away.

The second guard laughed. "It's just an owl. The great threat has been defeated." Laughing, the men returned to their patrols.

The tension drained from Marc as he joined Valeria on the branch above. —*Thanks. Where did you find that owl?*—

—*Flying around me, no doubt curious about...*—

A sudden commotion erupted in the southern part of the camp. "Help," a man shouted. "The prisoners have escaped."

Marc looked at Valeria with raised brows, tipping his head in the direction of the sound. —*Let's see what this is about.*—

Together they Floated south, finding another tree from which to watch. A short, stocky man stumbled slowly toward the center of camp, a bloodied hand held against the back of his head. A tent stood fifteen paces behind him. Others ran his way. The first to reach him briefly examined his wound. "How did this happen, Varro? They were but two girls."

"Someone struck me."

"And the prisoners?"

"Gone."

The man pointed at the rest. "Go. Find them."

As the others scattered into the woods, Varro touched his wound once more, wincing. "One man, maybe two, came up behind me and knocked me out."

Marc felt the lie.

"Is that so?" called out a commanding voice. The man seeing to Varro bowed as a tall figure dressed in black strode forward, followed by the remainder of the camp. A bolt of fear struck Marc. Thaddeus! Although very faint, he saw magic's glow about him. Barely stifling a gasp in time, he glanced at Valeria. Her incredulous expression told him she noticed it as well. Thaddeus had magic? How could this be?

Varro dropped to one knee. "Lord Thaddeus, I was overcome by an intruder who rescued the prisoners."

Thaddeus looked him over, then curtly gestured toward the man's middle. "Do you often guard prisoners with your pants undone?" The man quickly stared at the ground. His interrogator leaned closer and sniffed his breath. "Do you also consume strong drink while guarding Lord Crowe's captives?" Putting the heel of his sandal against the man's forehead, Thaddeus pushed him over backwards and, stepping over the prostrate Varro, continued on and entered the tent.

Marc Envisioned the interior, careful to hide his magic the way Oren had taught him lest Thaddeus detect his presence. Thaddeus picked up a spear and examined the blood on the butt end of it. Tossing it aside, he moved toward the back and plucked four leather strips from the dirt. With a snort of disgust, he tramped outside and kicked the prone form hard in his stomach.

"Stand before me, you wretch." A cold, dark anger flowed from Thaddeus, causing the hairs on Marc's arms to prickle—a vile, greasy presence that stank of rot and the grave. The *Nothingness* within Thaddeus dwarfed the amount inside of Tomar. Regaining his feet, Varro lowered his head as Thaddeus moved around him like a wolf circling its prey. "You lied to me and everyone else. Those girls were not rescued." He dangled the leather straps before the man. "If they had, these bindings would have been cut. You untied the eldest to have your way with her. As you dropped your pants, she struck you with a spear. It would have been better for you if she had run you through."

Thaddeus' face grew ever more livid while his voice remained icily calm. "Did you think no one would find out? Fool. Traitor. Those girls were for Lord Crowe's pleasure, not yours." He thrust the straps toward the nearest man. "Bind this dog. If we regain the girls unharmed, kill him quickly. If we do not, let Tomar slowly peel the skin from him."

Varro bolted but the other guards were prepared and had him held fast before he could take a second step. As he begged for mercy, Thaddeus turned away and, finally releasing his rage, harshly addressed the other men. "Find them!" They immediately fanned out in all directions, disappearing into the night.

Disgusted, Marc risked a weak Link to Valeria. *—We have to find those girls first.—*

—I already have.— She shared her vision of the two making the best speed they could through the trees. At once they Floated up high, clear of the trees, and headed after them.

Marc alternated his view of the girls with that of the closest pursuers. One of the men seemed likely to reach them first. He drew Valeria's attention to him. *—We need to distract this man. Can you Push a sound or image into him?—*

—I'll try.— Sharing the illusion with him, Valeria created a voice of a girl saying, "This way. Run this way."

Marc watched the man come to a halt and cock his ear. *— He heard you. Well done.—*

—I don't know how to make him think the sound is coming from a certain direction.—

—Let me try.— Marc rustled a bush thirty paces to the man's left and he immediately slunk toward the noise. Going further out, Marc snapped a few twigs and branches. Valeria's magic swelled for a moment after which the man ran in the new direction. Marc made several more noises well along the man's path. *—That should put him far enough away.—*

—We best return to the ground. It's faster than Floating and I'm beginning to tire.—

—Good idea.—

In a matter of minutes they caught up with the girls, their magic allowing them to better move through the dark forest.

244

Seeing Marc, the eldest girl urgently told the other, "Keep going." Skidding to a stop, she spun about and took on a fighting stance, deep gray eyes glaring in anger. As he slowed, Valeria passed him on the right.

—*I'll get the other one.*—

He gestured for the girl to stay still. "Easy. I won't hurt you." With a growl of rage she came at him, fingers held claw-like. In a flash he recalled a time when he had angered Gwen and how she demonstrated that a woman's fingernails made surprisingly effective weapons. He still carried the scars.

With a sweep of his arm, Marc softly commanded, "*Volitā.*" Instantly, the girl lost her footing and rose several feet, her long, curly, light brown hair floating weightless about her face. After a moment of panic her fire returned. "What is this? Who are you?" Although angry, she knew enough to keep her voice low.

"I am the wizard, Marc, here to rescue you, Barbara. Men from the camp are near. If you cry out, they will come this way."

"A wizard?" She lowered her hands. "What will you do with me?"

"We will take you and your sister to the safety of Oak Creek." Feeling her fear abate, he lowered her to the ground and drew near. "Did they... hurt you in any way?"

She shook her head. "You said 'we'. Who else is here?"

"Valeria," Valeria said, walking up with the younger girl in tow. Barbara gave her a respectful nod.

Marc scanned the area. "Two men are close by." He turned to Barbara. "We will Float both of you away from here. Hop on my back and remain silent." While she complied, Valeria had the other girl do the same. As one, he and Valeria softly said, "*Volitā,*" and rose up high.

Barbara's sister let out a gasp of fear, closing her eyes tight. "I'm... I'm scared. I don't want to fall."

"Hush, Rufa," Barbara whispered. "These are wizards and we are safe."

"Wizards?" Rufa opened one green eye and looked at Marc. "Like Oren?"

"Yes," Marc said. "Valeria and I are his apprentices." Hearing that, the girl visibly relaxed.

Drifting slowly in order to conserve their magical strength, they passed within view of the camp. Marc spotted Varro below, tied between two trees. Barbara saw him as well for her fingers dug deeply into Marc's shoulders, making him wince. At the northern edge of the camp, he became aware of strong emotions from beneath them, but the distance and cacophony of many thoughts made it difficult to immediately sort things out.

—*Val, what do you feel from the men below?*—

—*Most are alarmed, excited. One is quite frightened. He seems familiar.*—

Marc began trying to Envision that person when Valeria's thoughts slammed through his mind. —*It's Don! They've captured Don!*—

Chapter 24

With shocked disbelief, Marc tried to understand how Donald came to be in the enemy's camp. The last time he saw him, his onetime-friend had finally witnessed clear and undeniable evidence Valeria cared for another. For Marc. He knew Donald had suspected this for a time—hence the ire directed Marc's way— but seeing them holding hands earlier in the common house proved to be too much for his pride. That, plus his father's rebuke at his volunteering to—

The truth hit Marc like a knife to his heart. —*Val, Don tried to spy on them.*—

Dread carried across her Link. —*We've got to rescue him!*—

A heaviness settled upon his heart as he realized the cost of the responsibility he and Valeria shared. —*We cannot. There are five men about him. If we defeated them, Thaddeus would know others were spying on him as well. Maybe luck will be with us and Don can convince them he's no spy.*—

Marc sought out the elder's mind. —*Master?*—

—*What is wrong?*—

—*Donald has been captured spying on the larger camp.*—

After a moment of surprise, then worry, the master's thoughts calmed. —*Do nothing to make yourselves known.*—

—*Can we not help him?*—

—*Possibly, but remember, he chose to ignore Garrett's wisdom. Do not let his foolishness become your own.*—

—*But they will kill him,*— Valeria Linked, deeply worried.

—*Not right away. Crowe would have immediately done so, but Thaddeus is more careful and will question him first. Our priority is the safety of Oak Creek. Tell Sean of Donald's capture and to prepare for possible attack. I will join you as soon as I am able.*—

After Oren broke the Link, Valeria drifted closer to Marc and took his hand. She shook with fear. —*Why did I not foresee this?*—

Barbara shifted position on Marc's back and whispered into his ear. "Is something wrong?"

He nodded gently. "A friend of ours has been caught spying on the men who attacked your village." Torn whether to continue on with the girls or stay and watch over Donald, he reasoned it would best serve his people to remain for now. —*Let's hide the girls and see what happens.*—

Valeria nodded. —*That tree I used earlier has a good view.*—

—*Fine.*—

Backtracking to the tree, they put the girls on an upper branch.

"Remain quiet and still," Valeria told them. "We will return for you soon." As they Floated toward Donald's position, Valeria Linked, —*Help me contact Sean. You lift the amulet and I will give him the message.*—

Envisioning Sean, he found him sitting with Garrett, Ethan and others, fashioning spears from freshly cut branches. When the amulet lifted from Sean's chest, the men stopped their work and stared warily at the stone. Valeria said:

Friend Donald is missing, not to be found,
Detected while spying, by Crowe's men bound.
Those who serve magic, will watch him this night,
Make ready the village, make ready to fight.

Letting the amulet drop, Marc felt Sean's agitation. Not wanting to witness Garrett's reaction, he released the Envisioning and turned his attention to Donald. Crowe's men half led, half dragged him deeper into their camp, his face bloodied, taking him to the large tent Marc saw earlier. One man forced Donald to kneel while another went inside, returning with Thaddeus. Marc's insides twisted into knots.

Thaddeus stood before Donald. "Who are you and why did you spy on my camp?"

Donald looked him straight in the eye. "Claudius, and I am no spy. While hunting I saw your camp and wondered who you were and why you needed three fires."

"Then you were spying."

"Just curious, no more." Donald pulled against the men holding him. "Now let me go."

Thaddeus struck Donald on the face. "You lie," he said, his voice calm and devoid of emotion. "Tell the truth or you will suffer the same death as that man." He pointed at a well-bloodied Varro whimpering in his bindings. "He lied to me as well. Tonight he will beg for death as his skin is slowly cut from him." Thaddeus produced a dagger, placing it under Donald's chin. "I will allow you one more chance."

Donald's gaze shifted to the ground, his face still elevated by the blade. "Yes, I spied on you, but my village knows nothing about it. I wanted to do so but my—but the village leader forbid it saying it would anger Crowe."

"*Lord* Crowe."

"Forgive me. I meant no disrespect." Thaddeus removed the dagger and Donald's head dropped to his chest.

"Then why did you disobey him?"

"I—I—" Donald slowly shook his head.

"Answer me." Thaddeus waited for a long moment and, seeing his captive remained silent, nodded at the man on Donald's right, who savagely backhanded him, knocking him to the ground. Marc was startled to feel some of the pain of that blow. Donald attempted to rise but the man put his foot on him.

"I have not been accepted as a man by my village," Donald said, his voice quaking with fear. "I thought by showing enough bravery, that might change."

Thaddeus gestured at the man, who removed his foot. "You have not been made a man because you think first of yourself, not the good of your people. You do not respect the wisdom of those more experienced than you. Because of your foolishness, your village will now pay the price."

Donald rolled to his knees, looking up at Thaddeus in anguish. "*No.* Please don't punish them for my mistake. Punish *me*. They want peace. I know they will serve Lord Crowe well."

This puzzled Marc. When Donald left the village the plans were to fight. So what made him think of the same ruse as his father? Marc knew he lied, but Donald hid it well, much better than when he claimed to be Claudius. Maybe Thaddeus' weak magic could not detect this current deception. For the sake of their home, Marc hoped so.

Thaddeus paced slowly for a time, watching Donald closely. "You asked that I punish you instead of your village. Do you know what that means?"

Donald wiped at the blood trickling from his nose, his gaze once more upon the ground. "I will die." He glanced at Varro. "Unpleasantly, most likely."

Thaddeus smiled coldly as the men around him nodded approvingly. "Surely you did not think that by disobeying your father's orders you would be thought of as a man." Donald looked up in shock. "Yes, Donald, son of Garrett, I know who you are."

Marc felt defeat come from his friend, who lowered his head once more. "There's a girl in my village I much desire." Several of Thaddeus' men smirked knowingly at each other. "She loves another, a friend of mine. I thought if I did something really brave, she might realize my worth and love me more. But instead, I destroyed our friendship and endangered my village. I would give anything to undo what I did."

Valeria's hand tightened on Marc's as tears flowed from her eyes. Marc's own were far from dry.

Thaddeus crossed his arms and studied Donald for a time. "You have gained much wisdom this night. If you were under my leadership, I would now grant you your manhood."

Donald managed a weak smile. "My thanks, but what good does it do me now? If you're going to kill me, please be quick about it."

"Not yet. I like your spirit. You may also be useful as a bargaining point with your father should that prove necessary." Thaddeus turned an iron stare toward the two men holding Donald. "Bind him well, guard him well. We do not want any other escapes this evening for Lord Crowe returns on the morrow." The men paled and bowed their heads in acknowledgement.

A wave of relief washed over Marc; Donald would remain safe for a time. The men took him to the same tent the girls had been kept in; one guard posted inside, four outside. Any rescue attempt would be quite difficult. If they *were* to try something, it would be vital that Donald was aware of it.

—*Val, we should let Don know we are near.*—

—*I'll Push a voice into him.*—

—*No, wait. He may react poorly to it, alerting the guards.*—

—*Then how else are we to communicate with him?*—

Marc pondered on that. Writing messages in the dirt would not work; Donald could not read well enough. Thinking back over the years he remembered when they used to... —*The acorn game.*—

Her mood perked up. —*Perfect.*—

He, Valeria, Sean and Donald used to play the acorn game in their younger days, years before the darkness came. They developed a simple language made up of acorns arranged in various patterns to represent things and actions. By using these symbols, they left messages for each other and played hide-and-seek type games. Marc hoped Donald would remember.

A nearby oak tree provided a handful of immature acorns. When the guards looked elsewhere, Marc lowered several dozen seeds in a vertical stream into the space between a support pole and the fabric. Taking care to avoid the gaze of the guard inside, he moved them along the roof and down the back wall to the ground. Startled at first, Donald remained silent, watching the procession of seeds with wide eyes. Marc arranged some of the acorns into his own symbol, a pyramid, followed by the sign for *watches*, an image of an eye. After several seconds, Donald must have realized Marc's intent for he rolled on his side, shielding the acorns from the interior guard's view. Removing the second symbol, Donald added two more. It read, *Marc help Donald.*

Marc wished he could. *Not safe many men*, he wrote, followed by *help later.*

Yes, Donald responded.

Marc formed, *Marc Valeria watch Donald.*

Donald repeated the sign for *yes*, then, with a look of determined hope, brushed the acorns into disorder.

Ψ   Ψ   Ψ

By the time Oren arrived, Donald slept. Pleased they rescued the girls without being discovered, the master sent them back to Oak Creek while he kept watch over Donald. They were about a quarter mile from the village when Marc suddenly felt the presence of others nearby. Holding out his arm, he stopped the two girls and motioned for them to keep silent. Envisioning ahead he immediately felt pain and fear, but soon understood the small group of people posed no threat. He smiled at the girls. "I believe some of your neighbors are on this path."

Overjoyed, Barbara grabbed his arm. "How many?"

"Twelve."

She darted a short way down the path, then stopped and asked, "Is it safe?"

"Yes." Needing no further encouragement, she ran off. Rufa took a few timid steps, then looked expectantly at him. "Go." He chuckled as she also vanished.

Valeria started after them. "The older one is strong willed."

"Just like someone else I know," Marc said, giving her a warm smile.

Putting his arm around her, they followed the path until reaching the others: one man, four women, six children and a baby. Three were wounded—the man had a gash along the right side of his head, a woman had a serious injury to her left thigh, and a boy had an arrow lodged in his arm. Barbara introduced Marc and Valeria to her villagers, explaining how they rescued her and her sister.

Valeria examined the injuries. "Our master may be able to heal these."

The man bowed his head. "It would be appreciated, but see to her first." He pointed at the injured woman seated on a large rock. A hastily made bandage, sodden with blood, bound the wound. "Every time we move her she bleeds more."

Because of the dim light, Marc could not see her color, but he felt her weakness and pain. "I will carry her safely to Oak Creek. All of you are welcome there."

"Praise God," one of the women said. "We feared Crowe had attacked them as well."

Marc addressed the man. "What happened at Fox Glen?"

A spike of hate erupted from the man's aura. "Crowe's man came to us yesterday. Said we must accept Crowe as our new king. When he returned this morning, we could not give him an answer. Angry, he left. A short while later he, Crowe and about twenty men approached. We thought we could fight them, but we didn't know twice that number hid on the other side of the village. When our men left to fight Crowe, his other men moved in. Hearing the cries of our families, we rushed back to defend them, but—" The man's jaw muscles tightened as he shook his head with several quick jerks. "We got there too late. I only survived because I was knocked out and taken for dead. Others fled into the forest and evaded capture."

The woman with the baby pulled two other children to her side. "We were picking berries. If we had been home...."

Valeria touched the woman's shoulder reassuringly. "Be grateful you were spared. All of you should be." Gently, she moved her along the path. "Come, warm food and beds await."

Casting the spell, Marc Floated the injured woman before him. Several of the others gasped and backed away. "There is no need to fear," he said. "She is safe in magic's hands."

Heading for the village, Marc felt Oren's Link.

—Good news. A messenger arrived to tell Thaddeus of Oak Creek's support for Crowe. Donald will live until tomorrow.—

Relief flowed through Marc. *—I am glad. We found twelve more survivors of Fox Glen.—* Marc told of them, especially the injured ones.

—I will be there when I am able. Then you both will practice what you learned about healing wounds.—

They reached Oak Creek without further incident. While the villagers saw to the other survivors, Marc and Valeria tended to the wounded in the common house. The boy and man gratefully accepted the porridge offered them, but the woman refused to eat. Remembering Oren had him pack a small container of honey, Marc dissolved a large dollop in a cup of warm water and had her drink it. He made a second batch which she swallowed then fell asleep.

Marc turned his attention to the boy while Valeria cleansed the man's wounds. Gently grasping the boy's elbow, he read the magic around him. "How are you feeling—James, isn't it?"

"I'm well enough, sir."

The arrow had pierced the outside flesh of the young man's arm a hand's width below the shoulder. "Did you bleed very much?"

"Some at first, but no more since then." He glanced over at the woman. "Will my mother live?"

His mother? Marc read the boy's magic more deeply and saw how she blocked a sword meant for him with her own body. "I do not know. My master, Oren the Wise, will use his skill with magic to heal her." The boy looked downward. "Your mother is very brave." Putting his fingers under the boy's chin, Marc raised it to meet his gaze. "We will do all we can to save her."

James gave him a sad but hopeful smile. "Thank you."

"Now, let's get this arrow out. Hold still." Waving his hand, Marc said, "*Discinde!*" and cleanly severed the shaft next to the boy's skin. James' eyes opened wide with awe and then even wider as the arrow slid from the wound.

"Ow." His eyes teared up but he cried out no more.

"Well done, James. Let's clean up your arm."

Ψ   Ψ   Ψ

When Oren returned, Marc immediately brought him to the injured woman, who lay upon a table in the common house. After a brief examination, the master took him and Valeria aside and quietly said, "Her wound is deep and serious. I do not know if she will live for she has lost much blood. You did good, Marc, in giving her honey water. It will give her strength for what she must endure."

"What can we to do to help?" Valeria asked.

"Go to the village garden and bring me two large onions. Wash them well." She left. "Marc, from your pack get the mortar, celery seed, lavender, feverfew and morpheus root."

As he dug for the items, Marc found himself excited about finally applying his knowledge of medicinal herbs. Oren also taught them about the makeup of the body and how their magic might be used to treat wounds and illnesses. While learning about herbs interested him, he found peering inside someone's body most unsettling.

"Here they are, Master." He held them out to Oren who waved him back.

"You prepare them. Tell me why I selected those herbs."

"The first three are good for easing pain, especially the feverfew, and the lavender also helps reduce swelling. The morpheus root is to help her sleep."

"Good, now prepare them quickly."

Under the watchful eye of his master, Marc took a small mound of the celery seed, ground it to a powder and poured it into the cup he used earlier. Next, he placed three pinches of powdered morpheus root in the vessel. Two would normally be enough, but because of her pain, she needed a stronger dose. Adding a handful each of dried lavender and feverfew, he filled the cup halfway with hot water and stirred the mixture without stopping. After a few minutes, he strained the liquid into another cup and handed it to his master.

Oren smelled and tasted it. "Good work. Give it to her."

Taking back the cup, Marc approached the woman and touched her shoulder. When her eyes fluttered open, she appeared more alert. "I have medicine for the pain."

With Marc's help, she lifted her head and drank all from the cup. Her gaze shifted questioningly to Oren, then back to him.

"Oren is a master healer and I am his student," Marc said reassuringly. She smiled weakly which pleased him, for now she had hope. "I removed the arrow from James' arm. He will heal."

She smiled again, this time more with her eyes. While he made no attempt to probe her thoughts, he felt them as clearly as if he did. Deep gratitude and relief flowed from... Merga.

He gently patted her hand. "Now rest, Merga, and keep very still."

Returning with the onions, Valeria handed them to Oren.

Seeing the woman look toward Valeria, Marc said, "And you remember Valeria. She is my master's other student."

With a gentle smile, Valeria lightly touched Merga's upper arm in a show of concern.

"Thank you all," the woman said weakly before closing her eyes once more.

Hearing the rustling of clothing, Marc glanced around and saw that some of the villagers gathered to watch. The master noticed them as well but, unfazed, motioned at Merga's leg. —*Look carefully into the wound.*—

Marc reluctantly Envisioned the savage injury, causing a woozy feeling to snake through his innards. Knowing that he soon had to apply what he previously learned only in theory did little to calm those feelings.

Oren continued. *—See how the large vena has been nearly cut in two. This must be healed now or she will die. I trust you both remember what we learned about healing flesh?—*

Marc nodded, wishing his first opportunity to apply that knowledge could have been on something less serious—or bloody.

—Marc, squeeze the appropriate pressure point for her leg.—

Taking care to locate the precise spot on the woman's hip, Marc pressed the underlying nerve firmly with his thumb. Groaning, Merga tensed then relaxed as the pain ebbed.

"Bless you," she whispered.

Looking from their patient and back to him, Oren gave Marc an approving nod. *—We must work quickly lest she moves. First, remove the set blood and air from the vena.—*

Oren's magic expelled several clumps of clotted blood from out of the vessel, the gore of which brought a swell of nausea rising through Marc's core. He quickly looked away, swallowing to ease the acrid taste at the back of his throat, not wanting to throw up before the villagers. Taking several deep breaths quelled enough of the urge. Why did this bother him? He had seen injuries before and never reacted this strongly. Whatever the reason, he had to get past this for healing was an important part of being a wizard.

—Now, to repair the blood vessel.—

Oren brought the severed edges together, then began making many tiny sparks along the joint, causing the flesh on each side to stick together. Marc found that if he very closely Envisioned the area Oren worked on, making it appear many times larger than normal, his discomfort was all but nonexistent. Thankful for that mercy, he focused all his attention on the master's work.

—Next, the wound must be washed out or it will fester greatly. What must we remember about using the juice of the onion? Valeria?—

—Only fresh juice will properly cleanse the injury.—

—Correct. Now for the difficult part of the task.—

Casting an impressive, longwinded spell, Oren Floated the onions before him and crushed them in mid-air, separating their juice into what looked to be a giant, milky raindrop. Even though Marc knew how the master did it, he found himself nearly as taken in by the show as the awestruck villagers around them. When the rippling blob neared the injury, the flesh opened up to receive it. Oren gently massaged the area, working the juice into every crevice, then released his hold, allowing the wound to close and expel the fluid.

—*Valeria, hold the edges of the muscles together while Marc and I Spark them.*

Slowly chanting, "*Coalescite,*" Oren waved his hand over the wound, sparking together the muscles nearest the woman's hip. Starting on the other side, Marc did the same. Difficult at first, he carefully took his time and soon became more adept at it. Understanding the good he did this woman greatly lessened his discomfort at viewing her injuries. After several minutes, all the severed muscles were mended.

Oren examined their work and nodded appreciatively. —*Very good for your first time, Marc.*—

Thrilled, he tried not to smile too much, but failed after Valeria Linked, —*Yes, excellent.*—

Seeing the eagerness in Valeria's eyes, Marc asked, —*Master, why not let Val try healing the skin? She can only make tiny Sparks so far, but are those not best for thin tissue?*—

With a warm smile, Oren nodded his consent. Beaming, Valeria came up next to Marc and took over chanting, "*Coalescere.*" Jointly, they held the skin together and sparked the juncture closed.

"Good work, both of you," Oren said as a number of villagers applauded. The pride in his master's tone meant more to Marc than the appreciation of the onlookers. "Wrap the leg with a clean bandage, Valeria, and keep it in this position for the next few hours. If she wakes in pain, you or Marc will need to use the pressure point once more. Tomorrow we will drain what pus has formed."

Next, Marc and Valeria healed the wounds of the man and James under Oren's watchful eye. After the healing was completed to his satisfaction, the master left to sleep. Marc got two skins and unrolled them on the earthen floor of the common house next to the table holding Merga. One skin was for James, who refused to leave his mother's side. In less than a minute after laying down, the boy was asleep.

Marc knelt on the other skin. "Why don't you sleep, too, Val? I'll take first watch." He stretched out on his side so he could rest yet keep an eye on their patient. Valeria gratefully accepted, cuddling up next to him, her head upon his arm. As she slept, he thought on what might happen come morning. Would Merga live? And what of Donald's fate? Could he be rescued without Oak Creek incurring the wrath of Crowe? Marc did not know any of those answers. He *did* know his test would be soon. If it happened to take place tomorrow, would his magic be sufficient for victory?

He looked upon Valeria's beautiful face. The peace he saw there did not reside within him, only doubt and fear. He wanted more than anything to pass the test. Not just to live another day, which was only natural, but also to give her joy. His spirit yearned for an eternity with her. Gently caressing her hair, he pledged to make it so.

Chapter 25

Marc awoke to a pleasant warmth upon his lips. Opening his eyes, he saw Valeria kneeling by him, her face inches away. She kissed him again.

"Good morning." Her voice was as soft as her lips.

Smiling, he caressed her cheek. "Good morning to you as well." Then last night's memories returned, tempering his mood. Rising to one elbow, he looked up at their patient. "How is Merga?"

"Much better. No bleeding and her pain has eased." Valeria's eyes positively shone. "Our magic saved her life." Her joy flowed through him.

"That's wonderful. And the other two?"

"Healing well." She gave him a small loaf of bread, still warm from the oven.

"Thanks." Tearing off a bite, he stood and stretched. The heavenly taste stimulated his appetite and he let out a little moan of appreciation. "I feel like I haven't eaten for days." He knew his greater-than-normal hunger was due to yesterdays magic use.

Valeria handed him the monk's robe. "Oren said to meet him south of the village."

Marc quickly exchanged robes, filling the pockets and secret places of the new one with wizardly things he might need, then embraced her. "Wish me luck."

She clung to him. "Be safe, my love. Bring Donald back to us."

"I promise."

Kissing her, Marc collected his staff and left the common house, passing a villager who, after pausing a moment at noticing his change of attire, bid him well. The faint pink in the eastern sky meant dawn would soon arrive. Envisioning ahead, he found Oren walking south and briskly strode after him. Just before entering the trees, he heard softly running feet approach him from behind. "Hello, Sean."

With a snort of amused irritation, his best friend slowed to walk next to him. "How do you do that?" Raising his hand, Marc was about to speak, but Sean answered his own question. "I know, it's magic, but *how* do you know?"

Suppressing a chuckle, Marc remembered asking his master that very question not long ago. "The simplest answer is the magic puts the knowledge in my mind much like how the amulet speaks to you."

Sean pursed his lips in thought for several moments. "Good enough. Oren allowed me to come with you. If Don needs to be carried, I can help."

"Not that your help, and company, isn't welcome, but I could Float him home in that event."

"I mentioned that to Oren but he said you needed to save your magic for later." Sean studied him briefly. "What did he mean by that?"

Marc's emotions threatened to rise, but he held them back. "Remember the test I am to face?"

"Yes."

"I think it might be today."

Worry creased his friend's forehead. "If it is, you know I'll help however I can."

Marc gave him a grateful dip of his head. "Thanks. I can ask no more than that."

Catching up with Oren, they journeyed to a densely wooded area north of Crowe's larger camp. Leaving Sean hidden away, Marc and Oren walked directly south, their downcast faces shaded by the spacious, hooded monk's robes. Within several minutes they were discovered.

"Hold there," a guard commanded, brandishing a spear. "What business do you have around here?" Marc ignored the whispers of fear trying to invade his mind and focused it instead on the mission.

"None, except that of our God," Oren said in a pleasing tone. "May we be of service to you this fine morning?"

The guard viewed them suspiciously. "You are holy men?"

Oren bowed slightly. "I am Brother Crotious and this is my initiate, Brother Gastus."

Marc smiled unseen in his hood at Oren's use of the names of the two guards whose remains flanked his home's door. A second guard moved in, deliberately positioning himself off to their side.

The first guard studied them more closely. "Why are you here?" Oren began to speak, but the man cut him off, waiving the spear's tip in Marc's direction. "No. Gastus, you tell me."

For a panicked moment, Marc worried about what to say; he assumed Oren would do most of the talking. What would Gildas do in this circumstance? Keeping his emotions in check, he bowed slightly. "We travel about, spreading the Word of God. We minister to those in need—the sick, injured and those unhappy of heart. All we ask in return is a meager portion of food and a place by the fire at night."

—*Very good, Marc,*— Oren Linked weakly.

Feeling both relief and exhilaration, he answered, —*Thank you, Crotious. You look well for a skeleton.*—

A flicker of amusement echoed back from Oren before he ended the Link and said, "Are there any in need of our care? Or should we be on our way?" Marc heard more guards approaching.

"We have some injured men. What can you do for them that we cannot?"

"We are trained in the healing arts and carry medicinal herbs. Bleeding and festering wounds are made better with our skills."

Marc felt the apprehension of the first two guards ease, followed by a rapidly growing sense of the foul coldness he first experienced the day he killed the wolf. Thaddeus neared. Quickly pulling back his magic, he did his best to conceal it, then whispered a Link. —*Master?*—

—*I sense him as well. Remain calm and follow my lead.*—

Thaddeus stopped several paces from them, his sword drawn, his gaze intent. "Who are these two?" The first guard summarized the situation. "Monks, you say. You, Crotious, show yourself."

"Certainly, my brother." As Oren pulled back his hood, Marc sensed Thaddeus studying the master's face. He also felt the familiar magic of Oren Pushing an illusion into Thaddeus.

After what felt like an eternity, their enemy shifted his gaze to Marc. "Fine. Now you, Gastus."

Marc's diaphragm tightened; it was comply or be killed. He had to trust his master would disguise him as well for he still could not do it himself. "As you wish, gentle sir." Concealing his distress, Marc lowered the fabric and looked at the man who had nearly killed him months before. An overwhelming sense of *Nothingness* hung about him like a burial shroud.

Thaddeus viewed him with no more emotion than one would show gazing at a rock. "Your voice reminds me of someone else."

A spark of panic flicked to life inside Marc's gut but he instantly quenched it, not revealing any outward sign of it. "A friend of yours, perhaps?"

"No."

"An enemy, then?"

Thaddeus shrugged. "A relative of mine. A son of a cousin. We... see things differently."

He and Thaddeus were *related*? More than intrigued, Marc deeply wished he could pursue the topic further but knew that now was not the time. "How unfortunate. I will pray for you both. What is his name?"

Thaddeus sheathed his sword, then waved his hand in a single dismissive gesture. "Do not waste your prayers. He worships magic."

"Oh. That is disturbing," Marc said, trying to sound disheartened. "Well, I will say some for you, then."

"If you must." Thaddeus turned to his guards. "Feed them and let them tend to the injured, but stay with them."

Marc lifted his hood into place and dipped his head. "Thank you, kind sir."

Ignoring them, Thaddeus returned to camp.

"Follow me," the first guard said. "Go only where I tell you is permitted."

Trailing after the man, Marc finally allowed himself to take a full breath. While the encounter frightened him, he also found it most exciting. —*Thank you for concealing me. I must learn illusion better. Who did Thaddeus see?*—

—*A young version of Gastus. You did very well as a monk. Now we must find a way to get them to let us treat Donald's wounds.*—

The guard brought them to four injured men. Two had what looked to be sword wounds, one had taken an arrow which was crudely removed, and the fourth had a broken leg. While Marc and Oren treated them, they Envisioned the camp, seeking detailed information about the number of men, their weapons, food stores and other key facts, then quickly gleaned what they could from everyone's mind.

—*I'm finished, Master,*— Marc said.

—*What is your assessment of Crowe's men?*—

—*At least half are quite unhappy and wish to leave but fear being killed if they try. About a quarter more do not like Crowe, or what he is doing, but stay because of the food and pay. The remainder are filled with the same evil corrupting Thaddeus and Tomar. They enjoy doing evil things.*—

—*My conclusions are the same. What does this tell you?*—

—*That well over half his men are not loyal, a major weakness. How might we exploit that?*—

—*Find a way for them to safely leave his service, or better yet, turn them against him.*—

Once they completed their tasks, the guard said, "You are gifted healers. There is one other in need of attention. A prisoner."

Marc contained his excitement. "We will heal all, be they prince or prisoner." Hurriedly Envisioning the tent, he found no guard posted inside and arranged the acorns into the symbol for silence. Picking up the water bucket and sack of herbs, he followed Oren and the guard.

"This way," the guard said, guiding them into the tent.

Donald looked at the ground, playing in the dirt with his hand. Seeing that the acorns were scattered, Marc knew he had received his message. The guard tapped Donald on the shoulder with the butt of his spear. Donald looked at his visitors, his face dispassionate.

"Two healers are here to look at you."

263

Oren looked at Donald, then the guard. "What was his crime?"

"Spying on this camp. Our lord Thaddeus has generously allowed him to live thus far, but Lord Crowe will soon be here to decide his fate."

Marc lifted the bucket and faced the guard. "Would you be so kind as to bring us some more hot water? This has grown cold."

"Very well." With a pained expression, the guard took the bucket and left.

Dropping his hood, Marc held a finger to his lips and whispered, "We have to be very careful. Guards are everywhere, and we don't want to give them any reason to attack the village."

Donald's mournful expression echoed the emotions radiating from him. "Yes. Thank you for coming. I was so stupid—"

"Tell us later. The village is pretending to support Crowe. We are not certain how to free you yet, but go along with whatever we do."

Donald nodded.

"And do not act like you know us," Oren said. "The guard returns."

Marc flipped up his hood as the man entered and handed over the bucket.

"Here."

"Thank you." Marc knelt next to Donald and went about cleaning the dried blood from his friend's face. They set his broken nose and treated the cuts to his face and had nearly finished when there came a flurry of activity outside.

The guard began to exit the tent but then hastily stepped back in, bowing as Crowe entered. "Good morning, my lord."

"So, this is our spy." Amused and confident, Crowe's pale blue eyes gazed intently down at Donald who remained silent. Nearly as tall as Thaddeus, Crowe had much more muscle on him. While his hair remained a deep brown, gray had invaded the sides and center of his beard. "Thaddeus told me of your discussion. Tell me why I should let you live."

His face full of regret, Donald looked at him. "I was a fool, but learned the error of my ways from Thaddeus. He is a wise man. I wish only to serve the people of my village," Donald lowered his head, "and my new king."

"Well said. Still, I cannot be seen as being weak when it comes to those who work against me. Maybe I should kill you as an example to others."

Donald tensed and drew in a ragged breath. "I appeal to your mercy and charity, my lord."

Crowe had the darkest heart of any Marc had felt—completely consumed by the *Nothingness*; there was no love or mercy to be found within him. He would kill Donald without the slightest reservation for the other was of no value to him. Marc feared that any moment Crowe would decide Donald's fate and that it would not be a good one. A sudden idea came to Marc. He prayed it would be well received.

"May I speak, my lord?" he asked respectfully.

The man's cold eyes flicked his way. "Ah, the monks have a voice. Which one are you?"

"You may call me Brother Gastus, my lord."

"Speak, then."

"If this man is to be punished for his crime against you, may I suggest one that would profit both of us?"

Crowe kept silent for a time, his face impassive. "Go on."

"As brothers of the Word, we are not allowed to work on the Sabbath. To do so is to be damned. If he is to be killed for crimes committed, then he is already damned. Would you be so kind as to give him to us as our slave? That way our labors could be done on the Sabbath as well. Our brothers would work him hard all day and every day for the rest of his life."

Crowe laughed. "It would be better for him to die today. I see how it profits you. Tell me how it profits me."

"He never returns to his village. No body will be found. No one would know what happened to him. The people will fear meeting his fate and thus remain loyal to you."

Crowe's brows peaked for a moment. "Perhaps, but you still fare better than I."

Marc's mind raced. What to do? Chancing that Thaddeus was not nearby, Marc lightly probed the man's mind and found him desirous of getting the most of Donald's fate. Another idea came to him. Perfect. Oren's body blocked the guard's view. "Although we are but poor monks, we might pay you something. What worth would you give him?" While Crowe further inspected

265

Donald, Marc Floated five silver coins from the man's purse to his own.

"Four silver coins."

"Oh." Marc gave the impression it was too high. "What do you think, Brother Crotious?"

"With respects, my lord, I feel he is only worth one silver. He is clearly a trouble maker, and we have to feed and clothe him as well."

Crowe looked at Oren then Marc. "Three."

Marc opened his purse and peered inside. Letting his shoulders sag, he said with regret, "I only have two silvers to give you."

"Very well. Two," Crowe said with a nod.

Another brief probe informed Marc this bantering pleased Crowe. Bowing his head, Marc handed over the coins. "You are most kind."

Crowe studied him. "I am a powerful man yet you do not fear me as others do. Why?"

"I know my God will protect me, as will you, too, my lord, for I serve you both." Marc felt the man's pride come forth.

"Travel with us, both of you. We could use your talents."

"We were headed south," Oren said. "If you are going that way, it would be our pleasure to do so."

"No, we are northbound. Farewell, then." Crowe turned to leave, then paused and faced them once more. "Tell me, which village were you at last?"

"We spent the night at Oak Creek. They were most hospitable."

Crowe's eyebrows rose. "And the mood of the people?"

"Cheerful. They said their new king would visit them on the morrow."

Crowe smiled as a cold breath of dark conceit came from him. "I'm glad they were so friendly." He handed the coins back to Marc. "Keep these for your travels."

Dipping his head low, Marc accepted them. "Bless you, sir."

Oren bowed low. "You are most generous."

"I am. Safe journey to you."

"I pray that God speeds you to your destination," the master said, crossing himself.

Somewhere fiery and filled with tormenting demons, Marc hoped as the man departed. Oren led Donald out of the tent while Marc gathered up their belongings. Once outside, Marc searched the immediate vicinity with his magic and found no threat nearby.

Their escort gestured toward the center of camp. "Please, eat something before you go."

"That is most generous of you," Oren said. "Come, Brother Gastus."

"Certainly, my brother." —*Master, we've got him. We should leave now.*—

—*And how would it appear for two wandering monks to refuse a free meal?*—

—*We would be suspect.*— He turned to Donald. "What is your name, slave?"

"Donald, sir."

"We need to give you another, one not so noble. Marcus. Yes, that is lowly enough." Marc struggled to keep the smile from his lips.

"Thank you, sir. That name is highly regarded in my village."

"It is? Well, we will find something else suitable. Remain silent unless spoken to."

The guard served them some of the delicious leftover boar from the night before. As they started to leave, Marc nearly collided with one of Crowe's men, each briefly seeing a flash the other's face. Marc instantly recognized him as the red-haired soldier accompanying Thaddeus the day he came to collect the honorarium.

"Pardon me." Marc bowed to conceal his face, hoping the man had not recognized him.

"No harm done," the man said, hesitantly.

Probing his thoughts, Marc found the man—Rutilus—confused, but not surprised or alarmed. Trying to act naturally, Marc walked southward out of the camp with Oren and Donald. —*Master, do you know who that was?*—

—*Yes. The question is, did he identify you?*—

—*I'm not sure.*— Marc told Oren of what he received from the man's thoughts. —*If so, would not many guards be after us?*—

—Possibly. When we reach Sean, I will stay at his hiding place and watch for any who might come after us.—

After the three of them were well clear of the camp, Marc scanned the surrounding area and found no one else nearby. He lowered his hood. "We are not being observed." Turning, he led them west until reaching the path that would take them north toward Oak Creek. During that time, strong emotions built within Donald—relief, shame, regret—flooding over Marc's thoughts. "Speak your mind, Don."

With downcast eyes, Donald walked on for over a minute before responding. "I don't know what to say. Of course, my deepest thanks to you and Master Oren at being freed. You risked your lives to watch me last night and rescue me today. It's more than I deserve. I was a fool, not just for spying and getting caught, but—" He paused, letting out a deep sigh as if suddenly freed of a heavy burden. "I treated you and Valeria poorly. Shamefully. I put myself and my desires above everything else. Because of that, I greatly trespassed against both of you. I cannot ask forgiveness for that because I do not deserve it."

Marc's heart went out to his friend knowing such a change, and the admissions resulting from it, did not come easy. "What are we if we cannot learn from our mistakes? I, too, have walked that road. None of us *deserve* forgiveness. Neither can it be earned. Instead, it is something that can only be given freely by the other."

"Yes, life's too short, Don. Ask him." Ahead of them, Sean stood off to the side of the path, smiling. They had reached the thicket already.

Donald briefly smiled at Sean, then turned to face Marc. Slowly extending his hand, Donald brought forth the words Marc waited to hear. "Is there any way you can forgive me?"

Ignoring his hand, Marc embraced him fiercely. "I forgave you long ago. It's good to have my friend back." Donald clung to him as well. When they separated, Marc looked him in the eye. "That past is behind us. Let us speak of it no more."

Sean put his arms about the shoulders of his two friends. "Let's go home."

"One word of caution, Donald," Oren said. "Keep hidden from view, for Thaddeus, Crowe and some of their men will visit the village today. If you are seen, our deception will be uncovered."

Donald dipped his head in respect. "I will stay with Ethan's swine, Great One, until you or Marc say it is safe to return. Perhaps we should return by way of the eastern path?"

Oren nodded. "Good choice. You and Sean go on ahead. I must speak with Marc for a moment." The master sat on a log and invited Marc to join him. He seemed pleased about something. "You did quite well today."

"Thank you, Master."

"Stretch out your magic. Tell me what you sense."

Marc carefully examined the area around them, especially the distance between them and the encampment they just left. "Nothing unusual. Why do you ask?"

"I sense something odd is at hand, but my magic is too weak to tell me what it might be. I used much of it yesterday evening and have had insufficient rest to rebuild my strength." Oren sighed. "My age betrays me."

Marc checked again, this time Envisioning much further out, and found the only real danger, Thaddeus, riding his horse in the direction of the far camp. "I find nothing odd, Master."

Oren pursed his lips thoughtfully. "Perhaps it is a future event that I am unable to see at the moment." He waved Marc away. "Go. I will remain here for a time. Be careful."

"I will." Rising, Marc started to move away, then paused and faced his master once more. "Yesterday, I wondered why Crowe kept two camps instead of one. It made no sense to me. After feeling his thoughts and emotions earlier, I believe I know the reason for that."

Oren looked up at him, interested. "Do tell."

"He—" Marc shrugged. "I don't know for certain, but I believe he thinks little of many of the men who follow him. Despises them, actually. But those closer to his own nature—the soulless, heartless ones—he prefers their company. Most of the men in *his* camp are unrepentantly evil."

Oren dipped his head respectfully. "I concur, my young wizard." The master then smiled and winked. "Excellent use of insight."

Trying not to be too pleased with himself, Marc turned and hurried after his friends. Linking to Valeria, he told her the good news. As they walked home, Donald had many questions about magic and what could be done with it. Marc patiently explained what he could. Donald also found Sean's amulet fascinating.

"And you say it speaks to you?"

Donald's doubtful tone brought the beginnings of a smile to Sean's lips, but he quickly suppressed it, then reverently lifted the stone from his chest and rolled its length in his fingertips. "Not the amulet. The magic does. It speaks to my mind in rhyme."

"A wonder, it is." Donald peered closely at it. "Does Valeria have one of these?"

Marc shook his head. "No. She hears magic's voice as I do."

"What magic does she command?"

"Much the same as I except she sometimes sees the future."

"You jest," Donald said in disbelief.

"She foresaw me returning with the buck I found at the waterfall. She knew years ago that we were destined for each other." Marc felt a pang of guilt come from Donald. "Do not be troubled, for magic willed it so." After a pause, Marc added, "I, too, have foreseen a few future events."

"How is that possible?"

"All things are possible to magic," Sean said with a sly grin.

Marc put his hand on Sean's shoulder. "Ah, my new apprentice."

Sean laughed. "I wish that were true. Still, I have been blessed by magic. Because it talked to Marc, I was not killed by that wolf. And hearing magic speak though the amulet is a true honor."

They came to the place where the eastern path to Oak Creek crossed a small stream. Its gentle gurgling filled the quiet of the forest. Donald bent and scooped up a handful of water. "This is as sweet as my freedom. Again, my thanks to you and Valeria for watching over me last night. I pray you have many healthy children together."

Marc immediately recalled the night she tried to seduce him. The powerful memory of her touch and breath upon him made his spirit ache for her. The sudden clatter of rapid hoof beats and shouting roused him from his thoughts. Pivoting, he saw Thaddeus on horseback, a mere twenty paces away, drawing back his bow.

"Die, wizard." With a wicked smile, Thaddeus loosed his arrow.

Marc's mind snapped to attention and his magic leapt from him, deflecting the missile while he voiced the unneeded command.

"You failed, Thaddeus." Marc carefully approached him. "You cannot harm me."

Reaching for another bolt, Thaddeus swiftly placed it to the cord and pulled it taut. "But I can kill your friends." The arrow flew straight at Sean's chest.

Heartbeat pounding in his ears, Marc ignored the shouts of his friends and repeated the incantation, stopping the arrow in mid-air. But Thaddeus readied another, targeting Donald this time. Again, magic halted the missile before it struck. Going on the offensive, Marc prepared to injure Thaddeus with the magic Blade, but concentration it required caused him to stumble over a stone and fall backwards.

"*Now* you can be harmed!" With a scowl of pure hatred, Thaddeus released his fourth shaft.

Too disoriented to find the arrow with his magic, Marc definitely saw it with his eyes. It seemed to float slowly toward him, like the time the wolves attacked months before. He braced for the coming pain but suddenly found himself jolted sideways. In horror he watched as the arrow meant for him plunged deeply into Sean's back. With a cry of rage, Marc blindly hurled a Blade in Thaddeus' direction. Missing the man, it instead slashed deeply into the horse's flank. Releasing a shrill neigh of pain, the animal streaked into the forest with Thaddeus atop.

"Sean!" Marc cried out. His friend lay over him, his face wracked with pain.

"Oh, God," Donald said with a gasp, bending to lift Sean off.

"*Wait*, Don," Marc said forcefully, quickly casting the spell, "*Volitā!*" Sean Floated upward and Marc stood. Envisioning the injury, he went all cold inside; the arrow had pierced the corner of Sean's heart. "Easy, Sean."

"Where's Thaddeus?" Sean gasped, his bulging eyes flicking around to look everywhere.

Marc searched outward with his mind and found the enemy still galloping away on the panicked horse. "Gone." Seeing the crimson stain spreading over his friend's tunic, Marc swallowed hard. "Why did you do that? That arrow was meant for me."

Sean fixed him with an unyielding gaze. "I had to save you. You saved me."

Bowing his head, Marc yielded to the truth of his words; Sean had kept their village's code of honor. "Let me try and heal you." He lowered Sean to the ground, placing him on his right side. "Don, hold him so he doesn't roll over." Donald knelt and supported him while Marc quietly said, "*Discinde,*" severing the arrow at the skin. From the Traces found on the shaft, he knew Thaddeus learned of their ruse because Rutilus later remembered him. Disgusted at his failings, Marc hurled the shaft away.

Sean looked up at him, teeth clenched in pain. "I *had* to protect you because you're the next wizard... and my friend."

Near tears, Marc knew the wound was probably fatal, and more likely so because he had too little experience with healing. "Quiet, now. Let me work the magic."

Donald wept softly. "This is my fault. If I had not gone to spy on Crowe, there would have been no need of a rescue, and no one coming to kill me and my rescuers."

Marc pushed his magic into Sean's chest and held the wound closed as best he could. "No. Thaddeus came to kill me only. The magic has spoken to me of it."

Donald looked at him, a mixture of relief and puzzlement. "Why?"

Marc shook his head. "On that it remains silent." Though he put much pressure on the wounds to Sean's heart, Marc could not stop all of the bleeding. He tried using the spark to hold the flesh of the wound together, but it immediately tore apart. A cold terror crept within Marc's core, coiling about his own heart and squeezing it mercilessly as the truth of the situation could no longer be denied. Sean could not be mended. Death would soon claim his dear friend.

"I think I know," Sean said, his face paler than before. "Oren will die soon, and if there is no wizard to protect our land, men like Crowe and Thaddeus will have free run of it." Wincing, he grabbed fiercely at Marc's tunic, pulling him closer. "You will have to face him soon and only one of you will live. Please make sure it's you."

"I'll do my best." He hated that his best was not enough for Sean.

"Can you not heal him?" Donald asked.

Marc prepared to admit failure when Sean's expression silenced him.

"No, he cannot. Death's shadow is already upon me." Sean smiled, breathing heavily. "Strange thing, dying. You learn many things." His gaze locked hard onto Marc's. "I know the secret of magic. You are wise to keep it hidden." Sean closed his eyes as a ripple of pain coursed over his body.

Had it not been for his friend's sacrifice, Marc knew *he* would be the one lying there, pouring his life into the dirt. He wanted to thank him, but trying to form the words proved difficult. "Sean, I—"

"Do not speak it." Sean opened his eyes. "I know your thoughts just as you knew mine the day I rang the bell. There is no need to thank me. I did what I was destined to do. Serve our people instead." He looked at Donald. "And you. Be the leader you were meant to be. Seek Marc's counsel as your father sought Oren's."

His face wet with tears, Donald's voice shook. "I will, my good friend."

Sean's breathing quickened, becoming more labored. "Marc, you will have need of my body once I'm gone. Do so with my blessing." He tried to chuckle, but winced and coughed, releasing a trickle of blood out of the corner of his mouth. "I have a message for Oren: Your plum tree blooms so beautifully."

Marc did not understand.

"He will know its meaning." His smile fading, Sean swallowed, his voice much weaker now. "Your father is here, Marc. He's very proud of you." A spasm of pain shot through him. Sean gasped for air and seized the amulet in his fist. "We'll always be close by." Another, more intense, pain wracked his body which Marc felt as well. When it passed, Sean's eyes fluttered open. "That's better. It doesn't hurt anymore." Then his gaze slowly went empty as his body slumped.

Marc was about to cry, but then, with a sense of amazement, saw Sean's spirit rise out of his flesh and stand next to his body. It paused and joyfully Linked to him.

—I am at peace, my friend. I can linger but a moment. There are many here from the other side who love you. Goodbye and give my love to Val. You both honor me greatly.—

Suddenly, Marc became aware of a magical force of such spectacular power that it seemed to go on forever. It enveloped Sean's essence and Marc felt him no more. Reaching out with his magic, he touched this power and an awesome jolt of white energy exploded through him, quickly followed by oblivion.

Chapter 26

Valeria made another slow Envisioning sweep around the village out to about a mile, finding no spies, soldiers, or anyone else not belonging in the area. Taking a deep breath, she let it out along with the tension she felt over the precarious position they were in with Thaddeus, Crowe and the lot. She glanced at her father, Ethan, and nodded. "Still all clear."

He beamed with pride. "Thank you, Daughter. If you ever tire of being a witch, you could be one of the best hunters in the land. With your ability to find game with magic..." He raised both hands in a gesture used to cede victory to another. "Fine skill, that."

Taking up her knife to sharpen another hastily made spear, she smiled back at him. "I was already a fair hunter before apprenticing to Oren. Who's to say I cannot remain so and be a witch as well?"

Ethan chuckled.

"A fair hunter, you say?" Domas' basso voice rumbled from behind her. "Ah, dear child, there's no need for modesty. I dare say you're better than most of the men hereabouts. You may not be able to shoot arrows as far and throw spears as hard, but you more than make up for it with better aim and stealth."

She felt her cheeks redden and knew the others saw it when they laughed good naturedly. Ducking her head, she let her hair fall over her face, hiding her grin. She liked the positive mood of the villagers. Ever since she passed on the message that Marc and Oren had freed Donald, spirits soared, none more so that Garrett's. Knowing that Donald had seen the error of his ways made her even more happy. For some time she'd prayed he would come to his senses, and now that he did, she felt she had witnessed nothing short of a minor miracle. Finally, the four of them—Marc,

Sean, Donald and herself—could return to the tight group of friends they had once been.

Suddenly, a hot, then cold, sensation, flashed through her chest, filling her with an intense dread. Glancing wildly around for a threat that wasn't there, she opened her thoughts and suddenly *knew* Sean had been hurt. Dropping her knife and the unfinished spear, she raced out of the common house as fast as her feet would take her.

"What is it?" her father called after her, concern in his voice.

"It's Sean," she yelled over her shoulder. "He's been hurt."

Ψ   Ψ   Ψ

Confusion filled Marc. Everything was dark—no, not *dark*, exactly. More like missing. He had no real sense of his body. No light came to his eyes or sound to his ears. His skin detected neither warm nor cold. It was as if he lay in the deepest of sleeps or—could he be dead? Disturbed by the idea, he fought to collect his thoughts. If he were dead, then only his spirit would remain, and spirits had no need of a body and the senses they contained. Or maybe his spirit had left his flesh for some other reason, like the time he and Valeria first connected magically. No, somehow he knew that was not it, either. During that experience he still retained a sense of place, of being, of Valeria's presence.

Valeria's presence! Yes! He immediately tried to Link to her—and failed. Then he tried to Envision her but couldn't. With a growing sense of alarm, he tried using other kinds of magic only to find he had none to command. That which he resisted and feared for so long was gone. Only in its passing did he come to realize how significant a part of him his magic had become. As he began to reflect on the irony of that fact, he felt a *shift* slide over his being.

Muffled sounds came to him. Were they voices? His face hurt as well. More sounds again, this time seeming more distinct, followed by a sharp sting on his left cheek.

"Marc, Marc. Wake up," Donald said, his tone worried and urgent. He slapped Marc's cheek again.

Opening his eyes, Marc looked around, disoriented. His pulse drummed painfully in his temples and his eyes couldn't quite focus. He lay flat on his back with Donald bending over him, his face fearful.

"Are you injured?" Donald asked.

Was he? The lack of any significant pain let him know nothing was broken or deeply cut. "I'm all right, I believe." Blinking several times, Marc sat up and saw Sean's corpse a good ten paces from him. Odd. Only moments before he knelt next to Sean. "What happened?"

"I'm not sure. After Sean... died, you flew back as if, well, struck by something unseen. It took over a minute to wake you, and for a short time you didn't breathe. I feared you dead as well. And for a moment a bright light surrounded you as if you were within a great fire."

The fog addling Marc's mind suddenly cleared, allowing his memory to return. He stood, put his hands on Donald's shoulders and met his gaze. "The magic let me witness Sean's spirit as it left him. It- it was wonderful. I know that sounds like a strange thing to say right now, but it was. He said goodbye and that he was at peace." Marc's voice softened, taking on a reverent tone. "I think... I think I felt him go into Heaven." Marc paused at hearing his own words, for they came to his lips at the same instant they came into his mind. The significance of that understanding rocked Marc to his core. "Then a powerful force touched me. That must be when I ended up here." Returning his thoughts to the present, he Envisioned for Thaddeus and found him on foot, running their way. "We must go. Thaddeus returns."

Donald stooped and lifted their friend's body onto his shoulder. "I'll carry him home," he said, his voice breaking.

Marc keenly felt Donald's sadness and grief. His own remained trapped deep inside, not yet willing to face the truth. "Thank you. I must find Oren and Val. Go to your father. Tell him Crowe will move upon us very soon." Seeing the amulet swinging from Sean's neck, Marc took it and put it about his own, then picked up Sean's staff and one of Thaddeus' arrows. He handed the staff to Donald. "Go with God." Donald left quickly.

Marc tried Linking to Oren but, strangely, just like in his dream, or whatever it was, he could not. Trying Valeria, he encountered the same difficulty, as if that part of his magic slept. Unlike his dream, he easily Envisioned both and found her closer and to the west, running through the trees in his direction, so he headed toward her.

Marc ran full-out, ducking tree limbs and jumping over rocks and roots, until his lungs ached, his legs heavy as stone. Many thoughts tumbled through his mind, all centered on what led up to Sean's death. With each passing moment he became more aware the fault was his. Had he taken greater care, constantly watching Thaddeus and his men, none of this would have happened.

Instead, he childishly ignored the wisdom taught to him by Oren, his mind wholly on other things. Talking with Sean and Donald. Rejoicing at not only saving Donald's life, but reclaiming their friendship. And the very moment Thaddeus attacked, vigilance lay abandoned, his mind instead occupied by matters of lust. If only he—

"Marc!" Valeria called out.

Clearing his thoughts, he watched her emerge from the trees. Her face showed the grief he had yet to permit himself to embrace. They ran into each other's arms, clinging tight, reaffirming the other was still there, alive and well. When they separated, he looked down at Sean's blood on his hands and clothing. It seemed so unreal, like a nightmare. "It's Sean. He's—"

"Dead. I know." Tears streamed down her face.

Marc looked up and caressed her cheek to clear away the dampness, leaving a faint trace of crimson behind. "I'm sorry."

She shook her head then wiped at her eyes. "I've had visions. I... I saw his death several times before. The first time when he overheard you telling me about being in the Vale and finding the buck. Another time when he came to tell us of the king's death. It wasn't clear to me then, but now—" She put her hand to her mouth, fighting back a sob. "And a short while ago I felt his spirit cry out. Who killed him?"

An overwhelming pang of guilt hit Marc, making him turn away from her. "I did."

"*You did?*" She arced around him and lifted his face to meet hers. Confusion filled her hazel gaze as she softly repeated, "You did?"

"Thaddeus' arrow killed him, but it was meant for me. I should of been the one shot, not Sean." Marc told her what happened. As he finished, the anger and sorrow exploded out of him in a bellow of pure anguish. "His death is *my* fault, Val! He didn't need to die."

Valeria leapt forward and wrapped her arms tightly around him once more. "But then *you* would have."

"I didn't sense Thaddeus approach. Sean's dead because I was distracted," he snapped, bitter regret in each word. He closed his eyes and tried unsuccessfully to will away the pain flooding his soul. "Because I was a fool," he added, just above a whisper.

Valeria stepped back and held his face tenderly. "No, that's not the reason. It was his destiny to save you. Sean knew that. I *know* it, too." She gripped his bloody tunic in her right hand and shook it. "I feel it in his blood. Open your mind and let the truth in, Marc. If you weren't destined to have your magic, he would have died months ago. He lived then so that you would not die today."

Relenting, Marc allowed the Traces almost boiling up out of the remains of Sean's life to enter into his mind, the knowledge piercing his doubt like the sharpest of blades. All of what happened *was* meant to happen. While true, it did nothing to ease the pain of losing his friend. He held her closer. "I know."

Bathed in her love, he shed his agony and grief onto her shoulder. At that moment, he needed her more than anything.

Chapter 27

Marc held Valeria close as they stood deep in the forest south of their village. Lifting his head from her shoulder, he looked into her eyes. Her gaze, as well as her magic, held a deep, abiding love for him. While still sad over Sean's death, the worst of the grief had passed. She healed the wound to his spirit much as he had done to her when she had the vision of him dying. "I love you," he said softly.

"And I, you." The truth of her words resonated to the very center of his being. She stepped back, looking him up and down with curious interest. "Your glow—it's stronger."

"It is?" He felt no stronger. If anything, maybe a bit weaker. "I wonder why?"

Looking him over once more, she shrugged. "Let's figure it out later. For now we need to return to the village." She took his hand and took a step in the direction of the path.

"One moment." Standing fast, he sought out Thaddeus and found him examining the area where Sean had breathed his last. Seeing the remote image of that evil man made Marc's anger rise. The fervor of it seethed within his soul like a great fire, growing ever more toward out-and-out hate. It was easy to let that hate come, to *want* it to come. After all, who deserved to be hated more than Thaddeus? Then, with what felt like a sudden, cool breeze, his inner voice pushed those dark emotions away, clearing his thoughts, calming him.

Again he Envisioned Thaddeus, this time keeping his passions in check. The man squatted where Sean had fallen and studied the ground with a smile, apparently pleased at taking another's life. Pushing out with his magic, Marc easily knocked him off his feet, even from over half a mile away, dropping him face-first onto the blood-saturated soil. With a curse, Thaddeus sprang to his feet and searched about, brushing the tainted dirt from him.

"Damn you, Oren."

Without thinking about it first, Marc reflexively Pushed the illusion of his voice into his distant cousin, concentrating hard on making it sound powerful. —*Not Oren. Marcus.*— Clearly shocked, Thaddeus drew his sword and pivoted in place, trying to locate Marc's position. Marc, too, felt surprise. Never had he Pushed a sound so well, so easily. On a hunch, he recalled the image of one of the demons Oren had frightened Portaeus with and tried Pushing it into Thaddeus' mind. At first he only accomplished a wispy and vague version of that form. Focusing harder, he managed to firm the illusion enough to be recognizable. Thaddeus gasped upon seeing the wavering, somewhat transparent demon before him. Holding the image steady in his mind, Marc had it speak to him, its voice deep and ominous.

—*Come, Thaddeus. We await you in Hell.*—

Fearfully backing away from the perceived threat, Thaddeus blanched and ran southward, crashing through the underbrush with abandon.

Valeria smiled slightly, her gaze alight with approval. "Very good. Why didn't you tell me your skill with illusions had improved?"

Releasing the Push, Marc looked at her, feeling a bit stunned. "I- I had no idea I could." He momentarily inspected his fingertips as if they might hold the answer. "Somehow my magic has changed." He shook his head, wondering how this came to be. After a moment, he returned his attention to the here-and-now. "Let's get to Oak Creek."

As they hurried toward the village, Valeria squeezed his hand. "When I felt Sean's death, I tried to Link to you. Did you not hear me?"

"No. I also tried to Link to you and Oren but couldn't."

"Try him now," she said.

With more than a little trepidation, he guided his thoughts toward Oren, half expecting the effort to fail. —*Master, are you there?*—

—*I am.*— The elder's mind came through as clearly as it ever had.

Relief shot through Marc. —*Sean... Sean has died. He saved my life. Thaddeus attacked and Sean sacrificed himself. He*— Marc couldn't bear to finish it.

—*I know, my friend. I foresaw it all.*—

His master's sorrow rushed forth over the Link, both for Sean's loss and for having withheld the truth. At first, Marc wanted to rail against Oren for doing nothing to save Sean. Surely some way could have been found to change things, to prevent his death. If Marc had known ahead of time when and where Thaddeus would attack, he would have been prepared to do battle, and Sean would have—

The amulet about his neck suddenly felt hot as Marc recalled seeing Sean's pale body lying upon the ground, saying, "I did what I was destined to do." Letting out a deep sigh of resignation, Marc hung his head as the anger and frustration he harbored crumbled away. He understood why Oren had to conceal that knowledge. Any interference would have surely changed things for the worse. To know that future and yet do nothing to alter how it would play out took courage, faith and wisdom. It took someone like Oren.

—*I am sorry you bore that burden, Master.*—

A flicker of gratitude came across their Link. —*Better me than you. Tell me what happened.*—

Marc detailed his encounter with Thaddeus. —*Then Sean told me to tell you these exact words: Your plum tree blooms so beautifully.*— A sudden, powerful sense of alarm, then joy, exploded from within his master, leaving the hair on Marc's arms standing on end. —*What is it? What does it mean?*—

—*Praise God.*— A moment passed before Oren calmed enough to continue, happiness effusing his every thought. —*It is a message. From my wife. Just before she died, she said she would try to communicate those words to me if she and our daughter made it to Heaven. For years I ached to hear her thoughts, to feel her mind, but I never did. This news gladdens my heart more than I can say.*—

Valeria warmly embraced Marc as the magnitude of the message amazed and humbled him into silence. After he recovered, Marc told the rest of the story including being struck by the powerful force that knocked him out. *—That might explain the changes in my magic.—*

—Changes? What kind?—

Marc told of tripping up Thaddeus and Pushing the two illusions into him. *—It seems I can do more now than I could yesterday.—*

—Try the Blade on something,— the Master urged.

Marc knew that meant something too difficult for him to cut before today. Looking about for a suitable item, he found a small, dead tree with a trunk as thick as the width of his palm. With the skill he had developed so far, he figured it should take him two or three tries to cut it down. But now? Aware that Oren Envisioned his actions, Marc firmly struck the tree with the best Blade he could craft, cleanly slicing it through. It crashed to the ground with a heavy thud, faint curls of smoke rising from the edges of the cut. He turned to Valeria with eyebrows raised, doubting what he had just done.

Oren's emotions rushed through him. *—Incredible. The strength of your magic has increased greatly.—*

Realizing what it cost for him to gain that strength, Marc's elation sagged. *—I would gladly give it up, give all my magic up, to have Sean alive again.—*

The master's thoughts turned serious. *—Would you, Marc? Would Sean agree with that? You are a powerful wizard for a reason. You can save many lives in the years to come.—*

— But only if I remain a wizard.— Marc, as did Sean, understood that necessitated something else. *—And only if I survive the test. I gather Thaddeus' attack was not it.—*

—No, your test is yet to come.—

A claustrophobic sense of dread closed in around him. What he just went through was horrible. What could be worse than almost dying *and* losing a friend? In all likelihood it would be his test.

—When will it come?—

—I do not know the hour or day, only that it is soon. Do not let Sean's sacrifice be in vain. Fulfill your destiny as he fulfilled his.—

The strength of Oren's words took hold of Marc's mind, stripping away his negative thoughts. He started toward the village once more. —*I shall.*—

Taking his hand, Valeria walked with him and addressed the wizard. —*How are we going to fight Crowe's men? They are skilled, seasoned soldiers.*—

Marc knew she had a valid point. While brave and strong, the men of Oak Creek were no match for Crowe's forces. Add in three wizards and the odds improved a lot, but even if they prevailed, he knew many in the village would die. Memories of the horrific images from Fox Glen surfaced and he quickly pushed them aside, but not fast enough to quell the barely suppressed rage he felt over that unforgivable massacre. Somehow they had to find a way to prevent that.

—*I have a plan,*— Oren Linked. —*When you both learned the Great Secret, I also told you about something that made our magic more powerful. Do you remember?*—

Marc and Valeria glanced knowingly at each other. —*We do,*— Marc said. —*What do you have in mind?*—

Ψ   Ψ   Ψ

Entering the village, Marc and Valeria found most of the people gathered within the common house, mourning Sean, who lay upon the table nearest the fire pit. Marc found it difficult to look at the remains of his friend. Seeing them, Garrett and Donald approached, their faces long and pale with grief.

"Thank you for bringing Donald safely home," Garrett said quietly, embracing Marc then Valeria. He gestured toward Sean. "It's regrettable we cannot celebrate it at this time." Guiding them to a quiet space, he asked, "Do you have any ideas to help us fight Crowe?"

Marc nodded. "Yes. Oren has a brilliant plan." He felt a gentle and familiar warmth brush against his senses. Glancing at Valeria, he saw she sensed it too. "The Master has returned to the village."

Entering the common house moments later, the old wizard joined them, and motioned for Ethan and several other men to come over as well. Once everyone had seated themselves, Oren addressed them with a quiet yet authoritative voice, "I fear that if we fight Crowe's men directly, many of us will be lost. I have an idea that may defeat Crowe while avoiding a full-out battle. It involves some risk, but I believe it will work. While in Crowe's camp this morning, Marc and I learned many of his men have no desire to die for him. *That* we will use to our advantage."

Garrett's face brightened. "Valuable information to have. Go on."

Oren displayed a thin, somewhat sad smile. "It is no secret I am getting old. I am not as strong as I used to be, both in body and my command of magic." The master's admission of weakness surprised Marc. "Even with the able assistance of Marc and Valeria, the task before us is daunting. We will need some help."

Garrett gave him a reassuring nod. "I trust in your judgment, Oren. Tell us what we need do."

Oren detailed the plan. The men smiled and Garrett clasped Oren on the shoulder. "You are indeed a crafty wizard, my friend. We will start on it at once."

As the men left to see to their tasks, Oren turned to Marc, concern in his features. "Are you ready for this?"

Marc fought down his fear. He had to do his part perfectly, otherwise he, and many of his friends, would die. "Yes."

Oren leaned closer and lowered his voice to just above a whisper. "Am I correct in sensing the men from Crowe's eastern camp are all moving toward the western camp?"

Marc carefully Envisioned the entire area around Oak Creek, then concentrated more closely on the space between them and the two camps. "Yes, and they are all heavily armed. I believe that after reaching the western camp, they will all head our way." He met the wizard's gaze. "I think we have at most two hours before they are here."

Oren grimaced. "That is what I saw, too. What of their emotions, Valeria?"

Marc watched as she centered herself and concentrated on the distant group of men. Half a dozen breaths passed before she spoke. "Anger and hatred from some, many others hold fear, desperation. But from all—" She opened her eyes and cast them a disheartened look. "I feel readiness for war."

Oren nodded in acceptance. "Indeed. Let us change into our wizard's robes and prepare to meet the enemy."

Ψ   Ψ   Ψ

Valeria stood at the edge of a flat stone outcropping high on the southern end of Rocky Hill. The brisk wind whipping against her robe had a cool bite to it. She hoped that chill would not usher in bad luck for her village. Below, and directly to the east, she saw Oak Creek's graveyard, where many of her former neighbors hurried to finish their preparations. Shifting her gaze southward, she made out the dust stirred up by the column of Crowe's men. And directly in their path lay Marc.

Her insides knotted with dread. Would this be his test? To confront Crowe was to confront death itself. For what must have been the hundredth time she said a quick prayer for the safety of Marc and the village.

To her right stood Donald. With a hand shielding his eyes from the sun, he searched the woods below. "Do you see him?"

"Yes, but with my magic, not my eyes. He waits at the wide meadow. Crowe's forces are about a thousand paces from him."

Donald's discomfort at being near her assailed her spirit much like a fire's heat would warm exposed skin. When Oren put both of them at this lookout, she suspected that action served a purpose greater than watching the movement of Crowe's men, something she could do just as well from the ground. Probing Donald's thoughts, she found he wanted to apologize for his treatment of her and Marc, but hesitated to do so from more than just embarrassment. He feared her. Saddened, she hoped he could someday find a way past that fear.

She turned to him. "You are troubled. Please, talk to me about it."

Averting his gaze, he kept silent for nearly a minute. "It's difficult to speak of. You command magic's power and I have wronged you... and Marc."

"You think I would harm you over your past actions? Do you not know me?"

"The Val I grew up with would not, but—" He shrugged apologetically. "You have changed."

Almost denying his observation out of reflex, she realized the truth of it and gently touched his back. "Some, but you have changed, too. I am much the same person I was before hearing magic's call. I would never hurt you for any reason." She looked south to the approaching dust cloud. "Now, Thaddeus—I'd gladly rip the heart from his chest."

His fear strengthened. "You could do that?"

"Easily," she said without emotion. Facing him, she took both of his hands in hers. "I bear no ill will against you. We are, and shall always remain, friends."

"We will?" he asked, his expression uncertain.

She gave him a smile and subtle nod in answer, much like those Oren had given to her and Marc many times. She suddenly wanted to laugh at herself for mimicking her master's mien of appearing all-knowing and mysterious. The mighty wizard Valeria. Ha!

"We've known each other all our lives, Donald, and care deeply for each other, as if we were brother and sister. Your feelings for me became... misdirected for a time. Clouded by your desires." Seeing the crimson flush blooming upon his face made her want to tease her friend, but doing so would be unkind at this moment. "And while you experienced intense feelings toward me, they were not love in the romantic sense. Not true love."

Letting go of her hands, Donald hung his head in acknowledgement. "But you feel such love for Marc."

A swell of warm emotion welled up inside her, threatening to burst forth from her skin in a shower of incandescent joy, and she fought not to let it show. "All my life."

Donald looked up in surprise, his thoughts pouring into her, clear and undiluted, but she answered before he could voice them.

"Yes, all my life. I didn't understand or question my attraction to Marc early on, just accepting it as normal. But several years ago, long before I started my training with Oren, I began having visions. Mostly of Marc. I knew then I would marry him some day."

Donald nodded. "Marc said the magic had predetermined your choosing each other."

Valeria shrugged. "Possibly, or God did. Either way, Marc is the only man for me. We not only love each other, we are *in* love with each other. There's a difference there I cannot explain very well, and I doubt can be truly understood until you experience it for yourself. Don't worry, you'll find someone."

She looked deep into his eyes and had a flash of a vision; Donald and Barbara sat together in the common house, each holding a child while a very pleased Garrett squatted before them, tickling the tummy of the eldest tot. A chortle of amusement erupted from her as she realized its meaning. "Well, that didn't take long," she muttered.

His eyebrows rose as he cocked his head to the side. "What didn't take long?"

She gave him a toothy grin. "The magic just revealed to me some of your future. I know who you will fall in true love with, who you will marry."

Donald's spirit brightened. "You do? Who is it?"

Valeria laughed softly. "I'm not telling. It's better you find out on your own. But I will tell you she's a strong woman. A beautiful woman," she added with a wink. "Your life together will not be easy at times, but it will be rich and filled with love." Turning toward the meadow, she checked on her own love, her humor quickly ebbing away. If only she could have a vision of today's outcome as easily as she'd done for Donald. Again and again she tried to no avail. Marc's future was blank to her, as was her own. When she Envisioned Crowe and Thaddeus on their horses, she set her teeth together in anger toward the men who wished harm upon her husband-to-be and the village. Taking Donald's hand, she began forming the bubble about the two of them so they could Float back to the ground.

"Crowe's men are nearly there. It's time we take our places below."

Chapter 28

Marc's heartbeat quickened. The time had come; the enemy would appear at any second. Taking slow, deep breaths like Oren taught him, he fought off the panic creeping into his thoughts and began walking eastward along the northern edge of the meadow, trying not to look hurried or aware that over sixty well-armed and dangerous men were all but upon him. His starting position had been carefully chosen, putting him far enough from the bend in the western path to be safe from arrows, yet close enough to be clearly spotted. The plan relied on Thaddeus' hatred of Marc—and possibly Crowe's as well—to cause them to pursue him eastward to the graveyard instead of proceeding further along the established path toward the village. This action would hopefully fragment the enemy forces by separating the foot soldiers from their leaders, while also tiring the men by running them through difficult terrain. It was also hoped that the attackers would arrive at their destination man by man instead of as a group, delaying the start of combat.

Those on horseback were the first to emerge from the woods. Hearing their cry of alarm, Marc spun about and pretended to be surprised. Thaddeus immediately kicked his mount into a full gallop. Dashing north into the trees, Marc did not have to work much at pretending to be frightened. If he failed to time things correctly, he would likely be the first of many to die. Fifteen seconds of running time ahead rose the rocky embankment that ran roughly east-west for a mile in each direction. Averaging over twenty feet high, its slope was steep enough that neither man nor horse could readily climb it. Twenty seconds behind followed Thaddeus. Plenty of time to spare.

Marc had practiced this move while waiting. The woods were thick here and one false move could cause him to fall or dash his head against a branch. Gulping down air, he swung around the large gray oak, under the branch and over the log behind it. For an ordinary man, the embankment would be impossible to quickly scale. But not for a wizard. With a bound, he Floated up and over the edge, landing on his feet just as Thaddeus' horse skidded to a stop, hampered by the dense growth. Marc sensed the arrow flying past several feet above his head. He'd timed it perfectly.

"You cannot hide from me, *apprentice*," Thaddeus shouted derisively.

Continuing east, Marc ran along the ridge's crest, creating a deep furrow in the thigh-high grass. "Of course I can, *murderer*," he answered loudly, knowing full well that hearing his voice would draw Thaddeus and the others after him. "I can outrun you or any of your men."

Envisioning the meadow, Marc saw Crowe draw up next to his evil cousin and shout, "A hundred silver to the man who brings him down!" while directing the entire column of men after him. Marc felt a surge of satisfaction—and relief—that Oren had correctly predicted their attacker's actions. At first, Marc crashed through the underbrush and snapped off small, low-hanging dead branches, making enough noise to ensure the foot soldiers would know where to follow him. Those on horseback, however, would have to detour far to the west to get around the impediment. By then Marc hoped to be at the graveyard.

Running hard, he stretched out his legs, taking full strides, his magic letting him avoid hazards hidden by the deep grass, ones deliberately placed by him and citizens of Oak Creek—many short, sharpened sticks buried vertically in the earth, foot-high ropes stretched between trees, carefully concealed holes and other devious traps meant to injure the unwary. He easily made it to the graveyard before any of his pursuers and saw the adults of the village gathered about a freshly dug grave. Valeria, her face concealed by her robe's hood, stood with Donald, Garrett and Oren. Nodding at the four of them, he took his place beside the master as the sound of rapid hoof beats approached from the west.

Bringing their horses to a halt several dozen paces outside the graveyard, the riders held back, apparently waiting for the others to catch up. Crowe and Thaddeus warily eyed Oren, who stood straight and tall, both hands firmly grasping his staff planted vertically on the ground, his stern gaze meeting theirs. A steady stream of soldiers emerged from the trees and clustered behind their leaders, panting heavily. Many bore heavy scratches and deep cuts, especially on their legs, thanks to the traps set for them. Two men favored an arm and a quick Envisioning told Marc those limbs were broken. Only after his men had assembled did Crowe lead them forward.

Garrett addressed Crowe as if no threat were evident. "Do you come to pay your respects to the dead, my lord?" Crowe and several of his men laughed contemptuously. Glancing at Oren, Garrett gave him a slight smile then turned back. "No? Then I ask you to leave us to bury our brother in peace."

Crowe responded with a cold, inhuman glare, and Marc shivered as the *Nothingness* swelled within the man, Thaddeus and others around them. The clammy, almost slimy, sensation of it against his spirit felt *wrong* in every way, as if it opposed everything good, even life itself. An equally cold sneer curled the man's lips. "We came to give him plenty of company."

Like you and Thaddeus, Marc thought hopefully to himself. He watched the two leaders carefully as Oren advanced several steps past Garrett. "Shame be upon you, Simon Crowe. I knew you as a young man. Then you were eager to serve the king and protect us from the invaders from across the sea. He once trusted you. Now you betray all that, destroying his land and people with your lust for power." The wizard pointed his staff southward. "Leave us, or die this day."

The corner of Crowe's mouth lifted in a dismissive smirk. "So you say, old man. Your magic did nothing to protect the king from his nephew. Now he's dead and left no heir. Someone must rule and it shall be me. Those who refuse to serve me will feed the worms." Crowe's gaze shifted lazily to the village leader. "Garrett, I give your people one last chance. Serve me or die."

Garrett looked at his neighbors. "What say you?" A chorus of emphatic noes rose loudly from them.

Oren pounded his staff defiantly on the ground and thundered, "They will *not* submit to a servant of evil."

Crowe shrugged as if his decision were unimportant. "As you wish." He nodded at his archers. "Kill the old man first."

As one, a handful of men drew back their bows and loosed a flock of arrows. The breath in Marc's chest froze as Oren simultaneously made a great outward sweep of his arms and calmly commanded, "*Mē dēfende!*" The shafts halted several paces from the wizard, then dropped harmlessly to the ground amid gasps of surprise from many villagers and even some of the soldiers. Visibly tensing, the archers glanced uncertainly at each other. Oren gave Crowe an unyielding look. "You cannot harm me."

Even knowing the master expected the assault, seeing how smoothly his teacher countered the threat amazed and impressed Marc. Outwardly, Crowe appeared unaffected by what happened, but Marc's magic told him otherwise; only the man's arrogance—arrogance supported by the evil within—held his fear in check. Crowe already thought himself king, believing he had the right to decide who lived or died.

Glancing at the fallen arrows littering the ground, Crowe leaned back on his horse, pursed his lips for a moment, then said, "Very well, but the others have no magic to protect them."

Struck by the eerie similarity to Thaddeus's earlier threat, Marc glanced over at the black-clad figure who glared hatefully at him.

Oren took a deliberate step forward, almost stomping his foot down, his gaze hard iron. "*I* will protect them." He faced the soldiers and gestured toward the villagers. "Whomever moves against these people will earn my wrath and that of the magic I command."

Thaddeus laughed. He tried to make it sound derisive, but it ended up coming across as hollow. The man deeply feared Oren and—Marc suddenly realized Thaddeus feared *him* as well.

"You? Protect *everyone* here from *all* of us? Ha. You are too feeble, old man. You are not long for the grave yourself. Why not save everyone the trouble of killing you and crawl into that grave there." He pointed at the hole next to Sean's prone body, an eyebrow arched in query. "Is that for the one I killed earlier? Pity. I meant to kill your apprentice." The man's gaze turned back to Marc. "I'll get him soon enough."

Thaddeus's malicious stare pierced Marc's spirit like an icy lance; he meant what he said. Some of Crowe's men gave Marc the same look, the *Nothingness* about their spirits directing its hateful attention at him, as if it were alive, a being unto its own right.

With a sickening sense of dread, Marc knew his test had come.

"Do not mock magic and the dead," Oren shouted with authority, "for this is hallowed ground. Do evil here and the dead will rise up against you."

Warm magic flowed outward from the master, momentarily blocking the evil focused his way. In the lull, Marc now felt many of the men considering whether they should flee, their hatred of their leader evident. He also felt the *Nothingness* knew this, too, and had just tried to prevent him from detecting it. Maybe it *was* alive.

Crowe looked questioningly to Thaddeus who shook his head. "The wizard is only bluffing, my lord. The dead do not rise."

Portaeus emerged from the ranks and, after a worried glance Oren's way, dropped to one knee before his commander. "He's a powerful wizard, my lord. He once broke my sword with only a twig and two demons serve him. Please, my lord, let us leave here now." For a moment, Marc hoped Portaeus' plea might find a receptive ear. Then the man suddenly stiffened, eyes bulging, then fell lifeless to his right, an arrow protruding from the left side of his chest.

Gesturing with his bow, Thaddeus glared malevolently at his men. "Any *other* traitors among you?"

Worry began to gain a foothold in Marc's mind. Oren's edge had vanished—the men now feared Thaddeus more. Seeing that as well, Crowe began to gesture for his men to attack when Oren raised his voice once more.

"Spirits of Justice, come inhabit the body of our murdered Sean so that he may bear witness against his killer. Take the evil soul of that man to the lake of fire where his flesh will be seared for all time. Come now, for I, Oren the Wise, *command it!*" —*Now, Marc,*— his teacher Linked.

Marc watched as all eyes shifted to look upon his friend's corpse. Doing his best to conceal his grief and revulsion at defiling his friend's remains, Marc reached out with his magic and, with great effort and concentration, manipulated Sean's body, making it sit up, open its eyes and look at Thaddeus. Even though he had practiced this before heading to the meadow to wait for Crowe's army, the effect did not look anything like a body coming back to life, its movements too jerky and uneven. A gasp rose up from both the villagers and soldiers. Crowe's eyes widened as Sean stood and walked stiffly toward him, the villagers hastily parting as he passed. When Sean stood beside Oren, Marc had the body first look at, then point to, Thaddeus.

Oren directed the end of his staff toward the accused. "By his own admission, and by the direction of the spirits within Sean's body, Thaddeus is to be condemned to eternal death. Those who follow him will earn the same fate." The wizard slowly swept his staff toward the soldiers. "Do further evil here and *all* the dead will rise. And not just those dead resting here, but those of Fox Glen and everyone you killed in the past. They will pursue you night and day, never stopping to rest. You cannot escape them. *Ever.*"

Close to panic, the soldiers muttered excitedly amongst themselves, anxiously glancing between Oren and Sean. Thaddeus gave out a thin, nervous laugh, his hands tightening on his mount's reins. "Do not let this concern you, my lord. It is all a trick. Oren cannot command that sort of magic. No one can. The boy is alive, I tell you. Watch." He put an arrow to his bow and pulled it far back, letting it fly. The shaft pierced the chest clear through. Of course, Sean did not flinch, and Marc had him look down at the arrow and slowly shake his head. Breaking off the tail, Sean cast it aside and trudged toward Thaddeus, an accusing arm raised, finger pointing out his killer.

Thaddeus' mouth hung open in disbelieving shock.

"He doesn't bleed," one of the soldiers exclaimed in terror.

"We should heed the wizard's words," said another, his voice wavering.

"Poor Thaddeus," Oren said sadly, turning to the men, his arms out to his side in a gesture of appeal. "Escape his miserable fate. Save yourselves. Turn against him and Crowe."

Highly agitated, the men fearfully looked about at each other, close to making a decision, one way or another. With a snort of disgust, Crowe pulled out his sword and held it up. "Atta—!" With a cry of surprise, he found he no longer held the weapon, which now flew through the air toward Oren.

Catching its hilt, the wizard directed the tip at the previous owner, the sun glinting off the blade and into Thaddeus' eyes. "You did not heed my warning, Crowe. Pay the price." Raising the sword above his head, Oren swung it down upon a large stone, concurrently cleaving it in two with his magic Blade. "Rise, all you dead," Oren bellowed with righteous anger. "Rise up against the evil that mocks your sleep. Rise up and take them to the grave."

Marc Linked to Valeria, —*Hold Sean upright while I make Portaeus move.*— When he felt her magic take hold of their friend's remains, he made the dead soldier stand, pull his sword and lurch menacingly toward Thaddeus. Tomar and two others stepped before their leaders, swords at the ready. All three reeked of *Nothingness.*

"Dead or not, you will not pass," Tomar growled. While the man's voice sounded firm enough, his eyes nearly glowed with fear.

—*When they draw near, swing Portaeus' sword at their weapons and arms,*— Oren said as Tomar cautiously inched closer.

When the man got within range, Marc acted, his manipulation of the man's body slow and awkward, but when Portaeus' blade touched Tomar's, the other's weapon broke in two with a loud clang thanks to Oren's magic. Jumping back in surprise, Tomar let the other two men have a go. As if repeating a often-practiced move, they simultaneously plunged their blades deeply into Portaeus' belly. Taking advantage of their positioning, Marc immediately swung the sword at their extended arms while Oren severed them. Shrieking in pain and terror, the men retreated behind the others and jerked around in pain. Spitting out a foul curse, Tomar seized a spear from a nearby soldier and hurled it at Portaeus' corpse, piercing his neck. Marc had the body reach up with its left hand, extract the shaft and flip it over into a throwing grip. With the two weapons still impaled in his chest, Portaeus advanced on Tomar, spear and sword held high. While sickened by the necessary mayhem, Marc found himself grateful it had the desired effect—Crowe's grip on his men was loosening.

—*Throw the sword at him,*— Oren Linked.

Marc flung the sword and sensed Oren take control of it. The blade sang as it flattened out and sped toward the man's neck. An instant later Tomar's head tumbled with a crunch into a nearby bush as his limp body fell backward toward Crowe, spraying the leader with a shower of blood. Many of the soldiers let out shouts of alarm. The weapon circled back to Portaeus and Marc had the body's hand catch it. As a group, the soldiers began to creep backwards, horrified gazes fixed upon their former comrade-turned-undead executioner.

"*Rise, RISE!* dead of the village," Oren said, his booming voice rich and sonorous.

Panic flowed from Thaddeus like a gust of chill wind—his men *were* going to turn. From thirty paces behind, Marc sensed seven bodies emerge from their graves. Arms outstretched before them, the dead staggered slowly forward, soil and debris flaking away from their shroud-bound bodies. The villagers screamed and retreated while Crowe's men also recoiled, bunching together in wide-eyed terror.

Oren Floated six feet into the air, his deep green robe fluttering in the wind like a battle flag. "What do you fear more? Thaddeus' bow, or the wrath of the dead?" He pointed Crowe's sword at the two leaders. "They must die *now* if you are to escape this fate."

With a great, bestial roar, the bulk of the men charged Crowe and Thaddeus, the crushing intensity of their emotions nearly overwhelming Marc's senses. Those who remained loyal—each steeped heavily in the *Nothingness*—tried to fight them off. Feeling a sudden sense of danger, Marc's back clenched tight as he found an arrow suspended in the air several feet before him. As it fell to the ground, he looked beyond and saw Thaddeus lowering his bow, cursing. Giving the man a look of cool disdain, Marc inwardly regretted his foolishness at letting the mêlée distract him. This was the second time he dropped his guard today. The second time someone else saved his life.

—*Keep vigilant,*— Oren said flatly, landing nearby.

Glancing hastily about for further immediate threats, Marc answered, —*My thanks, Master, and my apologies.*— Resolving to stay better aware of his surroundings, he returned some of his attention to Crowe and Thaddeus, whose followers had retreated to form a semi-circular shield about their leaders. Marc guessed their number to be a little under one-third of the total force. Crowe sat upon his mount, closest to his men, with Thaddeus behind him, furthest from the threatening forces. Thaddeus's gaze caught his for just an instant, and in that moment, Marc knew the man was about to run. Incensed, Marc had to stop him, but how? Other than the knife on his hip, he had no bow or spear. Casting about, he spied one of the piles of hastily made spears concealed beneath some bushes. Releasing his hold upon Portaeus' body, which crumpled limply to the ground, Marc uttered the unneeded spell and brought one of the spears to him with his mind. He heaved it at Thaddeus, who easily parried it with his sword. Retrieving another, Marc was about to try again, but could not get a clear shot because his target constantly moved due to the fighting around him. As he spotted an opening, Marc drew his arm back to throw only to be nearly knocked off his feet by Donald slamming into his right side.

"Sorry," Donald said, huffing loudly, then springing away from him, "had to dodge a spear."

"No problem," Marc said.

He knew one could easily avoid a spear if one saw it being thrown, even if cast by a skilled warrior. They were only dangerous if a number arrived at the same time, or if one was caught unaware. Realizing the futility of using traditional weapons instead of his magical gifts, he tossed the lance aside and thought about how best to neutralize Thaddeus and Crowe. He didn't want to kill them outright, even if that would be easier than finding a less permanent way of stopping them. First thing, though, he needed to get them off their horses to prevent them from fleeing. Just as the idea formed in his mind, he watched Thaddeus maneuver his mount next to Crowe, lift a leg and, planting a foot on his leader's back, shove Crowe off his horse and into the fray below.

Thaddeus quickly spun his horse about and started forcing his way west and toward freedom. This action was repeated by the two companions that always seemed to be with him. As Marc started to send his magic outward to pull down Thaddeus, he sensed a sudden flash of anger and hate from his right. Casting a spare glance that way, he discovered one of the evil soldiers had flanked around the village defenders and now headed directly for Donald, his bloodied battle axe swinging up into a killing strike. Redirecting and strengthening his magic, Marc aimed for the attacker, shouting, "Donald. Down!"

Pivoting his way, Donald saw the direction Marc looked at and, apparently seeing the urgency on Marc's face, writhed in a manner that would make a ferret proud, flinging himself down and to the side. At the same moment the soldier swung the great axe and it would have buried itself deep in Donald's gut if the force of Marc's magic had not impacted against him. With a deep grunt of expelled breath, the man suddenly changed direction and became airborne, flying for over twenty paces until slamming violently into a tree with a muffled crunch of many breaking bones. The man then fell silently to the ground, either unconscious or dead.

Scrabbling to his feet, Donald looked to his attacker and, seeing the deformed heap, said, "Dear God." Facing Marc, he lightly bowed his head. "Thanks."

Seeing the light of fear in his friend's eyes distressed Marc, for he knew it was not due to the death Donald narrowly avoided—too little time had passed for Donald to fully realize the threat the soldier presented—but due to his fear at witnessing the level of power Marc possessed. At how much different—and dangerous—Marc had become. Setting this concern aside, Marc gestured toward the battle raging nearby. "Back to the fight."

Nodding his acknowledgement, Donald sprinted over to the fallen attacker and took up his axe.

Marc returned his attention to finding Thaddeus but became distracted as a volley of six or seven spears headed for where Oren and Valeria stood. Shouting a non-verbal warning to them, he stopped all but two, but because of his action, the other wizards safely intercepted those. Quickly assessing the scene, Marc found the repentant soldiers had just engulfed Crowe. Seeing their leader's defeat, the unrepentant soldiers now came at the villagers, determined to take some lives before their own were lost.

Marc immediately joined Oren in Blading the bows and swords of those attackers nearest the people. Not able to Blade very well, Valeria instead used her magic to hurl spears with deadly accuracy and force. Garrett, Ethan and others picked up their own bows and sent arrows into the mob. The attackers in the rear continued to throw spears over the fighting and toward the villagers. Marc managed to deflect all but one. To his horror, that missed spear struck Valeria's mother, spinning her about, taking her to the ground. Sprinting to the downed woman, he expected the worst and cursed himself for not being able to use his magic better. He reached her the same time Valeria did. Together they dropped to their knees, reaching to find Aula's wound. Then, suddenly, he and Valeria looked at each other and briefly laughed; fortunately, the spear had only caught the edge of Aula's garment.

His humor just as quickly passed. Standing, he seized the weapon and, from the Traces upon it, sought out the one who threw it only to find him lying headless in the dirt. The Trace upon the body was unmistakable. —*Thank you, Master Oren.*—

—*You are welcome.*—

Scanning the scene, Marc could not find Thaddeus, alive or dead; the man had escaped during all the confusion. Deeply frustrated, he wanted to slam the butt of the spear he held into the dirt, but instead calmed himself because that action would not serve any purpose except to upset him further.

In less than a minute the few remaining attackers fell. The men who heeded Oren's warning now knelt in ranks before him. The old wizard strode purposefully down the line—tall, vital and in charge—looking into each man's eyes. Only upon reaching the last man did he speak.

"Face south," he commanded tersely. "Look at the ground. Remain silent." After all the men complied, Garrett and Donald rounded up the seven villagers who had risen from their graves and moved them out of sight.

Marc found it difficult not to smile for the seven were quite alive. When Oren told Garrett of his plan to turn Crowe's men against him by making the dead rise, he explained he could bring only a shadow of life back to the freshly dead. The long dead would remain so. With only one fresh body on hand—Sean—he asked if some villagers might pose as the dead to further frighten Crowe's men. Oren hastened to add that magic would not normally allow such trickery, but because of Crowe's evil acts, it would be permitted this one time. There were no shortage of volunteers. After digging out shallow depressions in which to lie, they were wrapped in mud-saturated shroud cloth, covered with old leaves, then a thin layer of dirt. While waiting for Oren's call, they breathed through a bundle of short, hollow reeds. The well-acted, horrified reactions of the other villagers completed the ruse.

Standing before the soldiers, Oren lifted his hands into the air. "Thank you, spirits of justice. Return now to your domain and leave our dead to rest once more. Take with you the souls of Crowe, Tomar and those who served evil. Show them no mercy. Take them now."

Marc heard the illusion the master then Pushed into the soldiers minds—a long, blood-chilling squeal of death, not unlike a pig being butchered. Many of the men cringed at hearing it, letting out quiet noises of terror. Marc knew the illusion served more than to just embellish the show; each man would long remember the sound, a reminder of how close death had come.

Oren waited until the men stilled. "Your lives have been spared because you repented and fought against evil. For now, you will be little more than slaves, working to undo some of the damage you wrought. Take this opportunity to examine your hearts...."

While Oren continued his lecture, Marc Envisioned the outlying area and found no remaining threats. Far to the south, Thaddeus and his two men rode hard. While he would have preferred they be punished for their crimes, he would settle for them to go and never come back. To ensure they got the message, he Pushed an image of himself into their minds and said, —*Return here and die.*— Seeing the fear on their faces made him hope they would heed his warning and, if he were honest with himself, gave him a bit of satisfaction as well. The newfound strength of his magic still surprised Marc.

After binding up the worst of the soldier's injuries, the village prepared to bury Sean. His heart heavy with sorrow, Marc gently removed Thaddeus' second arrow from his friend's body, then Floated him back to the grave site. Valeria came alongside of Marc, nestling both her body and spirit against his. Her silent sobs pulsed through him as Sean's parents wrapped their eldest child in shroud cloth while Scipio, their youngest, watched with clenched jaw, desperately trying not to cry. They placed Sean in the ground, then each took a handful of dirt and dropped it on him, saying their tearful good-byes. Each villager in turn did the same. When the last of them had passed by, Marc stooped and gathered up some of the rich, dark soil that would soon forever embrace his friend. Looking down into the hole, he wondered whether Sean's sacrifice was worth whatever he might do in the future. Twice today his life stood in peril, and twice another had saved him. Facing considerable danger, he used his magic to help defeat those wanting to harm him and his village. While he may have passed his test, he took no joy in it.

Marc turned to the people, meeting their gazes. "What lies here is not Sean, only his empty shell, a memory of his life among us. His spirit lives on. He—" His throat tightened, not wanting to speak the words that must be said. Forcing his grief to retreat, he steadied himself, drawing in a calming breath. "He gave the full measure of himself for the good of his neighbors, saying I was to be the next wizard that would protect all of you. In honor of his sacrifice, I pledge that I will do everything in my power to keep the people of Oak Creek and the surrounding villages safe. For now, I will work alongside of Oren the Wise who has served you well for generations. When he decides the time is right, I will humbly take his place. This I do for all of you, and for Sean." Marc sprinkled the dirt into the grave, crossed himself and walked past.

Valeria, too, faced the people, her eyes sad but proud. "I, like Marc, have been called to serve magic. And, with him, I will also serve you." Reaching toward Marc with her right hand, palm up, she uncurled her fingers one at a time in a rippling motion while saying, "*Surge venīque, amulētum.*" Rising off of his chest and over his head, the amulet flew to her grasp where she then held it up for all to see. "When he died, Sean's spirit passed through this amulet on his way to his reward. The magic that lives with us all has a gift for you. Close your eyes. Quiet your minds. Be calm and listen to magic's voice."

When all was still, Valeria let the Trace Sean put upon the stone go from her mind into everyone else's. A multitude of gasps came from the crowd as they experienced what Marc had witnessed earlier—Sean's peace and joy as he transitioned from life to afterlife. After a minute she released her Push. A wave of gratitude and relief flowed out of the crowd and through Marc's mind. Everyone murmured excitedly, amazed at what took place.

Filled with intense love, Marc held Valeria close. —*That was wonderful of you.*—

Pulling back a bit, she kissed the stone and placed its lace around his neck once more. *—I had to ease their pain and let them know what we knew.—*

He kissed her tears away, sniffing back his own. *—And you did.—*

Sensing a sudden surge of pride, they both turned toward the source. Oren looked their way, a faint, sad smile upon his lips and he gave them a small bow of respect.

For the remainder of Sean's funeral, many spoke kind words about him, recalling how deeply he touched their lives. Afterward, Oren brought Garrett before the captives.

"This is Garrett, leader of Oak Creek. Follow his orders as you would mine. Please him and you will enjoy my mercy. Displease him—" The Wizard's voice and gaze hardened. "—and you will not." Crowe's men heard him well. Oren walked over to Portaeus' body and gestured at it with his staff.

"Portaeus and the remains of those who fought against Crowe will be buried here with honor and prayer. Those who sided with Crowe will be carted off for the scavengers to feast upon. They were evil and no hallowed ground will be wasted on them. Only after they have become the dung of animals may they return to the soil from which they came. The remains of Crowe and Tomar deserve even less than the wolves and foxes. Ethan, have some of these captives carry them to your swine. Both sows have blessed you with many piglets. They will make short work of their flesh."

Ethan warily eyed the grim remains of Crowe before nodding to Oren. "As you wish."

Marc, too, felt some discomfort at the idea, but agreed that such a profound insult would make a strong and lasting impression upon the soldiers. He only regretted that Thaddeus would not be joining his friends in the pigs' bellies.

Oren stepped back, motioning to Garrett, who stepped up to address the prisoners. "All of you who are able-bodied, divide yourselves into two groups. The first group will go at once to Fox Glen to bury the dead and return with what supplies and possessions you did not steal or destroy the first time you were there. Those items will be given to the survivors who will live with us for a time. Once back, you will begin building them homes here. The second group will remain here to bury the dead and cart off the refuse as Master Oren has commanded. Then you will go to Crowe's camps and return with all the supplies and spoils you have taken thus far."

As the men separated themselves, Marc watched the old wizard pull one of the captives aside. "I have a special task for you, Petros. Take a horse and visit the two villages north of here. Inform them of Crowe's defeat. Tell them they are welcome to come celebrate this good news with us on tomorrow's eve."

Tall and lean, yet strong, the soldier's black hair and eyes made his tanned skin seem all the darker. The man bowed his head. "I will do as you say, mighty one, returning before nightfall."

Oren smiled slightly. "Then be off with you."

Marc approached the man as he vaulted onto a horse's back. "Seek out a monk named Gildas who is among their people. Tell him he is needed here."

"I shall, Wizard Marc." With a kick to the animal's sides, Petros thundered off leaving a wake of dust.

Garrett came near, gesturing at the departing man. "Can you trust him to return?"

Giving out a satisfied grunt, Oren nodded. "Yes."

After a moment, Garrett glanced questioningly at Marc. "What is Gildas needed for?"

"So I may wed Valeria, of course."

"Of course," Garrett echoed with a smile.

Chapter 29

Marc, Oren and Valeria treated the injured soldiers in the village worship area, the benches providing the men places to lay. Of the three most severely wounded, they managed to save two. The remaining men were in no immediate danger, but even so it took hours of continuous use of their magic to heal them. Marc found himself nearly exhausted by the time they finished. Spotting Oren seated on a log in the shade, he joined him.

"What a day it has been," Marc said with a sigh, rubbing his aching temples. "I feel as if I moved a mountain, one stone at a time."

With a weak chuckle, his mentor nodded. "Indeed."

"So much has taken place. A lifetime of experiences."

For a moment the master remained still, watching as Valeria brought water to the wounded. "You did well today, with one exception."

Marc knew that issue would come up sooner or later. "Vigilance, I know. But I passed the test, thank God." Oren looked at him curiously, but said nothing. "What is it, Master?"

"You will always face tests of one kind or another. The most difficult aspect of each will often lie within you." Closing his eyes, the wizard chewed on a piece of dried fruit. "You did not kill today." Oren's calm voice held no admonition; he simply stated a fact.

"I used my magic in the least harmful way, just as you taught me. I could have quickly beheaded them all, but what would that gain? You gave the men enough chances to save themselves. I tried to do the same. Because of that, many lives and souls were saved."

The old man gently squeezed Marc's knee. "You have a peaceful, noble heart. But as we discussed last night, some men deserve to die. Valeria knows that."

The image of her heaving spears at the attackers rose in his mind. At the time her actions were justified. Still, he found it almost contradictory that the same woman who had earlier dealt out so much death now tenderly cared for others.

Marc took a deep breath and let it flow from him, releasing some of his stress and fatigue with it. "I understand, Master, I do. Since last night I have witnessed much of the violence and evil found in men's minds. I have experienced death, too—the poor souls of Fox Glen, Sean, all the soldiers today. The last thing I wanted was to make more of it." He looked at the blood-stained dirt by his feet. The many Traces upon it crowded at the edges of his perception—fear, pain, hate, anger, despair. They would overwhelm him if he let them all into his mind at once.

"I felt temptation today, Master." He told how the hate for Thaddeus came upon him and how his inner voice pushed it away.

Oren smiled, the crinkles around his eyes deepening. "Your goodness prevailed. The evil of the world wanted you dead, but Sean prevented it, bringing about many changes. Donald finally matured, putting him on the path to his destiny. Sean told you to use his body, which gave me the idea that defeated Crowe without any of the village coming to harm. Many worthy future events will come about because of his sacrifice."

The sadness coming from Oren equaled his own. "You did tell him he would play a large part in my destiny. I hope to be as wise as you some day."

"Live as long as I and you shall." The old man looked upon him with admiration. "You are much wiser than I was at your age. Arturius had not told me the secret yet, not for another two years. I was stubborn and did not accept all of his philosophy. I thought I knew better, and sometimes, when in a less than charitable mood, I considered him an old fool. But he remained patient with me and I eventually understood." Oren patted Marc on his knee. "Now it is *my* turn at being the old fool."

He looked at the man in surprise. "Nonsense. I have never regarded you in that way, Master."

"And so revealing your greater wisdom." The old wizard's eyes sparkled. "I told you that one day your magic would surpass mine, that I would no longer be the master. That day has come. From now on call me by my given name."

Marc felt a smile forming on his lips. "It would be my honor to do so, Oren, but we both know you have much more to teach me."

Oren chuckled and returned the smile. "Absolutely. I have gathered much knowledge and experience over the years and it is yours and Valeria's for the asking. But I cannot teach you any more about magic. All that remains is for you to sharpen your skills." Releasing a labored sigh, the old one struggled slowly to his feet, dust shedding off his robe like smoke. "I need to sleep. Look in on the wounded once more before you retire for the night, *Master Marc*. Be at peace, my friend." Giving him a small wave, Oren headed into the village.

Ψ   Ψ   Ψ

Marc and Valeria settled the soldiers into the east end of the common house before dark, charging the more able-bodied among them to care for those less so. True to his word, the rider Oren sent out returned, reporting to Marc that both villages now knew of Crowe's defeat.

"And what of Gildas?" Marc asked.

"I found him on the road north of Bitter Well. He said he will come this way with morning's first light along with many from the villages."

Their gaze met causing Marc to see a flash of the man's future. He would be a good man, a leader. Reaching up, Marc grasped Petros' forearm in a warriors grip. "Well done, Petros. See to the horse's needs, then tie it up with the others and take your supper."

The man hesitated, eyes downcast, clearly wanting to say something else but afraid to.

"Is there more?" Marc asked, giving him an opportunity to speak.

"I... we..." Petros paused, swallowed nervously, then gathered his resolve. "Many of us who rebelled against Crowe did not know who he really was at first. We and our families were starving and he offered a fair wage. We all knew he held a high and honored position with our late king—" He fully bowed his head, quietly adding, "—may the merciful Lord bless his soul." Straightening, he continued. "Crowe told us that together we would keep the peace and protect the land. Not knowing his true

306

nature, we swore allegiance to him. But all too soon—" Shaking his head, Petros looked away in shame. "Madness... cruelty... and...."

"Evil?" Marc finished for him. Petros nodded. "Then why did you not leave?"

Rubbing a hand over his face, Petros closed his eyes and slumped forward, regret ebbing from him. "A few did at first. Crowe had Thaddeus, Tomar and others like them hunt down and bring back the deserters who would then be killed slowly while we were forced to watch. One of the deserters had a family. He was kept alive until—" Petros took a ragged breath as his hands balled into tightly clenched fists. "Until riders returned with the heads of his wife and children."

While his outward expression remained impassive, Marc's gut quailed at the horror of the thought. Dear God, if that were to happen to him, if someone brought him the heads of his mother and sisters—of Valeria!—he would surely go insane. Careful to keep his voice calm and even, Marc said, "So you and the others were little more than conscripts; serve or die."

"Yes. I wish I could have found the courage to flee. If it were only me, I would have chanced it, but—"

"—you have a family," Marc finished for him. Pulling thoughts off the surface of Petros' mind, Marc said, "You'd rather keep your wife, Cana and your sons, Silus and Ocella, safe."

Petros suddenly straightened in surprise, then bowed his head once more, deeper this time, and said with a shaky voice, "You are indeed a mighty wizard. Please forgive my sins against you and your people."

A pang of discomfort squirmed inside Marc. He hated this part of being a wizard. "Look at me," he said, gently. The man complied to a degree, not quite meeting Marc's gaze. Marc continued, "Only the Almighty may judge you and forgive your sins. The Word says that those who truly repent and change their ways will be forgiven. As for me, I have seen your change of heart and any trespass you may have made against me is forgiven. Go in peace." Marc stepped away from the horse and gave Petros a little bow.

A small, tentative smile developed on the man's face. With a nod to Marc, the man lightly kicked his mount into a trot and left. After clearing away the emotions generated from his talk,

Marc sought out Thaddeus and, after a couple minutes of Envisioning down several of the southbound roads, found him and his two friends making camp more than a day's walk away. It appeared they heeded his warning. Turning, Marc headed around the common house and for the home of Valeria's parents. As he approached the doorway, Valeria stepped out to greet him, a knowing smile on her lips. Taking her into his arms, he drank in her essence. Holding her felt so right, as if only then was he fully whole.

They were betrothed, yet not in the traditional manner; the parents were not consulted, no permissions given. He worried that Ethan might feel insulted. Taking her hand, he entered the hut. Her mother, Aula, looked up from her sewing and smiled; something in her gaze made him take notice. Valeria gave him such looks at times, too.

Aula stepped over and hugged him. "It's good to see you, Marc."

Ethan stood and shook his hand. "Welcome." The man studied him then grinned slightly, putting his arm around his wife. "It appears you wish to ask something."

Marc swallowed and nodded, gripping Valeria's hand a little more firmly. "I do. I suppose by now it's no secret I love Val and she loves me." He kissed her hand. "I seek your blessing. I wish—we wish to marry."

Aula looked at them warmly. "When Sean returned from Oren's home, he told us of your love for each other. Valeria, do you know what your father said when he heard that?"

"It's about time," Ethan said, smiling.

Marc and Valeria looked at each other in mild surprise. He turned back to Ethan. "Then you approve? I have your permission to marry her?"

Ethan let out a hearty laugh. "Of course. Magic aside, I cannot think of a better man for her than you."

Marc's heart leapt. "Thank you. I will always love and care for her."

Valeria threw her arms around her parents, kissing each. After chatting for several minutes, Marc and Valeria took their leave and headed for the common house. They surveyed the room.

A multitude of snores greeted their ears like a giant swarm of bees about their hive.

"It's too full," she said. "And loud. I'm bone tired and need a quiet place to sleep."

He felt the same fatigue weighing him down. "Well, we can't sleep in our beds. Barbara and Rufa are using them."

"Wherever I sleep," her gaze settled softly on his, "I'd prefer it be next to you."

He smiled. "I have the perfect place in mind."

Leading her out the southern door, they made their way to the piles of goods brought back from Crowe's camp. Sifting through the items, he found two large skins. "These should do nicely." He rolled them up and hefted their weight onto his shoulder. "Follow me."

"Where are we going?"

"The tanning shed. There we will find plenty of quiet."

"And privacy." She squeezed his hand. "No unpleasant thoughts of others to invade our rest."

They walked north out of the village under a sky streaked with the vibrant pinks and violets of sunset. A lone cloud blazed overhead with a deep orange glow along its western edge, the last embers of a dying sun. Reaching the pens holding Ethan's pigs and sheep, they turned east and continued several hundred paces into the oak grove until they reached the shed. When they were younger, they used to play here with Sean and Donald. Marc opened the door and half a dozen mice scattered for cover.

Unused for over two years, the odor of flesh, oak leaves and leather was absent. The tanning barrels, once filled with a potent brew of leaves and bark, stood empty. The drying racks leaned against the far wall, barren, mute skeletons of wood and rope. To the eye and nose, little remained to give voice to the many hours spent working and playing here. But his magic found it to be richly populated with Traces of his father and friends. After the day's events, these good memories were most welcome.

Valeria stepped inside and looked around the dim interior. "I haven't been here since the darkness came." She closed her eyes and smiled. "I feel such comfort here. It is filled with love and friendship." She hugged him. "This *is* perfect."

He cleared off the large table his father used in his leather work and spread out the skins. Picking her up, he gently laid her on them. "Would you like a fire?"

"No, the skins and my robe will be warm enough." Shimmying away from the edge, she made room for him.

He climbed onto the table and pulled the other skin over them. Slowly drawing her near, Marc kissed her, lightly rubbing her back. She sighed and closed her eyes, saying, "Your touch is heaven itself and your love for me is like a bright light."

"As is yours for me." He continued to rub her back for a while, feeling her body relax. "Gildas will be here tomorrow," he said, breaking the silence.

"I know," she mumbled, snuggling closer.

"Sleep," he whispered, lightly kissing her forehead. Marc realized that for the rest of their lives they would be together like this, sharing everything, everyday. He could barely believe his good fortune.

As she drifted off, he silently offered up his usual nightly prayer, adding to it his gratitude at surviving his test and asking for guidance to ensure his friend's sacrifice would not be wasted. When that final thought entered his mind, the immense power he felt at Sean's death moved upon him once more. It did not come with force or dominance, but the most delicate gentleness. Although awestruck, Marc felt no need for fear. Apparently Valeria agreed for she sighed happily in her sleep. He wondered if she also knew *whom* the power represented.

—*Thank you*,— he Linked into it. —*Please take care of Sean.*—

As if in answer, peace filled him. Not an ordinary kind of peace, like falling asleep in the warm sunshine with a full belly, but a complete and total peace. Marc knew no words to describe it. Then he realized he'd been told that Sean knew this peace as well. Gladness surged within him and it echoed back from the power a thousand-fold stronger. His skin felt strange, as if ants crawled over him. Opening his eyes, he saw that a vibrant rainbow of colors buzzed around him, akin to the blue glow of magic only far more intense. Valeria giggled, but did not wake, equally covered in the beautiful light.

Amazed, he held up a hand and wiggled his fingers, causing the colors to swirl and flicker like flames. A thought entered his mind—no, not a *thought*, actually, more of an understanding. No words were heard or Linked to him, yet he comprehended the meaning just as clearly. They were being blessed, as individuals and as a couple. Valeria lay still, a wide smile on her lips, tears leaking from her eyes. Marc hesitantly reached out to the power with his mind, very heedful of what happened when he did the same thing that morning. This time he had better results. The nature of the power made him gasp in astonishment. Earlier, it overwhelmed him because he did not expect or understand it. Now he did. It was love. No, *Love*. Immense, complete, *eternal* Love.

Humbled beyond measure, he withdrew his mind and clung to Valeria. Moments later, the colors around them faded and, as the presence departed, he felt a sensation similar to a caress move over him. Now alone, he trembled as if very cold or frightened, yet neither applied. Why did the Almighty have reason to visit *them*? What made him and Valeria so special? Dozens of similar questions jumped around in his mind, each equally unanswerable. Doubting any explanations would come forth tonight, he believed it best to think on it for a while.

And what of Valeria? Wake her, or not? While he desperately wanted her to know what happened, he wondered if he *should* tell her. If she were supposed to know about it, would she not have awoken during the visit? Telling her now might also result in them staying up all night talking and that would not be good. They very much needed to sleep, to regain their strength, magically and otherwise. Tomorrow, then, he decided. Tomorrow.

Chapter 30

Valeria couldn't be happier. The love of her life was safe now that Crowe had been defeated, leaving them free to be wed. She thrilled that Gildas would be in the village before nightfall and able to perform the ceremony the next day. When she woke earlier that morning, she still lay beside Marc in the tanning shed, his arm protectively about her. Safe, warm, loved. She wanted to stay there forever. But just after Marc woke, the master Linked to them and asked them to return home to take care of things; Oren had not rested enough to make the trip there and back in the same day. And so they made their way home first thing.

During the journey, she told Marc of the fascinating dream—or vision—she had last night. It was so unusual, different than any before. While much of her memory of it seemed muddled and indistinct, parts of it remained clear. She remembered seeing many colors, rich and intense, some of which seemed strange yet wondrous, as if they were new to the world and could not be viewed with eyes alone. She also saw an unbelievably bright light, far, far stronger than the midday sun. It blazed so bright that putting a hand before her eyes did nothing to lessen its power. Within its radiance she felt love, especially love for her—Marc's love, her parents', her friends', love from everyone she'd known and would ever come to know, and much more. She didn't try to make sense of it, but meekly accepted its presence, and gladly, too.

Marc laughed and put his arm about her shoulder. "You had no dream, my love."

As he told what he experienced the night before, she found herself more and more amazed and, if she were to be honest, slightly anxious. "So you truly think the Holy Father actually came—" The final words fought to remain unsaid for fear they might be thought of as blasphemous.

"To us?" he said softly, tightening his grip ever so gently.

She nodded, welcoming the assurance he projected.

"I am certain of it. On the day I learned the Great Secret, Oren said he believed our abilities came from God."

She blinked as his words practically chimed deep within her, their truth undeniable. Her anxiety waned to be replaced with acceptance tempered with a bit of incredulity. After a long moment she said, "And he was right."

Ψ Ψ Ψ

Humming to herself, Valeria headed out the door to draw water from the well, her chores almost finished. What a beautiful day. Soon she could return to the village and prepare for her wedding. Dropping the bucket, she watched it land squarely on its bottom. Not waiting for it to tip to the side and slowly fill, she used her magic to quickly submerge it and raise it back to her hands. She liked having magic. It made everyday life easier. To not use it felt unnatural.

Setting the bucket on the edge of the well, she looked upon Marc as he inspected the fruit growing on Oren's trees. Each movement of his handsome body awakened a multitude of desires deep within her. And magic's glow shone brightly about him, part of it proclaiming his love for her. And to think she almost lost him yesterday.

Her thoughts turned back to the day when Sean brought them the news of the king's death, to her vision of a dagger killing Marc. The weapon's image seemed so clear at the time, detailed as to the length and shape of the blade and the scrollwork on the antler-bone handle. But somehow she must have misread the image, it being an arrow instead. The master had said that objects in visions sometimes were not as they appeared, instead only representing an idea. As she once more recalled seeing the blade fly toward Marc, a cold terror shot through her, instantly snapping her back to the present, her attention now fully upon Oren. With a grave sense of dread, she saw him standing upon a ledge on Rocky Hill, not far from where she stood yesterday. Far below him, sharp, jagged rocks bordered the stream that flowed by Oak Creek.

Why did she feel such alarm over seeing this? Envisioning about the master, she immediately understood. About forty paces behind him, halfway up the slope of the hill, Thaddeus hid amongst some holly bushes. Slowly drawing back his bowstring, he aimed carefully at Oren. Naked fear seized her gut and squeezed hard.

—*Master! Behind you!*— she screamed in her mind.

Thaddeus let the arrow fly just as Oren spun about and arched his back. With perfect clarity she observed the bolt speed past her master's chest, a hair's breadth away. Wheeling his arms in large circles, Oren unsuccessfully tried to right himself. Horrified, she watched as he fell backwards over the edge.

"Marc!" she cried out, hastily Pushing the image into his mind. He quickly understood and joined her in Envisioning the scene. Oren lay sprawled face up on the rocks, a red stain creeping outward from beneath his head. He did not move. —*Master?*— she Linked to him. No reply came. Thaddeus stood and gazed down upon Oren's still form. With an arrogant smirk of satisfaction, he turned and headed down the hill.

"He's *dead*," Valeria said with a sob, her heart breaking.

"I think not." Marc held her hand reassuringly. "I did not feel his spirit move from him. But he *is* injured. We must hurry to help him." Pivoting in place, Marc reached toward the house as the door swung open. His small pack of medicinal supplies swiftly flew out of the doorway and into his arms. "Let's go."

Together they ran toward the gate. She repeatedly tried to rouse Oren with a Link, but he remained unresponsive.

"Val, Thaddeus is meeting up with his companions, Rutilus and Atellus," Marc said. "Try to find out why they have returned." He hesitated, then added, "Besides attacking Oren."

Companions? How many enemies had returned? Hastily Envisioning them, she watched Thaddeus boastfully inform his friends of killing Oren. Her ire spiked. If only she had Marc's command of the Blade. Forcing her emotions aside, she strained her magic to the limit, Pulling what she could from Thaddeus over the distance. What she got sickened her. "He's filled with hate and revenge. The lust for murder consumes him. A lust—" A stab of fear struck deep into her soul. "—directed at *you*."

No fear came from Marc, only a heavy sadness. "We must stop him for good. Today."

Yes. Thaddeus *had* to be stopped for he would never change his ways, remaining a deadly threat to anyone who crossed his path. Now that he had attacked the master, he would soon move upon Marc. Valeria desperately hoped Oren had survived his fall for they needed his help, his wisdom. Once more she tried a Link, pleading, —*Master, wake up.*—

—*I am, Valeria.*— His pain coursed heavily through the Link. —*My thanks for your warning.*—

Her spirits soared in relief. —*Marc and I are coming to help you.*—

—*No. Return to the house. Thaddeus will be going there next.*—

—*But your head is bleeding,*— she said.

—*My injuries are not life threatening. I cut my head against the rocks as I fell but landed softly due to Floating. I feigned death to fool Thaddeus. Now go.*—

Marc took her hand and they reversed direction, hurrying toward home.

"It is I who must go up against him," Marc said, resignation coloring his voice. "Now I understand what Sean meant about Thaddeus and I. He said only one of us would live. *Today* is to be my test, not yesterday."

Valeria let out a panicked gasp. "No, Yesterday was. You nearly died twice. It's not fair."

Marc squeezed her hand. "And yet it must be."

—*Marc is correct.*— Compassion flowed from the master. —*You must face him alone, Marc. Valeria and I may not interfere. This is your time. Be the wizard you are, not only to yourself, but to all.*—

—*I'll be ready,*— Marc Linked, —*and this time I'll be more vigilant.*—

—*I pray you will,*— Oren said, breaking the Link.

So do I, she thought to herself.

On the way, she and Marc discussed how they might defend themselves. Jogging up the path to the house, they stopped before the door and Marc glanced back toward the gate, concerned.

She reached for his cheek, brushing it with her palm while letting her love spill into him. "There is no need to worry, Marc. Your skill with the Blade is such you could kill him well beyond an arrow's reach."

"Yes, but—" He pursed his lips thoughtfully for a moment, then said, "I somehow feel the need to do so differently. Make his death serve a larger purpose."

She hated the idea of Marc risking himself again, but she also felt taking the easy solution would be the wrong thing to do. "What kind of purpose?"

Understanding grew on his face. "Oren said for me to be the wizard I am for all. He wants me to make a big show of it, to defeat Thaddeus face-to-face." He drew in and released a heavy breath then met her gaze meaningfully. "Before witnesses."

She nodded, his intentions now clear. "Like he did at the graveyard. What are you going to do?" He told her. While good, the plan held much risk. "Facing him in the Vale is dangerous."

"I know, but that's why it is a test of my skills with magic, my cunning and bravery."

He gazed into her eyes. Within him shone a steadfast resolve to do what needed to be done. Several months ago she heard him tell his mother he could never be a leader, could never shoulder the burdens of others. A leader now stood before her, having unquestioningly accepted that mantle. She couldn't be more proud of him.

He gently placed his forehead against hers and sighed. "I need to do this. I... I almost feel compelled to do so." He gave her a tender hug, then pulled away. "We must leave now if I am to face him."

"But is not Thaddeus coming here?" Seeking him out, she found the three men halfway to Raven's Gate, riding hard. They needed to be delayed to give Marc time enough to reach the Forbidden Vale. A means to do so quickly formed in her mind. She smiled and kissed him. "You are not the only one with a good plan. Thaddeus and his men are on horseback while you are on foot. I'll stay here and keep him busy long enough for you to get to the Vale and prepare to welcome him." She detailed her plan.

"You are a devious one, my wife-to-be." He tenderly placed his hand to her cheek.

She kissed the proffered palm. "No more than you, my husband-to-be."

"But will not Thaddeus recognize you?"

"No. I kept my hood up at the graveyard yesterday. Oren insisted on it."

Marc smiled. "He must have foreseen today. Good luck." Giving her a hug and a quick kiss, he ran for the southern wall and bounded over it.

Trying to calm her jangled nerves, Valeria set about putting her plan in motion. First of all, Marc needed witnesses when he confronted Thaddeus and Oak Creek had a ready supply of those. She wondered how to catch their attention, to tell them where to go. Yes, she could simply Push a message into a small number of them, but doing so alone might frighten them unnecessarily. No, she needed something to catch their attention first, some kind of *show*. She quickly settled upon making something move. Given her physical limitations with magic, it needed to be small, lightweight and able to be manipulated from her current location. As she thought on it, a gust of wind blew past her, stirring a thigh-high cone of dust to life as it flowed around the stone ring of the well. With a chortle of amusement, she said, "Perfect," and turned her attention to the center of Oak Creek.

Envisioning it from high overhead, she located the largest concentration of people and, gathering up her will, caused a whirlwind of dirt and leaves to grow into a tall column before them. At first the villagers hurriedly stepped away from the disturbance, apparently not wanting to have dirt blown in their faces. They did not realize it was artificial as such things were fairly common sights. So Valeria made it move in little circlets, copying the steps of a popular dance that everyone knew. Before long, over a score of people watched in fascination as her odd vortex playfully flitted about amongst them. Quickly doubling the whirlwind's size, she Pushed a message into their minds:

Listen all to magic's words,
Stand and hear it speak.
Make haste you all and travel now,
Go to Wiccan Creek.

The witnesses jolted into an excited state; a few reacted with fear, but most seemed accepting, even delighted, at hearing the message. They hurried away and immediately began telling their neighbors. Pleased with their reaction, she released the whirlwind. Seeking out Gildas, she found him heading their way with many from the northern villages. She repeated the message for them, then Linked to Oren and told him what they were up to.

—*You and Marc have well learned what is means to be a wizard,*— the master responded, not even trying to hide his pride. —*I will be there, headache and all.*—

After unlatching the gate and leaving it slightly ajar, she went into the house and bolted the door. Running to the kitchen, she poured some distilled spirits into the round iron stew pot and Floated it back to the workshop. Opening the door to the cave, she quickly grabbed some skulls of bears, wolves and hawks and put them around the edges of the large table. Returning to the cave, she brought out the silver dagger and the oil lamp. Lighting the latter at the fire, she placed both items on the table as well. Securing the cave door, she hoisted the cook pot onto the table, placing the dagger and lamp on either side.

By then the three intruders arrived and had began searching the compound outside, moving ever closer to the house. She had to hurry. In her room, she put on the ragged clothing she wore for the dirtiest of chores. Going to the fireplace, she lightly smeared her face and arms with ashes, then tousled her hair. She was now the perfect lowly servant.

She knew Thaddeus wanted but one thing—to find and kill her Marc. The man would do anything to accomplish that and would likely leave no witnesses behind. So, in the next few minutes, she had to do two things. First, manipulate Thaddeus into thinking he discovered Marc's whereabouts and, second, survive his attempt to kill her.

Three loud thuds came from the front of the house. Just in time. Muttering a quick prayer of protection, she hurried to the front door and scanned the other side. No drawn weapons. Still, her heart thrummed madly in her chest. From fear? Excitement? Both? No matter. She had to be careful to conceal her true emotions—and magic—from Thaddeus.

"Who is there?" she said, timidly. "What do you want?"

"Send him out," Thaddeus demanded.

"The master has gone away. Come back later."

One of the other men chuckled and muttered, "He's gone away, all right."

"We're not here to see Oren," Thaddeus said less forcefully. "We want to see the young wizard, Marc. Send him out."

"He's not here, either."

"Where might we find him, then?"

"I don't know where he went. They rarely tell me."

"I see." His voice had become more friendly. "May I ask who you are?"

"I am Oren's housekeeper. May I ask who you are as well? I will tell Marc you came by when he returns."

"He and I have some unfinished business to take care of. Let us meet with him to settle our accounts so we can be on our way."

"I told you, he's not here."

"Then let me give you the payment owed him and we will take our leave."

She easily felt the deception but it was no surprise. She counted on it. "Well, I'll open the door only if you promise to stay outside."

"I promise," Thaddeus lied reassuringly.

Steeling her nerves, Valeria wiped the dampness from her palms, keenly feeling the men's evil intentions. They wanted to get what information they could, then rape and kill her, partly because she "belonged" to Oren, the wizard who humbled them the day before, and partly because they enjoyed such things. Only her wits would let her survive this encounter. She unbolted the door and the three men burst in. She squealed in terror—convincingly, she hoped. The last of them, a taller, red-haired lout, roughly grabbed her arm and pulled her after him as he followed the others. They searched the whole house, upturning anything which might possibly conceal a young wizard, and ended up in the workshop.

Thaddeus pointed to the cave door. "Open it." The man holding her shoved her toward it.

Pretending to stagger forward, she reached the wall to the right of the door and faced him, shaking her head earnestly. "I cannot. There's no latch. Only the master knows the secret of that door." She edged fearfully away from it and spoke in a tremulous near whisper. "There is some sort of great evil on the other side.

I've heard breathing come from behind there, like a large beast in much pain. Let me leave this room, I beg of you. It's bewitched. Things move on their own. Strange sounds, voices and smells spring up from nowhere. I do not like it in here."

Thaddeus gestured his men toward the door. "See if you can pry it open."

Both tried to wedge their blades between the door and the frame, but the gap proved too narrow. While they struggled, Valeria Pushed an illusion into the black-haired one and he jumped away from the door in fear.

"Did you hear that?" Atellus said, nervously pointing his weapon at the door.

"Hear what?" Rutilus asked.

"A growl of some kind."

"I heard nothing. Let me see if I can hear it." The man held his ear to the door and she put a different thought into him. Eyes widening, he scooted three steps back. "By Jove. There *is* something in there. I heard chains moving and great claws scraping upon stone." He looked at Thaddeus, worried. "Should we still try to open it?"

"No." Thaddeus put a hand to the back of her neck and the cold steel of his sword to her throat, his eyes hard and demanding. "Is Marc in there?"

She tried to look terrified at the thought. "No. He couldn't be, for if he were, he'd be dead." When he released her with a sideways shove, she deliberately stumbled back into the table, her hand striking the cook pot with a muted ring. Recoiling in horror, she scurried behind Thaddeus and, kneeling, clung to his leg, trembling.

He peered down at her, half amused. "Why are you afraid?"

Flicking her terrified gaze between him and the table, she whispered, "The demon. I may have roused the demon."

Shaking her off, he moved to the table and rapped his knuckles on the iron surface, eliciting another dull ring. "You mean this? It is only a cook pot. There is no demon there."

She vigorously shook her head. "It is enchanted. The master calls it his cauldron of knowledge."

Thaddeus' brows arched and his lips pursed in surprise. "Cauldron of knowledge? What does that mean?"

"It speaks to him, tells him things he wants to know." Valeria felt a surge in Thaddeus' emotions. Her plan was working. "How is it used?"

Flinching as if struck, she backed away. "I must not say. The master will be furious if I do. I will be punished most severely."

Rutilus grabbed a fist full of her hair and yanked her head back, exposing her throat. The sudden pain made her gasp. Bringing a knife to her neck, he said, "Tell us, or die."

After several moments of frantically eyeing the man and Thaddeus, she closed her eyes, swallowed, then nodded in compliance. Releasing her, Rutilus propelled her toward the table. Rubbing her aching scalp, she faced Thaddeus while avoiding eye contact and spoke quietly.

"I have seen the master use it several times. You must light the lamp, then wave the tip of the sacred knife through the flame three times. Use it to prick your finger and put a drop of blood in the cauldron. Next, cut off some of your hairs with the knife, light them with the lamp, and drop them in the cauldron. As long as the flame burns within, the demon can answer your question, but only one is allowed each day."

"So it can tell me where Marc is?"

"It knows all that is knowable."

With a snort of pleasure, Thaddeus grinned smugly at his companions and began the ritual. Valeria hurriedly decided what the demon would say. It would not be her best poetry, but certainly the most quickly composed. By the time he lit the strands of hair, she was ready.

Thaddeus stepped back as the cauldron burst into blue flame. The stench of burning hair made Valeria regret her choice of ingredients for a moment, but she had to put that concern out of her mind. Concentrating on making all three men hear her thoughts, she began her act.

What ask you?

growled a low, unfriendly voice from the depths of the pot.

While Thaddeus' men stiffened in alarm, he seemed quite pleased. "Where will I find the wizard Marc this day?"

Valeria made the voice become louder, more authoritative.

By Wiccan creek a Great Tree stands,
None larger in all the lands.
Standing on that cursèd ground,
Shall the wizard Marc be found.

Thaddeus grinned wickedly. "I know that place." He faced her, bringing the sword to her throat once more, just as she expected he would. "You have been quite helpful. Unfortunately, I have to kill—" He spun about as the cauldron spoke again, this time quite angrily.

You are not my master, Oren
But another, someone foreign.
You have magic and a heart of ice,
For this knowledge, you must pay the price.

"Price? What price?" He glared at her, raw hatred in his eyes. "You did not say anything about a price!" He drew his blade back in preparation to strike her down.

With a loud boom, the door to the cave flew open and a great roar, mightier than from the largest bear, erupted from the darkness beyond. Valeria made objects fly off the workbench and pelt against the men, who cowered against the onslaught behind raised arms, while the voice bellowed with seething rage:

Pay me now in blood that's fresh,
Yield to me a gift of flesh.

Thaddeus seized her arm and hurled her through the opening. Using her magic, she slammed and latched the door, then screamed as if being ripped limb from limb. Her death was quick. After a few moments of silence, she repeatedly slammed her shoulder against the door, making it shake violently, adding a few more roars to her illusion.

Atellus cried out in fear, "The beast wants more!"

The sacrifice's soul is hexed.

322

Be gone, be gone, or you'll be next.

A flood of pure terror poured off the men. They wasted no time in running from the house, mounting their horses and galloping away. Valeria sagged against the cave wall as the repressed fear and tension briefly surfaced. At the moment she couldn't enjoy the thrill of fooling the men, her thoughts too fixed upon her close brush with death. Only her magic and guile kept her alive.

Her guile. She gave out a snort of amusement. The master was right. Deception *could* improve their magic. *Did* improve it. Thaddeus and the others reacted just as she had wanted them to. Firming up her wobbly knees, she cast off the rags she wore and moved into the workshop.

—*Marc?*— she Linked.

—*Everything all right?*—

—*Yes. They are heading your way. Are you ready?*—

—*I will be by the time they get here. You feel excited and nervous.*—

—*I scared them out of their skins. Not bad for a dead woman.*—

—*Dead woman?*—

His sudden concern made her smile and she ached to tell him of her success, but knew he didn't need the distraction right now. —*I am fine. I'll explain later.*—

—*Hurry, Val. I want you to see it all.*—

—*I'll be there with many witnesses.*— She told him about contacting the others. —*Don't begin until they arrive.*—

—*As you wish, my mistress.*—

Valeria cleaned the ashes from her skin, then brushed out her hair. Donning her as yet unfinished wizard's robe, she locked the front door and gate, and made her best speed for the Vale. She would not miss Marc's show for anything.

Chapter 31

Sweat trickling down his back, Marc slowed to a walk as he approached the fallen tree that lay across Wiccan Creek. While catching his breath, he tried to determine the best way to move it—or if he *could* move it, even. No other way to cross the steep banks of the creek existed for at least a mile in either direction, and removing that bridge would delay Thaddeus and his men from entering the Vale until the witnesses arrived. Difficult or not, Marc had to do it.

The task presented a difficult challenge. Never had he attempted to move anything as large, heavy or oddly shaped. Yet from deep within him came an instinctive feeling he *should* be able to manage it. In theory, if he could put a bubble around it, he could move it. Concentrating upon that thought, he pushed out his magic and carefully formed an elongated bubble, straining to encompass the tree's entire length. Once enveloped, he attempted to Float it off the ground, but only the top of the tree moved, lifting less than a foot. Was the bubble formed wrong? No, it seemed properly made. Something kept the base of the tree from moving. Quickly Floating himself to the western side of the water, he Envisioned the part of the upturned root ball still in contact with the earth and found several roots remained intact. Wielding his magic Blade, Marc chipped away at the anchors, cutting through both wood and soil, casting up billowing clouds of debris.

Now that it was freed, he again put a bubble about the tree, but this time it took all of his effort, his magic temporarily weakened from using the Blade so much. With perspiration beading his brow, he completed the task and could not help but grin as it ponderously rose and slowly drifted to his side of the creek, the shadow of its bulk falling over him as it passed. After it fully cleared the creek's bank, he released the bubble and the tree fell hard, landing with loudly snapping limbs and a deep thump he felt in his bones. Once the wildly swaying branches calmed, he walked up and placed a hand upon the thick trunk, half-doubting what he just accomplished. He grinned again thinking how pleased the master—no, Oren, his friend—would be. So, too, would Valeria. He wanted so much to share this with her right now.

Remembering his duty, Marc put that desire aside, tempered his thoughts and Envisioned the area to the east and northeast. Those approaching from Oak Creek were past Broken Rock, putting them about fifteen minutes away. To the north, he found Gildas and those from the northern villages twice as distant. But Thaddeus and his men were about to emerge from the woods east of the falls. His stomach soured. What if his plan did not go as expected? What if Thaddeus or one of his men did something unforeseen? Marc knew the danger of making the face-off with his enemy into a grand show, especially with as little experience at being a wizard as he had. One false move could mean his own death. He had to trust himself and Oren's training. Dropping to his knees, he crossed himself and said a quick prayer for strength and wisdom.

Now in the clear, the three men spotted him and rode his way. As they drew near, the *Nothingness* flowed out ahead of them, its rank corruption fouling his senses. Marc fought down the chill of fear rising within him; such evil must not be allowed to live another day. And yet doubt continued to pull at his conscience, his reluctance to kill as strong as ever. The conflict grew until Thaddeus dismounted and stood across the creek from him. Inspecting the depth of the creek and its sheer, rocky banks, the man glanced up and down its course.

"Well, Marcus, we meet again. Unfortunately, we cannot cross over here." He looked at where the fallen tree had been, studying the depressions in the soil on either side. Shifting his gaze, he saw where it now lay. "It seems you removed that tree," he said mockingly, pointing at it. "Afraid, are you?"

Concealing his inner discord, Marc casually leaned on his staff. "Not in the least. I have no need of a bridge. If you wish to enter the Forbidden Vale, make another. But do so at your own peril." Marc met the gazes of Rutilus and Atellus, and hardened his voice. "To enter here is to forfeit your life. I warned you not to return." The men heard every word.

Thaddeus threw back his head and laughed. "Brave talk for a lowly apprentice."

Marc gave him a loose smile and nodded his head toward the fallen tree. "An apprentice with magic enough to hinder your progress. You command some magic, Thaddeus. Please, return this tree to its resting place and cross over. The sooner you die, the better for all concerned."

Hatred, pure and hot, poured into the man's eyes. "Do not mock me, *boy*. It will be *you* who dies this day." Spinning about, he strode angrily downstream, his dark brown hair fanning out behind him like a lion's mane. His men shot Marc a guarded look and followed.

"Flee now and live," Marc told them. "Remember Tomar at the graveyard?" Making a slicing motion in front of his neck, Marc perceived only mild apprehension come from the companions. Strange, he expected a stronger response. Stranger still, their emotions rapidly changed to a sense of smugness about... what? Trying to probe deeper, he found no immediate reason for it. In fact, he sensed far less information from them than expected, and that disturbed him. Was something wrong with his magic? Smiling, the men turned and followed their master.

Walking south along the bank, Marc kept up with them. They selected a tall, narrow pine much smaller than the tree he removed—at most three hands across—and began hacking at its trunk with their swords. Slow work at best. Moving a safe distance away, Marc sat upon a large rock and watched them, ever alert for an arrow or spear sent his way. During this time his magic regained its strength. Several minutes into their labors, Marc felt a very subtle sensation come over him, much like being Envisioned, but somehow different. If he had not been idle at the moment, he doubted he would have noticed it at all. Could someone be watching him? He knew without a doubt it was not Oren or Valeria for their magic had a bright, clear feel to it, even when they tried to conceal their Envisioning. This magic felt wrong in some way. Very wrong.

Bending to pick up a twig, he surreptitiously looked around for someone else in the area, but found no one. Reaching out with his mind, he immediately collided with the unknown force and the sensation instantly swelled in strength, revealing a malicious intent to the magic. Then, just as quickly, it vanished leaving no Trace for him to follow. A brief Envision from high above showed no one unexpected in the area. Someone possessing strong, wizard-level magic just spied on him. But whom? Thaddeus had a little magic, but nothing like what he just felt. Did another wizard live nearby? Might it be one of the people coming from the north? He had no clue. Maybe Oren would know, but now was not the time to be thinking on other subjects. He returned his focus to his enemies. Vigilance.

When Thaddeus and his men had cut a quarter-way through their tree, Marc saw the people from Oak Creek come into view. With them were the survivors of Fox Glen and the soldiers who renounced Crowe. Leading the way, Garrett waved at him. Returning the greeting, Marc pointed to the north with his staff. Nodding, Garrett turned the column that way. Moments later, he felt the comfort of Valeria's presence.

—*I see I am not too late to witness murderers become woodsmen,*— she Linked.

His tension did not allow him to share in her levity even though he knew she meant to lighten his mood. —*I moved the bridge to delay them. Would you mind guiding our friends from the village to the viewing place we agreed upon earlier?*—

—*My pleasure. I'll keep them at a safe distance.*— Her demeanor turned more serious, communicating her concern and love. —*Be careful.*—

Marc continued to watch the men whittle away at the tree until Gildas' group entered the meadow and joined those from Oak Creek several hundred paces upstream. By now the uncut portion of the trunk was about a hand's breadth wide, small enough for him to Blade. Standing, Marc approached the creek. "I tire of waiting. Move aside." When they complied, he raised his staff high and brought it down in a chopping motion as he loudly commanded, "*Scinde!*" At the same moment, he cleanly severed the remainder of the trunk with one blow, then pulled the upper part of the tree toward him so it fell across the creek in a shower of dust and needles. Thaddeus' men looked uneasily at Marc.

—*It begins, Val.*— He beckoned to the three, his voice foreboding. "Come, enter my realm."

Marc backed away, watching them closely. Thaddeus motioned for his taller companion to go first. After a slight hesitation, Rutilus held his spear high and made his way through the now vertical branches jutting from the tree, breaking off several lesser boughs blocking his passage. Once he was safely across, Thaddeus and the other man followed. Immediately thereafter, Marc lifted his hands, palm up. *"Volitā!"* The tree Floated up and over to the far side of the water, eliciting gasps and cries from the witnesses, though muted due to the distance. His enemies watched the tree's movement with nervous interest. Once it settled, they looked at him questioningly. "I insist you stay."

Assuming aggressive postures, the men spread out wide and circled around him, inching closer. Marc had anticipated they would try to attack him simultaneously from different directions, thinking he could only handle one attacker at a time. "Confident, are we?"

Atellus, the short, dark skinned man, pulled an arrow from his quiver and put it to his bow. "The wolves will scavenge your carcass before the sun sets—unless you yield to us."

"Yield? Why would I do that?" Again, Marc felt that same smugness emanate from him.

"If we die, so do your sister and brother." A wicked smile spread across his face revealing stained and broken teeth.

Marc immediately Envisioned the crowd of villagers gathered across the creek—the act taking far more effort than normal for some reason—and found Gwen was not there. He did see his mother and Stella wandering around, searching for something. Coincidence? He quickly tried Envisioning Gwen and got—nothing. It was like she didn't exist. What about viewing something else, like the village? Straining, he barely sensed anything. What was happening?

Keeping his momentary flare of concern from showing on his face, he assumed the man only bluffed. After all, Marc had no brother, so Atellus had to be lying in order to upset and confuse him. Just to be sure, Marc probed his mind—or tried to. His efforts only yielded a weak sense of the man's state of mind and emotions, but enough to learn Atellus spoke what he believed to be the truth. A heaviness settled over Marc. Why did his magic almost fail him *twice* now, much like it did after Sean died? The Almighty caused the latter, he believed, but what, or who, caused this current lapse? Had he displeased God somehow? Should he have dealt with Thaddeus at the graveyard yesterday? Was this a punishment for that failure?

Unsure, Marc tried using other forms of magic. Looking past the men, he easily moved a branch on the newly fallen tree. Relieved, he found making a bubble about himself had not changed, either. But when he tried reading the Traces upon his father's whistle hanging about his neck, the images were much harder to draw out, as if his magical abilities had lessened. Apparently, only those gifts associated with reading and sensing were weaker. Strange. Trying to set his worry aside, he pressed on.

"How will that happen if you never leave this place, Atellus?"

"They are all but dead now." Rutilus hefted his spear, watching him closely.

"They do not lie," Thaddeus said with more than a touch of ridicule. "Your magic should tell you that."

Marc instantly realized Thaddeus said *your* magic, not *the* magic. Did he know the truth, or only suspect it? Or was it just the turn of a phrase? "What do you hope to gain by telling me this?"

Thaddeus' steely gaze locked with his, the black of his eyes matching the stain upon his soul. "If you want them to live you have two choices—leave here and never return, or let us kill you. We will be swift and merciful."

Marc tried reading Thaddeus' thoughts but got even less from him than from Atellus. It reminded him of—of course! Oren could shield his thoughts and emotions from others. Marc, along with Valeria, were just beginning to learn that skill, but surely Thaddeus did not posses enough magical strength to do so. Or did he? Unsettled, Marc turned to Atellus, prompting him in order to bring memories to the surface.

"I hope my brother at least put up a good fight."

Immediately, the man recalled several indistinct flashes of Gwen and James, the boy from Fox Glen, being clubbed unconscious, bound and thrown over horses. If Marc had his full strength he could have gotten more detailed information from the man's mind.

Bitter anger welled up inside Marc, an unquenchable fire that demanded the injustice visited upon his sister and James be answered with swift, merciless wrath. Barely keeping his temper, he again tried very hard to Envision Gwen and felt only the vaguest sense of her existence and nothing else. About James he got nothing. Why had his magic forsaken him? Despair festered in his heart. Gwen's *life* was in danger because of *him;* a fool who thought his magic could solve everything. He was no wizard, only a feeble pretender. If Gwen died, it would be *his* fault. *His* failure.

Thaddeus pivoted his sword in swift, tight circles, his lustful smirk revealing he thought himself near victory. "What will it be, apprentice? Banishment, or death?"

For a moment Marc's hope faded as the temptation to cede to them grew strong. Then, suddenly realizing something didn't seem right about his shifting emotions, he struggled to center his thoughts and suppress his passion. Nothing was *ever* hopeless, Oren had told him that many times. A solution could always be found if one looked hard enough. Bolstered by that thought, he straightened his back, firmed his grip on his staff, and decided that now was not the time to give up.

"Neither. You know I cannot abandon my people to your kind. That would make me as cowardly as you."

"Then they die," the tall man said, his soulless grin partially hidden behind greasy red locks.

Marc shrugged. "If they must." Narrowing his eyes, he slowly extended the end of his staff toward the man and said with calm power, "But I promise, *you* will die before they do."

Rutilus spat on the ground, hate radiating off him as he jutted his chin toward Marc. "Empty words. You will not let them die. You are weak."

"I am stronger than you know. It is *you* who are weak. Three against one," Marc said with contempt. "Does it make you feel strong to strike down unarmed children and steal away with them like a thief? Tell me where they are and I will be merciful."

Growling, the man stepped menacingly toward him and Marc blasted him with a wave of magic, knocking him off his feet to tumble to a stop fifteen paces away. Spinning about, he did the same to Thaddeus and the other man. "Follow me to the other side of the hill if you choose." Floating rapidly skyward, Marc tried again to seek out Gwen. Her presence came to him, but still much weaker than it should. Gladness filled him. As he drifted higher and to the north, his sense of her grew clearer and more potent—she was east of the village. It appeared Thaddeus himself somehow affected his magic.

Marc found that she and James were in a dark place, tied at the wrists and ankles. Laying in a foot or so of water, neither moved. Pulling his perspective back, he saw they were in an old, shallow well. He recognized the place. A skin had been stretched over the opening with dozens of tree branches piled on top. Straining hard, he probed Gwen's mind and found her groggy, cold and in pain. James was unconscious and a dried trickle of blood lined the side of his head. Both needed help right away.

Anxious, he started to Link to Oren for advice, but then stopped. As the wizard being tested, he was expected to meet all challenges alone. So, what could he do to help his sister? Maybe he could wake her up. But how? An unexpected hunch made him think of Linking to her. Was that possible? She's destined for magic and her aura is fairly strong, but was it too soon for her gifts to come forth? No harm in trying. Clearing his thoughts, he attempted to Link with her mind.

—*Gwen? Gwen, can you hear me?*—

He felt no reaction from her. He repeated the effort several more times with the same results. By now the Great Tree lay directly below him. Maybe its power could help. Dropping swiftly to the ledge, he ran up and hugged its trunk. With a resonant thrum, the energy of the place entered him, prickling the hairs on his arms.

—*Gwen?*—

—*Who... ?*— came her weak reply.

He let out a breath of relief as the Link firmed up. —*It's Marc. Magic is letting us talk.*—

—*Marc?*— Her emotions spiked with both hope and alarm. —*Help me. Help us.*—

—*I will. Try to be calm. How is James?*—

—*He fought bravely, trying to protect me, but got hurt. Thaddeus and some men took us.*—

—*I know.*—

—My head hurts bad. It's dark and very cold here. We're sitting in water.—

—Yes, you're in the old well east of the oat field.—

—Free us.—

—I will, but it will take time to get someone to you, so be patient. Now hold still.— Marc examined the ropes about her. At first he thought about Blading them in two, but worried that even if he could sever the bindings from so far away, the distance may not allow him the control needed to keep from injuring his sister. Even with the power boost from the Tree, it took much effort and time to untie her hands. When the rope dropped into the water her anxiety ebbed. *— Undo the rope by your feet then free James.—*

—Can't you do it?—

—I don't have time. The men who took you are trying to kill me right now.—

—Kill you?— Her fear rebounded sharply, but this time it was felt for him.

—Trust that I will prevail. Help is on the way. Try thinking this way to Val or Oren. They should hear you. I love you, my sister.—

—I love you, too, Brother. You're going to win,— she added after a moment, pride infusing her Link.

He hoped so. Releasing the tree, he ran north down the path to the area near Hell's Gate. Could he contact Valeria or Oren now to dispatch help, or did he have to wait until after the test? Gwen and James might not last that long. He'd rather fail the test than put their lives in jeopardy. Trusting his hunch, he Linked to his former master.

—Oren, may I instruct others to do something not directly related to my test?—

—Indeed you may.—

—Thank God.— He explained the predicament Gwen and James were in. *—Can you send several men on horses to rescue them?—*

—Gladly. And your mother has been in a panic over Gwen's absence. I will allay her fears. Well done.—

Oren's compliment did little to ease Marc's concerns, his plans falling more into ruin with each passing moment. Glancing across the creek, he saw the crowd gathering by the water's edge with Valeria and Oren at the forefront. All would witness his success or failure. Having so many depending on him for their freedom weighed him down, and yet their faith in him also gave him strength. A curious contrast. Seeing that the wind came out of the east, he ran to a point fifty paces east of Hell's Gate, then watched his foes approach from along the shore of the creek.

As before they encircled him, not only with their bodies, but also with the hate and violence of their minds. As he turned to face each man, fear and doubt grew within him. They held their weapons tight, ready to strike at any moment, predatory gazes fixed intently upon him. What should he do and whom should he fight first? Rutilus possessed only a heavy spear, the least dangerous of the weapons threatening him. Normally, Marc could safely dodge a spear if thrown from a distance. But the man stood just five paces away, giving Marc little time to jump clear of a well-timed thrust. Atellus and Thaddeus had arrows, far more difficult to avoid, especially from this close, plus short swords. Marc briefly though about Floating high into the air, attacking them from afar. No, that would be the coward's choice. He would not shame himself—or Oren—that way.

As the malevolence in the men peaked, Marc again felt the numbing coldness of dread invade him. They were seasoned warriors who enjoyed fighting and killing. How could he expect to be victorious? They would attack simultaneously—he saw it in their merciless eyes. No wizard could stand against that. He had but one choice: take to the sky and flee. Just as he was about to give up, Marc felt a slender wedge of reason slip into his mind, prying open that which until now had blinded him to the truth— these emotions and negative thoughts were not his own. They came from outside him, from the *Nothingness* that infected Thaddeus and his men. An evil that hungered to make him its own.

Pushing his spirit out as far as he could, he desperately Linked to that infinite power he felt before. —*Lord, please help me fight the evil that tempts me.*— Brighter than a thousand suns, a white-hot flash of power and hope slammed through him, blasting away every trace of despair. Gone, too, was the weakening effect Thaddeus had on his magic. Marc's mind came alive, knowing everything around him. He *felt* the spear behind him as it left

333

Rutilus' hand. It moved slowly, like a fluff of down buoyed upon a gentle breeze. Unable to turn his body in time to see it, his magic surged forth and raced to meet the weapon mid-flight, striking it with the strongest force he ever created. The blade and shaft of the spear shattered into dust as the energy sped on toward the tall man's head, which suffered the same fate, exploding in a shower of flesh and bone. The power continued on until it struck the slope of the hill far beyond with a thunderous noise, casting up a great cloud of stones and dirt. Rutilus' corpse crumpled forward to land in a slack heap, spilling it's blood onto the earth. A raucous cheer rose up from the people across the creek.

Suddenly weakened from the energy he expended, Marc shivered when he sensed the fear and panic of the man's spirit as it left his body. The *Nothingness* around them momentarily swelled a hundredfold, the energies within it fouled with the most negative emotions Marc had ever known. He suddenly understood that was due to the evil which formerly occupied the man's body, now freed upon his death. As Marc thought in the graveyard yesterday, this evil felt alive in a way—intelligent, aware and purposeful. Several dark wisps flew past Marc and toward that evil and Rutilus' essence. With a hunger beyond words, they voraciously consumed both like ravening beasts and Marc sensed them no more. It felt completely unlike the serenity of Sean's passing. The wisps quickly gathered before him, bowed, then vanished. Too stunned to react, he put what he saw aside and returned his attention to the remaining enemies.

Thaddeus and the other man shrank back, first nervously eyeing their companion's remains, then regarding Marc with great caution. While Thaddeus's emotions remained mostly in check, Marc felt Atellus' escalating fear and played upon it. "You poor fool. Your mistake was listening to Thaddeus. He thought he could sway me by taking my sister and brother hostage. I *have* no brother. You made another mistake in thinking you could defeat me and magic's will. That cannot be done for I am a mighty wizard. Tell me where they are, Atellus, and I will let you live. Thaddeus, on the other hand, will die here and now. But speak quickly for my patience wanes."

Wavering, the man slightly lowered his bow, the realization of his doom only now registering on his face. Marc knew he would talk, just as he knew Thaddeus would not permit him to. Before the dark-skinned man could speak, Thaddeus' blade whipped up and outward to cut deeply into Atellus' throat, sending him to the ground to lie beside his friend. Seizing the bloodied sword with his magic, Marc flung it away behind his cousin. Glancing after it, Thaddeus appeared faintly amused, which caused Marc a moment of confusion—why did he not seem concerned at losing his weapon? Marc had no time to think about it because Atellus' spirit came before him, appearing as a misty reflection of his earthly form.

—*Help me, save me,*— he begged, frantically looking around for some means of escape. —*I'll show you where your sister and broth— the boy are hidden.*—

Momentarily startled at seeing the ghost—his second after viewing Sean's—he gave him a single, firm shake of his head. —*You willingly chose to sow the seeds of evil, and now you shall reap the harvest.*— He drove the shade back with his mind, fervently adding, —*And tell the evil you so loved in life that I serve only the Almighty. Tell it I will fight it and all who harbor and serve it until my dying day.*—

The *Nothingness* peaked once more and the wispy *things* returned to claim it and Atellus' spirit who, with a pitiful shriek, vanished from the world. As before, the things bowed to him, then left. *What are they?* he wondered.

Apparently ignorant of what just took place with Atellus, Thaddeus backed slowly away, holding his arms out at his side to show he was unarmed. "Now only *I* know where they are. If I die, they die." A quick probe told Marc he felt nothing about murdering his comrade.

Marc gave him a contemptuous smile. "That makes two of us. Very clever of you, using that old well. But don't worry, several of your finest men, or should I say, *my* finest men, are on their way to rescue them."

His adversary's smirk melted. "How did you—?"

Riffling his fingers in a casual gesture, Marc said, "I am favored by the magic."

Thaddeus snorted in disgust. "We both know there is no such thing as magic."

Marc probed him once more; Thaddeus only suspected the truth. "With ample evidence to the contrary," Marc paused to wave his staff toward the headless man, "what makes you say such a thing?"

"I have some power, but it comes from within me, not from *the magic that is all around us*," he added mockingly.

"That is because you serve evil. The magic shuns you, not allowing your power to grow stronger as mine has."

"You lie." As the man's fingers tightened upon his bow, Marc felt his intention to reach for an arrow.

"*Discinde!*" Snapping his fingers, Marc Bladed Thaddeus' bow in two. Startled, Thaddeus cursed and threw down the useless remnants of his weapon, grinding them beneath his heel. Taking advantage of the distraction, Marc hurriedly sought out the cracked stones deep within the soil beneath him and moved them wide apart to let the gasses begin their journey to the surface. If he timed it correctly, they should erupt as he finished the incantation.

"Take heed, Thaddeus, and see the might of the magic you scorn." Facing the nearby pile of stones, he loudly commanded, "*Aperīte, inferni portae!*" while slowly spreading his arms in a grand gesture. With a deafening roar, the vapors escaped their earthly bonds, causing the multitude behind him to gasp in awe.

Thaddeus abruptly retreated several steps from the cairn, his face paler, eyes darting about nervously. Pointing at it, his hand trembled as he gasped, "What is this?"

"Magic is angry at being mocked," Marc said loud enough to carry to the waiting crowd, his voice harder and displeased. "Watch and fear it's power. *Ārdē!*" he shouted. Bracing himself against the coming blast, Marc sparked the base of the gas causing it to explode into boiling flame. Prepared as he was, he remained fast, the pressure wave flowing around him, his robe jerking to his rear while Thaddeus staggered back, nearly losing his footing. The thunderclap raced past the stunned witnesses, echoing multiple times off the nearby hills.

For the first time Marc felt true fear surge within Thaddeus. The man edged closer to the inferno, circling around it some, his cloak raised to shield his face from the great coils of fire. "How can this be?" Marc remained silent. Even though his enemy felt some panic, that smugness remained within him; Thaddeus still believed he had the upper hand. After a moment, Thaddeus regained control of his emotions and faced him. "Let me live," he said, a subtle, crafty smile blossoming on his lips, "and I will tell you how your father died."

Those unexpected words found a home deep within Marc's soul. Closing his eyes, the image of his father's cold body bent backward over that log became fresh in his mind. Somehow, Thaddeus knew he ached for that knowledge.

"He was betrayed by someone familiar," Marc said, his voice rough. "Murdered." He opened his eyes and regarded Thaddeus, who looked away. "The coward plunged his sword into my father's heart without warning, then placed the buck's antler in the wound to conceal his treachery."

Thaddeus' head snapped Marc's way for a moment, eyes wide with surprise, then, squatting, he turned to face the fire once more. Marc paused. Had not Oren said that only he and one other knew how Marc's father had died? If so, then Thaddeus could be that other. Had he witnessed the event—or played a part in it? If the latter were true, he would be a fool to admit it.

Turning about, Marc slowly moved toward the falls. Maybe Thaddeus lied, trying to change Marc's mind about killing him. Or was it something else? No matter. Marc would not barter away the justice due his father. Marc sensed the magic about Thaddeus seemed different at the moment, as if he tried to hide something from him. He recalled Valeria foresaw that his enemy would be *crafty, hiding its weapons away* and that *no one knows its true strength until too late.* Did she mean Thaddeus the man, or the *Nothingness* that corrupted him? That she chose to say *its* instead of *his* implied it might be the latter.

In a sickening instant, he understood the meaning of her words. His magic flew from him and found the dagger speeding his way. Stopping it several feet from him, he set a smile on his face and, emotions in check, turned back to Thaddeus.

"A gift? Why, thank you, cousin."

Thaddeus froze, his posture clearly indicating he had just thrown something. "How—?"

Marc took it from its invisible perch in the air and felt the Traces upon it rush into him. Without warning, a moment of agony, hot and bright, passed through Marc's chest, and his strength suddenly left him as he crumpled to his knees in the snow. With eyes not his own, Marc watched Thaddeus plant a foot on his chest and shove him off his sword. Falling backward, Marc landed arched over a log, staring into the gray-brown sky. The man's face drew close and smiled with dead eyes as he said, "Marcus is next." Marc desperately struggled to reach for Thaddeus but his arms refused to move. His mind screamed *NO! NO! Please, God, no*, as blackness overcame him.

Blinking in surprise, Marc found he still stood facing Thaddeus while holding the dagger. Never had he felt a Trace so strongly. This was his father's dagger; Thaddeus had kept it after murdering him. Fierce power gathered in his mind as he digested the knowledge just learned. His back stiffened and his hands balled up so tightly that his fingernails cut into his palms. Breathing deeply, he again fought to keep his actions suppressed, but this time let his anger show as a cold and tightly contained wrath.

"I already know how my father died." Lightly fingering the decorations on the weapon's pommel, Marc slowly advanced toward the man. "You came upon him and the fine buck he had felled. Covetous, you helped him clean it, intending to wait until the task was finished to knock him out and take it. But after he told you, with some pride I might add, that Oren had revealed my destiny to him, you killed him in cold blood, giving him no warning or chance to defend himself. What disgusts me the most is knowing we are related. You murdered your own cousin over some meat!" Slamming the end of his staff into the ground, Marc slowly growled out, "You lazy waste of flesh."

His face burning with hatred, Thaddeus spat in his direction. "I should have killed *you* that day as well. My mistake was in thinking that without a father to provide for you, the cold and hunger would end your miserable existence. But due to Oren's meddling you survived. That old man should have died years ago."

Pushing aside his anger, Marc let a knowing smile come to his lips. "He lived to protect me the day you came to kill me. You had no interest in collecting any honorarium, only using it as an excuse to justify murder and steal the village's food. Oren outsmarted you. That very day I became his apprentice, studying hard and learning fast. I am now a master wizard."

Thaddeus sneered at him, his actions almost childlike. "At least I have the satisfaction of knowing the bastard is dead."

Marc laughed heartily, and upon seeing the man's brows narrow in confusion at his reaction, he laughed some more. "You failed for he lives." Stretching out his arm, he indicated the crowd on the eastern side of the creek. There upon a large rock stood Oren, tall and powerful, his robe gently waving in the breeze. The old wizard nodded Marc's way, telling him he was Envisioning all that transpired. That pleased Marc.

Thaddeus, fists clenching, gasped angrily. "It cannot be!"

"Yet it is. You may not choose his time to die, only the Almighty can. You have killed many innocent people, among them my father and best friend Sean, who gave his life for me. Their blood cries out for justice."

"Justice? You hypocrite! You seek to rule those people just as much as I." Blocking the glare with his hand, Thaddeus slowly sidestepped away from the raging flames.

Marc regarded him with pity. The man's twisted, self-centered viewpoint couldn't understand anything but brutality and domination. He wondered if that was one reason why evil had gained purchase to the man's soul, or if it came about as a result of it. "No, Thaddeus. I only wish to serve them."

With a rude noise of disgust, Thaddeus once more glanced at Oren across the way, then stiffened in recognition. Cursing, he pointed that way and said, bitterly, "Does that whore next to Oren *serve* everyone as well?"

Marc looked to see who Thaddeus insulted; only Valeria stood nearby. With a chortle of amusement, he crossed his arms over his chest. "I see the two of you have met already. Her name is Valeria, my wife to be, and she, too, is a wizard. As she bested you, so shall I." Marc turned back just as a sharp spike of hatred came from Thaddeus.

The man sprinted forward, extending his right hand out to his side. Marc saw his foe's aura peak momentarily as the sword taken from him earlier flew rapidly into his grip. Shocked, Marc held his ground as everything around him slowed down like it did when Rutilus threw his spear. Thaddeus had abilities *far* stronger than he had previously assumed. The way the sword moved into his hand appeared too smooth, too practiced to be the result of a suddenly awakened talent on Thaddeus' part; it was second nature to him. What other skills did he posses?

This, also, must have been part of Valeria's vision. Anyone non-magical would have been stunned into inaction by what they saw, even if for an instant. And such a hesitation would have given Thaddeus a lethal advantage. He was wise to keep his power secret.

Now four paces away, Thaddeus held his sword high overhead, preparing to bring it down in a single, killing blow. The man had been given multiple chances to change his ways before now, but never took them. No more time remained.

Thaddeus had to die.

Right now.

And, sadly, Marc knew the task to be his. At first he considered striking him as he had Rutilus. Such an end would be swift and merciful. But also too simple. Marc had to make this confrontation more than just ending a man's reign of terror, ending a man's life. He needed to make a bold and unforgettable statement—Marcus the wizard was powerful, to be respected, and for those who served the *Nothingness*, to be feared.

Marc momentarily closed his eyes. So be it.

Flinging his arms wide, he bellowed, "*TĒ ĒICIO!*" and bodily hurled Thaddeus upward into a high arc that led him directly into the crest of the plume. Falling through the flames, his cousin landed at its base, breaking both legs. Shrieking in pain from within the inferno, Thaddeus desperately clawed at the ground, dragging himself clear of the blaze, but not before being severely burned.

A stab of regret went through Marc when he saw what he had done, even though Thaddeus deserved this end, having killed many at Fox Glen in the same manner. Marc suddenly felt an intense spike of hatred briefly directed at him. Thaddeus? No, someone else. Someone far away. It was that mysterious Envisioning presence he felt earlier. Again he tried to trace it back to its source but failed. Could it be the *Nothingness* itself? He wished he knew. Composing himself, Marc turned toward the creek and, as he lifted his staff overhead in victory, a great cheer erupted from the crowd. Gazing upon Valeria, he felt the warmth of her love wash over him, easing his heavy heart.

—I'm so glad you passed the test, my love,— she said, not trying to conceal her ebbing tension. *—Oren would not allow me to link to you until now. Hurry to my side.—*

He returned the love in kind, basking in her growing joy. — *In a moment.—* Facing Thaddeus once more, he raised his palms upward and said, loud enough for the witnesses to hear, *"Volitā!"* Moaning and cursing, the man Floated up to eye level and drifted eastward across the creek, dropping to the ground before the crowd, parts of his clothing still aflame. Lifting himself higher into the air, Marc started toward the people, trying to look authoritative on the outside while feeling self-conscious and a bit frightened of himself on the inside. As he crossed over the churning waters he felt Valeria's Push flow into his mind.

—Beware the Magus of power!— Deep and mighty, the voice blew like winter storm winds from out of the heart of the flame. The crowd gasped, then stirred nervously, watching him in awe.

—Impressive illusion,— Marc told Valeria as she beheld the people's reactions.

Fascinated and mildly amused, her mind joined his. — *Seeing you Floating before the flame that way made me remember the vision I had when I passed out at the Tree. I heard those words when I saw you draw near with fire behind you. Was it wrong to make that part of the vision come true?—*

—No. I suspect you were to do so all along.— Marc landed beside Thaddeus' writhing form and gazed upon the people. The eyes of many were filled with gratitude, others held fear, and a few showed naked hatred toward Thaddeus. Most of the latter were the survivors of Fox Glen who clumped together as if uncertain their oppressor was truly vanquished. Recalling how Oren had behaved before Crowe, the soldiers and the people of Oak Creek the day before, Marc knew he should act accordingly. Gesturing toward Thaddeus with his staff , he addressed the survivors, his voice peaceful, comforting.

"He is the last of those who did violence against you and did not earnestly repent. Let go of your anger and pain, for justice has been served. Do not let the likes of *this* ruin anymore of your lives. Instead, look forward to better days ahead."

As Valeria moved his way, Barbara hurried forward and, kneeling before him with head bowed, softly said, "Thank you for our lives and avenging our people, mighty one."

A ripple of shame moved through him. "Please, stand and face me." The girl did so, taking several moments before allowing herself to shyly meet his gaze. Taking her hands in his, he felt her tense up. "Call me by my name or my title, and never kneel before me. No one should kneel for I am here only to serve." Hearing that, Thaddeus moaned louder, but Marc ignored him.

Cocking her head to the side, she looked genuinely surprised. "Serve? Serve whom?"

He gave Barbara's hands a gentle squeeze. "Why you and all these people here. The magic that lives all around us compels wizards to offer aid, wisdom and protection to all who need it. And more importantly, so does the Almighty."

Barbara smiled radiantly and hugged him tight. "Then thank you, Marc."

"You are most welcome," he said with a chuckle, lightly patting her back.

No sooner had the girl released him than Valeria took her place, holding him tight while giving him a deep, soulful kiss. The warmth and comfort of her embrace enfolded them both within the aura of her love, her remaining anxiety over his test slipping away to leave a grateful joy in its stead. Bathed in that calming peace, neither wanted it to end, but he had duties to finish. With an angelic smile, she separated from him, moving several paces away. Turning toward the flame, he raised his hands and, after moving the slab to quench the vapors, commanded in a great voice, "*Claudite, inferni portae!*"

The crowd gaped in wonderment as the flame died down, pointing after it while murmuring excitedly to one other. Afterward, Gildas caught Marc's eye, nodding first to Thaddeus, then the crowd. Marc dipped his head slightly in affirmation and the monk moved to Thaddeus, then turned toward the people.

"Behold the wages of sin," he said loudly over the man's cries. "Let he who fears the Lord remember this day."

"Kill me," Thaddeus begged, quivering with pain. "Please."

One of soldiers stepped up and tentatively looked at Marc. "May I have a sword? We should show him mercy."

Marc motioned him back. "Grant him the same mercy he showed to the people of Fox Glen." A heavy wave of guilt and regret rolled off the man as he glanced down at his former leader. Marc met the soldier's gaze. "If you are truly sorry for your actions and change your ways to serve what is good and right, you will be forgiven and find peace."

A flicker of hope glimmered in the soldier's eyes. With a slight bow, he returned to his place.

Turning to Gildas, Marc put a hand on his shoulder. "Those who once served Crowe need to know the error of their ways. When everyone returns to Oak Creek, talk to them, preach to them the Word."

The monk gave him a respectful nod. "I will. They need not end up as this one." Gildas gave Thaddeus an uncharitable glare. "Chaff to be cast into the furnace."

Marc looked sternly upon the soldiers. Many had fear in their eyes—fear of him. These emotions disturbed him but he knew that fear was necessary for they would not change their ways lightly. Only an external influence could do that, a figure of power and strength compelling them to move their lives in a new direction. *He* had to be that figure. Their fate, their reclamation, lay partly in his hands. Such was being a wizard.

"Heed this holy man's words. He speaks truth and has my favor." He gestured at Thaddeus with a slow sweep of his staff. "When this wretch dies, let him join Crowe in the bellies of Ethan's swine."

"Damn you!" Thaddeus choked out through gritted teeth.

Marc shook his head sadly, feeling the cold *Nothingness* lingering near once more. It feared him. "Arrogant to the end." Squatting, he spoke so only Thaddeus could hear his words. "Can you feel your fate approaching, cousin? Can you sense the cold, empty despair that wants you for its own? I do. When Sean died, I felt his spirit enter paradise, his payment for how he led his life. But your two friends did not make that journey. They went... elsewhere. As soon shall you. You're a clever man, Thaddeus. I'm certain you can figure out where that might be." Marc stood, looking upon him with genuine sadness. "And for whatever it might be worth, I *am* sorry for you."

"You—" Thaddeus lunged at him, but just as quickly curled up in a ball from the pain the action caused.

Paying no mind to the man's string of vile, near breathless curses, Marc lifted his gaze to the crowd, raising his voice so all could hear. "Remember this day to your children and grandchildren. Teach them well to live a peaceful life. Tell them not to trespass into the Forbidden Vale for only those chosen by the magic can survive it."

Garrett bowed his head slightly. "It will be done by those in Oak Creek."

Leahenfehr, a slender giant of a man with sandy blonde hair, moved out of the crowd and stood next to Garrett. "So, too, in Bitter Well, Wizard Marc."

Marc looked at both of them and inclined his head. "You serve your people well." Moving next to Valeria, he put his arm around her side and addressed the people once more. "Peace to all of you."

A voice came from their midst. "Thank you, Marc." It was Willie. Others echoed their thanks and soon the crowd came about him. Their gratitude and acceptance deeply moved him, reminding him of the day he and Sean gained their manhood. That day would always remain a happy memory.

This one would not.

For this was a day of profound changes. He had killed two men—three if he counted maneuvering Thaddeus into silencing Atellus. He had accepted the responsibility of protecting those of the villages nearby and overseeing the soldiers. But the greatest change of all was *becoming* a Wizard. Not the kind of wizard he felt himself to be on the inside, but the external one seen by others—powerful, wise, someone to be respected. To be feared, or if not feared, to at least be kept at arm's length for few would allow themselves to consider him a friend or equal. Certainly some would see Marc the man—his family, Valeria's family, Garrett, Donald and a few others. But many would only see the wizard. The one who was different. Dangerous.

Just like how *he* used to feel about Oren.

"Peace, my love," Valeria gently told him, shaking him loose from his thoughts as their teacher came over to them.

Oren put a hand on his shoulder. "I could not be prouder of you, Marc." Unshed tears pooled in the elder's eyes. He put his other hand on Valeria's shoulder. "I am equally proud of you, Valeria. In a way I feel as if you were the children I was meant to have."

Weeping, Valeria threw her arms around her master. Fighting off his own tears, Marc hugged him as well, more than proud Oren felt that way about them. For some time he had thought of the old wizard as a surrogate grandfather, as family. *Family!* With a start, Marc let go, suddenly remembering his sister's situation.

"Gwen! I have to go to her."

"Take ease, Marc, she's already free of the well," Valeria said, sniffing back her tears. "Donald and two of the prisoners took the horses tied up by the tree bridge and got there quickly. Gwen and James are safe." She gave him a questioning look. "When, and *how*, did she learn to Link?"

Joy filled him. Lifting Valeria into his arms, he kissed her and said, "I'll tell you later." He called out to the monk. "Gildas, I need to speak with you."

Chapter 32

"Of course I will marry you," Gildas said as he approached them, a warm smile spreading on his face.

Marc smiled back, surprised. "How did you know?"

"How could I not? I need no magic to see your love for each other. When do you wish to be wed?"

"Soon." Valeria squirmed free of Marc's grasp and briefly hugged the monk. Letting go, she looked upon him and compassion filled her gaze. "I would ask you to do so immediately, but you have more important duties to attend to."

"What duties?" Marc asked.

A gentle sadness emanated from within Gildas. "To pray over the dead. Valeria told me of the past few days. I need to bless those killed at Fox Glen, the graveyard and—" Pain filled the monk's eyes as he tenderly gripped Marc's forearm. "Your good and faithful friend."

For a moment grief overcame Marc, but the touch of Valeria's hand in his dispelled it as swiftly as it had arrived. The love within her spirit was life itself to him.

"Would tomorrow be too soon, Brother?" Valeria asked, her voice soft, yet hopeful.

The monk's mood brightened. "No. While yesterday and today have been filled with death and loss, let tomorrow be a day of life, joy and most of all, love." He took their joined hands and held them to his chest. "The day we met I could tell you were married already, not yet by spoken vows, but by the love that bound you to each other." Letting go, he stepped away. "I best be on my way for the journey there and back will take the remainder of the day. I will try to return in time to preach to the soldiers."

"One moment, Brother. I can help with that." Marc sought out the soldier who served them the day before. "Petros, come here."

Running to him, the man dropped to one knee. "Yes, Wizard Marc?"

Marc gestured at Gildas. "Accompany him on his duties. My friend Donald will meet you with two horses so you may travel to Fox Glen and back. Arm yourself. See that no harm comes to him."

"With my life, Great One." After bowing his head, he looked toward Gildas. "Command me."

The monk extended his hand. "Rise. I am but a servant myself."

Petros took it and stood. "My thanks, sir."

"Call me Brother Gildas." Gesturing in the direction of Broken Rock, the monk led him away.

Marc looked toward his friend and once master. Despite the dried blood matted in his hair, a vital spark shone within the wizard's eyes, belying his earlier brush with death. "Thank you for teaching me well. I could not have passed my test otherwise."

Oren gave him a subtle nod of agreement. "And what did you learn today?"

"I expected to confront my enemies in battle, testing my skill with magic. What I did not expect—the *Nothingness*, the evil within them—surprised me. I found it to be a foe far greater than Thaddeus and his men. It tried to... cloud my mind, to alter my thoughts, to weaken me. Resisting it, and my own shortcomings, proved to be my true test."

A satisfied smile widened upon Oren's face. "You are indeed wise. God chose well upon whom to bestow His gifts."

Humbled, Marc momentarily bowed his head. "Again, I have you to thank. While I should be pleased about today's events, I must confess my heart feels otherwise. I killed two men and even though their deaths were justified, my actions weigh heavily upon me." He met Oren's gaze. "Does it become easier?"

Momentarily closing his eyes, the elder slowly shook his head, then sighed. "No. But in time you learn to accept its necessity."

Valeria rubbed Marc's back. "Share the burden with me."

Marc did not wish to. Why make her feel bad as well? His concerns ebbed as her love flowed into him.

"You cannot hide your feelings from me," she said. "Even if that were not so, I would still want to share all with you, good and bad."

Gathering her into his arms he kissed her tenderly. "I promise there will be more of the good." He paused, then pivoting to face the elder wizard, said, "Oren, I experienced two odd occurrences during my battle with Thaddeus." He told them about the strange Envisionings. "Is there another wizard in the area?"

"No. The closest lives about nine days travel away."

"Well, someone with strong magic watched me. I felt their hate, their evil. This person wants me dead. If Thaddeus wasn't bad enough, now I have someone else after me."

"No, *us*," Valeria said, giving him an affectionate squeeze.

Shaking his head, he smiled. "I suppose so. Together we are stronger, right?"

"God have mercy upon those who oppose the wizards of Raven's Gate."

Oren chuckled. "Amen."

Marc was about to add his own quip when Gwen's thoughts interrupted his own.

—*Marc? Can you hear me, brother?*— Uneasiness tainted her Link.

He reached over and held onto Oren's arm so the three of them could share in the conversation. —*I hear you, sister.*—

—*Val told me you were fighting the men that took us. It worried her. Did you win?*—

—*YES.*—

A rush of joyous relief came across the Link. —*I'm glad. Thanks for telling the magic to let us talk this way. I like it.*—

He laughed. —*You are welcome. I see you are nearing the village. You and James must rest until we arrive. Do nothing, including talking this way.*—

—*Yes, Marc,*— she answered reluctantly.

—*When you get home, tell Don to meet Gildas on the path to Broken Rock with two horses.*—

—*I will.*—

—*And speak to no one else about us talking like this.*—

—*Does that mean Valeria and Oren, too? I... I can tell they are with you. I'm not sure why.*—

Marc laughed again. —*You can talk with them.*—

—*I promise, not a word. Or thought,*— she added merrily.

Breaking the Link, Marc heard Oren chuckle. "What amuses you?"

"Gwen. I underestimated her gift. She quickly learned to Link, which by itself is impressive. But when I consider how young she is—" Oren eyes twinkled. "While her power is less than yours and Valeria's, it *is* strong enough that one day she must also be told the Great Secret."

Intense pride for his sister burned within Marc. *Two* wizards in the family. His father would have been greatly pleased. And what of Stella? She, too, has a faint aura. Would her gifts also grow stronger with age? Part of him hoped so.

Valeria clapped her hands. "That's wonderful. Who will train her, Master? You, or us?"

"Soon I will pass my responsibilities to both of you. Therefore, as the official wizards of the land, *you* will train her."

A sly smile popped up on her face. "Ah, but since you will then have much free time, you would be the better choice for that honor."

Oren laughed. "You argue well, Valeria. Perhaps we should share the task?"

She gave him a wink. "Agreed."

Epilog

Marc looked around his village, pleased at all the activity. Oak Creek buzzed with excitement as everyone prepared for a grand celebration. Villager and visitor alike worked side by side, joyful in knowing they were safe for now. The women harvested carrots, onions, turnips and other vegetables from the village garden. They ground much grain to make many loaves of bread. The children gathered baskets of wild berries. Marc accompanied some of the men on the hunt, using his magic to locate a magnificent stag and several geese which they brought home singing spiritedly. The other men gathered firewood, hastily built tables and benches to hold the extra number, plus did other tasks.

Marc spent the remainder of the afternoon tending to the wounded. For a while Valeria worked alongside him, then left to help the women with some preparations for their wedding. While he worked, the breeze often wafted the wondrous fragrance of the roasting meat and baking bread his way, intensifying his hunger. Today was the first time he had seen this many people gathered in one place—well over two hundred. Soon they all would feast like he had never known.

As the sun sank deep into the western sky, Garrett climbed atop the talking stone in the common house and addressed the throng crowded within. "Welcome, everyone. Tonight we celebrate life and freedom, thankful for our deliverance from the hands of evil men. Let us all thank the wizards Oren, Marc and Valeria, whose bravery and skill with magic kept us safe. We owe them a great debt." The crowd cheered loudly and Marc tried hard not to let his embarrassment show.

Leahenfehr moved up next to Garrett. "My village also owes these servants of magic our thanks, and not just for defeating Crowe and Thaddeus. For as long as I can remember Oren has been there during our times of need, sharing his wisdom. Let us never forget how he saved us all from starvation. Now there are two more wizards to watch over us. We are indeed fortunate." After the cheers and applause died down, he placed the palm of his hand on his chest and faced Oren. "And I must confess, Valeria is far more pleasant to look upon than you are, my friend." Everyone laughed, especially Oren. Marc loved the way Valeria blushed.

"Indeed," Garrett said, lightly punching Leahenfehr in the shoulder. "Now Brother Gildas will bless us and our meal." Both men stepped off the rock to make way for him.

The monk, who had returned only minutes before, ascended the stone and looked out over the crowd before him. "We should all be grateful to be here this day." His gaze stopped upon Marc and Valeria, the warmth in his eyes reflected also in his spirit. Gildas looked forward to marrying them.

Turning his head, Marc regarded Valeria's angelic face. Magic suddenly engulfed him and he found himself elsewhere. Glancing about, he saw he stood on the grounds outside of Oren's house, with everything bathed in a faint blue hue. The sun shone too brightly to be real. A cool breeze carried the herb garden's heady scent to his nose, striking it more strongly than he had ever known. Clearly a vision had come upon him.

The old wizard sat upon the bench by the well, gently bouncing a year-old boy on his knee. An older lad of not quite three years held onto the other leg, laughing. With a start, Marc realized these boys were his sons. He saw Valeria's features in their faces mixed with those of his mother and father. What a wonder! To know they would be born filled him with pure joy. Eagerly reading all he could from the moment, he discovered their names, Sean and Oren. Of course. And Valeria? Where could she be? Casting about, he sought her. A touch on his hand made it all flee, replaced with Gildas standing before him, a loaf of bread in his outstretched hand.

"The honor of first bread is yours, Wizard Marc."

Momentarily confused, Marc realized the vision had caused him to miss the monk's blessing. Taking the loaf, Marc bowed slightly. "Thank you, Brother." Holding it over his head for all to see, he moved to break it open, then stopped. "This honor belongs elsewhere." Walking to Sean's parents, he hugged both of them then put the loaf in their hands. With sad smiles, they nodded their thanks and broke it, holding the halves high as Sean's father said, "For Sean."

"For Sean!" the crowd thundered back as one.

Garrett jumped back onto the rock and shouted, "Let the feast begin."

With a jubilant noise, the crowd made their way to the tables. Ten people remained standing. Earlier, lots had been drawn, and these ten were selected to serve the food. As they started to distribute the meal, Marc approached the one nearest him, a tall, thin girl with dark brown hair. His magic revealed her name, that she was thirteen years old and Leahenfehr's niece.

"Sit, Magrit. I will take your place."

With a smile she bowed slightly. "My thanks, Wizard Marc."

As he took her serving bowl, he found Valeria, Oren and Gildas had done the same. Walking down a table, Marc gave each guest their portion, nodding and smiling in response to their thanks.

—*May I help, too?*— Gwen asked. —*Or am I too young?*—

—*You are never too young to be kind to others.*— With love, he watched her rise and change places with a server. Something made him look toward his mother. She, too, saw Gwen's selflessness; pride for her daughter shone from her. Reading his mother's thoughts let him feel her joy at how well her children were turning out, tempered with the soul-deep ache that their father, her husband, would never see any of their accomplishments. Later on he would tell his mother the good news that Sean told him as he died; that Davidus remained nearby, which meant he *did* see how well his children were turning out. It surprised Marc just how intensely his mother loved his father. Yes, he always knew they loved each other, but being exposed on a daily basis to their affections made him initially think everyone enjoyed such a relationship. As he grew older he realized how incredibly lucky his parents were. He glanced around for Valeria and found her passing out slices of venison two tables over. As if feeling his gaze on her, she smiled his way then returned to her work. He smiled as well realizing he, too, was incredibly lucky.

His serving bowl now empty, Marc returned to the cook house. As he filled it, Gildas came along side to do the same.

The monk nodded at him. "It pleases me to see you humble yourself before others."

"It is the role we have both accepted, my brother."

Marc felt a change come over the other. "Now I understand the error of my earlier thoughts. Magic is *not* evil. What matters is those who wield it. I cannot deny that you, Valeria and Oren are truly good people. Godly people. Can you forgive my lack of understanding?"

Marc gave him a gentle shrug. "There is no need to forgive something I never took offense to. To be honest, I must thank you for your earlier misgivings. It made me question my own relationship with magic, leading me to greater wisdom. As Oren once told me, we never stop learning." Marc knew Gildas' destiny and while he could not share that knowledge or influence his actions, it would do no harm to plant a seed. Meeting his gaze, he said, "Write down the things you learn during your journeys. They may prove useful one day."

Gildas paused a moment to consider Marc's words. "That I will do." Hoisting the basket of bread onto his shoulder, he walked back to the guests.

Humming a song, Marc followed him.

Ψ Ψ Ψ

After everyone had eaten their fill, they stood about involved in pleasant conversation. Marc looked upon them. The day before, many here feared for their lives and now peace filled their hearts. Numerous changes took place, not only within him, but within others as well. No one had changed more than Donald. Marc decided it was time to recognize that. Seeing Garrett heading for the rock he used earlier to address the crowd, Marc intercepted him.

"Garrett, may I speak with you?"

"Of course."

"It concerns Donald."

The man's eyebrows narrowed. "Is there a problem?"

Marc smiled. "Not at all. I think it is time to change his status."

Garrett returned the gesture. "I agree. Since I am his father, it might be better for one of the other men to speak to the village of this." His gaze softened some. "I would be honored for you to do so."

Marc nodded in acknowledgment. "You were about to speak to everyone—"

"It can wait." Garrett waved him toward the rock. "You first."

Marc scaled the stone and gathered his thoughts. Though he made no sound, a hush rapidly came upon the people and they drew near, waiting to hear his words.

Valeria's thoughts touched his. —*What is it?*—

—*Bring Don to me.*—

She laughed through the Link. —*Yes, he deserves it.*—

As she moved to fetch their friend, Marc fought down the emotion rising within him; a wizard needed to appear calm at all times. "Did you enjoy the meal?" The crowd earnestly voiced their appreciation. "Good. Among us is someone who has proved his worth, putting this village before himself, even being willing to die for us. I wish to recognize that bravery." Marc's gaze fell upon Donald as he approached the stone. "Donald, son of Garrett, stand before me." His friend complied.

"Two nights ago, Donald left this village to spy upon Crowe's encampment, doing so against the wishes of the village leader. His actions were those of a child, seeking only to satisfy his own wants and needs. Captured and brought before Thaddeus, Donald then changed. He told Thaddeus he acted alone, against the wishes of his village. Donald pleaded with him, asking that he be punished instead of the village, knowing well such punishment meant an unpleasant death. And yesterday he just as bravely fought against Crowe's forces. Men of Oak Creek, I ask you, are not these changes the actions of a man worthy of our respect?" A great din of agreement rose from the men. "Should we grant him his manhood this evening?" The sudden cheer was deafening. Donald looked at the ground, smiling, his cheeks flushed. Turning to Garrett, Marc motioned that he join him. "It is time for the oath." Extending his arm, he helped Garrett onto the rock.

Gratitude shone in the leader's eyes, his hand warmly squeezing Marc's arm as they shook. "My thanks," he said quietly. Turning toward Donald, Garrett proudly rested a hand upon his son's head. "All here have witnessed your deeds...."

As Garrett continued with the ceremony, Marc recalled the day he and Sean became men. The thrill and pride of that moment surged anew within him. It had changed his life, physically and emotionally, putting him on the path that led to today. Many responsibilities fell upon him and Sean. He felt the weight of the amulet hanging about his neck—a reminder that his friend kept his promise to protect his village and people. His gaze fell upon Donald. He, too, proved worthy even before taking the oath.

Tears ran from Garrett's eyes. "Face your village." While Donald turned about, Valeria's spirit touched Marc's; her pride for Donald equaled his. Garrett raised his voice once more. "Citizens of Oak Creek, it is my great honor to welcome this man into our village. Do you agree?"

With a roar, the crowd moved forward and swallowed Donald into their midst. Even those from the neighboring villages congratulated him. When all had quieted down, Garrett retook his perch upon the rock. "This is a day to remember. We are safe, my son has become a man, and tomorrow morning the wizards Marc and Valeria will marry. All this calls for a celebration. Two days ago, when the wizards arrived here to help us face Crowe and Thaddeus, Oren asked me to start two casks of beer. At the time I did not understand the reason for his request, but now—" He grinned widely, nodding toward Oren. "Never argue with a wizard." Laughter roiled out of the multitude. "The beer may be weak, it may not be the best, but we have plenty of it."

Marc could not help but laugh, too, as many of the people whooped and jumped about as they followed Garrett to the cookhouse. Those who could not find any cups brought their dinner bowls along. Taking Valeria's hand, Marc headed for the end of the line, but Donald blocked his path. He held out two large cups.

"Marc, Val. Take these with my thanks for everything you've done for me. I owe you my life several times over." After they took the cups, he hugged them and left.

Finding an open bench, they sat facing each other.

Valeria sniffed at her cup. "Can we drink this?"

"Only one way to find out." He took a sip. "Not bad. Try it."

Taking a little taste, she smiled and took a swallow. "It's good. The bubbles tickle my tongue."

Laughing, he held up his cup. "To you, Val. I look forward to our life together."

She kissed him, the earthy aroma of the brew tasting even better on her lips, then raised her cup to his. "As do I, my love." Looking into each other's eyes, they drank some more. She smiled knowingly. "You have something to tell me."

Marc found himself eager to share what he foresaw. "I do. When Gildas gave the dinner blessing, I glanced at you and had a vision—a wondrous vision." He told her of seeing Oren with their two sons. "Everything seemed so real, yet strange. Is that how you see visions?"

"Yes." Sighing, she cuddled up to him, a calm joy pouring off of her. "Two boys. I've foreseen myself holding a girl as well."

"So we'll have three children?"

"At least. I love you enough to bear a hundred," she said with warmth and love. "Drink."

Chuckling, he did. "Trying to ply me with drink, eh, woman?"

Her eyebrows bounced playfully. "Garrett *did* say to celebrate."

"Indeed."

He tipped her cup up and she eagerly took a mouthful. The delightful shine in her eyes filled him with love. Content with each other's presence, they sat for a time and watched the merriment around them. When several people began to play flutes and drums, Marc and Valeria joined with the others and danced. The more they danced, the more he felt the weight of the day lift from his shoulders. The more the responsibilities of life and magic ebbed away, leaving behind a quiet kind of peace.

He never felt so free.

ABOUT THE AUTHOR

Scott Robert Scheller is a California native, married with two children. He entered college with the grand purpose of becoming an astrophysicist, but NASA had other plans, laying off massive numbers of similarly inclined souls. Scott therefore chose a radically different career path: television & film production. This field also let him express his creative side. Later, he returned to the world of science, specifically air pollution monitoring and research. In his spare time he writes Paranormal Urban Fantasy, the first effort of which you now hold in your hand.

More information on Scott and his books can be found at: www.scottrobertscheller.com

Made in the USA
Coppell, TX
17 September 2021